THE
CHILDREN
OF THE
SUN AND THE MOON

C. S. VANBEEKUM

DEDICATION

To my darling friend Nicole; my kindred spirit of the woodlands.
Adventures and cups of tea are only best when shared together, and
every story should be written for the thrill of a dear old friend.

CONTENTS

BOOK THREE:
SUN

PROLOGUE

Long ago, in the forgotten days of magic, there lived two fair maidens.

Near as sisters, all their years were they bonded to each other; twin spirits of the heathered meadows. As they grew, each admired so for their beauty and their virtue, the maidens were called upon before the kings of the land. The first, given in marriage to the king of Valta, the province in the north, and the second, given in marriage to the king of Hämä, in the south. Seasons came and went, and many years passed on, though neither had brought forth any children. Ruthlessly pressed to bring forth heirs, the women grew restless to appease the indignation of their husbands.

The queen of the north waited such long years for a child, so impatient was she, that finally, she sought the wisdom of the Spirit of the Forest. Hirthir, the Great Guardian of the Wood; one who possessed the power of old magic, and was said to have brought forth the forests of the world in the beginning. Finding him would prove its own journey, for the footsteps of the idle were blinded from his true presence yet the feet in great need were surely guided to him.

Upon entering the Blessed Wood of Hirthir, the lady bowed low and made her humble request to seek his counsel. Graciously, he sat upon his leaf-laden throne and heard her cause. Teeming with such compassion, he implored her to seek the Sun, and present to him an offering. The Spirit of the Rising Sun was the crown of all light; surely he would accept her offering and hear the lady's plea, should he find it worthy. The queen was advised to venture deep into the forest and remain there for three full days. At the first light of the third morning, she should offer up gifts of gold and sing to the Spirit of the Rising Sun. If he condescended to accept her offering, having found pleasure in it and in her song, she might present her request.

Still, all this came at great risk, for although Hirthir was gracious and wise, the Sun was his Ancient Master, and this Master was not one to tolerate the folly of the race of men. For many an age, he refused to tarry with them. Yet the Sun was not so cold-hearted, for he was passion, and flame, and the very breath that quickened even the faintest firelight. Now, all that Hirthir instructed the woman to do, she carried out. On the third morning, deep within the untamed forest, she presented her offering and sang such a bold and unyielding song. The Spirit of the Rising Sun, resplendent in his crown of light, listened intently to her melody. So captivated by her singing, and the bounty of glittering gold at her feet, he graced her with his magnificent presence.

"Fair daughter of the earth, what is your heart's desire?" He called.

"O King of the Scarlet Dawn, my only desire is for a child of my own," she bowed humbly.

"For your grand gifts, and sweet song, I shall grant you a child," he answered.

Soon, the lady conceived and shared with her friend the joyful news.

The second queen felt such conviction at the entreatment of her dear friend, and sought to gain the counsel of the Forest Spirit; for she too had longed many years for a child and to be free of her husband's wrath. Hirthir instructed her, as the other before, that she must make an offering to the Spirit of the Rising Sun. And on the light of the third morning, she must sing to him and make her request. If he found her offering and song pleasing, he would surely hear the lady's plea. So the queen set out, as her dear friend before. As she possessed no gold to offer the Sun, she brought silver in abundance and appointed this her offering.

On the third morning, dawn drew swift across the skies. The woman lifted up her voice in song, as the Sun's rays pierced through the branches of the forest. Yet her song proved too gentle for the Sun to hear it, nor did her offering of silver catch his eye. Still, she sang all through the morning, and through the midday's heat, and all until the final crimson hues of the Sun lingered above the horizon. As the last light of day had passed away behind the mountains, the queen fell to her knees and wept. Yet, she was not alone. The Spirit of the Moon, enveloped in locks of silver hair, rose above her and saw her weeping. Seeing the lady's great despair, the Moon took pity on her.

"Fair daughter of the earth," the Spirit of the Moon called down to her, "Why do you weep? What troubles your soul?"

"O Queen of the Starlit Heavens," she bowed humbly, "I have come to the forest to make an offering to the Sun. At the first light, I began my song, and all through the hours of the day I have sung, but he did not perceive my offering, nor did he hear my voice."

"And why is it that you have made such a quest?"

"My only wish is for a child... a child of my very own. I have waited such long years for a child."

"Come," the Spirit beckoned, "The Sun is greedy for gold, yet I am honoured with silver. Pray, let me hear your song, that I may consider your plea."

And so, the woman lifted her voice, so soothing and tranquil, the Moon was overwhelmed with peace. No song could have been more worthy of the Spirit's magic. At this, the Moon was very pleased with the woman's song and offering, and therefore granted the lady's wish. Soon she conceived and told her friend of all that had transpired. The first queen bore a son and called him Auringon. The second queen bore a daughter and called her Kuun. Conceived and born of such ancient magic, the children carried with them forever, the essence and blessing of the Great Spirits.

As the first queen brought forth her son, the people rejoiced, for an heir had finally come. Her husband found joy in her again, and there was peace once more. Yet, for the second queen, as she brought forth her daughter, her husband grew all the more bitter, for she had failed him. The woman soon succumbed to grief and died before the child was yet old enough to remember her.

Years passed, and as the girl grew into a woman, and the boy into a man, so their affection blossomed into their love. Auringon and Kuun desired each other with such a passion, and so pledged their everlasting love.

For this reason, they sought out the Great Spirits, with offering and song, to seek their blessing. Generously, the Spirits bestowed it. The Spirits of the Sun and Moon entrusted Vasar with the crafting of two brooches as a symbol of their union. The first, engraved with a rising sun over the forest; the second, with a moon calming the seas. Auringon and Kuun exchanged their vows in secret, and under the starlit night were they wed by the Spirit of the Forest. Yet, their happiness was but a mist, for upon the maddening seas, the ships of war were coming.

Lóknir the Wolf's Fang, the fearsome warrior, led his men across the waves, pillaging, and raiding, and making ready to challenge Auringon's rule. But for a time, Auringon would not hear of such a tale, for he esteemed it folly and so dismissed the warning until the hour grew too late. In great haste, the beloved king pleaded with the Guardian of the Wood, to aid in the protection of his people. But Hirthir refused; he would not condescend unto the wars of mortal men. Auringon must face his foe alone.

As the ships of the enemy drew upon the shoreline, Auringon cautioned Kuun to remain in the forest with the other women, and the children; but his wife was of such stubborn blood, she would not yield. Secretly, she stole unto the battle, a bold shield-maiden. As she fought, the dread Wolf's Fang caught sight of her; the fair queen who bore the silver brooch. And he would have her. Savage as a wild beast, he overpowered her, and as his men retreated beside him, with their hoards of treasures taken, Lóknir took Kuun upon his ship. Though she cried out for her beloved, Auringon could not hear her for the thunderous battle, until the ship had fled. Despondent, he watched upon the shore, his darling stolen from him across the seas. There, Auringon cried out to his father, the Sun, for the loss of his wife. He then swore to seek her, day and night, and bring her home once more. At this, the Spirit of the Rising Sun roared so fiercely in anger at the wickedness of such reckless mortals; appalled that any mere creature would seek to mar that which the Great Spirits had so richly blessed. The Spirit of the Moon rushed to the Sun's side, and together they wept over the destruction of such a union. They would curse the land with darkness, for in the darkness of man's evil did Auringon and Kuun suffer such a fate. Thus, for a time, the land lay in shadow.

Far away over the raging seas, Lóknir took Kuun as his bride. And as the wolf howls to the moon in vain, so too did Lóknir lavish Kuun in empty promises of love; yet she would never love him, and would never heed the call of the hound.

Soon, she bore a daughter of her own and did bequeath the moon brooch to the child, in hopes that perhaps her daughter would have more luck than she. In time, as the long years wore on, Auringon grew weary of searching over land and sea. So lonely in his heart, he found comfort in a simple wife. She bore him a son, and to the child was the sun brooch given, in hopes that he would find his true love, though his father did not. As the centuries passed, the moon brooch was handed down from mother to daughter, as the sun brooch was handed down from father to son. And while these two lines grew far apart, what held each together, though unknowingly, was the Ballad of Auringon and Kuun, sung ever in their remembrance. Though each had come to live well and die in peace, the shores of their kingdom, they never saw again, and how the people waited earnestly for the return of the king.

Now far in the shadows of the forest, Hirthir was summoned by the Sun and the Moon. Out of their great anger, they rebuked him, for it was he who counselled those queens to seek the magic of the Great Spirits, and out of this Auringon and Kuun were created. It was he who was appointed to guard them, yet had come to abandon them in their weakest hour. Finally, the Spirits of the Sun and Moon gave Hirthir this command: he must restore that which was broken. The vows forged by Auringon and Kuun would not be so abandoned, for it was out of magic they were brought forth, and sealed with magic was their union.

Thus, the Spirits sang forth their final warning, to their servant of the earth:

Upon thine shoulders, this thy portion,
Reconcile the vows left broken,
Beware, servant, lend ear to our call,
For if the children of Light should fall,
Should the Forest fail his quest,
The earth shall lay forever in rest.
The lands laid waste under blackened seas,
The darkness of night shall never cease.
If one should succumb to death's dreaded gate,
The second shall fall, intertwined in death's fate;
The third shall remain only to breathe,
A final breath at the curse's eve.
O Lord of the Forest, cling to what is said,
For a moment unwatched shall bring forth the dead.

The Great Lights hovered no longer over the land, and returned high above into their heavenly realm, as their servant awaited the appointed time.

But a secret remained, for in the first the age of the realm, Hirthir found love in a daughter of the earth. A maiden who dwelt by the riverside, with hair of bright, golden hues. She conceived and bore a son who grew to inherit the guardianship over the forest. He ruled by his father's side until his earthly body faded, though his spirit ever remained in the Blessed Wood with his beloved father. The bloodlines continued, and the eternal bond between the children of the Sun, the Moon, and the Forest, could not be shaken.

The descendants of light would be protected by the Forest; the descendants of Auringon and Kuun ever guarded, until the appointed time when the lines should be reforged once more, in hopes that their love would one day be redeemed.

BOOK ONE
FOREST

CHAPTER ONE

JUSTICE AND MERCY

"For these crimes committed: high treason against his royal majesty Prince John; aiding and freeing criminals of the law; and the murder of Sheriff Rothgar of Nottingham, you are found guilty." Callously, the plaintiff lowered his parchment and sneered at the criminal. "Does the condemned have any final words?"

Harrowing, the guards stood about the criminal as he fell subject to the weight of it all; the crowds roaring indignantly over him as the stone walls of the courtyard closed in about him, and the heat from the sun, blazing.

Until this moment, the man had let his head hang so that his dark locks fell about his face like a cloak. Wearily, he lifted his gaze, with hard eyes locked upon the woman before him. Her stature grand, her face fair, and her eyes an icy fury.

"Have you anything to say?" The woman inquired proudly, towering over the wretched man.

"If you were not such a coward, you would have my head roll before your feet this day," he glared. "If you despise me so, why wait? Why not be done with it?"

Now Lady Claudia could no longer mask her revulsion of the man before the court. "You fool," she muttered, drawing down her hands in fists at her sides. "You really believe I would give a black-hearted murderer a quick death? Why should I make any gesture to spare your humiliation? What justice is there if the people are robbed of your glorious demise?"

Gisborne knew, even in some small measure, this was what he deserved. Still, in the heat of his anger, he spat at the woman's feet. "Guards! Take this traitor to the dungeons!" She commanded, her gaze narrowing fiercely, and how her words did pierce as a knife in his ear.

Whether by the folly of impulse, or violent inclination, Gisborne's life had crumbled into a chasm of darkness. All manner of goodness that dwelt within him was snuffed out, and he had quite forgotten the taste of anything but bitter revenge. Anything worthy was but a vapour of a past life.

Grasping his shoulders forcibly, the guards ushered the criminal towards the castle. They advanced under the high stone arch and into the grim hall. As they did so, the man stole one final glimpse of the afternoon sun, and he would never feel its warmth again.

Dark halls, dark passages, dark stairways. So often had Gisborne walked them as the captor, proud and arrogant, but now, the captive; fearful and self-loathing.

As they made their way through the dungeons to his cell, the guards sharply swung open the metal bars, cast the prisoner malignantly inside, and slammed the door behind them. It was hastily locked, then the guards left him. Cut off far from the others, seldom used or maintained when vacant, stood the cell. No openings for sunlight; no bench or bunk. Iron bars, stone, and the foreboding cold would be his only comforts.

Languid, he rested upon the stone floor, leaning his back against the wall. His long legs stretched out before him, and his tired arms folded across his chest. He stared into nothingness and after a while, fell asleep, diving into a sea of his own eternal torment...

The restlessness of nightmares haunted him to consciousness as he awoke that first morning.

No guards came, and the day drew on, silent and hollow. Time flowed on, and the prisoner soon felt the stinging pangs of hunger.

He considered how much longer he would endure, or how swiftly starvation and thirst would end him.

How greatly he desired death to greet him.

***

On the morning of the third day, Gisborne lay worn; his lips parched and his stomach aching; his cheek roughly pressed against the unforgiving cell floor. Sluggishly, he arose to discover something he did not expect. By the slot, at the base of the cell door, there was food. A half-penny loaf, an apple, and a flask of water. Awe shocked him, then desperation drove him.

Ravenously, he ate until every morsel was devoured; and yet, he convinced himself to stretch the life of the water, sipping just enough to make it last throughout the day. There he lay for a time, pondering who or how. Perhaps Claudia felt some pity for the wretched man.

No. She craved my suffering. It would not be her, the man determined in his thought.

Night fell, morning rose, and all day Gisborne hoped for another source of respite.

Nothing.

On the following morning, he feared to open his eyes and disappoint his aching stomach. Yet, as he turned to face the entrance, he discovered a fresh half-penny loaf, an apple, the flask of water refreshed. Beside the food, lay neatly folded garments and a basin of water with a small cloth beside it. His trembling hands gently lifted the materials. Unfolding them, he revealed a tunic, a pair of trousers, and a blanket of flax. Raising the fabric to his face, he inhaled the sweet scents of lavender. Breathing deep, he shut his eyes, as a glimpse of kinder days swept over his mind. And as soon as the vision came, it vanished. When his thirst was quenched, and his stomach satisfied, the prisoner undressed, dipping the cloth in the cold water and drawing it over his body. Though he was given very little, the man contemplated who his mysterious benefactor could be, and why they came. He only knew that this creature or spirit appeared as he slept, unhindered by any of the guards. Gisborne then considered the deafening reality, how this would not be a lasting kindness.

The days beyond were humbly anticipated, though, in his heart, his great unworthiness choked any hope.

***

Beneath the cool and tranquil mists of the early morning air, alone, Robin arose and departed from his men, far from the comforts of the forest unto the village of Locksley.

As he followed along the path between the huts and hovels, he looked upon the slowly waking world, breathing deep the scents of the dew-covered earth and listening well to the faint, rumbling thunder so far off yet drawing ever nearer.

How soft and sober his pale green eyes shone as he surveyed the village; his dark blonde hair whisping across his brow in the wind's sighs. Tall and lean, he stood; his cloak of earthen hues waving as a banner behind him, and his hood drawn up, concealing his features.

While the world lay so still and quiet below such grey skies, suddenly, his keen ears heard the whimpering of a young child from a simple cottage not far behind him. Halting in his steps, the man turned to find the child, thin and pale, clinging to the garment of a frail young woman who held in her hand a small satchel.

"Please mama," the child cried. "Can't I have a bite? I'm hungry."

"Shh," the mother consoled, kneeling down before him and holding his little face in her tender hand. "I know, my love, but we must bring this to your father."

"But I'm hungry!" The little boy rubbed at his tearful eyes, as his mother held him in her arms, holding back her own tears.

"Now, we can't be selfish," she chided. "Papa has been waiting very patiently for us to bring him food-"

"Why can't he come back home? Why did the soldiers have to take him away?"

"Darling, we mustn't let your father go hungry. We will eat tomorrow, I promise."

"But when will papa come home?"

"Soon, soon. But for now, we must be strong and wait," the mother reassured, as the boy nodded, his little head hung low as he let out a sigh.

Witnessing all this, Robin could not restrain himself, for his heart bid him hence. "Wait!" He called out, running back to where the woman and the child stood.

Finding a strange man bounding toward her, the woman stepped back in fear, her hands firm upon her son's shoulder. "Who are you and what do you want?" She pressed.

"Forgive me, I only wish to help," he answered gently, revealing a loaf of bread from his satchel and holding it out towards the woman. "I am Robin Hood. Please, take the bread, and eat," he entreated.

"Robin Hood," she whispered, her eyes wide. For a moment the woman hesitated, but glancing down at her son, she let out a sigh and nodded. "Thank you," she answered, as she retrieved the loaf of bread and tore away a piece for the boy. "He's not eaten since yesterday morning," she confessed.

"And how long has it been since you've eaten?" Robin wondered.

"Does it matter?" She shook her head, though a simple light grew behind her eyes as she watched her son eat.

"But you said you were taking some food to the boy's father. Is this all you have?" He pointed to a simple satchel with just a few apples inside.

Silently the woman nodded, glancing away from the outlaw's eyes. "We've been rationing our food since my husband was taken weeks ago. I wanted to be sure he was given something."

"Taken? By who?"

"The sheriff's men," she answered, "He was taken to debtor's prison, and as it is we've scarce enough to keep us going. I've been doing what I can, trying to save enough money so they might release him, but we... we," suddenly amidst her words, she burst into tears, drawing her hand over her mouth.

Compassion in his eyes, Robin laid a tender hand upon her shoulder, "What is your husband's name?"

"Errol," she answered, wiping away the tear upon her cheek. "But, we were only given so long to pay the debt. If the debt cannot be paid in full, in two days..." pausing in her confession, the woman glanced down at her son, at such innocent eyes, and daren't continue. But looking back to the outlaw, the man readily understood. "Please, Robin, would you help us? Could you not speak before the sheriff on his behalf?"

Drawing his hand up to his bearded chin, the man thought. "That I cannot do, for I am as much a threat to the sheriff as any outlaw," he began, "but, I would not have you travel alone with the child to the castle. It is too far. Here," he revealed from his purse a sum of money, "this should be enough for you and your son to buy some food this day. Remain in Locksley. I shall go in your stead and bring provisions to your husband."

"But can you free him?" She implored, her dark eyes grasping for any hope.

"You have my word, I shall bring the matter before my men, and certainly, you and your son will be well looked after," he promised.

At length, the man bid farewell to the woman and her child, having given them what other provisions he already possessed, and made his way beyond the village toward Nottingham and the daunting castle. Along the way, the rebel of goodwill purchased what provisions he had means of gaining, and cautiously, he entered the courts of the castle.

Daylight had been dismantled behind the thick storm clouds overhead, the rain speckling the stone of the courtyard, as he reached the steps. Having enough coins to satisfy one of the guards the man was led under the high stone archway and down into the dungeons. Unnatural darkness and the stale stench of the place was inescapable. Then, being directed passed the cells of wailing prisoners, finally, the guard unlocked the door to one man's cell. Before the outlaw, a man of such stature stood, his ankle shackled and the chain secured to the wall behind him. The man only looked on in anger and fear, yet as the cell door shut, and the guard was far off, Robin removed his hood, and laid the provisions before the man.

"Errol," the rebel whispered, "I have come on behalf of your wife and son."

"Who are you?" The man wondered.

"I am Robin Hood," he answered.

"Robin!"

"Shh!" The outlaw scolded, bringing a finger to his lips.

"But what business have you here? Shouldn't you be galavanting through the forest in search of wealthier pockets to pick?"

"I am here because the suffering of your family has been made known to me. Your wife spoke with me of what the sheriff has done, and I am come to give you my word that she and your son will be looked after."

"But how... how did they come to find you?"

"I found them," he answered, "but if I am to free you, I must know all that has happened."

"You would truly do this? You would set me free?" Errol stared, astonished.

"I can do nothing if I do not know the full account," he answered honestly, as he sat and motioned for the man to sit before him and eat. "Now, we must be quick. The guard will return shortly."

"Yes, yes," the man agreed, tearing away a piece of bread and drinking from a flask before he began. "Not four months ago, a new tax was enforced on the surrounding villages; a farmer's tax. Once a month the guards would come to collect payment. A month

ago, we simply didn't have enough, certainly not enough for us to
have anything left. As we hadn't the sum, I was taken until the debt
could be paid off, but then because I was taken, the debt was
doubled."

"And the sum?"

"Twenty crowns," the man sighed. "No farmer could produce that
in one month. That is why the others were taken."

"Others? What others?" Robin's brows furrowed.

"Five other men were taken from the village that day, along with
myself, and for greater debts even than my own," Errol shook his
head. "We will be hung soon if we are not reprieved. But what can
be done? Who would have such a sum to release all of us?"

Contemplating all this, the outlaw sat in silence, for in his
estimation, this would be a difficult task, but one he could not cast
aside. Something must be done, for it was injustice in itself that
such a tax be made upon those who could never yield the means to
pay it. As the thought rose to his lips, Robin made as if to answer
the man, but before he could speak his mind, the guard had
returned. Throwing his hood over his head, Robin concealed
himself from any suspicious eye.

"It is time," the guard declared, swinging back the iron door.

"Promise me you will consider this cause?" Errol entreated the
outlaw.

"You have my word," Robin bowed his head, as he departed from
the dungeon.

***

Returning to his men, deep within the forest, the outlaw brought
the entirety of the matter before the company, urging them to lend
their mind, for if anything was to be done, it must be done with the
utmost care.

"We cannot stand idly by," Robin determined, "If you had only
been there to see the young lad. He could not have known more
than four winters, and now he starves because the sheriff has so
oppressed his family. And we do not yet know of how the other
families have been afflicted."

"Master, you do not see reason," Tuck petitioned, "*All* of this land
has been oppressed, by sheriff after sheriff, guard after guard, all
the very servants of the dread prince, and he, the one who would
see every poor farmer cast into prison to meet his gain!"

"And so because these men are a few amongst many, we have no
cause to defend them?" Robin rebutted. "They will die if we do
nothing."

7

Stepping forward, Little John folded his arms across his chest, his grey and wild hair falling about his shoulders. "Think. Even if we set this one man free, the others will grumble that we have not considered them, and it will not be long before Rothgar uses this as fuel to defame our cause; to slander us as nothing more than common outlaws."

"We must do something!" Robin insisted. "I gave the woman my word that she and her child would not be left to starve."

"Aye, and we'll not let them starve," Alan agreed, "but we cannot free her husband."

"Then what shall *she* say if we do nothing?" Will added, standing firm amidst the men. "It is according to practice that the sheriff so condemns us, but the people will not believe such lies if we uphold our honour. Surely, we have enough treasures in our hoard to appease the debt of the six?"

"Scarlet, this is madness!" Alan roared, his dark eyes blazing. "Would they not suspect that the sum came from the coffers of the Rebel and his company? And how do you suppose we are to deliver the sum to free the men? Would we give such gold to their wives and so allow them to be taken as they were aided by outlaws?"

"And do you not trust that our master already has a plan?" Will defended, then stepping back he watched as the outlaw sat silent, "You... you do have a plan, don't you, master?" He questioned.

Twisting the golden ring upon his finger, the man stared at the earthen floor before him and shook his head. "No," he mumbled, "No, I don't."

"Then it is settled," Tuck determined, "We will bring provisions to this woman and her son, and perhaps discover the other families in need, but nothing more can be done."

For a moment the men stood about the camp, so conflicted. At length, Robin stood with stern eyes as he looked on each of his men.

"How can we be so divided?" He sighed, "Is this not the very reason we took up oaths? To protect the people from such tyranny? Is this not the reason you appointed me your leader?"

"Robin, surely, you are a man of conviction and compassion beyond all of us, but you must see that we risk far too much in this endeavour," A'Dale thought.

At this, the outlaw could not bear the sight of them, and storming away from the men, he drew farther into the forest, to be alone. There, he did sit beneath the boughs of the wood, the night skies shrouded under cloud, as he pondered the circumstance. Downcast, he thought on his men, and on his people, and on those of greater consequence from whom he had departed, so long ago. Then, just as his heart took such steps towards despair, following its tempting call, Scarlet drew near and sat beside him; his long copper hair hanging down his back and his soft eyes looking out into the cheerless night.

"Master," he began, "whatever you decide, we are with you."

"Truly?" Robin challenged. "It would seem, that while the world teems with people, with minds and eyes to perceive many things, I am the only one who sees these people in their need," he sighed. "There are too many minds that do not think; too many hearts that do not feel. Why is it that I must bear this burden alone?"

"You consider this a burden? To care for others as you do?" Will questioned.

"No, no. The burden is not my care for them, but my sight. I alone see and have sacrificed much indeed to meet such need, and yet, none other sees in this way, and thus I stand with a weight upon my shoulders with none to lend me aid, and with many swift to afflict me for it."

"Master, how can you reason in this way?" Scarlet thought, "Indeed, it is an evil that many have so gluttoned themselves on wealth and power while the people suffer to supply it. Yet, you have arisen and taken up this banner, to be a light and a hope to this land! This is not to be taken lightly. And while the men and I have not sacrificed what you have sacrificed, nor have we been so afflicted as you, all the same, we stand beside you!"

Comforted, Robin glanced up at Will as the man concluded this thought and rose to his feet. "Whatever you decide, master, we will follow you," he encouraged.

Returning to the camp, Scarlet let the man alone for a time, to ponder all that laid upon his heavy heart.

***

At length, the men held council once more and came to an accord.

As Robin had only spoken with Errol and his family and had not come to know the names or the faces of the other men, they would free this one man. For if the sum for the six were to be presented, Rothgar would indeed discover the company's influence and they could not risk the lives of more people under such wrath. Moreover, it would be better to show mercy to one, than to show no mercy whatsoever.

As dawn awakened the men from their slumber, each readied himself for what work could be done in Locksley village, as Robin, along with the woman and her son, ventured to Nottingham. Having given the woman the sum, he accompanied her and the child as far as the castle, but beyond that point, he dare not go, for he had already risked being discovered when he sought out the prisoner the day before. There, at the entrance to the courtyard, he waited with the child, as the woman went before the sheriff to present the money. Thus was it granted that the man be set free.

Finally, descending down the steps came Errol and his wife. Looking up with such joy, the child bounded toward his father, and the man caught him up in his arms.

"Robin, I don't know how I shall ever thank you," the man proclaimed, as he reached the outlaw by the gates.

"Do not forget me," he answered plainly, a simple grin upon his lips.

As he and the family departed, the man and his wife and the child returning to their home, Robin and his men completed what work was to be done that day. Soon, it was brought to the attention of the company, the other families whose men were taken, and whatever they needed, the company was quick to supply it. Yet all the while, the thought of those other men weighed on the Rebel's mind, and how he wished there were some means of freeing them.

As the final light of day faded beyond the horizon, suddenly, a great cry of joy resounded through the village, at the sight of five men marching down the road. The men had been set free! Amongst all the wives and children who embraced the men, Robin drew forth in such wonder.

"How has this come to pass?" He asked of them.

"It is a miracle!" One farmer answered, his smile broad as he held up his child in his arms. "Ready to face the gallows we were when suddenly the guards came into the dungeons and had declared all our debt had been paid in full! They removed our chains and bid us return to our homes!"

"But how can this be? Who presented the sum?"

"They did not say," the man shook his head, "Only some noble had come with money enough to acquit us, and the debt was more than two hundred crowns between us. All the same, whoever the noble was, we'll thank our stars for him tonight!" He beamed.

At this, the rebel company was astounded and in such mirth did the whole village celebrate.

**

Though the night had given each one some comfort, how the morning would rise on a day of blood, and the cries of the people could be heard from afar. That very night when the six were pardoned, and each home lay quiet, Rothgar and his men did ride hard through the village, with force and power, searching for the six. When the six had been found, the soldiers slaughtered them before the people, for it was not their own money by which their freedom was rendered, and therefore, they were still in opposition to the law. Yet Robin and his men did not discover this treachery until the morning, and how they did weep over such innocent blood spilt.

Yet before they could devise any means of avenging the people, justice had taken hold the reigns, for the very next morning, the sheriff was declared dead; murdered in his own bed. And to everyone's astonishment, the deed was done by Sir Guy of Gisborne.

CHAPTER TWO

OCEAN AND IRON

How the silence of the air felt as a void, creeping into the prisoner's mind, consuming him.

Neither voice, nor breath, nor the gentle whisper of the wind met his ear, and he was beginning to forget the sounds he had once known so well. Nought but the heavy thud of ironclad footsteps marching through the corridors beyond could remind him of his humanity. Soon, Gisborne could no longer decipher the nightmares from his waking.

Finally, one night, the man determined he would not sleep. Submission to sleep was submission to madness. Indeed, it fared far better to brave the silence than to be captive in his memories. Adamant, he remained awake as long as possible, attempting to witness the secret spirit, for he was resolved to discover whether it was of his own imaginings. As the evening hours crept on, he waited in agony. His heart sunk as he doubted he would ever see it. Positioned closer to the entrance of the cell, he hoped to catch a better glimpse of this creature, though he remained at a sensible distance if perchance this being proved to harbour any malcontent.

Considering all that could unfold in such an encounter, the man sifted through his thoughts as his eyes followed the faint and flickering light from a far off torch. Much as the tide washes up against the shore, so the light advanced and retreated over the uneven stone. Gisborne studied the rhythm of the firelight and its shadows, his pale blue eyes seeking out impatiently. His very breath resonated in the flow of the dancing light.

At length, nothing happened.

When he could no longer cling to curiosity, and all his doubting fostered disappointment, he suddenly heard a peculiar sound. Soft, timid footsteps approaching. Nearer and nearer they came as if the very anticipation and unquenchable longing of the man drew them. Every muscle tensed as he listened to the ripples in the air, quieting his anxious breath.

Opening his eyes slowly, cautiously, he saw... her.

A young lady of delicate stature hovered before the entrance, her figure draped in a cloak as dark as the sea. Hastily, she knelt down and set to work, arranging the food and drink, and preparing the new garments. So desperately did the prisoner desire to see her face, to truly know whether she was just a hopeless vision.

Impetuous, he sprung to his feet, thoughtlessly clinging to the bars of the cell and staring at her with such intensity. Yet in so doing, he startled the lady so that she cried out in fright and dropped one of her belongings, frantically running back into the darkness.

"Wait!" He cried out, reaching his arm through the bars, his face pressed up against the cold iron. "Please... come back!"

Whoever she was, she did not answer, nor look back. The spirit had vanished.

"Idiot," Gisborne rebuked himself angrily, hurling a kick at the bars, and gritting his teeth.

Then, at the base of the entrance, something caught his eye. Kneeling down, he reached his hand through the bars. Groping towards the object, the tips of his fingers slowly drew it closer until he could firmly grasp it. "A silver brooch?" He murmured, tilting his head as the fragile light from the distant torch illuminated the treasure.

Engraved upon it was a great wave of the sea and a full moon devoutly guarding the wave from above. In an instant, a memory swept fast across his mind; a memory not wholly his own. In the hollows of his thought, he beheld the face of a woman with hair as black as night and eyes as bright as silver; there she stood upon a shoreline, her ivory hand reaching forth. As she looked on him, she whispered something; something which his ears could not hear, yet his heart understood and all at once forgot. As quickly as the memory came, it fled, and as he was left to ponder his vision, he craved all the more to know of who this maiden was that had left this treasure.

***

All through the hours beyond, Gisborne thought on the young lady, determined more than ever to see her again. As night approached, he remained positioned closer to the entrance, and the treasure never left his hand. There he waited so still; listening. His heart pounded within his chest, as everything in him yearned so fervently to break through those wretched bars. And as all those nights before, she came! His longing was not in vain, for her footsteps beckoned him and he was ready for her.

According to her way, the lady knelt down before the cell to set out the provisions, but amidst her work, she was suddenly stopped by a quick hand, reaching through the bars, gripping firmly about her arm. Letting out a gasp, she shuttered under the man's touch, her breath hastening.

"Don't be afraid," he whispered, "I only wish to see you."

Under the touch of his hand, the lady lifted her face, so her eyes of a brilliant silver hue met his enamoured gaze, yet she did not look on him in wonder, as he, but in fear. Realising he had frightened her, the man gently released her arm.

"Forgive me, I've no wish to harm you. Who... who are you?" He wondered.

Yet, she made no answer.

"You're the one who has come to care for me. But why?" He asked. "Please, tell me your name? Or are you a vision that you cannot speak?"

For a moment, the maiden seemed so unsure of what to do, though she knew she must requite his curiosity in some measure.

"First, I am no vision. If I were, you would not be able to grip my hand," she said, her subtle French accent lingering on the tip of her tongue. "And my name does not matter."

"But it does matter," he said. "How can I thank you if I do not know your name?"

Again the maiden delayed in giving an answer, for though he had released her, she hardly looked on him, but only as she must, and how she kept her distance from him, nervous he would reach out toward her again.

"You are afraid of me?" He sighed.

Timid, her eyes glanced up but a moment, as she hurried about her work. Finally, as she found the courage to speak, she answered the man. "I...I know who you are, and why you are here," she whispered.

"I see," he folded his arms across his chest, his voice rough and angered. "If you are so enlightened, why do you bother coming at all? Have you come to taunt me?"

"That is not my purpose," her brows furrowed.

"Why, then?" His jaw tensed, "To prey on my humiliation?"

"Surely, if my coming has angered you so, I will leave you this instant," she stood, emboldened. "But to accuse me of such a motive as to mock you-"

"Answer me," he demanded. "Why have you come?"

Letting out a deep sigh, the lady lowered her gaze. "I... made a promise," she confessed.

"A promise? To who?"

"It is a secret," she resolved.

As he stared hard at the maiden, his eyes shone cold, "Was it Lady Claudia who sent you? To spy on me?"

"What?"

"Hoping to find my corpse?"

"No," she returned, gripping the iron bars as she looked on him. "And how can you think such a thing when I have been giving you food and drink all this while? If Lady Claudia had wished to send anyone to spy on you, it *would* be for the sake of finding your dead body or else one might put you out of your misery."

"Then who has sent you?" He pressed.

Cautious, the maiden thought, for she must be careful with what words she spoke to him, "I was sent by one who knows you of old."

"An enemy?"

"A friend," she answered. "He bid me come. Therefore, it is for his sake that I have made good on my promise."

Pensive, the man remained, rubbing at the back of his neck as he searched every name in his mind. Yet, he could deliver none, for who would defend his cause or take compassion on him at such an hour?

"This *friend of old*, what name has he given you?" He pondered.

"Forgive me, but I cannot tell you," she shook her head.

"And yet he sends you in his stead, on my behalf? Why?" Gisborne thought aloud, wholly perplexed. Glancing back at the young lady, he perceived the gentleness in her eyes; how young she was, and how she must have been frightened, being forced on such a horrid errand. "Did this friend tell you the dangers of coming here?" He questioned, "Do you not understand? If the guards were to discover you-"

"I knew the dangers full well. Now I must go," she gazed down, slowly backing away from the cell. "Farewell, Sir Guy."

"You mean to say, you have fulfilled your promise?"

"Oui, peut être..." she said.

"Go on, then. Leave," he hissed, turning his back to her.

Still and silent, the maiden lingered a moment; her fists clenched. Looking on the man, alone in the dark, she could not depart so heedlessly. While her head persisted most arduously that she withdraw, it was her heart which coaxed her to stay. Try as she might, she could not ignore her heart, for it grew heavier and heavier, as if it were anchored where the man remained.

"Perhaps," she hesitated, "I could return tomorrow."

Turning about, the prisoner faced her once more with doubting eyes. "I thought you had fulfilled your promise?"

"Yes, but I cannot... I could come again if you so wish it," she answered.

The prisoner nodded, then looking up at her, his eyes shone cold once more. "I would not wish you come again, save it was of your own will, though what risk you take troubles me. But, how can I be sure that you will return?" He challenged.

Kneeling down before the cell, the lady gazed upon the prisoner curiously. "You have it with you, do you not?"

At first, the man was unsure of what she meant, then upon understanding her, he revealed the brooch she had left the night before. "Yes," he nodded, holding it forth in his hand. "It's a rare treasure, indeed."

Though she had retrieved it, she thought a moment, and then, quite unexpectedly, held it out toward him. "Keep it. It is my promise that I shall return," and in his hand, the maiden placed her gift.

"Thank you," he said, smoothing his thumb over the patterns upon the silver. "But please, tell me, what is your name?"

Ambivalent, she turned away. Then after a pause, she finally acquiesced. "The brooch tells you my name. Regardez," she said. Reaching her hand through the bars, she traced the carvings on the silver with her little finger. "This is my name."

"Your name is *the moon*?"

"No, no," the lady permitted a gentle grin, "My name is Múriel. It means a bright sea."

"Múriel," he echoed with a soft smile on his lips, "It's beautiful."

"Now, I must leave," she rose to her feet.

"I know," he stood, gripping the bars. "Until tomorrow, Múriel?"

"Jusqu'à demain, Sir Guy. Until tomorrow," she bowed her head.

At these parting words, the prisoner watched as her cloak swirled and tossed about, down and away beyond him.

And Gisborne would wait for her; unwavering.

***

Two weeks had passed, and after having made a proclamation before the people of Gisborne's death, though none made good on determining this, Lady Claudia returned to more pressing matters at hand. Swiftly after Rothgar's demise, she was appointed as sheriff over Nottingham, for she was an intimate of Prince John, and he trusted her well enough to give her such power.

As the sun arose on that bright summer morning, the woman awoke to all the luxuries of her chamber in the castle. Maids came padding across the stone floor and drew back the scarlet curtains, the cheerful sunshine beaming through the panes, caressing every golden lock upon the woman's head. Swift, the maids laid out fine clothes and jewels. No sooner had the woman wakened than she bounded toward her dressing table. Brushing her long hair over and over again, she admired what fair reflection she found in the mirror.

Suddenly, amidst her calm and comfortable reveries, a ferocious fist blundering against the door startled the woman. Before she was given leave to find her feet, a guard came bursting into the chamber.

"What is the meaning of this?" Claudia shrieked, drawing a shawl from the end of her bed as she clutched it over her chest. "Am I to be so maltreated in my own castle?"

"Forgive me, your grace," the guard bowed, "but your presence is needed at this very moment!"

"Why? What has happened?" She implored.

"The taxes from Locksley, everything is gone!"

"Gone? What do you mean *gone*?"

"My lady, the sum taken up from Locksley has been stolen!" He panted, anxious as she drew near, staring hard at the man.

"You mean to tell me, you let near three hundred crowns slip through your fingers?" She whispered, "Who did this, Dumont?" She glared fiercely.

"We do not yet know," he answered.

"Well have the thieves yet fled? Could they still be in the castle?" She wondered.

"I have ordered my men to search everywhere, and they are seeking out the blackguards even as we speak-"

"Then what are you doing pestering me before I've yet dressed?" The woman huffed, waving her hand in the air. "Away with you! Do not trouble me with this again until-"

Instantly, as she had been scolding the guard, she halted her breath, for through the crack of the doorway her eyes fell upon two hooded figures carrying a weighty trunk as they crept down the corridor. Drawing a finger to her lips, the woman gave a warning glance to her guard, and he did wait and listen.

"What else have you to say, Dumont?" She raised her voice, motioning with her eyes for him to advance into the corridor.

"My- my men have petitioned that the armoury be expanded. And we require more weapons," the man called back, keeping his breath as he silently followed the faint sound of the treasures rattling about in the wooden chest. "We've another ten men set to join our divisions come autumn, and we simply do not have the means to supply them."

"Very well. Deliver a full report by tomorrow of what is to be altered and what is lacking. I shall review it, and arrange everything accordingly," the woman continued in elevated tone, her eyes seeking out this way and that as the guard departed from her chambers.

"Don't be frightened, your grace," he whispered, "No harm shall come to you."

Without another word, the woman gave a sharp nod, watching as the man continued down the corridor where the thieves had traversed, and three of the guard's men caught up behind him. Retreating back into the chamber, Claudia ordered her maids to make haste to dress her, for she loathed the thought of missing the amusement of a menacing enemy's capture.

Emerging from her chambers, fully adorned, the woman scurried down the corridors with her maids, as the drumming of every soldier's foot and the roars of the men echoed through the halls.

Reaching the high arched window of the east tower, overlooking the courtyard from high above, the woman stared with wide eyes as she beheld the riot before her. How the guards did battle against the Rebel company. Robin Hood with his mighty bow loosed arrow after arrow upon them, as each of his men drew up their own blades and felled many a man of the division. Watching in such fury the woman's fists clenched tight, her eyes fixed upon the Rebel, for he was indeed no match for any of her guards.

Then, as each guard lay wounded and weary, scattered across the courtyard, a cavalry began to drive through, making as if to hedge them in, but the thieves were far too cunning to be so thwarted. Casting the great chest back against the fray, the men weaved their way through the braying horses and out into the city streets, winding here and there and everywhere into the thick of it. At that moment, to all who had warred against the dastardly outlaws, they seemed wholly vanished.

"Hah!" The woman laughed, drawing up her gown as she descended down the winding staircase, through the corridor and out unto the great stone steps beneath the archway of the keep.

"Well done, Dumont!" She grinned, flying down the steps as she greeted the man, though he stood half breathless. "Your men may have suffered some, but indeed the scoundrel shall not so easily gain our prize. Have your men fetch it here, if you please, and return it to the treasury."

"Aye, m'lady," he muttered, "Bring it forward!" He called out, as the only two of his guards who were well enough to stand gripped the chest and heaved it up to the final step. As they did so, Dumont unhinged the lock and opened the trunk, only to find that it was filled with rocks.

"No," he sighed, shaking his head.

At this, the Lady Claudia stared horrified, and so slapped the guard across his face.

"You realise that every coin in that chest belonged to Prince John?" She howled, "Now what word shall I send to him in lieu of the payment demanded? Men!" She called out unto the aching crowd, "Let these wounds be a lesson to you! Bleed if you must, but you shall not rest this day until every coin is returned from the filthy hands of those outlaws! Find them!"

***

The day drew on as it had so many times before; unyielding and empty. This time, Gisborne had reason for hope; his eagerness mingled with willing patience. As night fell, he listened for her footsteps.

"Please come," he whispered, with lips pressed lightly against the coolness of the silver brooch, as if to summon his enchantress.

Meditating on the movement of the light from the distant torch, taking in how much the light touched beyond its source, he waited. Indeed, the flame was at a considerable distance from his cell, yet, the stones before the entrance were somehow being illuminated. No sooner had the idea sprung in his mind, than he took up the flint and steel to light the candle she had left for him. Perhaps this could be a way for her to observe his readiness. The candle did not add much light at all to the cell, yet it flickered faithfully through the watches of the night.

He had not paid so much attention before as he had assumed for he suddenly heard the creak of a door, almost certainly a door, and then, like the ringing of raindrops came her light and agile footsteps.

"Múriel?" He called through the bars. "Múriel, is that you?"

"Shh! We must take care lest someone hears us," she rebuked in a whisper, hurrying to the entrance of the cell.

"You've come," he said, his eyes beaming.

"Of course. A promise I make is a promise kept," she smiled warmly, "And, I could not bear the thought of leaving you hungry."

As she spoke, the lady pulled back the hood of her cloak, revealing a waterfall of soft brown hues. "Here, I've brought you some water, and bread," she said. Removing the food from her basket, she slid each item under the slot of the cell door.

"I don't deserve this," he mumbled, his expression darkening.

Graciously, the maiden looked on him. "Let me be kind to you," she said.

"Thank you," he answered softly.

Gisborne's eyes remained so fixed upon her, a reserved grin lingering upon his face. To satisfy the lady, he took up the flask of water and tore away a piece of bread, but as the warmth of her words vanished, darkness reclaimed its grip.

How could anyone care? How long could she endure this?
He thought.

"I still think you risk too much in coming here," he said. "Perhaps you shouldn't have come at all," he swallowed; his heart aching at his own words.

"You say you wish for my company, yet you admonish me for coming?" She stared hard at the man.

"I am grateful for what you've done, truly-"

"If I had not come at all, you would be dead already."

"But coming here, helping me... it's foolish," he shrugged his shoulders.

"Then let me be a fool," she resolved. "I have come of my own volition, with no desire to find you dead. If the duty has befallen me, to be *foolish* so you might live, then I must yield."

The man shuttered a moment under her words, reflecting on what he had spoken against her and warring against such thoughts.

"Forgive me, I've no wish to offend you."

"Then don't," she concluded.

Gisborne nodded, picking up another piece of bread, and so unsure of what to say. "But, if you are bold enough to come here despite the danger, and keep a prisoner company, I must insist you answer my questions."

"Questions?" Múriel pursed her lips, "Trés bien alors... but I will only answer three of your questions tonight."

"I am only to ask you three questions?"

"I cannot stay here all night," she raised her brow, "Moreover, while you may insist upon satisfying your curiosity, I am bound both by time and matter. You may ask more of me another day, but for tonight, choose wisely. Do we have a deal?"

"Deal," the prisoner agreed.

Reflecting a moment, he studied how the light from the small candle was just enough to draw delicately over her features, and she was lovely to behold. Bringing her hand down to her lap, she used the other to prop herself up as she knelt before him.

"What weighs on your mind?" She wondered.

"First, why is it that you come here?" He asked, "Truly?"

"I don't understand, I have already given you my answer," she said, "I made a promise-"

"But you said yourself that you come of your own will. Why, then?"

"Do you still not know?"

"I don't understand why you trouble yourself, all for some worthless, forsaken wretch," Gisborne huffed, his eyes fixed upon the cell floor.

"How can you say that?"

"Say what?"

"That you are worthless and forsaken," Múriel drew closer to the cell, wrapping her fingers around one of the iron bars. "Every night I have come to supply your need, have I not?"

"Just answer my question," he rolled his eyes.

"And how can you think that you are worthless?"

"Because... it is so," he sighed.

"And who spoke such things to you? Who told you such a lie that you believe it so willingly?"

"I don't have to answer this-"

"But how have you come to so despise yourself?" She pressed.

Embittered, the man shook his head; his jaw tense. Turning his gaze away from the maiden, he remained silent. "Do you have no trust in me?" She dropped her shoulders.

Sombre and sullen, the man tilted his head back, staring up at the ceiling of the cell. "Why should I trust you? We hardly know each other."

"Oui, you are right," she acknowledged, "We hardly know each other at all." At this, the man drew forward, his eyes calculating. "But, have I not shown you much of myself in my coming here? In my willingness to tarry with you?" she asked. "Do you think me deceitful or false?"

Observing how steadily she spoke, and finding some comfort behind her eyes, he let out a deep breath and reclined once more against the stone wall.

"With all that I have done and all that cannot be undone, it would have been better if I..." he hesitated, his lips fearing to bear his thought.

"And what have you done?"

"Are you mad? You know why I'm here."

"No. Murdering the sheriff, it can't be all that is weighing upon your conscience," she determined; her sight keen. "Tell me, the things that cannot be undone... what have you done that has deprived you of any hope?"

"And why should I tell you anything?"

"Because I alone am here and willing enough to listen," she replied.

For a moment the lady waited, her fingers falling away from the iron. Parting his lips a moment as if to speak, he couldn't find the words to say. Then the words found their way to his lips.

"I took Rothgar's life because he forced me to kill someone," he said.

"You were an assassin?"

"No," he shook his head, "Oh, this is useless."

"Please," she reassured, drawing nearer. "Tell me."

The prisoner remained; his eyes shut tight, and his breath strained. There they sat for a time, in the stillness. Then as he lowered his head and opened his eyes, he spoke.

"He forced me to kill her," his voice cracked, breaking the silence.
Múriel's face flushed pale, as she stared at the confessor. "Who?"
"The woman I loved," he whispered.
"You loved her, yet you took her life?"
"No, you still don't understand-"
"Then what happened?" She implored, gripping the bars.
The prisoner closed his eyes a moment, composing his words, then opened his eyes once more, keeping his gaze away from the maiden.
"Not a year ago, I asked for her hand. But, when I confessed my love, she revealed to me, in confidence, her secret. She had already pledged herself to an outlaw, and the marriage had to be kept hidden. She swore me to secrecy, begged me to protect her should anything happen. She said if I loved her, I would do this, and I could not deny her. I gave her my word. If anyone discovered her connection with the outlaw, it would mean death. And so I took every precaution to keep the matter concealed. I pleaded with her over and over to leave, to remain in Sherwood with her husband, yet she refused. She fought to find another way to keep the marriage hidden, to keep... but when she had finally decided to leave, it was too late," Gisborne paused, bringing his hand over his mouth.
"Too late?" The maiden questioned. "What do you mean?"
"Somehow, and I don't know how, she was discovered," he continued, "She was making ready to flee the castle and a letter was found in her chamber, signed by the mark of the outlaw, detailing plans to conspire against the prince. It was enough evidence to prove her alliance with the Rebel, and because the marriage had been kept secret for so long, I had to continue in my pretences as if I never knew. That very night, I was called upon by Rothgar, to arrest her for high treason... I'll never forget her eyes that night," he confessed, "The next morning, the trial was held. She was found guilty and was sentenced to death."
Múriel's eyes welled with tears, as she gazed upon the man in horror. "You executed her?"
"She committed treason and was found out. I had no other choice."
"Yes, you did! Mon Dieu, you could have helped her escape, you could have defended her! You swore to protect her, and yet you abandoned her! Did she mean so little to you?"
"How dare you!" Enraged, Gisborne shouted through the bars, clutching the iron in his white-knuckled fists. "Rothgar is the one who sealed her fate. It is for this reason I put an end to him."

"And murdering him has brought her back?" The maiden rebuked. "Has it avenged her death or healed the pain of your heart?"

"You ignorant child, you know nothing of pain! What would you know of the pain I have suffered?" He roared, "Are you yet satisfied, *listening*? Do you now see why I wish death would take me? Why I loath my very life?"

Terrified, Múriel withdrew from the cell, staring in fear at the man before her. A man, so horribly broken. Gisborne released his hands from the bars, drawing his hand up to cover his face. Múriel knew she must speak, searching ardently for the words to say. Any words to break the deafening silence.

"I... I'm sorry-"

"Leave me."

"Sir Guy, please-"

"I said leave me!" He snarled, his glare raw and raging. Picking up the brooch, he cast it through the bars at her feet. "Go!"

Without another word, the maiden shuddered in fright. Taking the brooch, she sprinted to her feet and fled.

Alone, the prisoner succumbed to his despair once more. The hope of ever seeing Múriel again was lost, and in such anguish did he weep.

CHAPTER THREE

THE RHYTHM OF THE TIDE

The next day came and went, in bitter emptiness.

Thoughts of anger and of fear and of the dreaded end that awaited, all such weights ceaseless, and what longing he felt for the blessed final breath. The second day came, and drew on, as so many days before. His lips were parched and the pangs of his stomach, a restless taunt as he lay caged. Night fell, and the dawn of a third day lingered but a few hours away. There the prisoner lay upon the stone floor, motionless; not quite asleep or awake, craving and loathing death altogether.

Suddenly, like the first rays of sunlight beaming over the horizon, came the sound of those gentle footsteps he thought he would never hear again. Rising up, he peered through the cell, as she knelt before him, with provisions in hand.

"You've come back?" His brows raised.

"I've no wish for you to think me capable of abandoning you," she sighed, lighting a candle she had taken up from her belongings. "I promise not to bother you. I'll leave the food and go."

Reaching his hand through the bars, Gisborne gripped the edge of her cloak.

"No, would you please stay?" His sad eyes pleaded through the darkness. "I feared I would never see you again, and I realise I should not have spoken to you in that way... that was wrong."

"I understand why you were so angry," she muttered nervously. "I shouldn't have reproached you so."

"No, you were right to," he acknowledged, drawing his hand back. "Please, forgive me?"

Múriel paused in reflection, and knowing the man to be sincere, she nodded. Then turning her gaze away, she withdrew from him. "I'll leave you now."

"Wait," he called out, "You have allowed me to confess something I have never spoken of to another soul. Can I trust you, never to speak of it to anyone?"

"You have my word," she promised, lifting her hood, "Until tomorrow-"

"Please, don't go yet," he urged, "You said you would answer my questions, remember?"

Pensive, the young lady halted, then removed the hood once more, "Oui, you're right. I shall stay, but only long enough to answer your questions."

Seeing how his hands did tremble, how his face shone so pale, the lady shook away all apprehension and handed him the flask of water.

"Please, drink something," she encouraged, as he took the flask from her.

Leaning his shoulder against the cell door, he drew the flask up to his lips and drank until his thirst was quenched. But as he did so, the light from the maiden's candle shone over his neck; the bruises and the blood. Horrified, Múriel stared.

"Those wounds," she whispered, bringing her hand over her mouth, "Those wounds around your neck... why did they do this to you?"

"*They*?"

"The guards," she said.

Silent, the man strayed his eyes far from her. Breathing deep, he parted his lips, as he stared ahead at the wall of stone.

"This was not of their doing," he whispered, and in such shame did he bring up his hand to conceal his face.

Distraught, Múriel could scarce take her eyes from him. Such an encumbrance of sorrow swept over her heart, for indeed she could not bear such a grievous thought. With tears in her eyes, she reached through the cell and held fast his hand, and he, in turn, gazed back at her, astounded and fearful; his eyes brimming.

"Sir Guy," she began, her voice so gentle, "Would... would you allow me to speak plainly?"

The prisoner nodded, anxious to know the maiden's mind.

"You have allowed your past to define you irrevocably, but to continue in it will destroy you. You must not allow guilt to be your master. Do not indulge the lie that you are a slave to it, for surely as you live, you are not bound to it," she said, her eyes fixed so unwaveringly upon him, as tears fell down her face.

Gazing into such compassionate eyes, and hearing such words, the man was overwhelmed. Looking down at her hand in his, he nodded; his heart aching and his mind wrestling so with shame and doubt. For how could such a maiden come to feel any compassion for him?

"Why is it that you come?" He whispered, "What drove you to do any of this?"

"You know I cannot answer that question," she shook her head, "Not yet."

For a time, they permitted the silence, brushing away their tears. All the while, he never let go of her hand, and she, so concerned for him, had no wish for him to do so.

"May I ask more questions?" He finally asked.

"Of course," she said, "What else have you to ask of me?"

"If you cannot tell me *why* you come, then how is it that you are able to reach the dungeons? This cell is far from all the others, and surely it would be impossible to find this place without anyone noticing."

"Oh, well, that is a secret," the maiden answered calmly.

"Will you answer any of my questions or do you insist upon vexing me?" He rolled his eyes, releasing her hand as he folded his arms over his chest.

"I've no wish to anger you. Indeed, I'll answer you, save you ask questions of which I am free to give the answer," she sighed, "But, what is your final question, Sir Guy?"

"Well, as you cannot answer why you come, or how you've managed to accomplish getting here, could I ask more questions instead?"

"Yes, but only two. I haven't much time," she admitted, glancing down the corridor.

"Right," the prisoner sighed. "Well, this should be simple enough to answer: whose clothes are these?" He tugged at the collar of his tunic.

"That I can answer," Múriel smiled, "They belong to my brother."

"Your brother?" Guy lowered his chin.

"I have one elder brother, Henri," she said.

"Isn't he concerned that his sister is going to the dungeons every night, to bring his clothes to some filthy prisoner?"

"No, no," the lady raised her brows. "My brother is at war in the east. He is not here to use them, and he doesn't have to know."

"And what of your mother and father?" The man asked, "Do they know you come?"

"They died long ago," she replied.

"Then, you are all alone?"

Múriel's expression drew from warmth to coldness, her easiness fading as she thought, staring down at the cell floor. "I am," she nodded, letting out a deep breath.

"Well, when your brother returns, you'll have to give him my thanks," Gisborne said. "So, I am allotted one more question?"

"I'm ready," she said.

"You may think it strange, my asking this, but why do the garments you bring always smell of lavender?"

At this, Múriel's brows drew up instantly. "Oh, well, I grow lavender. It's how my family made their wages when we first came to England. We brought it with us from France, and I now have a garden full of lavender. I never thought of it before, but you are right! The clothes really do smell of lavender," she smiled sweetly.

"Yes, I've grown accustomed to it," the man fought away a grin upon his lips, "The fragrance makes me think of you."

Glancing back at her, Gisborne betrayed his fascination and yearning, though the lady did not immediately know it herself. Dodging her eyes between the man and the floor, she was so uncertain of how she felt, or whether such feelings could be trusted.

"If you are finished with your questions, there's still food for you to eat, and fresh garments," she remembered, searching through her satchel to retrieve the clothes. "Please, eat first, but when you are ready, you can change, and I can take the other clothes."

"But I thought you had to leave?"

"I could stay a little while longer," she nodded.

"Good," he grinned gratefully.

The prisoner ate until his aching stomach was contented, and he talked more with the maiden of her brother, and of the war, and of the people their king had quite forgotten because of it. As he finished eating, no sooner had she suggested he change, than the man stood up instantly grasping the hem of his tunic, pulling it over his frame.

"Here," he said as he held it towards her.

Swift, the maiden stood to retrieve it, and in so doing, beheld his stature. "Forgive me," she blushed, handing him the other garments just before she turned about. Staring at the stone wall before her, she waited.

"You can turn around now," he said.

As she faced him again, the maiden took in how the wine-dark tunic draped over his broad shoulders, and how a natural light gleamed in his eye.

"Let me take those for you," she held out her hand as he gave her the other garments.

"I must thank you," he sighed, his expression growing serious once more. "Truly, for everything. I don't deserve any of this."

"I am glad to be of some help if I can be," the maiden bowed her head. "But I really must leave you now."

Gisborne looked on her solemnly, tilting his forehead against the bars. "Must you go?"

"Wait," Múriel thought. Unclasping the brooch from her cloak, she held it out to him, as he accepted it. "I meant for you to keep it. As long as you have it, I will return."

Without thinking, she brought her hand to his face, brushing his stubbled cheek with her thumb. It was not quite so long to be a beard, yet not quite so short to be a mere shadow; it was somewhere in the middle as if it had not made up its mind whether it ought to be a true beard or not. And something subtle, something quiet behind his eyes shone differently.

What am I doing? She thought.

Perplexed by her own actions, then not wishing to entertain the thought of his touch any longer, she pulled her hand away. Yet, before she could retreat, the man took her hand in his, and she stood still, her heart racing madly.

"Please, be careful," he cautioned. "As much as I am forever in your debt because of your kindness, it is dangerous coming here."

"I know. But I will be careful, you have my word," the lady nodded.

"Until tomorrow then?" He asked as before, still holding her lovely hand in his.

"Oui," Múriel bowed her head, "Jusqu'à demain."

With their parting words, she relinquished her hand and vanished into the darkness.

Carefully, he listened as the sound of her footsteps faded, then, a strange noise struck his ears again; the slight creak of a door, open and shut. The prisoner knew of no other entrance than the dungeon doors at the top of a flight of stairs, which could only be accessed within the first level of the castle. And the dungeon was always thoroughly guarded. It seemed strange altogether that the maiden could happen upon such a place without being discovered.

While Gisborne was wrought with curiosity, sleep soon took hold. Though he laid upon the stone floor, neither the coolness nor the unyielding way of it could deter him from his newfound felicity. How he dreamt of Múriel and of seeing her smile again, for he could not bear to be parted from her presence. She, of such a gentle nature and a compassionate spirit, so beckoned him in slumber's woods, and he desired so fervently, to venture to deserve her.

***

Afternoon drew to evening; evening drew to nightfall; night fleeted, and there was no sign of Múriel.

Every cause for her absence fed his anxiousness, as the waning hours pulled at his heart. Overcome, the man could do nothing save close his eyes to hope and to rest. Then, he remembered the candle she had left for him, and quickly, he lit it; his beacon. Though for such a time, the candle burned in vain. At length, she had not come and utterly spent as he was, Gisborne fell asleep, though it would be only one more hour before the silence was suddenly broken.

"Sir Guy," Múriel whispered before the entrance, "Are you awake?"

But as she had approached the cell, she saw that the prisoner had fallen asleep, waiting for her. There he lay by the entrance, the crown of his head just touching the iron bars, his breath deep and steady. The candle's flame went out just as she had appeared, its string of smoke rising into the air, creating smooth swirls of grey and white. She was very late that night, and in truth, this errand was proving a difficult feat indeed. Hurriedly, the maiden arranged the provisions, and when she had finished, she determined to leave and let him rest.

But then, as if by magic, she felt such an overpowering, compelling urge to remain. Kneeling down, and finding him to be fast asleep, the maiden began to hum a pleasant, sleepy tune. Soft and melodic was her voice, like the sigh of an evening breeze, sweetly coaxing the world to rest.

At the sound of her voice, the man began to stir, his heart casting aside all its former uneasiness. For she was safe; she was near.

"You've come," he whispered, a smile upon his lips.

Múriel's heartbeat hastened. Withdrawing from the cell, she drew to her feet. "Forgive me... I thought you were asleep," she said, lifting her hood up to conceal her embarrassment.

"Wait," Gisborne sat up, "Please... don't stop."

As she relinquished her apprehension, the maiden followed her heart. Drawing back to the cell, she knelt before it, and as she returned, the man laid down as before; waiting.

"Would you sing to me?" He entreated.

"Of course," she smiled.

The young lady let the melody rise from her lungs again, soothing his heart. Then recognising her song, the man raised his brow. "Of what are you singing, Múriel?"

"It is something my mother would sing to me when I was little," she answered. "*Le Soleil et Sa Chérie.* But I don't remember the words."

"I... I do," he said as he rose up, staring into such silvery eyes. "*The Sun and His Darling*, yes?"

"Yes!" Múriel said, her eyes lightened with such excitement, as she beamed sweetly and wrapped her fingers around one of the iron bars. "Si vous plait, do you remember the words?"

"Oh, well, if I remember any of it, it is only in English," he mumbled, leaning against the entrance as he gazed upon her.

"Please teach me the words," she smiled. "Perhaps as you sing, I will start to remember some in French. But I will listen first."

"But I've not the voice for-"

"Come now, have I not been bold enough to sing for you? It is your turn," she insisted. "Would you sing for me? Please?"

Timid, his heart pounded within him, thinking on the words of how the song began.

Then with measured breath, his voice deep and calming, he began to sing.

Fashioned of purest light,
Her eyes, a starlit night,
O maiden come, come be mine,
For my heart is yours, my darling.

Whispering soft through the trees,
His voice, as dawn calling me,
O lover be, lover be mine,
For my hand is yours, my beloved.

Vows spoken in the night,
Forged of the Blessed Light,
O sweet promises, promises we hold,
Tonight we are one, my darling.

Where has he taken you, dear?
So far away from here,
O maiden where, where have you gone?
The warrior stole my darling!

Will you come to me?
Will the path ever find your feet?
O lover swift, be swift as the dawn,
Forsake me not, my beloved.

The crimson sky of the eve,
Bleeds o'er my suffering,
O maiden hold, hold fast the vow,
For I shall recover my darling!

There, upon the shore,
I dreamt of him in the storm,
O lover find, find me here,
Across the sea, my beloved.

All such rays of light now far gone,
And moonlight, her song undone,
O yet hope remains, remains for the day,
The lover finds his darling.

How his voice struck her, and she, so stirred by him.

"I remember now," she whispered.

Out of her heart, she began to sing, and as the man recognised her foreign tongue, so he joined his voice with hers. The midnight aura teemed with their song, echoing softly in the night. In such pure harmony did they sing, as if their very souls were dancing. As their song ended, the man could hardly find what words to speak, for he thought his heart would burst. Taking Múriel's hand, he laced his fingers with hers. Bashful and besotted, he gazed so affectionately into her grey eyes.

"I did not think I would ever hear that song again," he sighed.

"I did not think I would remember the words again," the lady blushed. "It's strange; it's such a beautiful song, but so sad. How did you come to know the words?"

"My mother sang this to me as a child," he said.

"I think our mothers would have been kindred spirits," she grinned.

"So they would have been."

"It was passed down for generations in my family, and I hope to continue this with my own children one day," the maiden resolved, her eyes glancing far off as if peering into another realm entirely.

"I must admit, I've often thought the very same," he grinned. "Continuing my line, passing down such songs as these to my children, and sharing with them such precious stories," halting his own thought, a shadow shone in his eyes, as he released her hand. "But those dreams died a long time ago."

Downcast, the man stared at the floor before him, and while she looked on him, the maiden felt such pity in perceiving so much more of his heart and his shadows.

"Múriel..." he whispered; a question on his lips.

"Oui?" She clutched the iron. "What is it?"

Yet whatever he was truly desiring to ask of her, he restrained it. "Nothing... forgive me," he shook his head. Brushing aside the thought, he composed himself closer to the entrance, facing her directly. "I do have more questions to ask of you... may I?"

"Of course," she nodded, "But remember, only three." She gave a little smile, resting her hands upon her lap.

"Yes, only three," he agreed. "First, how did you know where to find me? This is a difficult part of the dungeons for anyone to find."

"All I can tell you now is... I knew that if I followed my feet, they would guide the way." She held her breath, shifting her eyes away, hoping this would suffice.

"As if by chance, then?" He tilted his head, not entirely satisfied with the answer.

"In a way," she said.

"Then I am glad you followed your feet."

"I never find fault in them," she returned with reserved smile. "And the second question?"

Closing his eyes, he thought, anxious to share what words lingered on his tongue. "Why have you continued to come?" He sighed. "I still don't understand why you've been so willing to endure in this."

As she drew her gaze downward, the maiden twirled a loose thread from her cloak in her nimble fingers. "The truth?" She hesitated, lifting her eyes to meet his.

"Please," he insisted, his intense gaze locked upon her.

"Bien," she nodded. The first night I came, to bring you provisions, it was, in part, because I sought to keep my promise. Just once. There you laid, asleep, but in such misery. Tossing and turning about, writhing and crying out through your nightmares... it was terrifying," she said, letting a breath escape her lips, wishing to hold back, but surrendering once more under his need for her answer. "I thought I had done my duty, and would never return. In fact, I had no wish whatsoever to return. Yet the promise I made, and the thought of you here... I thought, an evil man never feels shame for his wrong, but a good man who does wrong will regret it. And abandoned to such loneliness; a man who has been so deprived of kindness can never have the strength to do what is right. That is not life, it is just lingering. I pitied you, and then that pity grew into a desire to show you, even in the smallest way, some kindness; to give you hope."

Gisborne's eyes widened in such astonishment, for it was as if her words pierced the shadow towering over his soul. Light, cascading in for the first time. After a long pause, finally, he spoke.

"Thank you," he whispered, "You've shown me a kindness, such that I have never known. It is your kindness, which has sustained me."

Múriel smiled gently, holding back tears, for her heart yearned so deeply for some means of freeing him from all his burdens. Yet, as was her nature, she drew back to save face, unsure if she had shared too much, and so continued with calmed inflexion.

"But, you have a third question?"

"Yes, my third question," the prisoner nodded, attempting to clear his mind. "Surely, this is a question I should have asked you long before," he admitted, glancing downward. "It almost seems a bit foolish to ask you this now, but Múriel, you are not married, are you?"

At this, the maiden blushed, taking a moment to conjure her answer.

"No, I am not married," she answered directly, her easiness retreating for a moment, though the man couldn't observe it.

"Good," he said. "I would be uneasy if my wife was visiting these dungeons at night."

"And you are not married, are you, Sir Guy?" She wondered.

"No," he shook his head; his tone solemn. "No, I never did marry."

The two fell quiet for a moment. If circumstances were different, their words might have settled more sweetly, but his end was sealed already. All that prolonged his fate was this maiden's boundless benevolence, but for how long? Indeed, any sweetness felt would not have held by a long road.

"But you have loved before, and that is a precious thing, is it not?" She asked.

Guy went cold at these words, staring bitterly at the stone floor before him; his countenance withholding. "Yes, I suppose," he obliged, "Have you?"

"Once, long ago," the lady admitted, the stillness unyielding. "Well," she sighed, suspending the heaviness, "As you are finished with your questions, I must go."

"The hour is growing late, I know," the man acknowledged. "But you will come again tomorrow?" His eyes begged.

"Oui, I will," Múriel nodded.

"Promise me something?" He asked softly as the lady's gaze met his, ready to hear this new request. "When you come, would you come a little sooner and stay a while longer?"

"You have my word," she promised.

"Until tomorrow, Múriel."

"Until tomorrow," she bowed.

His eyes fell away from her so reluctantly while the maiden made her way down the corridor, as she had so often, and to Gisborne, it seemed his life was only worth living when she was near.

CHAPTER FOUR

TIGHTENING THE NOOSE

Searching in vain, and with nought to bolster their cause, the soldiers of Nottingham had returned to the keep, for the Rebel and his comrades had surely vanished into thin air, their present course ever as a nagging mystery.

Upon the men's return, Dumont along with two other guards met with the sheriff in the gardens of the courtyard. There to the west of the keep lay the grounds, with a row of young trees guiding the way to where the woman stood. So poised and delicate, she lingered in the sunlight. Her complexion was soft and fair, her graceful hands gently plucking what blooms caught her eye upon the rose bushes and lifting up to inhale was pleasant aromas they gifted. Whatever flowers were deemed most pleasing, full and bright and fragrant, the woman placed them in the basket she carried.

Now turning to find the guards approaching, Claudia gazed on anxiously.

"What news, Dumont?" She asked.

"Your grace," the man bowed his head, "He is nowhere to be found."

"Is not Sherwood his domain? Have you not yet searched it?" She pressed, stepping nearer the guard.

"Those woods are treacherous, my lady; full of wild beasts and wild men. We have done all we could," he said.

"But what of Locksley?" She thought, her eyes searching about nervously. "Are there not Saxons enough on the street to be bribed?"

"Sheriff," the man sighed, "While there may be some who do not loathe the outlaw, none are willing to divulge any information, for the few who know anything know very little and even less than ourselves."

One by one, she tore away leaves from the stem of a rose, her eyes growing steadily darker as she thought on the matter. "Well, we have until the end of the month to produce the sum," she mumbled to herself. "Perhaps the prince will be lenient."

Suddenly, the blaring of a horn resounded across the courtyard; the guards and the sheriff abruptly halted in their audience, for a messenger drew forth unto the gardens, on a white horse. Though the messenger uttered nothing, he lowered his bannered horn, and held out a length of parchment; a scroll sealed with the mark of Prince John himself.

"For the Sheriff of Nottingham," the messenger proclaimed.

Gracefully, the woman bowed and retrieved the scroll from his hand. At this, the man upon the white horse swiftly departed beyond the gate.

"What is it, sheriff?" Dumont questioned, gazing on her sternly as her eyes scanned the page.

As she lowered the parchment, Claudia could not bring herself to look upon the man, but stared into nothing, her hands trembling.

"My lady, what is the matter?" The guard wondered.

"The prince shall arrive in two days," she whispered. "He is eager to receive his tribute from Locksley, and to see Sir Guy's body."

"Fret not, my lady," the man consoled. "Indeed, we may not have the sum, however, when the prince sees that you have put an end to the wretched traitor, he is sure indeed to show mercy."

"Perhaps you are right," the woman nodded, as a light in her eyes restored. "Yes. The prince will surely be glad to see he is rid of Sir Guy, and all under my hand," she smiled. "Well then, Dumont, when you are given leave from your other duties, go and fetch the body."

"Very good," the man bowed. Motioning for his men to follow, Dumont and his men departed from the gardens.

***

That very evening, Dumont appointed the most trustworthy of his men to accompany him into the dungeons, to retrieve the corpse of the traitor. It would be a gruesome task; not for one who had little stomach for such horror. All the same, Dumont knew Roland to be of a tempered mind.

Far down below such stone, the two men marched.

The silence of the night felt as a secret dread, a haunt upon them as they descended deep into the castle, down the steps into the dank corridor. How the dungeons were a ghastly place; of iron and stone and shadow. What prisoners who remained too long, grew frail, their bodies haggard, their minds wasted, and their very names, long forgotten. What prisoners who had succumbed to their end, were heaped in piles; their mouldering flesh dragged out and burned to be rid of the stench.

Through such a grave as this, the guards continued, passing by the walls of iron bars, through the thick of the dark, and onward toward the final cell.

Yet upon their errand, Dumont halted, his keen ears listening.

"Wait," he whispered, holding up his hand, "Do you hear that Roland?"

"Hear what?"

"Shh!" Dumont rebuked.

"What is it?"

"Well, neither of us will hear anything if you do not keep your mouth shut!" The man huffed. "I thought I heard someone talking."

"And what of it?" Roland scoffed. "Anyone who's been here long enough babbles on and on-"

"Wait," Dumont halted in his steps, straining his breath. "He's calling out for someone!" He proclaimed, sprinting on ahead.

"Who? Who is calling out?" Roland questioned, as the man before him advanced into the dungeon.

At last, reaching the cell of their pursuit, the guards stared aghast, their lips silenced, for their eyes fell upon something which they did not expect.

***

Múriel returned to visit Guy night after night.

The man grew so increasingly fond of the maiden and ardently longed for her companionship. As much as she longed for his presence in return, her head did chide her heart so against his affections. Yet, she could not dissuade how his heart was unwaveringly captivated.

Each night, the prisoner would ask his three questions, and in turn, the maiden would give her answer, only as she was free to divulge what secrets she kept. From such nights as these, the man came to discover that he had been imprisoned for near a month, and to the public, he was already, much forgotten. For the Rebel and his men were making trouble enough for the new sheriff, and so kept her eye far from Gisborne's condition.

That very night, Múriel came again with food, and drink, and her gentle spirit.

"You are late tonight," Guy said, leaning his head against the bars as he stared up at her.

"Forgive me," she said, kneeling down before him. "I was afraid someone was following me, but I lost him, I think."

"Someone was following you?" He raised his brow.

"Yes, but I am here now... oui?"

"Múriel, when will you tell me the truth?" The man looked on her in earnest. "You cannot keep your wanderings a secret forever. I want to be certain you'll not get caught."

"Don't worry so much," she sighed. "This is only the second time he has attempted to follow."

"This has happened before?" He questioned, gripping the bars. "The same man has been following you?"

"Please, don't scold me-"

Suddenly, they were interrupted by the sound of guards fast approaching. Anxious, both listened as the clanking of metal marched closer down the corridor, and Gisborne's eyes waxed with worry.

"Go! Quickly!" He ordered.

In an instant, Múriel, and all traces of her disappeared down the corridor. Gisborne knew not where she went, but he could not think on that now. For as the guards arrived at the entrance of the cell, before them, leading the way, was Lady Claudia.

"Alive!" She howled fearsomely. "How can you still live?" Her fingers coiled around the bars of the cell so that her knuckles went white.

"What do you want, Claudia?" Gisborne said.

"Don't presume you may be so informal with me," she scowled. "I am the Sheriff of Nottingham, and as such, you will address me as your sovereign." Examining the man's clean and simple clothes, and how he fared well, the woman digested the evidence of what guileful circumstances had been prospering. And how she did loathe the prisoner all the more. Narrowing her eyes, she glared with all contempt. "Who has done this?"

"Done what?"

"You imbecile, who has given you aid?" She pressed. "What devil have you conjured that calls you *master*?"

Rising to his feet, Gisborne stared through the bars, his fists down at his sides, "If I gave the name of such a spirit, would you seek to ensnare it? All that troubles you is that I remain alive despite your conceited attempt of revenge."

"Sentencing a murderer to death is justice," she gritted her teeth. "Well, if I could not starve you to death, then I shall have you hanged. Tomorrow!"

At this, all colour ran from the man's face, and though in such shock, he found his response.

"Go on then and hang me! Fill the courtyard with what cattle heed your call and let them praise your works!"

"No," she shook her head. "You shall meet your end here in these very dungeons. None shall see you die, none shall hear you gasp your final breath. You're not worth an audience," Claudia sneered, as she turned to leave.

"Oh, I see," the man said, folding his arms across his chest as he leaned his shoulder against the iron bars.

"See what?" The woman turned back, her nose, wrinkled.

"It's not worth your humiliation," he said.

Marching toward the cell door, the woman faced him once more. "And what humiliation would I suffer having you hung in the dungeons?"

"Oh, Claudia," he grinned slyly, "All of Nottingham believes I am long gone. To discover now that I am yet living merely proves how you are so wholly lacking in what power has been given you."

"How dare you!"

"You're far too much of a coward to bring me forth and have done with me. Would it not mar your little *understanding* with the prince?" Gisborne lowered his chin, eying the vile woman boldly.

"You dare call me a coward?" Claudia questioned, her face pressed up against the bars. "You, who faltered when Lady Marian was to be arrested? You, who feared to exact justice upon her when the duty was put to you?"

"Stop."

"Even when you discovered her alliance with that treacherous outlaw to plot against your future king, still, you made as if to justify her!"

"Shut your mouth, you wretch!" Gisborne hissed viciously through the bars.

At this, Claudia could no longer restrain her anger. Flame and fury in her raging stare, she looked at her guards as she stepped back from the cell.

Instantly, a guard marched forward. Removing a set of keys from his belt, he unlocked the cell door. With the creak of the iron swinging back, the frame knocking hard against the stone walls, two guards rushed in. Though the prisoner wrestled, two more guards came blundering in such that there was hardly any chance to overpower them. Finally, amidst the struggling, the guards managed to pin back the prisoner's arms. Thrust to the ground, the guards swung their fists against him, beating him until the stone floor was speckled with his blood. Doubtless, they would have beaten him to death save for the woman who raised her hand and halted their brutality.

"Enough," she stepped forward, towering over the prisoner. "Perhaps now you might learn to hold your tongue."

Indisposed and unable to summon any further defence, Gisborne stared up at the sheriff; the blood dripping from his lips. "Do as you wish with me... my conscience is clear," he whispered.

"Have you such a conscience?" Claudia said. "You are nothing more than a pathetic waste, scraped from the very dregs of humanity."

"That may be, but I am no grovelling dog, begging for scraps at the prince's table," he muttered. "You know well enough the prince won't indulge your howling much longer."

Outraged, the woman's eyes shone fiery. "It will be a pleasure dragging away your putrid corpse to the rot-heap, and watching your flesh burn," she jeered. "Seek your stars while you can, lest the morning devours them."

As she departed from the cell, the guards were swift to follow, the iron bars locked behind them as all the clamour fled away, leaving the man alone again.

Weary, he lay upon the cold of the unforgiving stone. His body ached, and the blood upon his lips was bitter. How all the silence of the void stifled his breath and taunted his mind. The unbound nothingness. Stagnant and starved and seeking; as the open grave.

How he had grown to loathe it, but now when he was to greet such an end, the longing for what fragment of nothing could be spared, afforded no comfort.

Slowly, the rhythm of his breath returned. Listening, he waited, concerned for what respite might still be rendered from the silence. Then, when his hand let slip near all hope, her voice rung out.

"Guy?" Múriel called; her soft voice travelling down the corridor, as her footsteps followed. Before the entrance, she looked down upon the man, and the blood; terrified. "Guy..." she whispered, her nervous hands holding fast the iron.

Peering up at the door, the prisoner slowly opened his eyes to see a foggy image of the maiden before him. Groaning, he lifted himself upright, and drew near the lady, and gently held her hand to give her some assurance.

"I am alright," he sighed.

Múriel brought her hand up to his face, staring at the blood that fell from his temple. "But you are not alright," she shook her head. "Don't say such things if they aren't true."

"It doesn't matter," he said. Though he would wish her innocent of everything, the man's eyes conveyed his sorrow far more than he had intended. "Múriel, I... we both knew this day was coming," he lowered his head. "Tomorrow I am to be hanged, and-"

"No! I'll not let them," she declared, unwilling to relinquish his hand.

"You must go... and forget me," his voice cracked.

"Forget you? How can you say this?"

"You must not think on me, nor ever think on this place," he sighed.

"No," she fixed her tearful eyes so passionately upon him. "How can you think me so heartless that I would abandon you? You have my word, I shall do whatever it takes to set you free."

"You have already risked too much. I would far rather face death knowing you are safe than to put your life in any more danger," he shook his head.

"Please, let me help you escape," Múriel insisted. "I can lead you through the passage I've taken to come here every night," she confessed; nervous yet ready.

"You mean, there may be a means of freeing me?" The man questioned, his eyes flickering with a hopeful light and his heart pounding fiercely.

"Long ago, before Lady Claudia, before Rothgar, this part of the castle was not a dungeon," she said.

"What do you mean?"

"It was the old kitchen," she continued. "There was a service corridor blocked off years ago when this was converted into the dungeons. The service entrance is by the old storehouses, and it leads directly here, to the old cook's quarters. The entrance to the corridor lies not far from here; left untouched. It took me some nights to remove enough of the stone on the outside to finally reach you."

"Unbelievable," he mumbled. "I had no idea, so certainly Claudia would not know of it. But how do you propose to free me from the cell?"

"Oh," the maiden thought. "Perhaps I could steal the keys from one of the guards; wait until the jailer falls asleep and-"

"No," Guy released her hand to clutch his aching side. "If I escape, surely Claudia will stop at nothing to discover me again."

"Then let her search! We must make haste, or we will lose our only chance," Múriel entreated.

"You don't understand," the prisoner said as he wiped the blood from his brow. "She would overturn every corner of Nottingham to find me, to find whoever helped me escape. She would use whatever means necessary. Would you truly want the blood of innocent people on your hands?"

"But we... we must think of a way," the maiden whispered, as a tear rolled down her face.

Though all this pained him so, Gisborne brushed away her tear, his hand framing her face as he smoothed his thumb over her cheek.

"Múriel," he sighed, "Please, allow a dying man to confess something?"

The lady listened in lament, her stormy eyes meeting his pain filled gaze as the man took hold of her hands.

"Allow me to confess how fervently I care for you," he forced a sombre smile. "You have been a light and a comfort, and I now know what it is to have hope. When I greet the end, I shall greet it willingly, for through you have I been shown such grace beyond what I could have ever imagined."

How the maiden's heart wrestled within her at such a thought. As she let more tears fall, the two succumbed to the bitterness of the hour.

"There must be another way," she said. "I don't want you to die."

"And I have no wish for you to die," he said. "Please, you must leave or else be taken."

"I'm not leaving!"

"Go, Múriel, before it is too late!" Letting go of her hands, the man and the maiden fell silent.

For little had come of little, and not a grain of hope could sustain the weight of it. Staring hard at the floor beneath her, so unsure of what else to say, if to say anything, the young lady lingered, for she could not bear to move, nor withdraw from his presence. If to be near in this hour was grief itself, how could any more be endured in her parting? In all her tears which fell, she thought, and nought was the remedy she did beg, and how it cut her heart.

Then, suddenly, amidst the woodlands of her mind, she found a clear path, one she had not considered, but upon the finding of it, she followed.

"Wait!" Her eyes lightened, "Quickly, you must tell me everything; everything about Claudia. Tell me of her weaknesses, her pursuits; everything!"

"Why?"

"I have an idea," she answered.

CHAPTER FIVE

FREEDOM IN SLAVERY

There remained but one chance to accomplish their end, for to fail would be death itself; thus would Guy and Múriel be parted, so unwillingly.

The silver treasure was returned to the lady, as the man could not be caught with it and it was fortunate indeed that none of the guards, nor Claudia had found it. Surely fate could not be tempted any further. Now all that could be arranged was discussed in full; the maiden, having her own duties to carry out, while the man must wait. And when the hours of the night had passed, and dawn drew in its first breaths, the man and the maiden knew the time was near.

"Tell me one last time, what was her cousin's name?" Guy asked.

"We don't have to do this," Múriel shook her head.

"Yes, we do. I must be sure you have the names right," he insisted.

"Very well," she sighed, "Jacqueline LeConte."

"And her mother?"

"Milicent, oui?"

"Yes," Guy nodded. "Promise you won't forget?"

"I won't," the lady answered, lingering a while by his side in the stillness. "It's nearly dawn," she thought aloud, looking on the man and not wishing to part from him.

With such affection, Guy laid a kiss upon her hand, as he stood behind the iron. "Please, be careful," he cautioned, "whatever the outcome, I could not bear it if any harm came to you."

"You know I'll be careful," Múriel reassured, drawing her hand to his face once more as she took in what faint light shone behind his eyes. "But I... I must leave."

"I know," he nodded, closing his eyes as he sighed under her touch. "Until tomorrow, my lady?" He whispered.

"Jusqu'à demain," she answered.

Slowly, Guy released her hand as she withdrew from the cell, watching as she stood far off from him; and how he loathed it. Gazing on her now, he took in what eyes had first given him hope, and knew well that if he never saw those eyes again, he was blessed to have ever beheld them. For the final time, the man watched as she disappeared into the night, the flame from the distant torch kissing the edges of her sea dark cloak. There, with her presence and her very essence gone from him, he clung to all the hope he had yet been afforded; all at once warring between trusting and fearing.

***

It was near the fifth hour when Múriel departed from the dungeons; never once looking back.

Dim, the skies of the early morn lit the earth below, its pale rays of light breaking through the dark clouds. How empty the streets stood; the dirt path silencing the lonely maiden's footsteps as she ventured out. So emboldened, she pressed on, for dawn was fast approaching.

Not far from the old storehouses, the maiden marched ever toward the Golden Tusk; a tavern heralding the first row of homes on the old street, and a former frequent of Robin Hood and his band of outlaws, or at least it was so rumoured.

There it stood, the panes roughly fitted in the walls and the frame of the building warped from age. As the cool of the breeze swirled down the street, the great sign hanging above the tavern door swung back and forth, creaking as the metal chains did grind against the hooks. Upon the sign was carved the image of a golden boar, with mighty tusks and a tongue of scarlet. An omen to those who would seek mischief, yet a privilege to those who had proved their mettle.

One of them must be there. They have to be there, she thought.

Advancing ever nearer the tavern, Múriel soon sensed a lingering presence behind her. Not a sound was made yet the feeling of two eyes gazing on set a chill in the air. So uncertain, the young lady hastened on, though the pace of the agent behind her was agile. Listening with sharp ears, she recognised more and more the pattern of step which followed. Undoubtedly it was the man who had attempted to follow her before.

Restless, Múriel's heart pounded, for she daren't look back, anxious the man would gain a foothold if she gave in to her fright. Finally, gathering together what courage she had left, she resolved to face the assailant.

Fearless, she turned and drew a dagger from her side. Now the man halted as the tip of the blade pricked against his throat; the vein beneath it, pulsing. From beneath his hood, soft brown eyes shone and tufts of earthen hair swept across his forehead. Swift, he threw his hands in the air and let out a gasp.

"You!" The lady scowled, taken aback.

"Múriel! I only-"

"Listen well," she ordered, "I will show mercy save you tell me why you follow me," she demanded, pressing the blade against his skin.

"And what cause have you to threaten me thus?" The man grumbled. "I confess I have been following you, but I would not have you presume me some wayward scoundrel nor treat me in such a manner as this."

Lowering her chin, Múriel squinted her eyes, searching the man's face. "Bien," she sighed, withdrawing her dagger as the man lowered his hands to his side. "Tell me, A'Dale, what are you doing here?"

"Now, I cannot speak a word with you of my errand until I am certain of your loyalties. You are still an ally of the Rebel company, are you not?" He questioned. "I must be certain you can be trusted."

"Oh, you know perfectly well, I'm trustworthy," she rolled her eyes. "But, I must admit, I am glad to have found you for there is something I would speak to you about. Something urgent."

"Something urgent?" Alan wondered, drawing nearer the maid as he saw what fear lay behind her eyes. "Múriel, what has happened?"

"I cannot tell you everything, not now, for I must make haste! I am losing time speaking with you already!" She implored, placing her hand upon his arm.

"Very well. Speak as you must," Alan nodded, drawing his hand to his bearded chin.

Without delay, the young lady related to the man of what had passed between herself and Gisborne; how he was to be executed that very day and how they had devised a plan for his escape. Yet for the outlaw, he would not hear of such a notion.

"And you went every night to give him food and drink?" Alan questioned, folding his arms across his chest.

"If you had only seen the condition he was left in-"

"He is a murderer! A blackguard who should have died long ago. What possessed you to do such a thing?" He rebuked.

"You think me mad for showing him mercy?" She challenged.

"I think you mad for intending to free him," Alan wrinkled his nose in disgust. "Do you not know the danger of attempting this? Do you have any idea what would be done to you if you were caught, never mind that making to free him only prolongs the inevitable? No, this is utterly insupportable," he scoffed, turning away from the lady.

"But you've not yet seen the change in his heart," she returned; her stance firm, her words unshaken. "Are you, being one of Robin's men, so incapable of mercy?"

"He's a vile wretch. His lot is well earned," he determined. "Don't waste your honeyed words on me."

"Please, you must listen!" Múriel petitioned.

As she darted forward, the maiden grasped the outlaw's arm and brought her lips up to his ear. Whispering so rapidly it seemed a mere second, she confessed to the outlaw all her heart had meant to say, and much of what she had been so careful to conceal from Gisborne. The outlaw listened carefully, his brows raised. As she pulled back, he gazed upon her dumbfounded.

"You believe me, do you not?" The young lady begged, placing her hands upon the outlaw's shoulders.

"I... I thought it was just," he shook his head in disbelief, as he lifted his hand up to his temple. Then gazing down upon her clasp, his eyes grew wide. "You're absolutely certain?"

"I swear it," Múriel brought her hand over her heart.

"Why did you not tell me of this before?" He whispered.

"I did not know of it then," she answered.

"Well, I suppose I understand a little why you need to... why you would want me to…" he paused, staring at the ground, as he let out a sigh. "Still, I fear this is too great a risk."

"Please! Lend me your aid!" The maiden petitioned. "Fais-le pour moi."

"Perhaps, there is a way we might strike a bargain. I could help you free Gisborne in exchange for some intelligence," he said, glancing down at her with a mischievous eye.

"What is it you wish to know?" She asked, staring curiously at the man.

"My master has another mission to carry out," he began, "The sheriff has taken a young lad hostage, hoping to lure my master into her midst. We need to find some means of freeing the lad from the castle before Claudia is given any chance to make Robin her captive. It is for this reason that I have followed you. Being clever as always, you clearly know a way to get in and out without attracting any guards. If I were to take this risk with you, to free Gisborne, I must insist that you supply me with what means are necessary to free the young lad," the man concluded.

Knowing the outlaw well enough, and finding what usefulness they could lend unto each other, the maiden could not deny him his want, for his quest was well worth her mind.

"Very well," she thought. "If you help me, then I will direct you to the secret passage, personally. It leads into the isolated part of the dungeons; to the final cell. Is that of any use?"

"Perhaps," Alan thought, "But this passage, who else knows of it?" The outlaw leaned against the tavern wall.

"It is an old passage; abandoned long before Claudia or Rothgar came to power," Múriel said, "I have told Gisborne of it, and he confessed he did not know of it, nor did the sheriff. I doubt anyone of significance would know of it."

"Then how is it that you discovered it?" Alan wondered.

"I cannot tell you," she shook her head.

"Múriel," he sighed, "if I know not the one who told you of it, then I may be leading my master into a trap. Now, who told you?"

"Truly, it is someone who is already well trusted, especially by Robin. But I've already said too much. You must trust me," she answered, staring up at the man as his eyes longed to unravel what mysteries she set before him.

Considering the cause, the man drew in a deep breath; the cool of the morning air making the hairs of his arms stand up, and the strands of his locks toss about the frame of his face.

"And you're sure of him?" He asked, "Such that you would risk your very life?"

"I made a promise... I must save him," Múriel's eyes stared heavily.

"Aye," Alan sighed. "I will need to speak with Robin first."

"No," she pleaded, clutching his cloak, "I will need your help *alone* to rescue him. We do not have time to await Robin's aid, nor would he be in favour of such a feat as this. You know that full well."

Reluctant, the outlaw took what little time could be spared, weighing once more what challenge was laid before him. He knew his master would unquestionably deny such a request, yet the risk must be taken; for her sake, for Gisborne's, and for Robin himself. Moreover, a new passage in and out of the castle would prove useful in meeting his own end.

"Come," Alan held out his hand, "In this hour shall I be your devoted servant."

The maiden shook his hand firmly and struck an accord. With that, A'Dale and Múriel set to work. The cunning outlaw, knowing the tavern as if it were his own, snuck in through a window. Once inside, he withdrew into the cellar to retrieve what treasures were hidden in the barrels by the Rebel company. It was from this hoard that he collected precisely the sum of gold needed, for he knew it could swiftly be returned. Múriel was only in need of an impressive garment, which did not take long for Alan to acquire, according to his sly ways, on her behalf.

By the eighth hour, all was set in place.

Clever man that he was, Alan managed to confiscate a horse and carriage, though the pair were much alike in age and haggardly condition, yet enough to convince any noble. Although the young lady was not so entirely approving of the outlaw's dubious methods, she could not deny it would add to the illusion. Thus, with Múriel dressed and seated within the carriage, they drove directly to the courtyard of Nottingham castle. Reaching the inner courtyard, how the wheels of the carriage cracked and crunched as it rolled over and over against the stone. There, the carriage halted, and Alan dismounted from the seat to aid the young lady. Her feet upon the cobblestone, the young lady stood at the very edge of excitement and fear.

Elegantly attired, in a deep blue gown with long flowing sleeves, she appeared quite regal. She wore a silver headdress of simple design and carried on her left wrist, a modest purse. Clasped upon her grey cloak, was her silver brooch, glittering in the sunlight.

Timorous, the maiden departed. In so finding her feet at the grand steps, her eyes fell upon a guard. Having taken notice of the young lady, the man descended unto her.

"Who goes there?" The guard addressed her, his manner cold as he came forth.

Shaking hands and a racing heart, the lady advanced, pressing on to summon what boldness lay so quiet within her.

"I am the Countess of Levisham, cousin of Sheriff Claudia," she lifted her chin, "As a matter of great urgency, I demand an audience with my cousin."

"Wait here," the guard ordered.

Ascending to the archway of the keep, he exchanged words with what other guards stood by; the pack of them speaking in whispers and glancing back down at the lady who remained unmoved upon the step. Restless, Múriel could scarce draw breath for fear her task was already lost, as she awaited an answer. At length, the guard who had met with her descended once more down the stone steps. He bowed his head, and then standing tall again, he outstretched his arm toward the castle entrance.

"This way, my lady," he said.

Relieved, she followed, as the guard escorted her under the arch and into the castle. As she passed, the young lady stole a glance back at the outlaw. Under his dark hood, the man gave an approving nod and a consoling smile. As she nodded, the maiden turned back to follow the guard.

Passing through such lofty corridors, they drew into a grand hall, such as the maiden had never seen. The whole of it was richly decorated with banners of vibrant colours and various textiles, ornate tapestries depicting historical battles, and brilliant suits of armour; irrefutably the hall was a magnificent sight to behold, and all the same, intimidating.

There, amidst such grandeur, the guard led Múriel directly to the banquet table where the sheriff sat; so still and reposed. The woman wore a gown of myrtle green, the folds of silk draping in great length about her feet. Her blonde locks were braided up so delicately, with strands of golden thread. Upon each of her slender fingers, she wore rings of gold and silver. But for all her beauty and presence, none could match what fortitude lay behind her lips, for as she rose from her chair, a coldness shone in her eyes.

"Your grace, may I present the Countess of Levisham," the man bowed.

"Do you not see that I am already occupied?" She scolded, marching past the guard and the lady. "The prince himself is expected to arrive this very evening. I've no time to spare."

"But your grace, she has requested an audience with you, and says she is your cousin."

"My *cousin*?" The woman sneered, as she looked on briefly to study the maiden. "And how am I to accomplish anything of significance if you insist on bringing some professing relation to my door before the sun is yet in the sky?"

"Your grace, do not be so unreasonable. Surely, you can spare this woman a thought-"

"How dare you! Do you forget who has the power over the breath in your lungs?" Claudia snarled, her voice ringing through the hall. "I am no more obliged to give her a thought than she is obliged to pester me! Now, I care not who she is nor what her errand be. Send her away!" The woman waved her hand in disapproval, giving no further notice of the young lady as she turned back and departed from the hall into the long corridor.

"But, your grace, I must speak with you!" Múriel pleaded as she followed Claudia, hoping desperately to catch her up. "S'il vous plaît, ayez pitié!"

"I said go away!" The sheriff called back, drawing up the train of her gown as she hurried down the corridor.

"But this is a matter of great import!" Múriel insisted, chasing after the woman with all haste and no ceremony, for the woman gave no heed to her pleas.

Although the innocence in the Múriel's voice gave the sheriff no leave to feel offended, the woman remained wholly determined.

"*A matter of great import*? How fascinating," she rolled her eyes, her voice obtaining several octaves of derision. "Pray, what is the grave matter for which some Français of no consequence must beg an audience with me and so herd me like cattle?"

Suddenly, the woman stood still and turned to hear what folly this guest could produce. How tall she was; a fury of such magnificence. Standing there, she glared at the young lady with cold eyes such that Múriel hardly knew how to answer.

"Oh, has the Français lost her tongue?" Claudia mocked with a smirk, "Do you know nothing else but to bow your knee on English soil?"

"I..." the young lady began, her lips trembling as her hands began to shake. Try as she might, she gave in far too much to her fear.

"Ha!" The sheriff laughed. "You really are a pathetic little creature. Go on, now. Go and disturb some other noble with your impudence."

"Your grace, please, let me speak," Múriel called, taking in a deep breath as she drew forward. "I have left my husband, and am in need of your help," she whispered. "I have risked much in coming here to seek your counsel and your security. My horse is weary from the journey, and I need supplies to take me as far as Portsmouth."

Tilting her head, the woman thought on this curious circumstance. Motioning for Múriel to draw closer, the young lady obliged. Lifting her chin, the sheriff searched the maiden's eyes. Then observing the expensive apparel and the extravagant brooch upon her cloak, something changed in the woman's expression, growing in her willingness to indulge the lady.

"Leave us," she waved her hand, as the guard who had followed amidst the pursuit bowed and departed from the corridor. "Now, if I am to give an ear to whatever scandalous tale you have to tell, know this: I have very little time to spare. I must have a prisoner hung by the ninth hour and no later, and I will not have Prince John arrive at my castle without all due ceremony. Now, tell me quickly, how did you arrive at the conclusion that you are my cousin?"

"Allow me to explain," the maiden began, "Your mother, Astride, was the cousin of my late mother, the Lady..." for a moment, Múriel had forgotten the woman's name. Faltering in her words, Claudia was swift to descend upon her.

"The lady who?" She pressed.

Searching her mind, she remembered how Gisborne had spoken the name over and over again, and how his lips formed each syllable. "Milicent!" The lady opened her eyes as the name burst forth. "Milicent of LeConte, she was my mother. And I am the only daughter of the house of LeConte."

"Jacqueline?" The woman questioned, her eyes fixed upon the maiden. "I thought you were a sickly thing; that you had passed long ago."

"No, your grace, though many rumoured it," Múriel answered. "But your mother was so fondly remembered by my mother as such a gracious woman, I was certain her daughter could not be without such graces. Therefore, I intended to venture here amidst my travels."

At this, Claudia's demeanour slowly softened. "Well, odd as our connection may be, I'll not turn you away now I am certain of your rank," the sheriff nodded as she lowered her voice, "however, to leave one's husband is a shameful endeavour."

"The very union itself was shameful," the maiden answered, gaining more confidence as the sheriff had accepted her identity. "Against my will, I was forced to wed him after the death of my mother, and my father believed it was a handsome match, that it would yield great prosperity. But, my husband is a fool. He has wasted all our fortune on gambling debts, he has neglected his duties unto the estate, and," she whispered, "I have of late, discovered his infidelity."

"Oh, Jacqueline," Claudia sighed, "I cannot imagine how long you have endured such a thing."

"Long enough, cousin. Thus have I resolved to leave him and return to France," Múriel sighed.

"Return to France?" The sheriff wondered, "But, with the prince arriving shortly, certainly you must stay. Undoubtedly, his highness would be most delighted to hear of another noble in favour of his rule. And I insist you stay at the very least until next spring."

"No, your grace, I could not so impose upon you-"

"I will hear of nothing less," Claudia said. "My servants can fetch your things here immediately."

"But my lady, you do not understand," Múriel said. "Already I have made arrangements, and my arrival is expected. I cannot go back on my word."

"Oh," the sheriff stiffened her shoulders, feeling rather slighted. "And my arrangements would not suit you?"

"Forgive me, I've no wish to discredit your immeasurable generosity and kindness," the lady fumbled, the shaking feeling in her hands returning, "but I must depart for France."

"And where would you go? Is your father to receive you?" The woman wondered.

"No, I fear for his discovery of my circumstance," the young lady said. "It is a distant relation who will receive me, and she has informed me of a vacant manor not far from her own estate. I only wish to plead upon your generosity for what food and supplies are needed for the journey ahead."

"Very well. You shall have it," the woman nodded. "And your horse looks more like a starving dog than a steed. I shall lend you one of my horses. A sound palfrey. I would not dare see any lady being dragged about as some bondsman," Claudia resolved. "Now,

I shall send for my guard to escort you to the courtyard once more where all will be arranged."

"But cousin," Múriel began, hoping to find some way of remaining a while longer, "I know this matter is rather sensitive, but tell me, do you believe this endeavour foolish?" She asked, watching as the sheriff remained silent.

Taking some time to think on the matter, finally, the woman spoke. "I believe you are wiser than you appear, Jacqueline," she said, "Why should you be so subjected to a lifetime of misery and humiliation? Seeing all your wealth squandered and your good name defiled? Men are such beasts."

"Merci," the maiden said, relieved for the ruse was so well received. "I had hoped you might understand."

"Well, even I have had my fill of the selfishness of men," the sheriff grumbled. For an instant, she seemed as if ready to reveal a great secret, importuning the ease to let it slip from her lips. Reflecting upon such hidden thoughts, Claudia brought her folded hands down, eying Múriel hesitantly.

"What is it, cousin?" The young lady pressed, placing her hand upon Claudia's as she conjured a sympathetic gaze. "What troubles you?"

"I've only known you these few moments," the woman said, "While *you* may feel free to share your troubles, I do not know how well I can trust you," she gazed back at the lady; yielding.

"I understand," Múriel replied. Though she let such natural words slip from her lips, she felt desperate for there could be no more delay in her errand. "My husband never trusted me," she continued, "He only spoke what words he wished to achieve his artless gain. But all men hold their secrets, do they not? For what else do they know if not to speak with forked tongues and so shame the gentler sex?"

"Yes," the sheriff thought, bringing her hand to her lips, then down to her lap again. "Jacqueline, perhaps as you were not so withholding, I could share some of my own tales," she said, as she kept her eyes away from the lady.

"Only if it would ease your heart," Múriel coaxed, looking on her with what compassionate expression she could muster.

"Well," Claudia began, "I was to be married once, to a lord. How he lavished me with gifts and words of praise. On the very day of our wedding, before the whole assembly, he confessed that nothing could entice him into such a marriage," she pursed her lips.

"Then, he did not love you as you loved him?"

"Love? What had love to do with it?" The woman wondered. "He disgraced my name and fortune before the court! Four-thousand pounds, he flatly refused."

"*Four-thousand pounds*?" Múriel raised her brows. "He must have been out of his wits to refuse such a match."

"Indeed! And he had once been revered as a man of invincibility, loyal to the prince and amongst his most trusted supporters. Suddenly, after he had broken our engagement, he was delaying executions, releasing debtors from the prisons, and giving money to commoners for bread! And then to dig his grave that much deeper, he murdered the Sheriff Rothgar. The poor old man was stabbed to death in his own bed. And," the sheriff held her breath. Though it seemed she was ready to confess it all, reluctance was catching up with her.

"Oui, my lady?" The maiden questioned, making all effort to contain her desperation for her confidence.

"Well, as it was, a month ago, I had him arrested and sentenced to starve in the dungeons. But last night, I had sent my guards to the dungeons to retrieve the corpse and discard it," Claudia's eyes swept this way and that, knowing the danger of even one capricious witness. Lowering her head and her voice, her whisper in that great corridor disappeared into its heavy silence. "Now we have come to find, he is yet living."

"How?" The young lady whispered back in all astonishment.

"Someone was helping him; bringing him food and drink, and fresh garments, mind!"

"Despicable," the maiden declared. "Certainly, your grace, there must be a remedy to all this. He must be executed before the people."

"Yes, and I would hold a hanging for him this very moment, if not for..." Claudia bit her lip. "Cousin," the sheriff took the young lady's hands in hers, "If I confess all this to you, will you swear never to speak of it to anyone?"

"Truly, you have my word," the maiden promised, nodding confidently as the sheriff released her.

"After the trial was held and his sentence carried out, all have naturally assumed him to be dead," the sheriff's wide and watchful eyes searched the corridor once more before she continued in hushed tones. "His death was intended to be my gift for the prince, and now I am bereft of my gift though Prince John has already accepted my invitation to Nottingham," she complained.

"Can you not give the prince another gift?" The maiden wondered.

"No," the sheriff answered defensively, "It was Sir Guy that I resolved to give him. Thus, the criminal must be hung in secret."

"Attendez," Múriel interjected, "Your grace, I may have a plan, one which may truly benefit us both."

"I don't understand," Claudia questioned as she narrowed her gaze.

"As I am to acquire new lands, there is a farm on the estate that will need tending," she said, "I have only one manservant who will accompany me to France, but he is not built for hard labour. Perhaps, I could purchase this felon from you?"

Pensive and entangled, the sheriff nodded in sly curiosity. "Go on," she encouraged.

"If I were to purchase him, I would have a slave to tend the land, and you would not be in want of a gift to give the prince," the maiden concluded.

"Hmm," she thought, drawing up her hand over her mouth to conceal her smile beneath it. "I may be willing to sell him, provided I knew he would be abominably treated for the savage he is; but what sum would you be willing to offer me? You understand I was especially fond of the idea of his head for the prince."

"Surely, I will give you all that I carry with me!" Múriel promised.

Glancing shrewdly at her guest, the woman reclined once more in her chair. "All that you carry with you? That's preposterous."

"Your grace, I do not carry *all* my wealth with me. This is but a token of my gratitude for having shown such compassion upon me," she answered.

"How much, precisely?"

"Three hundred crowns," the maiden lifted her chin proudly.

Immediately, Claudia's eyes sparkled with amazement. Weighing the matter, she stood in perfect silence for one whole agonising minute.

Múriel felt quite hot, the palms of her hands perspiring as she waited. It felt as if the walls of the corridor were closing in about her, and all light faded into shadow. The lady wasn't sure whether she should break through the silence to beg an answer. How her mind dashed to Guy; what he was enduring that very moment; whether Alan would wait long enough for her and hold up his end of the bargain; ultimately, whether the sheriff would acquiesce.

Finally, when she could no longer wait, the maiden set her hand upon the sheriff's arm. "What do you say, cousin?" She urged.

The seconds that passed seemed endless, for Claudia would not readily give her answer. Then, at length, the woman spoke.

***

In the darkness of the cell, sat the man whose fate hung by a single thread.

With his back against the wall, Gisborne remained; his lean legs stretched before him and his arms folded across his lap. His long dark hair brushed lightly over his broad shoulders, as he closed his eyes; hidden in deep thought. If he could not summon hope from his maiden's gift, he would devote every thought upon her; holding fast to her essence.

Bursting through the silence came the sound of footsteps.

As a great wave unyielding, they came. The torch from beyond was brought near, as three guards approached the entrance. As the door of that miserable cell was opened, the man rose to his feet, though to freedom or the end, he could not tell.

The first of the guards stood before the door, as the second took hold of him, and the third brought forth chains to bind his hands.

"Where are you taking me?" Guy asked.

Yet the guards made no answer. Forcing him out, the door of the cell slammed hard behind them.

"Where are you taking me?" The prisoner questioned again, this time wrestling against the guards, though they would not answer. "I demand you tell me where I'm being taken!" He shouted, his heart sinking, his eyes despondent.

While he persisted, the guards tightened their grip upon him, marching faster and faster through the dungeon, until they reached the centre of it. Breaking their mission, a guard from beyond held up his hand to the men who drew near.

"Halt!" The guard called out, "We need this rat of a lad over 'ere to be taken up as well," he said, as he pointed to the cell on his right.

Within the cell sat a young man, a very young man to be sure, who somehow appeared quite familiar and different all at once. Staring at the young prisoner, Gisborne pondered who the lad could be, for surely he had seen that face before. While he rattled his mind about the prisoner, on either side of him stood a guard, not loosening their grip for a second, though the one who was at the back took it upon himself to unlock and retrieve this new captive. The lad, who was already bound, spoke not a word, though he gave such a bewildering, examining look at Gisborne. Instantly, and for what particular reason he knew not, the man felt a flame of guilt. In that very moment, the guards returned to their pursuit, as both of the prisoners were rushed out of the dungeons.

Out of the darkness, into the light.

Emerging from the castle, they were brought forth, and how the man took in the reality of the sun's warmth on his face, for it felt as a strangely welcome comfort. Then gazing across the courtyard, he saw her. So adorned as he had never seen, Múriel was a vision of light, bathed in the soft glow of the morning. While such joy overwhelmed him, he could not let any expression betray him, for he could not tell if all had gone as they had planned. Then, as Múriel caught a glimpse of his bright eyes, her complexion illuminated. How she wished to rush to his side, but she mustn't falter now.

Looking on her with a shadow behind his eyes, Guy pondered their fate. At that moment, the maiden knew his mind and nodded. Relieved, the man sighed, though the journey was far from over. So unwillingly, each retreated back into indifference.

Remaining as the driver of the carriage, Alan played his role unenthusiastically, yet he played it all the same. Finally, the outlaw's keen eyes caught sight of Múriel descending from the castle; the train of her dress flowing down the flight of sunlit steps.

As the lady approached the carriage, Alan leaned down toward her. "Has it gone well with the sheriff?" He whispered, "What's happened?"

"He is freed," she answered, nervously looking over her shoulder. "She has promised us a new carriage and horse. Look," she said as a host of servants drew forth with a modest carriage and a strong horse of a bronze coat. "Now, fetch the chest so we may be on our way," the lady said, shifting back from the old carriage.

"Aye, your grace," Alan grinned as he descended from the seat. "You over there! I'll need a hand," The outlaw called to a nearby guard.

"Do as he says," Claudia encouraged, as she stood not far from Gisborne.

When the outlaw and the guard had hoisted the chest out of the carriage and unto the final step, the men bowed before the sheriff, and she then motioned for her servants to deliver it into the keep.

As this was settled, the woman whispered to the guard at her side, "Dumont, did I not say he must neither be seen or heard?"

Without a word, Dumont motioned for his men to force the prisoner to his knees. Gisborne fought against the guards as they struggled to gag him and throw a hood over his head. Finally, when the guards had carried out their orders, they proceeded down unto the cobblestone; the sheriff following behind.

"Chain him to it," the woman said, as she directed the guards to secure the prisoner to the back of the carriage she had supplied. Turning to the young lady, the sheriff set in her hand a set of iron keys. "Well, cousin, a fair exchange indeed," she smirked.

But for such a sight as this, Múriel fought to keep her composure, for she hated to see the man so oppressed. "Your grace," she began, her worried eyes fixed upon the man, "Is this necessary?"

"Nonsense," the sheriff hissed. "He is a worthless beast who must be treated as such."

"Must he be? Surely he does not-"

"Oh, you are too naïve," Claudia stared harshly. "Do you not understand that he is an abominable murderer?"

Disgusted, Múriel fell silent; her fists clenched at her sides, as she held her tongue for she must comply, though it gave her pain to do it. Observing the maiden's displeasure and how she looked on the captive, the sheriff's eyes narrowed.

"Be sure of this, my dear, anyone who fails to uphold a bargain struck with me, will be found out," Claudia whispered in the maiden's ear, her lips brushing against her skin.

Taking a deep breath, the young lady faced the woman. "All shall be as you wish it," she bowed her head, restraining her tears of offence.

"Yes, it will," the woman jeered.

As the guards had finally secured the man to the carriage, Alan ascended to the seat, eager to be done with such an odious errand. Then far in the distance, he observed the young man who was also brought out to the courtyard, standing before the archway. His hair was light brown, wavy and wild; and his blonde stubble further marked his youth. He did not look afraid, rather, he carried himself with an air of courage. The young fellow intently examined all that was transpiring in this puzzling exchange, with eyes that were knowing and not merely curious. As the lad's eyes fell upon the outlaw, his stare grew stern; and the outlaw feared his understanding.

"We must leave, now!" Alan leaned down, whispering to Múriel as she came near the carriage.

"Your grace," she turned to face the sheriff, "I must take my leave, and I give you all my thanks," she bowed.

"You are always welcome here, Countess. It was a pleasure coming to this little arrangement, although I do believe I've gained the better end of the bargain," she smiled. "I bid you a safe and successful journey. Send word to me when you arrive in France!"

"Adieu, cousin!" Múriel bowed her head once more before Alan hastily aided her into the carriage.

Swiftly, the carriage exited the courtyard, with Gisborne following behind, trying to stay caught up. Watching as they departed, the sheriff turned to Dumont and Roland who stood behind her.

"Men," she said, "Follow them. If you find anything unusual, anything out of place, bring word to me directly. Understood?"

"Yes, sheriff," they answered.

"Now I must tend to my other duties. Go," she shooed them away.

Standing before the young prisoner, she roughly grabbed his face, so that her nails scratched at his cheeks. "Poor boy," she shook her head at him devilishly, "If the Rebel does not come, I'm afraid your scrawny body will be dangling from the gallows," she mocked.

While Claudia and the lad remained at the keep, Dumont and Roland set out to follow the carriage, and after a few minutes passed, Alan grew suspicious.

CHAPTER SIX

THE GATE AND THE MESSAGE

With all deliberation, through the bustling streets, the outlaw, the maiden, and the captive rode far and away from the castle.

Never ceasing, never yielding.

Holding tight the reins, A'Dale set all this thought upon reaching the gate. Maddening, the horse's hoofs drummed fierce against the dirt road, as great puffs of dust were kicked up into the air. Within the carriage, Múriel remained, leaning her head out the opening on the side every chance she could manage, looking on Guy to be sure he was safe as he raced to stay caught up.

Amidst their errand, Alan felt a bewildering feeling; a warning. Just as he had deprived his sensing, he heard a most unusual sound; a steady rhythm of metal clanking. Heavy and dull, it rang differently than the rattling of Gisborne's chains and followed wherever the carriage ventured. Peering over his shoulder, the outlaw could not find from where the strange noise came amongst the crowd and so faced the road again. As the sound of the clanking metal quieted, Alan turned around once more, his eyes seeking out.

Nothing.

Expelling the very thought of it, he set his mind firm again upon the task at hand, his eyes careful as he directed the carriage down the streets. Dimmed by the clouded sky overhead, the morning light fed what shadows dwelt beneath the eave of every home. Row after row, dark and obscure and shrouded they stood, and for all his speed, the outlaw could not be rid of the lingering premonition.

Now, though no strange sound could be heard, for the third time in that instant, Alan felt the urge to turn around, if only to be absolutely sure. His dark eyes looking over his shoulder, they set on something he feared to find. There, not so far in the distance, were two castle guards, hastening on toward them. His heart pounding, he set the horse driving heedless. Recklessly, the carriage jolted as he drove around a curving street. Thrown against the left side of the carriage, Múriel hit her head. Startled and disgruntled all at once, she hurdled to the partition at the front, where she could gain a better view of the outlaw.

"Alan, what on earth are you doing?" She shouted, rubbing at her temple. "You're driving like a wild beast!"

"I fear we are being followed," he answered.

"Followed?" The lady raised her brows, "How can you be sure?"

"There are two guards following us as we speak-"

"You think Claudia has discovered us?"

"I cannot tell," Alan said, "but she'll soon discover us if we do not make haste."

Quickly, the maiden peered out of the carriage, though her eyes fell not on the guards but on Guy who had fallen, and was dragging behind. Horrified, her eyes went wide, as she shouted through the partition.

"Stop!" She cried, pounding her fists against the wood with all her might, "Stop!"

"Stop the carriage? Are you mad?" The outlaw scolded. "If we stop now, those guards will-"

"Guy has fallen! Please, stop!" Múriel pleaded.

Brash and discontented, the outlaw brought all to a halt, the horse neighing and wrenching its head this way and that. "Hurry," Alan ordered, "We haven't much time!"

As the lady flung open the door, the hinges knocking against the frame, she leapt down. Ignoring whatever words the outlaw had spoken, the lady rushed instantly to Guy's side. Frantic, he panted, his hands trembling as she aided him to his knees. Swift, the maiden revealed the dagger from her side and cut away at the hood and the gag. His cause of affliction now gone, Múriel saw how the iron shackles had scratched against his wrists, and how his arms were bruised. Hot and pale the man's face shone, and he could not speak a single word, nor look on the lady.

Lifting her hands up to hold his face, she searched his fading eyes. Frightened, Múriel gripped at his shoulders. "Guy? Please, look at me," she urged, though he could not meet her gaze. "Help!" She shouted toward the outlaw, "Help! Venez ici!"

As swiftly as his feet permitted, Alan sprinted down from the seat, hurrying to aid the lady. Strained, the lady could hardly hold Gisborne in her arms, though she would not let him fall. And the sight of the captive's condition and the strange lady who aided him was enough that the people passing on the streets were beginning to take notice, and stare at the scene unfolding before them.

"Alan, you must help me bring him into the carriage," she begged.

Anxious, the outlaw looked across the way as his eyes found the two guards again, their shining helmets weaving their way all the nearer. Fearful, the lady's eyes dashed between Guy and Alan and the distant shadow, knowing both the outlaw's expression and his fear all too well.

"Fetch the keys!" Múriel commanded, her silver eyes piercing.

Giving a quick nod, the outlaw ran back to retrieve the keys from within the carriage. Without delay, he returned and knelt before the captive. Unlocking the shackles about Gisborne's wrists, he cast them aside. Throwing the man's right arm about his neck, Alan lifted the man to his feet, as Múriel took his left arm about her neck. Slowly, but inevitably, the outlaw and the maiden brought him into the carriage. There, upon the base, the man lay breathless and weary.

"Can you see them?" The lady asked, "The men who were following us, are they still there?"

Leaning his head around the side of the carriage, the outlaw scoured the busy town and could not find them, though he knew they were certainly there. "I swear they were not far behind us not a moment ago," he said, "We must fly or else be caught. You think Gisborne can manage the rest of the journey?"

"Let me worry about him," the lady answered, "We must reach the gate. Now go!"

Shutting the door, Alan mounted the driver's seat and brought the reins up in his hand. As an arrow loosed from a bow, they flew across the way, the wheels creaking and the horse's hoofs stamping the earth; fleet and fierce and firm.

While no respite could be afforded upon the road, Guy felt some peace in being near Múriel. Unfettered, and so wonderfully free of all hinderance, she was with him; and the iron wall, as a distant memory. Sitting side by side on the base of the carriage, the lady retrieved a flask of water.

"Here, please drink," she said, bringing the flask up to his lips.

Having quenched his thirst and finding the strength to speak, the man gazed on her in awe.

"Thank you," he whispered, looking down at her hands and how he longed to hold them. "I... I can't believe you did this. That you risked your life to save me," he sighed.

"I couldn't let her..." she shook her head, closing her eyes a moment.

Opening her eyes once more, she stared up at the man, and then suddenly, was caught up in his warm embrace. Holding her fast, Guy wrapped his arms about her, his right hand entangled in her hair as he nestled his head in her neck. Yet what eased his longing heart beyond measure was Múriel's touch; her slender arms reaching around his torso, and her hands pressed against his back; holding him so close. For the little time that passed, this moment seemed as if it would know no end; and neither would wish it flee from them.

"How could I ever repay such a debt?" He thought, pulling back only to look on her with such a deep, joyful smile as she had never beheld.

"You have been made free, that is all the reward I have desired," she answered.

Her face held so tenderly in his hand, Guy's heart raced within him, looking down into such soulful eyes, and she, smiling all the brighter.

Without warning, the carriage halted, and the sound of men's voices and marching footsteps drew near.

"Shh," the lady whispered, bringing her hand to Guy's shoulder as she withdrew from his embrace; listening.

"Whoa now!" A guard called out. "State your name and business!"

"I speak on behalf of the Countess of Levisham," Alan declared, "Her business is to travel on to Portsmouth."

"Travelling to the Portsmouth? That's a long way from here," the guard grumbled, eying the man with a narrow gaze. "I don't remember this carriage entering the gates. When did you arrive in Nottingham?"

"My lady was a guest of the sheriff not a week ago, and the sheriff is the one who supplied us with this carriage," the outlaw answered.

"No matter, I cannot let you pass until I have a word with your mistress," the man advanced toward the door.

"Quick, hide!" Múriel whispered as she motioned for Gisborne to hide under the bench opposite her.

Instantly, the door of the carriage was swung open. The maiden hardly knew what to say, staring with wide and uncertain eyes at the guard. Bitter and begrudging, the brute stared back at her. Then upon seeing such a graceful yet frightened lady, his expression shifted.

"Oh, em, pardon me, your ladyship," he bowed carelessly, "Didn't mean to frighten you. 'Tis my duty to be sure no strange folk are passing in or out. One can never be too careful with that blasted Rebel and his band of reprobates on the loose."

Regaining her composure, Múriel fixed her eyes on the guard so as not to give away Gisborne's position, though Gisborne's eyes strayed not a moment from her.

"It's quite alright," she finally answered, "But as you can see, I am no outlaw. May we pass?"

"Aye, your ladyship," the guard managed a smile of crooked teeth under a thick moustache.

Calmly, the young lady bowed her head, and the door was shut once more. Instantly, Guy nudged his head out from under the bench, only to be hindered by Múriel's raised hand.

"Is it clear?" He asked.

"Shh, not yet," she chided, as she lowered her hand. Pressing her ear against the door, she listened again.

"Move along!" The muffled voice of the guard called out.

As the wheels of the carriage began to turn, the lady nodded and motioned for the man to return to her side. So near her once more, Guy took her hand, "Múriel," he began, looking down at her hand in his; yet whatever he had meant to say, he could not persuade himself to speak, but gazed into her silver eyes, and all the gentle understanding within them teeming.

"Don't worry," she said, holding fast his hand, "I know."

Breathing deep, the man smiled softly, then closing his eyes, he tilted back his head and rested; never for one moment letting go of her hand.

While the carriage rocked and swayed over the dirt road and onto the rippling stony path, the man and the maiden sat silent, perfectly content in such a quiet moment, knowing neither would depart. There, upon the road, the air whipped around the frame of the carriage, the rush and constant of its breath carrying the song of the waking earth and all manner of dew-covered thoughts as all that was green increased about them. And as Guy drifted, Múriel watched as he slept so peacefully, and how the light of day gave such warmth to his face; and something about his spirit fared far brighter. For she could see that in his very heart, though much time would be needed to mend it, he was free.

At length, half an hour had passed, when finally they arrived, and there the great woods greeted them.

"We're here!" Alan called, climbing down from the seat as he swung open the door, grinning broadly beneath his dark beard.

As the hinges struck against the frame, Guy was suddenly woken, taking in a stuttered breath as he urged his eyes open. Before the lady could descend, he gathered what strength he yet harboured and leapt out of the carriage. Standing there, though his eyes shone so spent, dutifully did he hold out his hand, waiting for her. Taking hold of his hand, she stepped beside him.

For the first time in so long, the man paused, breathing deep the scent of the forest. As grand arches, the arms of the trees hung in the atmosphere, each leaf upon the branches as little wings of green; and how the breeze sifted through the boughs and filled the air with the fragrance of the morning. The man had not fully comprehended how greatly he had longed for these woods. Returning his mind to the present moment, he knew not what to say, but watched as the outlaw spoke with the lady.

"Well done, Múriel," Alan said, "You're a lass far more bred for adventure than I'd wagered. Now, I've my own duties to carry out, and so must bid you farewell and return to my master before he loses his wits."

"Trés bien, et merci pour tout," the lady bowed her head.

"A'Dale," Gisborne held out his hand, "Thank you."

"Oh," the outlaw hesitated, then shook the man's hand. "All the thanks really goes to Múriel. This lass here struck a good deal. Mind you keep out of trouble from now on."

"I shall," he nodded, turning his gaze to the maiden.

"Wait, I've nearly forgotten!" Alan raised his brow, "Before I leave, you must tell me about the passage, or else all this will be for nought!"

"Oh, forgive me," the lady gasped, lifting her hands to cover her cheeks, "I was supposed to bring you-"

"There's no time," Alan shook his head, "Tell me what you know."

"Very well," she lowered her chin, "the secret entrance to the dungeons is by the old storehouses on the east side of the castle. A great row of stone pillars, standing side by side. Between the second and the third storehouse is the entrance. The entrance itself is narrow; you will need to remove some stones before you enter, and do not forget to place the stones back when you have fled. Now, when you enter, the passage is very dark, and the steps are not level. You will have to bring a torch."

"And how long will it take to get through, precisely?"

"If you are quick, you'll find your way through in less than ten minutes."

"Is there anything else I should know?" Alan asked, folding his arms across his chest.

"Oui," she answered, "At the end of the passage, you'll reach an old door, but you must be very careful when you open it for there is a torch attached to the other side. Take care not to let it fall, and you must keep quiet. Once you have made it safely inside, the corridor will lead you directly to the restricted end of the dungeons. Can you remember all of this?"

"In between the second and third storehouses; dark, narrow passage; bring a torch; got it," he grinned.

As the lady related all this to Alan, Gisborne stood astounded, realising all Múriel had done for him.

"Thank you, now I must go," Alan said.

"Remember, you can't say a thing... he can't know," Múriel paused, holding her breath.

"Don't you worry, it'll be our secret. Farewell!" Alan called as he hurried off into the woods in pursuit of the company.

Silent upon the road, the man and the maiden stood, watching as the outlaw made his way through the forest, and swiftly disappeared. Alone, the two remained, so still. Finally, Múriel turned to Guy, looking on him sombrely.

"Where will you go?" She whispered.

"What do you mean?"

"Well, you're free now. You can travel wherever you like... see the world," Múriel stared off into the forest, dreading the words as she spoke them. "So where will you go?"

Tenderly, Gisborne drew nearer the maiden and took her hand. "I have seen enough of the world, and have found little pleasure in it. I wish only to go wherever you go; to dwell in *your* world," he said, "So, where will you take me?"

Finding such solace in his thought, Múriel beamed up at him, "Well, my cottage lies in the forest, a few miles outside of Locksley. I've no great palace or garden, no servants or-"

"Do you take pleasure in it?" He asked.

With a sweet grin upon her lips, the maiden nodded, "It is my sanctuary."

"Then take me with you," Guy gazed into her eyes with such a look of passion and adventure.

Excitedly, taking the carriage, the man and the maiden sat together on the driver's seat and started their way through the woods. Secretly, the maiden clung to this hope; that the journey would not end upon the roadside. And how contented was she, to know the fulfilment of it.

***

Resounding through the streets, thundering in every ear, came the call of a trumpet.

Tempestuous, the herald upon his grey-dappled steed rode forth, his robes of a deep scarlet and his hair billowing behind him in the wind. The horn lifted to his lips, the call rung out again amidst the crowd.

"Make way!" He commanded; his voice so clear and strong, "Make way for the prince!"

Their eyes widened in fear, Dumont and Roland halted in their pursuit as the peoples about them whispered and hurried off the road. With the carriage of the damned so far beyond them, the guards doubted whether they should continue the chase, or depart for the castle.

"The prince?" Roland murmured, his eyes bulging as he stared at his captain, "What shall we do?"

Looking to the gate, and then back to where the herald had passed, Dumont squinted his eyes.

"Well," he thought, scratching at his beard, "the countess and the captive are surely a suspicious pair, but there is no chance we will catch them up now," he paused, his moustache curling as he gave a sharp nod. "Come along, Roland," he said, "Let us return to the keep."

Without another word, the two guards followed the trumpet's call and the heavy stamping of the horse's hoofs, back along the way they had come. Indeed, it would prove a worthless feat if they did not heed its warning, and for all their suspicions, the matter of the countess and the captive must wait.

At length, when the afternoon sun shone hot above them, the guards had reached the courtyard, awfully weary, and so took their ease in ascending the great steps. But then, just as their feet touched the landing, the herald withdrew from beneath the stone arch, and scurrying past him, the sheriff herself.

Bowing but a moment, the guards stood nervous as Claudia wrinkled her nose at them.

"I would have a word with you before the prince arrives," she whispered crossly. "Tell me quickly what you saw."

"Well, we followed them as only we could, your grace," Dumont began, "We watched until they reached the gate, but as the herald came, we departed."

"That is plain," she rolled her eyes, "but what of the countess? What of Sir Guy? Did you find anything curious? Anything strange?"

But before the man could conjure any further answer, Dumont was suddenly interrupted as a guard rushed forward unto the steps, while several other guards were rattling about frantically behind him.

"Sheriff! We must speak with you at once!" The man called, bowing his head as he approached.

"Can you not see that I am already occupied? What could have possibly induced such a disturbance as this?" Claudia's brows raised contemptuously. "The prince is to descend upon us before the sun has set!"

"But your grace," the man continued, "I must warn you, whatever is said, do not tell the prince of your plans to capture the Rebel-"

"Do you think me a child that I must be so censured?" The woman tightened her lip, "The prince must know some of my designs against the outlaw for he has entrusted me with the task. Now, what of it?"

"Sheriff," the man whispered, "He has escaped."

"Escaped?" She lowered her chin, stepping further away from the herald, "Who has escaped? The Rebel?" She whispered.

"No," the man shook his head, "We've not yet lured him; it is the lad, your grace."

"Blacklock?" She gulped.

"Aye," the man answered nervously. "We… we don't know how, but somehow he's vanished."

"Vanished?" The woman snarled, grasping at his collar, "You imbecile! He was our only means of gaining the outlaw! Now, listen well for I will only say this once," she cautioned, lifting her eyes to glare at the band of guards. "I want every single one of you searching for the lad, but so help me, if any of you creates a disturbance, if I hear any noise greater than that of my own breath, I shall have you all hanged! John Blacklock must be found before nightfall, and the prince cannot have any whiff of suspicion! Do I make myself clear?"

"Yes, sheriff," the guards uniformly answered and bowed once more.

"Now, leave me... all of you!" She waved her hand with an air of such impatience.

As all of the guards dispersed from the steps, the search began. Not one corner of the castle was left unchecked, not one table unturned, not one door left closed. Passing through the corridors, when the other guards had fled this way and that, Dumont and Roland paused momentarily.

"With all this commotion, do we dare tell her anything of the countess? " Roland wondered, tilting his head back in the direction of the arch.

"No, I fear we'd only be tormenting the hornet's nest," Dumont nodded, leaning closer to the man and lowering his voice. "We must keep the matter to ourselves, save she asks of it again."

"But, wouldn't that be dishonest?"

"No, indeed," Dumont puffed up his chest, "Keeping quiet is not always idle, and be sure, she will press us again. Now, we must catch up and find this lad!"

CHAPTER SEVEN

THE TRAVELLER, THE RANSOM, AND THE WITNESS

Seven long years had passed after young John Blacklock bid farewell to his father in the mighty forests of Sherwood.

All the lad clung to in his remembrance of that final parting, and the legacy of his brave father was his sword. It kept his thought centred, his feet agile, his spirit strong. For as he grew in stature and understanding, so too did his longing grow, to leave behind the simple life he had come to know, and take on a grander feat.

At the arrival of his fifteenth birthday, John resolved to tell his aunt and uncle of his desires to venture beyond his home. That very evening, as the sun was setting in hues of crimson and burnt orange, the quiet family sat at the table of their modest home. As each morsel was taken, each cup drunk, John grew all the more anxious to declare his conviction.

"Aunt Agnes, Uncle Harold," he sighed, leaning forward over the table. "I have something I would tell you. Something that's been weighing on me for quite some time now."

"Well, and what's that, eh?" His uncle managed through a mouthful of bread, a simple grin on his lips.

"I've been thinking," the lad looked down soberly, "I'm a man now. And I think it is time I've found my own way in the world. That is to say, it is time I found my father again." John swallowed, nervous to hear their answer.

"And has your uncle meant nothing to you all these years? He's been more of a father to you, right *here,*" Agnes placed her hands firmly about Harold's shoulders.

"You know what I mean, aunt," John said, "I've been living here and working here for a time. The work is good, but I've not done much with my life, have I? With all the injustice happening in our very own land, I cannot let it all go by. Not when my father is out there making some difference while I am stuck here!"

"You say we do nothing?" Harold questioned, placing his elbows on the table.

"You don't understand," John shook his head, "*none* of us is doing anything."

"Now hold your tongue just a moment! We're doing plenty in minding our own," Harold tapped his forefinger on the table. "Living at peace with our neighbours; working hard; caring for each other. That's what makes a country. Your father, and Robin, and the lot of them... what they're doing is noble to be sure, but-"

"But what?" The boy rolled his eyes.

"Here is where you belong, lad. Here is where you're needed," the man said.

"Uncle, I cannot stay here forever. I shall suffocate if all I am ever to do with my life is plough a field and dig in the dirt from dawn until dusk, all for another quiet meal, at a quiet table, in a quiet town. If I am needed here, it is for work that any old dobbin can do. I want to fight!"

"Take care what you say, John. Do not forget, your father entrusted you to us after your mother's death so you could live a good life, away from all the outlaws," Harold placed his hand upon John's arm. Pausing a moment to think, he then raised his finger, "However," he thought, as Agnes looked on nervously, jotting her glance between the two. "You're truly determined to go? To fight alongside your father? To fight for England?"

The lad tensed his lip, broadening his shoulders and staring hard at his uncle's hand, then back up to such gentle brown eyes. "I am," John nodded.

"Well, I'll say this, then," Harold squinted his eyes, "You must consider the risk; mind, take a day or two to think on the matter-"

"But I have already thought on-"

"Wait," the man raised his hand, and the lad listened once more, "First, take time to think on it, and if you're still set on going... then you may go with my blessing." Harold sighed, reaching his hand across the table, grasping John's shoulder firmly, and at this, both Agnes and John's eyes lit in astonishment.

"But, Harold, that's dangerous sending him off amongst a lot of outlaws!" Agnes thudded her hands upon the table.

"My father is not some common outlaw. He is one of Robin's men!" The lad interjected.

"Agnes, you and I both know the Rebel company is not a band of mischief-makers. They're trying to stop the troubles of our land, whether we would agree with that way of life or not," Harold admitted, looking down at his meal.

"Aye," the lad stood from his chair, "You must see they fight for justice."

"They fight, I'll not deny it, but they care not who is cast aside in their battles," the woman said, "Let them heap what guilt they may glean from their thieving and double-dealing. Stay here where you are safe!"

"No! And how can you judge them as such devious criminals? I cannot stand by any longer to watch our whole country fall to pieces because of some prince who would see us all bled dry for his own satisfaction! And neither would my father stand by for it!"

Agnes made as if to respond, but Harold halted her gently, as John marched away from the table, stomping off towards the entrance of the home.

"I will fight!" He proclaimed. Swinging open the door then slamming it shut behind him, the lad left his aunt and uncle to hold council over the matter.

"I'm afraid we must let him do as he must, Agnes," Harold shook his head, as he reclined in the chair. "He only wishes to make things right for other folks, to make England right again, just the same as any of us. We ought to let him be, in his own way. Let him be a grown man-"

"I don't care how grown he is, he's like a son to me! A son who has filled his head with all these silly notions. He's still that innocent, frightened little boy I took into my home," Agnes sat down, her hand upon her heart.

"Oh, come now," Harold sighed. "You cannot treat him as a child-"

"So you are content to have him leave us and join the Rebel company?" She asked.

"Don't do this, Agnes-"

"You are content to let him be caught in their first mission? To be thrown in a dungeon or worse?" She argued, "You remember how that wretched sheriff killed his mother... my own sister," Agnes's voice rung with fear as the lump in her throat couldn't be held much longer. "How-how they took her to pay off John's debts," she whispered, drawing her hand over her mouth as the tears rolled down her face.

"Oh, Agnes," Harold said. Taking to her side, the man held her tenderly within his arms. "John came home with us for good reason, but he is not that little boy anymore. Brave men do brave things, as is their nature. If our nephew has that fire, to be brave, we must let him be, eh? And you know Little John's a trustworthy man, just as Robin, and Will, and the others. If it weren't for those men, we might not be here right now, you see?"

"But I don't want to lose him," she said.

"Neither do I," he comforted, "All the same, we need to give him the chance to grow up, to become the man he must be."

The two held onto each other a while, discussing and weighing the entirety of the matter. Finally, Agnes and Harold were in agreement. John would be given a full week to come to his conclusion, and if he truly felt he must set off to fight alongside his father, then they would support his decision.

At dawn on the seventh day, it was time for the young man to decide whether he would make off for Sherwood, or stay. Utterly determined, John would not hear any more of staying. Although his aunt implored him one final time to reconsider, he declared all the more his resolution. He would go.

With reasonable belongings packed, and his sword in his hand, the young man was ready to depart. Reassuringly, he embraced his aunt and uncle, and bid them farewell.

"Aunt Agnes," the lad smiled, pulling back from her embrace and leaving a kiss upon her forehead. "You were a second mother to me... I'll never forget that."

"You stay safe, mind. And keep close to your father at all times, you hear me?" Agnes stared hard at the lad, as her eyes brimmed with tears.

"I will," John promised. "Uncle Harold," he moved to embrace the man. "Farewell."

"Make me proud, lad. Make us all proud," the man grinned.

Harold and Agnes watched as the lad set on his journey; beyond their home, beyond their merry neighbours, beyond everything safe and familiar; into the forest.

"Harold," Agnes whispered, wrapping her shawl tightly about her shoulders, "Do you suppose we shall ever see him again?"

"You know, love, I think we shall," he said.

***

John delved deeper and deeper, into the woods.

As the days passed on, with the trail beyond still guiding the traveller, the young man decided to leave the road in pursuit of the more untamed paths, nearer the woods of Locksley. For he was confident that if he were to go there first, he would surely find his father.

Taking a turn onto a stranger path, the young man came upon a row of three grand elder trees. All three were of equal magnificence, of sturdy trunk and furrowed bark; the branches reaching out as if to praise the heavens, yet their roots so deeply set in the earth. Glistening, every leaf shone together as a crown and thus adorned, the trees swayed beneath the breath of the wind. There was something quite peculiar and familiar about those three elders; perhaps he may have only caught a glimpse of them in his childhood years, and somehow still remembered them. Far from the village, those grand trees stood, and far from the deeps of the forest. Constant, in between the worlds. It gave John an air of peace in his heart, and his countenance fared more hopeful as all trace of doubt faded behind him.

Finally, beyond the thickness of the woods, he arrived. Locksley, at long last.

The homes, the people, the scents; everything drew him back as if he had never left at all. And just as he breathed in so many memories, the dark ones crept through the shadows, for they had never left, though the lad was too young to observe it.

As John approached the village, he perceived a few guards standing in a threatening stance at the end of the first row of huts and hovels. The lad sifted through his thoughts, wondering whether to advance or retreat. Yet, he resolved to err on the side of caution, remaining at a safe distance as long as he could while he continued on his way.

As he stepped cautiously onward, he heard the voice of a woman from afar; a voice so soft and clear, giving orders to the guards. For an instant, he grew excited, believing the woman to be someone he had remembered from long ago. Still, he drew nearer, and his eyes fell upon a woman in a gown of pure white, laced with golden ribbon; her long hair glistened in the sunlight, and her bonny face captured his eye. But he did not recognise her face. No, surely this could not be Lady Marian, as he had remembered her. Lifting his hood over his head, John carefully made his way through the village, searching for any sign of Robin or his father. Suddenly, and most unluckily, he was spotted by the woman in white.

"You! You there!" She called to him, as she waved her hand at two of her guards so that they followed behind her. Lifting the train of her dress, she marched towards the young man. He, quite unsure of what to do, heeded her command and stood awaiting her audience.

"What is your name, young man?" She questioned, her eyes clear as the water of a rippling brook.

He did not answer but remained silent, lowering his chin to keep his face hidden from her gaze as his sandy locks shaded his features.

"There have been many travellers of ill repute who have been seen wandering through this village," she said, "I only wish to be sure you are no foe."

"As you have done me no harm, I cannot be your enemy," John stated plainly. "I am only a humble farmer's son. But, a woman so lovely as you, must be a lady of nobility."

"I am the Sheriff of Nottingham," the woman answered, smiling as she was a little flattered. "But you have not yet told me who you are... pray, what is your name?"

Nervous, the lad hesitated to make his answer. Yet, being drawn in by the woman's gentle speech, and believing her to be sincere, he obliged her request as only he could manage.

"I am called John. John Blacklock, your grace," the lad answered, as he removed his hood and bowed.

At the mention of his name, the woman's brows scrunched together in thought and curiosity.

"John Blacklock... John Blacklock... why does that name sound familiar? Let me see," She paused, a hand at her chin as her eyes scanned the blades of grass. Studying the young man before her, she then noticed the sword he carried, and the mark carved upon it.

"Ah! Now it has come to me!" She smiled, as something softened in her expression. "Little John Blacklock! Surely you know of him, do you not?"

"Yes, indeed! He is my father," he nodded.

"How fascinating," the woman thought, "But did you not say that your father was a farmer?"

"Oh, yes. Well, I meant my uncle is a farmer," John said, taking in the woman's beauty. "I've lived many years with him, but my father was a farmer too, a long time ago."

"Ah, I see," the woman said, "He is a good man, Little John Blacklock. Very brave to fight alongside Robin Hood."

"Aye, and that is how I see it," John's brows raised excitedly. "It was difficult persuading my aunt of it, but she came around in the end. Certainly, my father had some trouble with Rothgar a long while back, that is to say, the old sheriff was. But my father is no common outlaw as many might reason."

"Of course not," the woman added, setting her hand on the lad's arm as he smiled.

"Well, it's grand to see there is a sheriff who thinks for the people," John continued. "It's high time we had one leader who understands us."

"Oh yes, Rothgar and Sir Guy have been long, long gone," she chuckled cunningly, waving her hand about. "And it is a privilege to rule."

"But, your grace, if you know of my father, do you suppose you'd know where he might be? I have come to Locksley hoping to find him, but it would seem he is nowhere to be found."

"You're looking for your father?" The woman wondered. "Well, I would be delighted to help you find him!"

"Truly?" John's eyes lit up under his fringe of tousled hair.

"Of course," she nodded, "In fact, it may please you to know that he and all of the Rebel company are to be my guests this evening in Nottingham castle. I've been very fortunate to have such allies and wished to thank them. I could escort you there personally."

"Thank you, your grace," John bowed his head.

Smiling broadly, the woman turned to call for her guards. "Fetch my horse at once, and another for this young fellow here. He is to be my guest this evening, and we mustn't waste any time."

The lad felt it was curious the sheriff should be in such a hurry to return to the castle, but his naiveté and eagerness to be reunited with his father quieted any hesitations. Before he could utter another syllable, he and the sheriff, along with several other guards, made their way to Nottingham castle.

***

Dismounting in the courtyard, the lad stood amazed at the sight of the castle. Grand stairs led to a beautifully carved archway, and the light of the sun cascaded over the stone, illuminating its

85

craftsmanship. Banners of deep hues hung from the ramparts, and all along the battlements, were guards clad in brilliant armour.

Yet, amidst the splendour, John had the most unsettling feeling in the pit of his stomach. As the sinking urge to flee swept over him, his feet knew to draw him backwards, but it was too late.

"Guards! Arrest him!" The sheriff shouted.

Suddenly, guards poured forth from the castle's archway, bounding down the steps, unyielding. All about the lad was a maddening wave of clanging metal, as they seized him.

"But I've committed no crime!" The lad protested, "You said you would take me to see my father!" John struggled angrily against the guards, though they successfully chained him, ripping away his sword, as well as his other belongings.

"Ha! Oh, you stupid little imp," she jeered, as she stood before him, "Did you really think that I would ever stoop to patronise a petty commoner, let alone have your traitorous father as a guest in my castle? I would rather dine in a courtroom of rats than speak two words with such depraved dogs."

"How dare you say that about my father!" John gritted his teeth.

"And what use is a commoner's son to you? Do you find it good sport to arrest innocent people?"

"Oh... you're precisely the pawn I need," she said murmured.

"Pawn? What do you mean?" He questioned, as the guards roughly held him back. "What are you going to do with me?"

"I'm going to kill an outlaw," she grinned.

"You cannot do this!" John wrestled against the guards, "You can't just take anyone you please and torture them for your own amusement!"

"And what are you going to do? Run and cry to your father about it? You don't even know where he is," she mocked, "What kind of son abandons his father like that? Oh, oh wait," she tapped her chin. "Or is it that your father abandoned you, and now you're hoping that when he sees you, he will wish to reconcile? Hmm?"

John fell silent, hanging his head, then lifting his gaze once more. "My father will come for me!"

"Oh, I'm counting on it," Claudia said. "Guards, take him to the dungeons!"

Shuffling the unfortunate young man through the corridors of the castle, the guards led him down into the darkness of a cold, ruthless cell.

***

For two days, John was left alone, but by no means frightened.

Far more furious than fearful, was he, yet he scolded himself for not having been more guarded in his actions. His only wish was to be given a chance to prove his himself; as a son, or simply as a man. The hours of the following morning dragged on, as the young lad sat pensive in the cell. Although he felt some heat of frustration, John would not let his circumstance overpower him. The more he kept to the truths in his mind, the more confident he grew in the trustworthiness of Robin and his men, and most especially, his father. But the dungeons, he would never forget.

Where he was placed in the thick of the cells, the morning dawned with the wailings of the prisoners, at least the ones who still had strength enough to cry out; begging for bread, for water, for any respite to ease their suffering. Menacing, the guards whipped long chains against the bars to silence the outcries, and just as one assumed the cries would cease, the howling would start up all over again.

Abrupt, a mingling of harsh voices resounded from the back of the dungeon, drawing nearer and nearer, and suddenly up to the very cell in which John remained. There, the lad saw three guards who were leading a prisoner through, but now, were interrupted.

"Halt!" A guard from beyond them held his hand out, blocking the procession. "We need this rat of a lad over here to be taken up as well," he said, pointing to the cell on his right.

As the lad looked up, he observed the prisoner being escorted. John was almost certain he knew that face. The young man's eyes stared keenly, racing over and over every face in his mind's eye, then, he remembered. Before him, was Sir Guy of Gisborne.

John could not fathom why the man was imprisoned, nor for what purpose he was being brought through the dungeons, yet it would not take much to convince him that the new sheriff had some part in this. John quietly contemplated all this, as the guard swung open his cell, and dragged him upward. Joining the other guards and their prisoner, they proceeded through the dungeons.

Determined of the prisoner's identity, John debated whether he should address Sir Guy; yet as he had no reason to address him other than simple recognition, he reasoned it would prove a hopeless business. Moreover, what else would he say if not that he loathed the man for all the oppression he had set on others.

Through the archway of the keep, the captives stood, as daylight broke against their tired faces. As the guards ushered John aside, beyond him, he witnessed the most extraordinary encounter.

The other guards thrust the man to his knees at the top of the stairway, then gagged him and forced a hood over his head. As the man was shoved down the stairs, the guards then secured his bonds to a long chain at the back of a carriage. The sheriff was there, greeting a lady, who was rather lovely indeed. The lady's hair was like the rolling sands of the seaside, her attire modest and delicate. While the sheriff had quite a sly smile, this woman seemed quite different altogether. Her countenance was something of innocence, or so the young man reasoned. And curiously, this young lady kept stealing restricted glances at Gisborne and looked on him as if she took pity on him. Odd enough as that seemed to the lad, the gentle lady looked horrified that the man was treated thus.

As the sheriff and the lady spoke, and of what John could not well make out, the driver of the carriage turned about to whisper something to the gentle lady. This man also struck a chord in John's memory, although that was a trickier mystery to unravel.

At length, the lady, the carriage, and Sir Guy, who ran behind, exited the courtyard.

Immediately, the sheriff whispered something to two guards, shifting her eyes in the direction of the carriage. The guards nodded, and as they marched in pursuit of the carriage, the wretched woman turned about, approaching John; disdain in her eyes, and something sinister upon her lips.

***

"Well you were the last to keep watch," Little John grumbled, gripping Will's collar as his eyes stared something fierce, "I find it very hard to believe you saw nothing."

"I swear, master, he was there as I sat by the fire, and by dawn, he vanished," Scarlet complained. "I didn't hear a sound!"

"Then where is he?" Little John shouted.

Suddenly, the arguing of the men died down as they heard a voice echoing through the woods.

"Master! Master!" The voice shouted.

Carelessly, Alan leapt through the woods, and upon reaching the camp, was utterly breathless. Stopping so abruptly in his tracks, he wet his hands on his thighs to support himself while the rest of the company surrounded him anxiously.

"Finally!" Scarlet called out, his brows in a straight line across his forehead, "Where have you been?"

"To the castle," the outlaw huffed.

"You found a way in?" Will asked.

"Aye," the man nodded.

"And yet you left without having spoken a word to any of us. You know that is against our code," Robin scolded, drawing near the man.

"Forgive me," Alan said. "I didn't want to waste any time. But believe me, it was all worth the trouble."

"Well, go on then, what did you find?" Tuck wondered.

"An entrance in between the old storehouses," he panted, standing up straight. "There's a narrow passage leading straight into the dungeons. No guards; no witnesses."

"But did you see my son? Are they keeping him in the dungeons?" Little John pressed, grasping the man by his shoulders.

But for lack of breath, Alan held up his hand, and stepping aside he leaned up against a tree. Presently, as he made no answer, John marched towards the man.

"Did you see him?"

"Well, I haven't actually gone into the castle yet," he confessed, letting out a deep breath. "I don't know where he's being held."

"It's doubtful the sheriff would keep him anywhere else save the dungeons," Tuck reasoned, "now if you've not gone through yet, how can we be certain the passage is safe? How did you even come to discover it?" He asked, folding his arms across his chest.

"An old friend," the outlaw grinned, rubbing at the back of his neck. "and a trustworthy ally to say the least."

"And what was his business?" Will wrinkled his brow.

Nervous to give his answer, A'Dale paused, and when he had gained enough courage to speak, he was glad to have been interrupted.

"That doesn't concern us," Robin shook his head, "All we need know is that the passage is safe and that this friend of yours will not betray your trust."

"You have my word, the passage is secure, and our errand is well concealed," the man promised.

"Good," the old friar nodded, "So, as we've found our new way in, how do we go about getting the lad?"

"Well," Robin thought, "Certainly, the sooner, the better. We've lost a good bit of the morning as it is, and we should strike during daylight."

"And only one of us should be sent," Tuck whispered, thinking aloud as the others stared at him perplexed.

"Only one of us?" Will questioned, "The task at hand is dangerous enough as it is, but to go alone-"

"Would give us the advantage," Robin corrected, stepping forth amidst the men, "With only one man set on the task, there's less chance of being discovered."

"And whoever is set to retrieve the lad, what if he be caught?" Scarlet wondered.

"You know your oaths," Robin answered.

"Send me, master," Little John said, "It is my son who's been taken. I must free him."

"John," Robin paused in his steps, facing his comrade. "I fear the task must fall to Alan."

"But master-"

"If we are to succeed in rescuing your son, we must act now," Robin said, "Already, Alan knows the way, and is proven most cunning if he has managed to slip by all of us who know well his step. We must let him try."

"Then if Alan goes to rescue the lad, what shall *we* do?" Scarlet asked.

"Create a diversion," Tuck said. "We'll need some sort of distraction to draw out the sheriff and her guards," he concluded.

For a moment, the men remained quiet in their thoughts. Finally, the comrades produced what wiles could be conjured, and so plotted until all were in perfect agreement of what was to take place. Alan was to return directly to Nottingham, alone. There, would he keep to the shadows and wait until Claudia had fled, while the rest of the company would make for Locksley village and create their wildly conceived diversion. Yet time would not oblige them, and so in much haste did the men retreat from their camp.

***

"Sheriff!" A guard's voice came bellowing into the great hall.

Directly, he advanced to the long table where Lady Claudia sat. Horrified at such a display, the woman jolted from her chair.

"Am I never to finish another thought while I live?" She growled ferociously, slamming her fist upon the table. "What is the matter?"

"Sheriff, all of Locksley is up in arms! The people are rioting!" The guard panted.

"Rioting!" She raised her brow, "I suppose you shall tell me next that all the guards of the manor have taken their ease, lounging upon the green, instead of tending to their duties. How is it that the people have not yet been reprimanded?"

"Your grace, the Rebel company has disarmed them-"

"What?"Claudia gripped the arms of the chair as she leaned forward, a wrinkle forming between her brows.

"They have rallied all the men of the village, and have fashioned an effigy of your ladyship," the guard swallowed, taking a step back. "They make ready to burn it."

Seething, the sheriff sprinted to her feet. "They have the audacity-" the woman huffed, her lips pursed as she could no longer fathom any coherent outburst, "Prepare my horse, and when you are finished, gather together the second division of the guards!"

"Yes, sheriff," the man bowed, hastily departing from the great hall to sound the alarm.

Claudia hurried off, storming her way down into the courtyard. There she joined her swiftly gathered regiment, the whole company departing for Locksley.

***

"My brothers," Robin stood before the assembly, a flaming torch in his hand. "We have seen oppression and wickedness and tyranny under this foul government. Over and over has justice been denied us, and freedom kept far from us! Have we not known more than the aching of our bellies? Have we not known more than the death of the innocent? Each of us this day has suffered; each of us has drunk deep this poisonous fount. And our oppressors? How they have been eager in their violence against us, all in the name of a prince who does not revere the *true* king of this land!"

"Aye!" The villagers called, each man gathering near with discerning eyes.

"Do not deceive yourselves, my brothers," Robin implored, "Even now, our sheriff has raised the taxes on this land, and has taken in more prisoners for the crime of their poverty. Amongst them, young John Blacklock, born and raised here in this very village is now held as ransom. The sheriff wants only to abuse her power over us and cares not for our affliction. I ask of you today, shall we stand for such a government?"

"No!" The men shouted.

"Should we tolerate this wickedness?"

"No!" The men roared all the louder; teeth gritted, and fists raised high.

Casting the torch at the foot of the likeness, Robin watched as the flames climbed higher. "I bid you now, to stand with me this day, and fight!"

Alit by the fire, scarlet hues shone swift across every face. As the chants of outrage continued, suddenly, the rolling sound of horses hoofs was heard, fast approaching. Leading fearless before the soldiers, the sheriff rode upon a white horse, and how her eyes shone wrathful. Then, as she beheld her own image, licked in flames, she halted; watching as her adversary drew forth.

"Take care what words you speak," Robin warned, readying his arrow, "For they may be your last."

"You may speak well, Rebel," she smirked, "But you know full well if you harm one hair on my head, the prince will have blood."

Though the woman advanced, the wall of soldiers behind her, the outlaw did not flinch; did not blink. Seeing his strength, the men of the village stood together, unshaken.

"And as for the runt, do you truly believe I will hold him ransom forever?" She lifted her chin, her jaw tight. "A shame, the lad is quite determined you will come for him."

With his sword at the ready, Little John relinquished all constraint, and so charged against the enemy; his sword raised high and his cry as a call unto war.

Now, the whole assembly of men followed, armed and ready to face their enemy. Standing back, Robin loosed arrow after arrow, felling four guards in one breath. Down they fell from their horses and the outcries of the men causing the horses to kick up their hoo.

Fearless, Scarlet swung his sword as three guards dashed forward. Wielding the sword low, he struck a blow to one man's leg, sending him to the ground in agony. The other two leapt upon the moment of distraction, lifting their swords to slay him when Tuck sprinted up from behind. Using his sword to skewer the second man, the third he conked on the head, before Will got to his feet, joining him in fending off another group of guards. Little John was undoubtedly the most terrifying. Growling as a ferocious beast, he hacked his sword against many a man, felling each without count.

The battle raged on, as each of the outlaws and the villagers overcame the division, the unfortunate ones left wounded and wailing in pain.

Dumbfounded, Claudia's skin grew white as snow, watching in horror as the Rebel stood amongst his men, victorious. At this, the sheriff turned about in shame, galloping back towards Nottingham. What guards who were left alive, weary indeed from all the fighting, slowly and begrudgingly followed the sheriff.

Cheering proudly for the battle won, the men stood together, and not one of them was lost.

***

As the strength of the evening sun beat down upon the earth, the friends of the forest waited, restless to hear of Alan's safe return and the fate of the lad.

How the thought of seeing his son again after such years filled Little John's heart with such joy. Indeed, when they had parted, it was borne from necessity. But surely, if the lad had returned, there lingered a chance to reforge what had been broken; or so the man hoped.

Soft, the winds swept through the woods as the men waited. Stirring at a pot over the fire, Will remained, as Friar Tuck sat near. So close to the fire John sat, staring at the flames and how they curved around the iron pot and watching as the smoke rose high above; his eyes unwavering, and brimming, and anxious. Placing a hand upon his comrade's shoulder, Robin looked on the man in understanding.

"They'll come," he reassured.

"I hope so," John sighed.

Waiting in the stillness, John listened to the crackling of the fire, a steady whisper against the emptiness of his mind. Then, he heard something; twigs snapping in the distance, coming closer.

"Father!" The lad shouted with a broad smile, waving his hands about, and racing through the trees.

Little John whipped his gaze around to find the young man, bounding toward him. "My son!" He cried. Now he could hardly keep, but sprinted out to the lad, and pulled him into a firm embrace.

"My son," John said, freeing all his tears, as he held the lad close in his arms. Pulling back, he set his hands upon now broader shoulders, to face the young man for the first time in so long.

How the lad had grown so much and was nearly as tall as his father. His locks of hair, unruly; his chin had but the faintest stubble; yet he was a man all the same. His countenance was dignified, his hands were rough from work, and his eyes shone bold and kind.

"I... I can't believe it's you," the man whispered, clasping the lad's face in his hands. "In a single breath I've said farewell to a child, and have welcomed home a man."

"I've still much to learn, father," the lad smiled back, letting some tears fall, "but it's grand to be home again!"

"But I don't understand, why did you risk so much to come here? What of your aunt and uncle? Do they know you've come?"

"They gave their consent," he nodded. "I wanted to see you again, and fight for the cause of the people; to stand by your side, to stand with all of you," he turned to address the company, "I wish to fight beside you. I know I shall need to train, and learn how to fight, but father, would you be willing to teach me?" The lad asked, looking back at his father's eyes; searching for an answer.

"Aye, that I'll do," the man grinned. "Now, there is something I would tell you, something that has been as a weight upon my mind for some time," he sighed, "I... I was not there when I should have been. You needed me when your mother died," he paused, closing his eyes as he took a deep breath. "It seemed right, sending you away to your aunt and uncle; that it was best for you. But I see now, that I have missed many a year with you; years I'll be hard pressed ever to gain back... please, forgive me," he stared steadily, his burdened eyes fixed on his son.

"I already have, father," the lad nodded.

And as they embraced once more, the men stood silent, for each understood that all was mended.

"Well, it would seem, my comrades, that there is another rebel in our midst," Robin declared heartily, as he held his hand out to the lad. "Welcome, young outlaw."

Shaking the man's hand, the lad smiled. "Now, you'll forgive my bluntness, but I already know of the dangers in joining this company. Please, I beg you would spare me of this warning; I am ready to take my oaths."

In such pensive stare, Robin nodded, then his eyes softened as he motioned for the young man to kneel. Bowing his head, John waited to hear what words the outlaw would speak; the words he spoke over and over in his mind as an endless rhythm; the very words his father taught him such years ago.

"John Blacklock," Robin said, "before these men, in this hour, you will disown any pursuit of glory, any pursuit of praise, any pursuit of comfort. No such worldly thing shall be yours. You shall know no poverty, but that of the poor; you shall know neither hunger or thirst, but that of those who starve and thirst about you; you shall know no want, but the want of those in great need. Fellow man shall be your keep, and you to ever guard them; in courage, in kindness, in wisdom, and in truth. Never take what is not yours, never cheat any man or woman, never lie, and never shed innocent blood; never be prey to greed or envy, to deceptions or hatred. For here stand men of honour, ones who will not fail to slay you if you so prove corrupt. Do you swear by these oaths, to cast aside self, to uphold what is fair and just according to the laws of Sherwood?"

"Yes, master," he answered.

Lifting his head, the lad watched as Robin held forth an arrow and placed it in his hands. The arrow was fashioned of silver birch and wound about the red-tipped feathers at the end of the shaft, was a bright green thread. Rising to his feet, he now stood beside the outlaw.

"My brothers," Robin said, "Here, in this hour, stands a man of Sherwood."

At these words, each head bowed, and the young man not knowing what to say, simply grinned, "It is an honour to know you all," he bowed graciously.

"It's an honour to have you with us," Scarlet stepped forward, shaking the lad's hand. "Nevertheless, I believe we've arrived at a small dilemma."

"And what could that be?" Little John grumbled.

"We must decide upon a new name for your son," Will answered plainly.

"I'm to have a new name? Why?" The lad wondered.

"I very well can't go about saying *John Blacklock* and *Little John* and then *John Blacklock* again, day in and day out," Scarlet reasoned. "Too many *Johns* is bad luck indeed! I shall soon be driven to calling someone *Little Blacklock* or *Blacklock John*, and my head won't know the difference."

"That is a good point," Alan tilted his head, giving a little grin.

"So, what shall we call the lad then, eh? *Johnny*?" He chuckled, as the friar and Will joined in the fun, though Little John rolled his eyes.

"You can't call him *Johnny*," Little John protested.

"Well, what about *Johnny Boy*?" Will laughed, then all at once, he and Alan both shouted "*Johnny Boy!*" in jest.

"Ah!" Hood waved his finger, with a smirk. "What about *Lack-beard*?"

At this, Will and Alan burst out in laughter. "How do you fare this eve, my Lord *Lack-beard*?" Will teased, feigning a dramatic bow toward Alan.

"Oh very well, my Lord Scarlet," Alan bowed, though, for all their bowing, the two managed to knock their heads together.

"I must protest to *Lack-beard*," the lad shook his head disapproving, though he was growing rather amused. "It is simply too ridiculous!"

"Balderdash! It's brilliant," Will smiled, as he rubbed at his aching temple.

"Oh, would you stop it," Little John glared at the two chuckling imbeciles from under his bushy brows.

"Wait! What about *Jack*?" The old friar's eyes lit up. "That seems suitable, does it not? What do you think?"

"I'm quite fond of it," the lad nodded, rather satisfied. "And in truth, my father and I both being called *John* would have become rather confusing."

"Jack it is!" A'Dale beamed with excitement.

"Jack!" The whole lot shouted merrily, as the laughter and carefree air of the evening flourished.

***

Night soon swept over the woods.

As a blanket of stars twinkled through the branches, so the light of a full moon bloomed over the leaves and brush of the earthen floor. The woods proved quite a different world at night, altogether a realm of peace and uncertainty, for a while the world lay so quiet none could tell what lingered in the darkness. Nought could be known but the voice of the wind, and the light of the heavens, and the calls of the creatures who dwelt in the shadows. At a turn, one could see a pair of bright red eyes blinking in the distance; silent and focused and wary. But on an eve that fared far brighter, one could look up and find great wings sailing smoothly across the skies betwixt the boughs overhead. Yet for all this, a fire blazed most faithfully and kept every uncertain thought and every dreadful rhyme of silence at bay.

While the rest of the men had long gone to sleep, Little John and his son remained awake, sharing their stories beside the fire, letting the crackling and snapping of the wood and the rush of flames sing behind their voices.

"What happened while you were in the dungeons?" John asked.

"Nothing," Jack said, "they merely cast me in, locked the iron bars, and left me. I spent the hours sitting and thinking and growing hungry, least before Alan freed me."

"Well, perhaps it was best you were left alone," John thought.

"Aye. But, father," Jack said, "while I was imprisoned, I saw someone rather peculiar. Briefly, when I was taken up into the courtyard so the sheriff could issue her demand, there was another prisoner taken up with me. It was Sir Guy, that tax collector or other. You remember him, do you not?"

At this, Little John's large eyes went wide in disbelief. "Gisborne?" He whispered, lifting his hand to his chin.

"Why do you suppose Claudia would have him thrown in prison?"

"It can't have been him," the man determined. "He's been dead a month now. You're mistaken, so I think-"

"No, father, it truly was Sir Guy," Jack insisted, "I couldn't forget that face, not by a long road. But it was so strange, for the sheriff had made it seem as if he were already dead, but there he stood beside me!"

"Shh!" John brought a finger up to his lips, looking about to make sure no witnesses were present. "Keep your voice down. I don't want anyone hearing this and getting any wrong ideas."

"I don't understand," the lad whispered.

"Listen well," John said, "Not five weeks ago, Gisborne was sentenced to death for murdering Sheriff Rothgar; set to starve in the dungeons-"

"So this is why Claudia was appointed sheriff," the lad sighed. "I simply thought Rothgar had died of old age. But Sir Guy was neither hung or executed; simply thrown in prison?" Jack leaned forward, the light of the fire flickering across his cheek.

Little John stared into the flames, resting his chin upon his fist, taking in a deep breath and releasing it once more.

"Father, surely if he were dead there would have been a body, yes?" Jack said. "If Sir Guy were dead, and I really am mistaken-"

"Stop," the man held up his hand, having reflected upon the matter. Then turning to face the lad, he placed both hands upon the young man's shoulders. "Son, would you stake your life upon it? That you saw Gisborne alive?"

"You have my word, father," The lad nodded soberly.

Bringing his hands back down to his knees, the man thought; then bringing one hand up anxiously, he stroked at his beard. "And what happened when he was taken up?" He wondered.

"Well, there was this lady who stood before a carriage in the courtyard," Jack recalled, "She spoke with Claudia though I couldn't quite make out what they were saying. The lady had a French accent." The lad paused a moment, grinning to himself as he scratched just above his ear.

"Pff," Little John rolled his eyes, "Very well, the sheriff spoke with a bonny french lass. Then what?"

"While she was standing there, speaking with the sheriff, the guards had Gisborne gagged and hooded, then they had him chained to the back of the carriage and ... oh!" Jack's brows raised, and his jaw hung loose.

"What is it?" John asked.

"I nearly forgot! There was a man, em, a servant seated at the front of the carriage! He looked quite like Alan," Jack furrowed his brows, reviewing his own interpretation.

"Alan was there?" The man lowered his chin, as his grey brows flared.

"No, at least I don't believe so. Either way, the servant, whoever he was, leaned down toward the lady to whisper something-"

"He whispered something to Claudia?"

"No, no the other lady. I didn't catch her name," Jack sighed.

"But you saw Alan helping that french lass and Gisborne?"

"Well, the man resembled Alan," the lad thought, "I can't remember quite clearly, for I only saw a corner of his face, and the man was wearing a hooded cloak," Jack shook his head, returning to his present thought. "But with absolute certainty, I saw Sir Guy. He was taken with the lady and driven out of the courtyard."

"Do you know where they could have gone?"

"No," Jack answered.

"Son," John began, leaning forward as his eyes scanned the camp, "Promise me you will say nothing of this to anyone. Master Robin cannot know that Gisborne is still alive."

"I promise," the young man nodded, "But why can he not know?"

Wrinkling his nose, Little John sighed as the ends of his moustache curled. With his elbows propped up on his knees, he drew his hands together as he kept his eyes upon the fading campfire.

"He cannot know because Gisborne is responsible for Marian's death."

Aghast, the young man stood, "Sweet Lady Marian? Why? Why would he do such a thing?"

"Would you alarm the whole camp and put us all at risk?" John rebuked the lad, pulling him back down. "It doesn't matter *why* it happened, but that it did happen. From that day forward, Robin's been boiling for revenge. It was a relief when he heard of Gisborne's sentence, and it seemed good enough that the blackguard had finally met his end. But to know it never happened would devour him. And if the other man you saw aiding that murderer was truly Alan…"

Jack sat still a moment, staring hard at the fire, then back to his father.

"I swear, I will say nothing," he promised.

"Good," the man sighed.

Both father and son remained silent; the sounds of the night filling the void, as they stared into the embers left from the once roaring fire. Suspicious, Little John glanced over at the sleeping outlaw, and contemplated whether he would rebuke Alan for such disloyalty; though as he could not be sure of the man's testimony, at present, he would keep the matter to himself.

Therefore, Jack contented to say nothing, though he secretly pondered how all this came to pass, that the Norman would be driven to murder, and yet live.

CHAPTER EIGHT

INTO THE WILD

Long and winding, the hidden path led through the forest, enveloped in the arms of the wild country.

Through the eaves of the forest, the sun's rays painted strokes of glittering light across the earth. Stripes of light, skipping fast over the branches and trunks and roots of the trees, and over every green and growing thing. The horse trotted ahead, its auburn coat reflecting the golden summer sun. As Guy breathed in the rushing breeze, his dark locks caught up in the wind's whispers, and his new air of ease swept over Múriel's mind.

Sensing her gaze upon him, Guy leaned to the right, still holding the reins. "How much longer until we turn left?" He asked.

"Only a minute or two, peut être," Múriel said, "We stay on this way until we see the three elder trees."

"But we've been riding for nearly two hours at the very least. You cannot tell me you rode all this way just to bring me bread?"

"I never said I rode," she murmured.

Now the man's eyes widened. "You walked!" Halting the carriage, he was met with a rather guilty silence from a guilt-felt maiden. "Alone? Every night?" His brows rose.

"You believe it so imprudent that I walked such a distance, *alone in the dark?*"

"It's not merely a question of your unguardedness, but that's miles of walking back and forth, never mind how you snuck into the castle dungeons," Gisborne's tone grew rather sharp, "Surely you must see…" he shook his head.

"See what?" She pressed.

"You must see how insupportable that is," he said.

"*Insupportable?*" Múriel stiffened her posture. "Well, while you may choose to judge my actions in ill favour, I will hold that for a worthy cause, such acts could be considered bravery."

"I did not mean," Guy sighed. Bringing his hand to the bridge of his nose, he thought, as both sat silent. Realising what he had implied, he offered his hand to her apologetically. Though reluctant at first, finally, Múriel accepted his hand. "Forgive me," he whispered, his eyes sincere.

So the maiden nodded, relinquishing what feelings would stave his reach, as she glanced up at him. Then as her eyes wandered beyond him, something caught her attention. "There! Over there!" She called.

Far to the left, the maiden noted the three elder trees. Standing side by side, their branches waved through the breeze as if to call them hence. The man permitted a soft smile and signalled for the horse to move on towards those three trees. Riding on, they passed beyond the trees, the elders acting as a gate. Before them, stretched a vast green field with walls of forest on either side and nestled far in the distance was a little cottage. It reached no more than two storeys high if one could surmise its height to be that of a modest two storey home. The thatched roof matched that of a small barn which stood not far from the cottage; a gentle mingling of such earthen-yellow colours. Behind the dwelling, lay the garden, with rows of herbs and bushes of lavender peeking around the corner of the eastern wall.

"Wait," Múriel gripped Guy's arm, causing him to stop the carriage. "Let me go on ahead to start a fire."

Without any answer from him, the lady removed her shoes and descended from the driver's seat. As her bare feet touched the cool of the grass, she sprinted merrily towards the little home. How the deep hues of her garment flowed in the patterns of the wind's breath, and her long hair followed.

Gisborne could not help but look on with such enchantment, watching her bound gracefully over the field and suddenly disappear into the cottage.

Soon, he reached the cottage and saw smoke rising from the chimney. The carriage was brought up to the barn, and as he dismounted, Guy worked to remove the bridle and reins from the horse, and bring it into its new home.

When the carriage was well concealed at the side of the barn nearest the woods, and the horse was settled, Guy thought how he would approach the cottage himself. It would be the first time he and Múriel would be alone and free. He had no wish to startle her with any undesired signs of affection, but his heart was yearning for her.

Nervous excitement brought him to a small door. As he lifted his hand to knock, the door swung open.

"Supper will be ready soon. S'il vous plaît, entrez," Múriel motioned for him to enter, as she fluttered back towards the hearth.

Bowing his head to enter in, the man took in every aspect of the home.

To his left, stretched a long table, comfortable enough for a modest household and most ideal for a small family, with five chairs at most. At the end of the table was a simple open fireplace, and a hearth before it, where Múriel stood, stirring a pot of stew and reaching around the mantle to retrieve what herbs hung there. Directly across from the door was a flight of stairs that drew straight upward against the east wall, though neither door nor any measure of the hall could be seen from that angle. As the man moved closer to the stairs, he perceived the beginning of a simple hall, with a small window on the right casting the afternoon light upon the floor. Making his way in the direction of the table, he sat upon the chair nearest the fireplace.

"So what are we having for supper?" He inquired shyly. "It smells delicious."

"Just a simple stew, I hope it will suffice," Múriel smiled up at him.

"Well, as I've had nothing but bread and water and apples all this while, I'll be happy to eat anything you make," he smiled.

"Bien," she said, "now, I'll only need a few more things-"

"I could help, if you like," Guy's words stumbled out of his mouth nearly as clumsily as he stumbled out of his chair.

Following the maiden, she led him directly across from the table, into the kitchen. There were simple shelves of simple dishes, and shelves which housed spices and little vessels of various sorts. Another table stood in the centre with some food in baskets set on its surface, and overhanging were all manner of dried herbs and flowers. Guy watched as Múriel hurried about the kitchen, grabbing this and that, and piling it all up in her arms. The glow of the sun beamed over her through the window overlooking the garden, highlighting her gentle features. The man now noticed how she had changed her attire. Now she wore a dress of flax, with long tight sleeves, and tied around her waist was a cream coloured apron. And in his mind, she was ever lovely.

Now as he loathed to feel idle by any means, the man stepped forth. "What can I do?" He wondered.

"Oh, here, could you set these out?" She asked, holding out a stack of dishes.

Taking the dishes, the man nodded and walked back to the table. But as he did so, he wasn't quite sure how to set it all up. In truth, the man had lived so long as a noble, such a time when he had ever set the table could not be recalled. All the same, the man soon remembered where things went, and once everything was prepared, he rushed back to the kitchen to receive his next instructions.

"What else would you have me do?" He asked.

"Well," she wiped her brow. "I can only imagine how tired you must be. Please go sit, I only need to fetch some more water for tea-"

"I can imagine how you must also be tired," he said. "I'll fetch the water for you."

"Merci. Here, take this," the young lady said. With a pleasant light in her eyes, she handed him a wooden pail. "Use the back door here and go straight through the garden; at the end is the well."

Nodding, the man set on his task.

Set on his task, the man opened the door, the hinges creaking as he stepped out. Walking through the garden, the air rustled through every fragrant leaf; scents of lavender and sage, rosemary and chamomile. An oasis of colour and life, and at the very end stood the well. When the man had retrieved the water, he returned to the comfort of the cottage. Múriel removed the pot from the hook over the fire; and when she poured the stew, she took her place beside Guy.

For a few moments, the two sat quiet; taking up a morsel of bread or spoonful of stew as they watched the sun's rays shine through the window, across the table. Indeed, for having been awake over a day, each felt the weight of it, and it did not seem so wrong that the world lay still for the passing time. Quite content, they enjoyed the quiet together. But, as the man looked on the young lady, he realised how much he had not yet comprehended, even in all their time together, and how greatly did he wish to know her more.

"Múriel," the man mumbled, serving himself a second helping of the stew, "Forgive me, but I would ask you something..."

"More questions already?" She grinned warmly.

"If you don't mind?" He asked.

"Ask anything you please," she encouraged. Setting down her bowl, she propped her elbow on the table and gazed on him.

"First, how is it you have all this food? It is just you living here, isn't it?" He wondered.

"Oh, it is only me, yes," she began, "but those are provisions for some friends who are quite in need of it. My garden yields more than enough, and I've been able to get by, selling herbs and flowers, so I prepare something to bring at least once a week. I was supposed to deliver those baskets this morning, but the evening will have to do."

"How many friends must you visit?"

"Three, well, it is three homes I'll need to visit," she answered. "Two are nearer to me in the forest, and one is in the village."

"Hmm," he nodded, readying another bite of the stew, "Well, as soon as we have finished eating, I'll accompany you on your errand. And before you go rattling on about being alright to go by yourself, as I'm sure you know the way better than anyone else, these woods grow dangerous after dark, and I'll not hear of you travelling alone."

"But, after last night... and today," Múriel trailed off, staring at Gisborne's bloodstained tunic.

"Trust me, I'll manage," he said, "I just want to make sure *you'll* be alright."

"It would be wonderful to have the company," she thought, resting her chin upon her hand. "Very well, I will let you come with me, but I must insist you take some time to rest and wash up first. I'll set out some new garments for you, and a basin of water."

While she spoke quite plainly, still harbouring some concern, time spent in his presence was precisely what she wished for. She wasn't sure of how long he would stay, whether he would stay long at all. Yet, anyway she could, she would make the most of every moment.

"But, do you believe someone might distinguish you?" She considered.

"Ah... I had not thought of that," he acknowledged, lifting a cup to his lips. "Perhaps, as I go with you, I'll stay at a distance. I shall be your guardian."

The maiden blushed a little at this thought. "Perfect," she beamed. Then fearing she may have revealed too eager an expression, Múriel resolved upon conducting herself as reasonably as she could, assuming her abrupt change in the topic would suffice. "And how do you like the stew?"

"It's incredible," Guy said, as he filled his bowl for the third time. "I haven't had a meal like this in so long, I could eat up that whole pot."

"You nearly have!" She laughed, rising from her chair just to peer into the almost empty pot. "But I'm glad you like it. Stew always seems a grand way to end a very long day."

"It has been a long day, indeed," he sighed.

Both he and the maiden stopped a moment to ponder just how long the day had been. It felt as if all that had happened the night before, drawing into that very morning, was just a story told by someone else long ago. Devising their plans in the cell, and happening upon Alan A'Dale; the interlude with the sheriff and the escape from Nottingham; even losing those suspicious guards who seemed to follow them a while. It all felt so distant and foggy.

"I can't believe we did it," Guy said, "How on earth were you able to convince Claudia?"

After a few moments of silence, the maiden broke through. "I don't know," she contemplated, tucking a lock of hair behind her ear. "It was terrifying and exciting all at once. I knew there was no turning back. I had to do it, and there wasn't a single moment where I wasn't thinking of you and..." her mouth stopped, suddenly no other words could come forth, and Múriel shifted her gaze away from Guy. "Forgive me..."

"No, you've no need to beg my forgiveness. I owe you my life," he said, taking her hand. His bright eyes stared so humbly at her, and for an instant, she was lost in them.

"Do you truly mean to stay?" She whispered.

"You have my word," he promised, "I'll stay as long as you need me."

Leaning forward, his eyes fixed upon her supple lips. Múriel's heart pounded within her, her cheeks blushing as she stared, yet her timidity of nature got the better of her. Within a breath's measure, she departed from the table before he could achieve his conquest. Fumbling about, she made as if to clear the table, rather awkwardly avoiding his advance.

"If you are to stay, you cannot sleep in the cottage," she said, as she hurried into the kitchen with dishes in her hands. "I do live alone, and so it would not be proper, that is, I mean-" she let out a sigh, biting her bottom lip as she stumbled over her words.

"I suppose you're right," he nodded in confusion, turning round to see her fussing about with the dishes. "Where may I sleep, then?"

"The barn might be suitable enough," she answered, fearful of facing him. "There's a large hayloft, so there would be plenty of room for you. What do you think?"

"Very well," Gisborne sighed.

"And there are only a few chickens there now. I could try to move them into the garden tomorrow, though."

"Lovely," he sarcasted.

For as long as she could manage, Múriel remained in the kitchen, still rebuking herself.

Taking a deep breath, she turned about to face the man again. Though her mind commanded self-control, her heart begged to let go. As she drew back to the table, she thought to listen, maybe just this once; listen to her heart and trust that her feet would lead where she needed to go. And as she looked on him, his expression faded from indifference to a wondering hopefulness, his own heart sensing her call. Then, her eyes observed the sunlight shining dimly through the glass; only a few hours lingered until evening. Thus, her heart must be made to wait a little longer.

"You should rest while you can," she kept her eyes on the shadowing fields. "We must bring those provisions to my friends before nightfall."

"Right," the man stood dutifully. "Well, I fear I'll not gain one wink of sleep in this light. I'll be well enough to wait until tonight. What's to be done before we leave?"

"Yes; first, I need to finish cleaning up from supper. I can do that while you wash up. As soon as that's all settled, we may make ready to leave."

"Brilliant," he nodded with a grin.

Into the garden, the maiden retreated to fetch more water as she prepared a basin in her brother's chamber. With garments laid out, and the water warm, she withdrew to the kitchen, where Guy sat waiting.

As the man heeded her direction, retiring to the first chamber of the hall, Múriel remained a while in the kitchens, clearing the table and washing the dishes and putting out the fire. At length, the man's footsteps steadily marched down the staircase, and the lady could scarcely help but smile. For she found the sound of his footsteps a surprising and delightful comfort. Drawing into the kitchen, Guy leaned his shoulder against the wall; his arms folded across his chest, and his long hair hung dark and damp.

"Are you ready?" He asked, watching patiently as she worked.

"Oui, almost," the lady nodded, binding some herbs in a length of twine, "This last basket is nearly done, and then we can make use of that horse!"

"Tell me what to do, and it shall be done," Guy insisted, a kind light in his eyes.

Múriel smiled, shifting her gaze away from his to redirect her thoughts. Rolling up her sleeves, she brought her eyes back to greet him.

"Oh, well the baskets are ready now," she said, "Would you take these out and prepare the horse?"

"Of course," he nodded, taking up the provisions and marching towards the door.

"Wait," the lady followed. "Are you sure you don't mind doing this? I'm not asking too much of you?"

"It's my pleasure," the man bowed his head, a small smirk upon his lips.

Hastily, Guy set to work. By and by, when the horse stood ready, the man returned to the cottage, and swinging open the door, he stood at the threshold.

"Everything's ready!" He called, yet there was no answer. "Múriel?"

Marching in, Guy had forgotten to lower his head and so conked his forehead upon the doorframe. Rubbing at his aching brow, he searched about the kitchens, and the garden, yet the lady was nowhere to be found.

Upstairs, he thought.

Eagerly, as he approached the bottom of the stairs, he then paused and stood for a while, contemplating whether to venture up or to wait. Then, the sound of her familiar footsteps came pitter-pattering down the hall, finally halting at the top of the steps.

Donned in a light grey cloak, she stood, graceful and enchanting as ever. Her silver eyes illuminated beneath the hood, and draped over her slender arms, she carried a cloak.

"Here, it will get cold before we return," she said. Descending the flight of stairs, she held out the garment; its shade a dark blue, with grey embroidery along the edges.

Receiving the garment, the man fastened the cloak about his neck. How his shoulders looked all the broader, his stature all the grander, and how the dark, sea-swept hues did make his eyes shine as starlight.

"To the forest, my lady?" Guy held out his hand.

"To the forest," Múriel took hold, as he guided her down the final steps of the staircase, and through the door.

The grasses of the field before them swayed in the sweetly sighing winds, as the evening shadows stole across its waves. The horse stood fast, as they made ready to ride.

"It will be easier if you put your arms about me," he suggested most cunningly.

"Perhaps," she admitted.

Wrapping her arms about him, Múriel blushed, and Guy smiled under her touch.

"Now, you'll have to direct me where to go," he said.

"First, we must reach the elder trees, and from there, we must ride straight across the forest for half a mile. After that, we will reach the first cottage."

"Excellent," he said. "Shall we?"

"Allons-y," she answered.

With that, the horse drew round, trotting across the field and towards the wilderness once more. The sun was beginning to set, as a lingering echo of its light still hung above them. Passing the elder trees, and entering into the thick of the woods again, the light grew dimmer and dimmer.

"We should have brought a torch for the journey back," he thought aloud.

"You're right," she confessed. "I had not thought of it. We'll have to make do without."

"Yes, but we must be quick," he said, "there is a long journey ahead."

They rode on for over half an hour, and finally, nestled amongst the trees, they found a little cottage. Of simple means, indeed, it appeared to be fashioned from the earth itself, with a veil of ivy climbing up the side, and uneven stones guiding the lonely wanderer towards its unusually curved door. A wisp of smoke swirled from the chimney, and an air of warmth and comfort filled the atmosphere.

Not so far from the dwelling, the man stopped the horse and dismounted; having aided the lady to her feet, he handed her one of the baskets.

"So, who lives here?" Guy glanced curiously at the cottage.

"An old friend of my father's. A healer, but in his old age, he's taken to living a far quieter life; been much like a second father to me," she sighed, reflective. "Would you care to meet him?"

"I think it would be best if you went in alone," he sighed.

"Oh," she dropped her shoulders. "You're worried he may recognise you?"

"It's not a risk I'm willing to take. But I'll wait here for you," Guy promised.

"Very well," Múriel said, "I won't be long."

In a few moments, she reached the cottage door. Before she could rap her knuckles against the wood, an old man, with a wild white beard and an endearing smile, swung the door wide open. He embraced the lady, welcoming her in, yet the width of the open door permitted him to discover someone in the distance, standing beside a horse.

"Múriel," the old man squinted his eyes, his whisper like a wave washing over stone. "That man... he-"

"Shh," she scolded, turning her head about to steal a glance at Guy before turning back to face the old man. "Tonight, he is but a friend," she whispered.

"A friend, indeed," he said, as suspicious, yet tender eyes questioned the maiden. "This is dangerous business. How did you-"

"Please don't say a word... s'il te plaît?" She begged.

Aldred let out a deep sigh, as his moustache curled up in disapproval. "Very well," he whispered, "He is welcome to come in if he so chooses."

"No, that is very kind but-"

"You, sir!" Aldred called out to the man. "Would you care to join us?"

Lifting his head, Guy stared out from the edge of the hood. The healer and the lady exchanged a tensed glance, waiting for his answer. Stepping back a pace, Múriel held her breath; nervous.

"Any companion of this lovely lady is surely welcome here," Aldred bowed his head.

And as the maiden nodded, Guy felt the weight of inescapable obligation, and so did he follow the stony path unto the door; the leather reins held firm in his grip as he led the horse. As he drew near, the maiden's gaze met his own but briefly, yet the old man already took notice.

"Tie your horse here," Aldred instructed, pointing to a ring of metal secured at the entrance of the cottage. Above it hung a lantern, with a single candle shining through the iron panes. "Come in when you please," he said.

After having settled the horse, the man entered the humble dwelling. There was a simple fireplace directly across from the door in the rounded corner of the room, a little table not so far from the hearth, and to the right was an open door which led into a modest bedchamber. Though the home was such of humble setting, it amply proved a welcome comfort.

Soon, Múriel had set down her basket, and each of them found their place around the table while the old man poured out a hot kettle of tea. With the steam rising in the air, and the earthy savour of sage calmed their palates, both the man and the maiden wondered at who might be the first to make any conversation, though all at once, both felt at ease, for the old man was eager to speak indeed.

"So, Múriel, you are quite late," Aldred lowered his chin.

"Forgive me, I was... delayed," she answered, as she snuck a glance at Guy before drawing the cup to her lips.

"Ah, I see," the old man sighed, darting his eyes between the two. "Well, what have you brought this evening?"

"Well, I've been fortunate enough to have yielded more carrots; and there are two loaves of bread, and-"

"No, no. I'll worry about that later, thank you, my dear," he gently chided, "I meant to inquire after this new acquaintance of yours." His thick, grey brows lifted up curiously. "Would you care to tell me his name?"

At this, Múriel blushed, as she clumsily gulped her tea. "Oh! Oui! This is em, em-"

"Hugo," Guy said.

"Yes, *Hugo*," the lady nodded. "And Hugo, this is Aldred."

"Pleased to make your acquaintance," Guy leaned over the table and shook hands with the old man.

"Delighted," Aldred said, "And... how did you come to meet this young lady?"

For a moment, the conversation had utterly halted. Guy and Múriel glanced at each other in hesitation, uncertain of how they might continue.

"I'm a traveller. From... the north," he stared at his drink, conjuring what to say next. "I've only just arrived in Sherwood, and we met... along the main road."

"Hmm," Aldred reclined in his chair, drawing his hand up to stroke his beard, with sagacious eyes fixed upon the man.

"Hugo had been travelling for many miles when I found him. He wished to know of a place he could lodge for the night, and so I offered he stay at my cottage," Múriel took a sip from the cup, masking her eyes behind it.

All the more did Aldred's eyes stare and all the more did his moustache curl over his frowning lip. "You allowed a perfect stranger to lodge in your home, while you are living alone?"

"No, no, no," Guy leaned forward, "In the barn. I've taken to lodging in the barn."

"Hmm, I suppose that is more agreeable," the old man said, "Múriel, I have no wish to discredit your generosity, but you should have referred him to me. That being said, for precisely how long do you intend to stay, Hugo?"

"As long as ever she needs me," Guy spurted the words out before he could think, and darted his eyes away from the healer, as he fumbled through his explanation. "I mean, as long as I can be there to help tend the land-"

"I see," Aldred said. "Well, I am glad to hear Múriel is being looked after in some way, for the time being," he reasoned, as he seemed to nod approvingly.

Their conversation drew on for a time as they tarried with the healer. They spoke of the weather, and the condition of England, and before long it grew rather late. For what light of the eve had shone through the window, now was wholly consumed in the darkness and the stillness of the night. And while they had remained, both Guy and Múriel had quite forgotten that two more homes lay ahead, before their task could well and truly end.

"Forgive me, but we really must be going," the maiden leapt from the chair, drawing her hood over her head. "I still have provisions for the Smiths and for Winifred-"

"Nonsense. I'll not hear of you taking anything to anyone at this hour. And *forgive me*," Aldred placed his hand over his heart. "I am the reason you are so late. Allow me to take the provisions to them in the morning."

"Are you sure?" She asked.

The old man nodded, his smile so tender and his pale green eyes shining. "Oh yes, I'll take care of everything. Be on your way home, and make haste! The woods at night are no place for any sane man or woman. Hugo, it was a pleasure to meet you," the old man shook his hand again. "And take care with Múriel, she is as a daughter to me."

"You have my word," Guy answered boldly.

Aldred watched as his two guests mounted the horse, the maiden at the front to direct their journey, as the man had his arms wrapped around her. The two waved farewell to the old sage and continued on their way back to the maiden's own little cottage in the woods.

"The horse will need water before we retire for the night," the man whispered.

"Oui, and then to bed," the lady said, her eyelids longing to close, as she fought to remain awake.

Drowsily, Guy nodded. "How close are we?"

Múriel shifted her gaze this way and that, as the once briskly trotting horse now dragged its tired hoofs along the uneven path. "I... I cannot tell."

"Over there!" Gisborne called, with an instant burst of energy, so startling the horse.

"What? What is it?"

"The elders, just ahead!"

"Finally," Múriel sighed. "My eyes cannot stay open much longer."

"Don't worry. I'll take care of the horse," Gisborne promised, as they passed through the gates of elders and approached the long, darkened field before the cottage.

Their journeys proved rather arduous, considering the length of their day and all the events therein. While the moon rose high above them, faintly lighting the tips of the grassy field and outlining the edges of the cottage, the night beckoned them to lay their heads to rest.

Guy dismounted at the entrance of the barn and aided Múriel down, his hands firmly supporting her about the waist, as her hands rested upon his shoulders.

"Merci," the lady whispered, staring up into his eyes as he released her tenderly.

"Before we say goodnight, may I ask something of you?" He began, his endearing gaze captivating. Múriel's heart galloped for miles, his pause vexing her anticipation at his question.

"I was deprived of something last night, something which I was greatly loathed to part with," he drew closer, "If by night we must part, perhaps, may I keep your brooch with me, that while I sleep, you may not be so far from me?"

The lady's eyes filled with surprise at his request, yet she was more than content to oblige him. "Oui! Of course, you may have it!" Gracefully, she removed it from her cloak, placing it in his hand once more. "It is yours to keep," she folded his fingers over the treasure.

Guy brought his left hand up to her cheek and held her face, his smile deepening as the starlight bloomed above them. "Múriel... I-" But before he could finish his thought, she began stepping back.

"Jusqu'à demain? Until tomorrow?" She managed.

"Until tomorrow, my lady," he bowed his head.

Holding fast the brooch, he watched her safely enter, and after, he retreated to the barn, remembering to water the weary horse. "You've brought us quite a bit of luck, haven't you?" Guy said as he stroked the horse's mane while it drank.

After the horse had been settled, Gisborne noticed a ladder propped against the right wall. Climbing up, he discovered the hayloft, and the mountains of dry grass piled high. There was ample room for him to create a bed of sorts and rest comfortably. Removing his cloak and laying it out over the hay, he positioned himself to face towards the window.

Through the high window, the light from the moon gleamed through; its light was cool and clear and calm. Upon reclining, he perceived in the distance, a small flame, flickering from within the cottage. Instantly, Guy shot up, dashing across the hills of hay to gain a closer view. Ultimately, he could only observe the flicker of light behind the pane, and nothing more, yet he knew that on the other side was Múriel; and how the thought of her presence comforted his soul.

Resting back upon the hay, the man brought his right arm behind his head, and in his left hand, clutched the brooch against his heart. Indeed, she was not far from him at all, and nearer still she would remain, or so he determined.

CHAPTER NINE

SECRECY AND SUSPICION

"What do you mean the Rebel has not been captured?"

Enraged, Prince John leapt up from his chair in the great hall, towering over Lady Claudia as she remained seated; fearful of moving.

Disgraced, Claudia bowed her head, "For-forgive me, sire. I did not think he would succeed in retrieving his ally."

"You *didn't think*," the prince mocked, rolling his dark eyes. "It's clear indeed you haven't any brains to think with or else the damned outlaw would be dead this very moment!" He snarled, slamming his fists upon the table, as the woman shuddered. Leaning over the table, he lowered his face, so his eyes met hers directly. "Claudia... I thought we had reached an accord," he said, "I cannot have a queen by my side who does not know how to obey her master. If you cannot fulfil these simple commands put to you now, how can I trust you as my wife?"

"But your highness, surely I am trustworthy to do your will!" She pleaded. Kneeling at his feet, she grasped his hand to kiss his ring and stared up at him with eyes brimming. "You must know I speak in earnest."

"And oft *in earnest* have you spoken such words, but I fear you have only proved the opposite," he grumbled, releasing his hand from her touch as he looked away from her. "Perhaps these failings have prevented me an ill match."

"My lord, I may require more time to obtain the Rebel, but I have proven my loyalty," she said.

"Truly? How so?" The prince wondered, with a sharp gaze.

"Already I have provided the sum taken up from Locksley, which you commanded. Moreover, I have dealt with someone else who had greatly displeased you," the woman whispered, "I have dealt with Sir Guy of Gisborne."

"Oh come, come, stand up. I'll have no more of this," he mumbled impatiently, as Claudia rose once more. "Do you think I am wholly ignorant of your feeble methods? Sir Guy should have been hung! And yet I have been informed that he has been permitted to live. Do you not think this confirms my doubts?"

"But my lord, he was not permitted to live," Claudia said, keeping her eyes fixed on the prince.

"He is dead?" The prince's brows furrowed. "I don't understand-"

"What you heard was true; I did have him thrown in the dungeons that he might suffer a slow and painful death. Yet, I knew you would not be pleased to hear of any negligence of justice. For a command once ordered must be carried out swiftly," the woman paused, only for a moment to think. Observing a guard far behind the prince, carrying a torch, she was given a spark of inspiration. "Therefore, I had him burned at the stake."

"When?" The man gripped her shoulders roughly.

"Two weeks ago," she answered. Holding her breath, she hoped desperately that her word would be accepted.

"I need you to say it; speak the words I have longed to hear," he begged, his keen eyes staring hard at the woman. "Tell me, truly... tell me Sir Guy is dead."

The woman nodded; her expression hard as stone. "He is dead."

Suddenly, the prince's expression grew from agony and doubt, to utter relief. His grip loosening, his eyes grew brighter as he held her hands and his smile grew all the wider so that he suddenly burst out in laughter.

"Ha!" He shouted, holding the woman's hands so fondly. "Oh Claudia, I am finally rid of the thorn in my aching side! I had no doubt of your abilities."

"Now we may all put our minds at ease," she smirked.

"And how you have proven your matchless worth," he whispered in her ear, his lips brushing against her skin as he left a kiss upon her cheek. "I shall never doubt you again, not for all the world."

"It is a great honour to serve you," the woman said. Grinning slyly, she held the jewelled pendant on her necklace, twirling it in her slender fingers. The prince and the sheriff snickered in conceited amusement.

"Now, I must be forthright," the prince said, "I was rather hoping to receive an invitation to the execution, or at the very least, to see some evidence."

"Evidence?"

"Oh, anything will do. Of course, the best proof would be the corpse, if you'll forgive my bluntness. But have you any proof of his most certain death?" The prince entreated, whilst he held her hands, drawing each one up to his lips as he laid kisses upon them. "You must understand, I must be absolutely sure."

"Of course, your majesty," Claudia nodded, her eyes darting here and there, searching for another idea.

High above the hall, the banners hung, each fastened with a golden ring. As the light from the windows shone through, its beams reflected on the banner's rings and so lit a fire of imagination.

"Your majesty... do you by any chance recall Sir Guy's ring?"

"His ring?" The prince tilted his head in curiosity.

"Yes, a family heirloom," she said, "He was never seen without it. In fact, it was his last request that he might die with it upon his finger. It is just in my study if you would care to take a look."

"What a ghastly thing, to take such a prized possession off a dead man's finger," the prince said, making a face as if something smelt unsavoury. "All the same, take me to it."

As the sheriff and the prince passed through the great hall toward the woman's study, Dumont and Roland followed close behind. As the prince and the sheriff entered the study, the guards took their posts before the door. Hastily, the woman searched about the drawer of her desk in pursuit of the ring.

"Here! Here it is your highness," Claudia presented the ring, holding it out as it sat in the centre of her palm.

Picking up the ring, Prince John held the trinket near the light from the candle upon the desk, to gain a better look. The ring was wrought of gold, with three garnets fashioned together at the front. The engraving of a vine stretched over the band, with leaves and curling tendrils all about it.

"I must say, this is quite an exquisite piece, even for a man of noble birth. 'Tis is a shame he could not keep it," the prince admired it, a grin slowly growing upon his thin lips; rather pleased. "Farewell, Sir Guy," he whispered.

"Please, keep it, your majesty, as a symbol that I always keep my word," the sheriff bowed gracefully.

"I think I shall," he said. Holding the ring taut in his right hand, he placed the ring over each finger of his left hand, until finally, he found that it fit upon his forefinger. Slipping it over his finger, he smiled proudly. "And ever I shall hold you to your word, fair lady. As for now, I must bid you adieu for I must ride onward to London to attend other matters of state, yet I shall eagerly return for the Winter's Feast!"

"Of course, sire. May I escort you to the courtyard?"

"No, indeed. I would rather say our farewells now," Prince John said, drawing so near the woman that his whiskers tickled against her ear. "Farewell, my dove."

Blushing, the woman whispered, "Farewell, my darling."

"Oh you fair mistress," he whispered desperately, wrapping his arm about her waist. "Would that my brother was dead tomorrow, and I could take you as my queen."

The Prince held his composure close to hers, and his countenance rather sultry. Then, upon holding out his hand for the woman to kiss his ring once more, he flew toward the door of the study.

"And Lady Claudia, " he called, with his right hand gripping the door frame, "When next I return, I expect a full, detailed plan for capturing the Rebel. Until the feast!" He called, lightly bowing his head just before he vanished down the corridor.

Claudia's stomach churned, and her head felt hot. Bringing her hand to her forehead, she had not known just how much she had perspired, nor how nervous she had truly felt all the while. As the prince could be heard calling out orders from down the hall, the woman motioned for Dumont and Roland to quickly close the door to the study.

"I had no idea of Sir Guy having a family ring. Surely, it is good luck you remembered that your grace," Dumont let out a deep breath, his broad shoulders slumping.

"He never wore it. It was made when he had intended to be my husband," she said, moving behind her desk as she sat down. "But mark my words," she warned. "If anything I have spoken finds its way beyond these walls, be certain I shall have your arms torn from your bodies and have you beaten to death with them. Do I make myself clear?"

"Y-yes, sheriff," both men stood at attention, the silence hanging heavy in the air.

"But, sheriff," Roland spoke up.

"What?" She asked.

"When last we had meant to speak with you, we could not give the full report of all that happened with the countess," the guard confessed, reluctant to look up at the woman.

"Oh yes," the woman reclined in her chair, recalling her orders to them. "What of the rotting pig and the countess?"

"Sheriff, we *did* see something strange happen just before they reached the gate," Dumont admitted.

"Go on," she said. Lifting her hands, she laced her fingers together under her chin; listening.

"Well, your grace," Roland began, "We had been vigilant, following them through the city, yet the heat of the day and the length of the pursuit grew too much. We did take one moment to pause and breathe, but we never lost sight of the carriage, not for an instant-"

"Get to the point." Her eyes squinted, as she pursed her lips.

"Suddenly," Dumont continued, "The carriage went faster and faster as that manservant drove the horse, mad through the streets, and so sent Sir Guy to the ground, dragging behind. Not a moment after the countess had discovered this, she ordered the carriage be stopped, and so descended from it looking quite upset. She and the manservant helped Sir Guy remove the hood and the gag, and just as he was beginning to lose consciousness, they brought him into the carriage. Can you imagine? A murderous criminal, *in* the carriage with her ladyship! Roland and I stood aghast. But then, the manservant took to his post again, and they carried on through the gate."

The sheriff weighed all this considerably, then spoke.

"Is that *all* you saw?"

The two men nodded.

"Well, that is a bit strange... although, Jacqueline did say she needed a slave when she returned to France. Dragging a dead body would be a waste of her end of the bargain, and she had paid quite a sum," she thought. Claudia's restless eyes searched about the study; thinking.

"Do you suppose anything's to be done, your grace?" Dumont questioned.

"No," the woman answered. "No, I think it is rather unusual, what transpired, but certainly nothing to investigate. Sir Guy is no longer my problem, and I have the prince's trust once more. Thank you both, you may leave me now."

The two guards bowed and retreated into the corridor, the door to the study shutting tight behind them.

No sooner had the guards left, than Claudia poured over the circumstance. She did think it odd that a woman of such noble rank would be perturbed at the idea of such a wicked and depraved man losing consciousness, and even being driven to descend from the carriage and tend to him herself. Nevertheless, the thought of the whole event soon became lost under far more pressing matters. Claudia could not fail the prince. Her mind was instantly set on how she might to lure and capture Robin Hood.

**

Weeks had passed since Gisborne had arrived at the cottage, beginning this new, uncertain life.

How each day was filled with so many things to learn and to discover. For he longed so dearly to listen to all of Múriel's stories, and she, in turn, waited patiently for him to share his heart with her. Over and over, her kindness and her gentle spirit fueled his admiration. Working the land together and walking with her amongst the garden, what beauty was beheld in this little world; yet for all the flowers of the field, to him, she was the only beauty to be found.

As the morning called his sleeping eyes to wake, Guy lay in the quiet hayloft, awaiting the maiden's gentle voice. It fared far calmer than his first morning there, for the lady had made good on her promise, and set the chickens out in the garden. Nought but the whistling wind and the low whinnies of the horse could be heard. Then slowly, the sound of the barn door creaked open, and there she stood, upon the earthen floor; her long hair braided to the side and her expression, sweet as ever.

"Bonjour," she waved. Drawing to the bottom of the ladder, she gripped her hands around it, smiling up at him with such bright eyes.

"Good morning," Guy bowed his head, beaming down at her as he lounged close to the edge of the loft. "I trust you slept well?"

"Oui, I did," she nodded. "But I must show you something. Come, quickly!"

Before the man could make an answer, the maiden fleeted from the barn. Hastily, Gisborne made his way down the ladder and out unto the open field. The early morning dew clung to every blade of grass, and the skies above stretched dim and cloudy. Breathing in the fresh grassy air, the man listened to the songs of the birds, heralding the day. Yet as he looked about him, he could not find the maiden.

"Múriel?" He called, stepping further out onto the field.

"I'm here," she whispered, her voice coming from the side of the barn nearer the forest. "Come!"

Turning about, the man found her laying low upon the field, her chin propped up on her hand and her arms folded before her in the tall, waving grasses. Kneeling down beside her, Guy looked out into the forest, unsure of what she saw.

"Come," she said. "Venez ici."

Grasping his sleeve, she pulled him downward, so that he lay beside her in the grass, staring out into the woods. Silent, they lay side by side, Guy's arm brushing up against Múriel's, as they kept their eyes forward. Then suddenly, the young lady took in a sharp breath and clutched his arm.

"Do you see it?" She whispered.

"See what?"

"Shh, look!"

There, not far beyond them, in the thick of the trees, stood a magnificent white stag. Bold and beautiful, his pure coat shone; his antlers, a crown of majesty. The very breath from his nostrils as a mystic vapour, and his black eyes, unyielding, stared. Stepping through the trees, he soon caught the maiden's eye. Fearless, he drew forth, until he stood at the very edge of the field, the blades of grass curling up over his feet. His height was far greater than they had anticipated, for his antlers stretched near as high as the branches of the trees, and his very hoofs could span the width of their faces.

Amazed, Gisborne rose up and watched as Múriel drew to her feet; her eyes fixed upon the wild creature. Fearing for her safety, the man moved before her, guarding her.

"We should keep back," he said, "It could be dangerous."

"No, wait," she turned to the man, nodding and giving a soulful glance, as she laid her hand upon his shoulder and stepped beside him. "I think he wishes to give us something."

Walking toward the creature, she bowed her head and lifting it once more, she outstretched her arm forward and held up her hand toward the stag. Bowing in return, the creature came near, until his forehead rested under her palm, the breadth of her hand like that of a fallen leaf upon his face.

Gisborne's eyes filled with wonder at her bravery, watching as she stroked the stag's pure white coat and smiled. Then, glancing back at the man, she looked on him with a secret thought behind her eyes. Turning back to the stag, she nodded and stepped aside. Slowly, the creature approached the man. Standing firm, waiting.

"What shall I do?" Guy wondered, not wishing to take his eyes away from the creature.

"Bow," Múriel answered.

Heeding her words, he bowed before the creature, then held out his hand as she had so done, toward the great stag. So, in return, the stag did bow his wreath of glory and brought his forehead under the man's fingertips. The man remained wholly bewildered. For in the very moment his hand touched the creature, something so ancient was stirred within him, though he could not understand it. Then a deep and steady voice reverberated in his mind; words that were not his own:

Remember.

For what reason he could not grasp, the man felt a curious sense of melancholy sweep over him, and altogether it seemed, he had once known this creature well, though it was so strange to him. Suddenly, the cry of a falcon echoed overhead, and the voice vanished. The stag's keen eyes searched out; his ears alert and his breath heavy. In an instant, the mighty creature retreated into the woods, his hoofs stamping the earth so lightly, almost none could tell any creature was there. Farther and farther away, he ran, and the land sang the song of the morn once again. There they were, the man and the maiden, standing side by side as such a wonderment filled the air about them.

"I've never seen a white stag before," he murmured, "I thought it only a myth."

"As did I... that is why I wanted to catch a glimpse before he stole away," she smiled, bringing her hand to her lips.

"But, how did you know he wouldn't harm you?"

"I didn't know, though I didn't want to miss my chance, either."

Guy gazed upon Múriel as the wind caught up in the wisps of her hair and her silver eyes sparkled. For a moment, it seemed she understood something, something his mind could not yet perceive as if the world she knew was far grander than he had estimated. And all he desired was to see, as she did.

"What? What is it?" She raised her brows, nervous as his eyes strayed not from her.

"You are the most enchanting woman I have ever beheld," he said, bringing his hand up to her cheek as the maiden blushed, sighing under the warmth of his touch. Then, a thought sprung into her mind.

"Forgive me," she backed away, "I... I forgot about breakfast. I hope it's not burning!" Sprinting, the lady made her way toward the cottage. "Oh and, you can come in if you like!" She called, as she threw the door open and left it ajar.

The skies growing heavy with cloud encouraged the man's eager footsteps. Soon he neared the cottage, within, its warmth and the maiden who awaited him.

Why must you keep turning away? You fear nothing, save your heart, but why? He thought.

All through the grey clouded morning, Guy and Múriel worked in the garden. She taught him everything about the herbs and plants she grew and the simplest of things set her smile blazing; the finding of a butterfly upon a blooming flower or watching as the birds sang cheerfully as they sat perched upon the garden gate. They worked what bit of earth they could, and when that was finished, the chores of the day truly begun. There were linens to launder, chickens that needed tending, a field of grass that was growing quite unruly, and a horse very much in need of a hearty gallop.

Though it took some convincing, Guy agreed to remain at the cottage and cut the grass, while Múriel rode the horse to deliver provisions to her neighbours. Though he insisted they ride together, the lady was determined to accomplish her task alone, and as there was no avenue to persuade the lady otherwise, he acquiesced.

Gallantly, he readied the horse for the lady and bid her a safe journey, gently cautioning that she return before nightfall. As the maiden made her promise, so the man looked on as she and the horse bounded across the field, disappearing into the forest. The sun hung shrouded behind the fog of the morning, and would not shine in the afternoon, and by the foreboding grey of the evening, a storm was brewing.

As Guy laboured in the fields, wielding the scythe in his hand, he heard the pitter-patter of raindrops fall against the blade. His eyes searching over the land, he could see no sign of the maiden.

What's keeping her? He thought.

Setting down his work, as the rain left little drops all over his tunic, the man withdrew into the cottage and waited. He could have easily let sleep caress him in the comforts of the hayloft, but seated at the long table, he kept watch through the window, and never stirred from it. Hours passed, the sky grew black, and the drizzling rain soon became a downpour. The rain beat so relentlessly against the window, the man could hardly see through it. Removing to the entrance, he swung the door aside, the thunder booming overhead and echoing against the walls of the empty house.

Then, as his foot touched the earth outside the home, he could faintly hear the sound of hoofs approaching. She had returned!

"Múriel!" He called amidst the storm, stepping farther into the rain as his eyes fell on her. "Múriel!" He called again, running out to her.

Holding out his hand, he aided her down before he led the horse to the barn. He could barely see her face for the pouring rain but felt an uneasiness about her.

"Let me handle this. Get inside," he said.

As the horse was finally settled, Guy returned to the cottage, so unsure of what to expect. Beside the hearth, the maiden sat; soaked to the bone and shivering. Now the man grew rather cross, for she should have returned long before nightfall, and it wouldn't have taken her so long given that she had the horse at her disposal. Letting out a deep sigh, he took his cloak from the hook on the wall and wrapped it about her shaking shoulders.

Moving toward the fireplace, he began to set the kindling in place, and reaching up to the mantle, he took up the flint and steel, to light the fire, blowing on its embers as the flames grew. When the fire was made ready, he took a chair away from the table and sat beside the lady; his eyes stern.

"Múriel, what happened?" He questioned.

The maiden remained silent, her lips trembling, as she clutched the cloak tighter about her.

"I was worried you wouldn't return, and you gave me your word you would come back before nightfall," he said, as the water droplets fell from the tips of his dark hair. "Well? Have you anything to say?"

Biting her bottom lip, she hesitated, then finally, she spoke. "I didn't even reach the village," she shook her head. For but a moment, the young lady brought her tired eyes up to meet his angered gaze; dropping her shoulders, she looked back on the fire.

"What happened?" He pressed.

"I went to Aldred first, then to the Smith's, but as I made for the road to Locksley, a division of the sheriff's men were proceeding. One of the soldiers caught a glimpse of me and followed after me on horseback, with two others gaining behind him," she said. "I rode as fast as I could to lose them in the woods and so took the longer path to come back here, away from where the guards would follow. It began raining just before the guards spotted me. Please know I had no intention of returning so late."

"Oh," he sighed, bringing his hand to his bearded chin. "Well, I'm glad you've returned, and you're safe. Be sure, the next time I shall be there with you. Had you a weapon?"

"My dagger," she mumbled.

"Carry it always."

"I will," she promised.

"Thank you," he sighed.

Taking her hand in his, he met her gaze as a strange darkness lingered behind her eyes. Considering how long she had been in the rain and how she had gone without any supper, he felt ashamed at having ever been angry with her.

"You need rest. Go upstairs, get changed, and I'll fix you something to eat."

"Don't worry," she shook her head, as she stood, removing his cloak and handing it back to him. "I've no appetite as it is, but thank you."

"But there must be something I can do," Guy stood swiftly, as he held the wet cloak in his arms. "A cup of tea perhaps?"

"Merci, but a good night's sleep should do the trick."

"Are you certain?"

"Yes, don't worry," Múriel nodded. "But, I almost forgot, do you have enough blankets in the barn?"

"Yes. But you ought to go up and get some rest. Allow me," he held out his hand, leading her to the bottom of the steps.

"Jusqu'à demain," she whispered.

"Until tomorrow, my lady," he said.

Guy let her slip away from his touch, watching as she rose to the top of the stairs and disappeared down the hall.

In the pit of his stomach, he sensed something, a looming shadow hovering in the distance, or so it would soon approach. Yet, he would not trouble the thought any further that night.

Letting out a deep sigh, he returned to the fireplace. After the fire had burned down to its final embers, he departed from its warmth, closed the door to the cottage, and returned to the barn. All through the night, nothing save his dreams of her would comfort his heart until morning.

***

Shining high above the cooling world below, the man awoke to the sun's pale light reaching through the window of the barn and the scented winds of early autumn sifting through the forest. From the look of the sky, it was well past the ninth hour, yet Múriel had not come to the barn to wake him as she had so done every morning before.

Finding the day begun so late, Guy quickly readied himself. Calmly, yet cautiously, he determined to enter the cottage. Before, he had been wary of helping himself in without her invitation, not wishing to act in such a boorish manner. Wrapping his dark blue cloak about him, he hurried from the barn to the entrance of the cottage, nervous to knock upon the door. All the same, intuition drove him to it.

"Múriel?" He called out. "It's me... may I come in?"

No answer.

Entertaining the notion that she may have let him sleep late, he thought she could perhaps already be working in the garden. Toward the rickety gate he went, but there was no sign of her. Again he called out her name, but for all his searching, it proved in vain. The emptiness of the world about him haunted between his calls.

Perhaps she left, and wherever she is, she didn't want me to come, he thought. *No, no she wouldn't go without saying something.*

Every possibility rattled about in his mind. Marching to the front of the cottage, he paced back and forth, when suddenly he looked up and observed the chimney. No smoke rose from it.

Perhaps she really has gone somewhere, and it would not be so bold to be sure she wasn't inside. Would it? He thought.

At last, he resolved to search the cottage before making any more assumptions; his thought of her overwhelming what convictions of propriety would stifle it.

"I'm coming in," the man announced himself as he entered the cottage.

The fireplace was bare, the whole home drenched in a chilling silence, and no evidence of her presence could be felt whatsoever. But such pure silence could not lend him any conclusion. Therefore, only as he must, he ventured upstairs.

"Múriel? Are you here?" He called out from the bottom of the stairs; his left hand gripping the railing, and his right foot set on the

128

first step, creating a ghastly creak. "I'm coming up," he coaxed the silence.

Still, there was no answer.

At length, he made his way to the top of the stairs and paused for a moment to listen. For a minute, nought could be heard but the breeze, blowing against the window panes, and the tensed breath from his own lungs. Then, a faint sound coming from the end of the hall echoed in his ear.

"Guy?" A weak whisper called out.

The man's footsteps hastened as he marched down the corridor. At the very end of the hall, two doors stood opposite one another. The first to his right, the second to his left. Both closed shut.

"May I come in?" He paused, listening again.

"Oui, entréz," the lady's soft voice beckoned from the door to his right.

Nervously, he opened the door. Directly before him, Múriel laid upon the bed, shivering, and the natural brightness of her silvery eyes faded. Instantly, he rushed to her side and knelt beside the bed.

"You're pale," he whispered. As she leaned on her side, the young lady closed her eyes again, and the man brought his hand to her forehead. Dreadfully hot. "Múriel, you are ill. Please forgive me for not calling upon you sooner," he said.

"Sooner? What do you mean? It is not yet the sixth hour."

"It is the tenth hour."

"What!" The maiden sprung up in the bed, turning to stare out the window at the late morning light. "Mon Dieu, I must get to work!" Casting the bed linens away, the maiden shivered, the cold air hitting against her like a roaring wave.

"No, you're not going anywhere," he said, drawing the blanket over her, "You're far too ill for any work this day."

"I'm well enough," she shook her head. "I only need a moment-"

"You have a fever."

"I shall manage. 'Tis only a little fever," she said.

"No. You shall lie here and rest."

"But I don't-"

His finger halted her lips. "Let me care for you," his soft blue eyes insisted. "Now, have you had anything to eat or drink?"

Sighing in defeat, Múriel rested her head back upon the pillow as she pulled the linens up over her shoulders, and confessed with a shaking head.

"I've not eaten since yesterday," she whispered.

"Well, while you rest, I'll fetch you something. I won't be long, but please, do try to get some rest," the man said. Without another word, Guy placed a tender kiss on her forehead and departed from the chamber, down into the kitchen.

Swiftly, he started a fire. One pot of water was set for the tea, and another was set for the porridge. He kept his mind so to working and buzzing about the kitchen, searching for this ingredient and that, distracting himself so much so that he did not notice a certain lady's determined footsteps sneaking down the stairway.

Múriel had thrown a simple cloak about her shoulders, hurrying out of doors to feed the chickens and the horse. For she would not hear of relinquishing all her responsibilities at once. The morning chores were simple enough, though the task drew on rather tediously for her rising temperature. Her mind was not so clear nor her hands as strong. Mad with a mission, the maiden tried to hasten along before Guy could notice. But she was growing weaker, and her stubbornness would not fuel her for long.

It was nearly eleven in the morning when Guy had finished preparing breakfast. Upon reaching the chamber, he knocked on the door with his one free knuckle.

"It's me, again," he said, "May I come in?"

No reply was given.

He thought this somewhat curious as he wasn't too long in the kitchen. But believing the maiden may have fallen asleep, he thought to quietly set the food by her bed so when she did wake there would be something there for her. As the man entered the bedchamber, he discovered the empty bed; the blankets and linens all lumped at the end of the frame. Rolling his eyes in frustration, he tensed his jaw and roughly set the tray down on the table near the window. Gazing down through the pane, he found her lugging a bucket of water in the direction of the barn.

"Headstrong lass," he muttered sharply under his breath. Retreating with all speed back down the hall and flight of stairs, he marched out toward the barn.

"Múriel?" He called, reaching the entrance of the barn.

No answer.

Pushing back the vast and towering doors, he saw her set the water down by the horse. Startled at his discovery, she turned about to face him and gasped.

"What on earth are you doing?" He scolded.

"Guy! I didn't-"

But before another word left her lips, her eyes went dark, and her stance weakened as she began to faint. Rushing forward instantly, Guy caught her in his arms before she fell to the ground. Holding her limp form tightly in his arms, he rose, carrying her back into the cottage.

***

Hour by hour crawled on yet she did not wake.

While he could not persuade her to rise, nor to eat or drink, Guy had no wish to leave her. As he remained through the watches of the night, lounging on the floor beside her bed, he tried to stay awake, resting here and there for but a while, then suddenly waking to tend to her. Faithful, he watched as her breath grew shallow and her body lay so still, that at moments he wasn't sure whether she was yet living, and so gently shook her arm a bit to hear once more a small breath in and out. Then, would he close his eyes again, if only for an hour or two.

At first light, he knew she must drink something; she must have enough strength to fight this. Stumbling down into the kitchen, he fetched a pitcher of water and a cup. Returning to her chamber, he set the pitcher and cup down upon the table, and stood by her.

"Múriel," he began, "If you can hear me, I need you to drink." Softly, he tried to stir her from her slumber, stroking her long hair. Yet she made no answer, and so after filling the cup with water, Guy sat on the edge of the bed and lifted her up in his arms. "Please, try to drink," he whispered, offering the cup.

As she began to wake, her eyes fluttered just enough to see the cup before her. Nodding slowly, the man brought the cup to her lips, and she drank.

"There, that's better," he encouraged, though she drank little and the very heat from her body was raging.

He persuaded her to drink sip after sip until finally, the cup was empty, and she nestled her head in his chest. Setting the cup down again, he held her and laid a kiss on the crown of her head.

"Múriel," he whispered, "I'm going to make you something to eat, alright?"

The lady made no reply.

"If I bring you some soup, will you try to eat?"

She nodded, but while still in his arms, she brought her hand up to lay it upon his chest.

"I'll only be a few minutes, I promise," he reassured her.

Throughout the day, the man brought the maiden anything he thought she could possibly stomach, yet she hardly ate a morsel for all her sleeping. While she slept, he brought small cloths and cold water to lay upon her forehead attempting to bring the fever down. As well as he could, the man made time to work the land as she slept, for he would not neglect it any more than he would the maiden; but all the while he had forgotten to eat much himself. He felt neither hunger nor thirst, save the aching to see her through this. As night fell, he knelt by her bedside. With his head resting upon the bed, and her hand in his, the man finally succumbed to sleep.

When the dawn of the third day ran swift across the sky, he awoke rather sore and stiff in the neck. The lady was still fast asleep, but he quickly listened for her breath. Quiet and shallow and slow. Her temperature raged fiery hot, and her complexion grew all the paler.

"Múriel? Múriel?" he stood above her, shaking her into consciousness.

"Oui?" She said.

"I fear you are in danger," Guy shook his head, "You've not eaten or had hardly any water for days. You need medicine. I must go into the village to find a physician."

"But... someone will notice you," she whispered. "If someone... sees you-"

"It doesn't matter."

"They will kill you," she opened her eyes.

"I don't care! Right now, your condition is only getting worse, and I cannot let you..." he paused, his fists clenched. "You need medicine, and I'm fetching it whether you like it or not."

The lady only nodded; her eyelids heavy. "Water?" She whispered.

Instantly, he sat on the edge of her bed and brought a cup of water to her lips; his brows furrowed, as she only took a small sip.

"Before you go," she mumbled faintly, "There, in the wardrobe, is a small purse. Take whatever you need."

Stepping toward the wardrobe, he found the leather purse, with a mere twelve pence inside. The man was so determined, yet he knew how cautiousness was vital. Several of the villagers in Locksley could recognise him, and there was always the risk of running into the Rebel. Nevertheless, he could not bear to see her so ill. Thus, would he brave the danger, for her. Returning to her side, he held her face so tenderly in his palm, brushing her cheek with his thumb.

"Will you be alright while I am gone?" He asked.

The maiden nodded, still shivering under the blankets.

"Just rest," he said. "If you have some strength to drink, please do so... but promise me you will rest?"

Lifting her hand to hold his, she nodded. "Please return," she whispered, opening her eyes to call upon his.

"You have my word," he answered. "Sleep, my darling," he comforted.

With these words, his stature of valour rose and fled from the chamber; his quest began.

Donned in a dark cloak, and his beard rather grown, Guy clung to remaining invisible. Entering the barn once more, he took up a walking staff, a flask of water, and attached the leather purse to his belt. The horse whinnied and trotted his feet, ready to fly. Off into the forest once again, the man made his way to the village of Locksley, hoping he could complete his mission as hastily and as discreetly as possible.

***

"What are you doing? Why are you rolling your eyes at me?"

"I was not rolling my eyes," Robin responded flatly.

"By and by, we should return to the camp by noon," Will continued, "if we linger here too long, we shall surely be seen by the sheriff's men, and then-"

"Wait," Robin held up his hand, "there is but one basket left to deliver to the family at the end of the lane. *I* shall deliver it. While I am gone, gather the rest of the men, and tell them we must make ready to depart."

"Very well, master," Scarlet nodded in agreement, remaining a moment as his master marched past him into the thick of the village.

Now, where's everyone gone? Will thought, scratching at the back of his neck.

Looking this way and that, the man paused, deciding which way he ought to proceed when suddenly, a heated conversation tickled his ears.

"Someone?" an older woman's stern voice spoke. "Who needs it exactly?"

"My... my wife. She has been battling the fever for days, and it's only gotten worse. She won't eat, she can barely drink... she needs medicine. Here, take the whole purse-"

"No, 'tis no good." The woman said. "I'll not be cheated."

"Cheated? But that is all I have!" The man protested.

"You've pestered me long enough. I do not make any exceptions for strangers. Go find a knave, base enough to let you barter with him! Away with you!"

At this, Will whipped his head around to find the healer, Winifred, speaking with a tall man in a hooded cloak.

"Pardon me," Will interjected, as he marched toward the two, slamming his hands upon the table of wares. "You're refusing to sell this man medicine?"

"How am I to know he truly needs it?" The old woman retorted defensively, her arms folding across her chest. "As it is, he doesn't have enough money to pay for it."

The man in the cloak stood quite uneasy, lowering his head so the outlaw could not see his face.

"How much have you charged him for the vial?" Will asked.

"One crown," she said.

"A whole crown! Are you mad?" Scarlet complained, his freckled nose wrinkled. "Not a single man in all of Nottingham could meet such a sum save a noble. And what kind of magic have you yielded to conjure such a potion? Have you gleaned a pocket-full of faerie dust? Or a vessel of unicorn's blood?"

"Oh come off it, will you!" Winifred huffed impatiently. "The ingredients aren't so easy to come by, and it isn't such a simple process to make the tincture, either. I have to charge a little more, you see," she nodded, feeling quite justified.

Turning his gaze toward the man, the outlaw lifted his chin. "How much money do you have, friend?"

"He only offered me twelve pence," Winifred complained, turning the outlaw's attention back to her.

"Well, seeing as this could save someone's life, *I'll* pay for it." He declared, producing his own leather purse from his belt, and so slammed the coins upon the table.

"No," the man began to refuse, "that is very generous, but-"

"My friend, do not prevent me the honour of aiding your family, especially given these difficult times and circumstances," Scarlet said. "Winifred, I am surprised at you, withholding medicine from poor farmers."

At these words, the old woman simply rolled her eyes and started counting the coins, whispering something rude under her breath.

"Did you-" he wondered, "did you just roll your eyes at me?"

"What's it to you?" Winifred narrowed her dark eyes at him.

"That is the *second* time this morning..." The outlaw muttered to himself; quite miffed.

"Thank you, I am truly grateful," the man in the cloak began, trying to keep the hood over his eyes as Will handed him the vial.

"No need to thank me, I only hope your wife fares better," he said, "And for all this woman's pettiness, she is a skilled healer. Mark my words, this will soon cure her," he said. "The name's the Scarlet," he held out his hand.

"Pleasure to meet you," the man remarked. Quickly shaking hands with the outlaw, he hurried his footsteps to retreat from the village, though the outlaw was swift to follow, not sensing the urgency.

"And may I know your name, friend?"

"Hugo," the man answered, keeping his eyes upon the road.

"Delighted to meet you," Will smiled, "And what is your wife's name?"

"Múriel."

Thoughtless, he burst out her name. While he was in haste and most anxious to return to the cottage, the thought of her being his wife warmed his besotted heart.

"Her name sounds familiar enough, why does it sound familiar?" The outlaw stroked his copper beard as he thought, "I believe she may have been a friend of, well, this lady I knew once. Eleanor." For a moment, Will trailed off, immersed in his own thoughts before he shook his head back to the present. "Say, how far from Locksley are you?"

"Not far." The man answered, quickening his pace.

"You live in a nearby village?"

"In the forest."

"Oh, splendid! Being one of Robin Hood's company and all, I quite take to the forest as well. You know, Hugo, you look quite familiar. Do you suppose we've met before?"

"I don't believe so," he mumbled.

"Even your voice! I'm certain I've seen you or heard you round the village, passing here and there," Will continued, tilting his head this way and that to try to find a better view of the man's face.

"Forgive me, but I must return home," the cloaked man was nearly racing to get back to the forest.

"Of course, of course, another time. Farewell, friend!" Will shouted out, as he waved the man on.

At that moment, the merry outlaw turned about to find Little John, Jack, and Alan. Placing his fists upon his hips, he glared at them with a scolding eye.

"Now, where have you lot been? Robin sent me to search for you. We're to return to camp immediately."

"The master just told us to look for *you*, you idiot!" Little John complained, "Said you'd gone off who knows where, and we've all been waiting about as a hen's council for almost twenty minutes!"

"Well, I wasn't *wandering about,* if that's what you're thinking."

"Oh no, we daren't think such a thing as that," Alan laughed, as he and Jack rolled their eyes.

"You... did you two just roll your eyes at me?" Will barked, most incredulously put off, his tone soared three octaves higher than what it could achieve.

"It doesn't matter! Now, let's catch up with Master Robin," John said, his grey brows raised.

"Fine," Will huffed, tensing his upper lip. "Still, I would have you know, I was helping a farmer. Fellow's name was Hugo. He needed to buy medicine for his wife, medicine that could save her life, mind. Winifred was charging him a whole blooming crown and wouldn't't hear of settling for a farthing less!"

"Hmm," John acknowledged, not paying too much attention and finding more pleasure in the walk than in the listening.

Once they had reached the centre of the village, they drew ever nearer Tuck and Robin, who stood quite peevish, and were within earshot of Will's audible thoughts, as the company gathered together.

"And you'll never guess his wife's name."

"What was it, Will?" The others unenthusiastically questioned in unison, as the outlaw droned on and on.

"Some maiden named Mariel or Múriel or something," he answered, "It was something quite strange, and I can't remember precisely, but I think she may have been a friend of Eleanor's."

Alan pricked his ears up and felt a sudden uneasiness at this mention. "Will, did you just say Múriel?" He asked, scratching at his dark beard with his left hand.

"Múriel? You know her?" Will asked.

"That doesn't matter," the outlaw shook his head, "But you say she is married now?"

"Have you been listening to anything I've said? Aye, she is married, to that farmer Hugo. I swear he could remind me of someone... his very voice rung so familiarly," Will thought for a minute, running his fingers through his unruly hair.

"Now where have you been, Scarlet?" Robin questioned, his arms folded across his chest, though Will paid not the slightest attention.

"I've got it! It's Gisborne!" Will finally shouted.

"What!" Alan's brows went straight as an arrow. "What about Gisborne?"

"Hugo! I swear that man could be Gisborne's double!" Scarlet smiled proudly, quite pleased with himself for having solved the mystery, though Tuck's brows furrowed in scepticism. "You saw some bloke who looked like Gisborne?"

"Ha!" A'Dale slapped Will on the shoulder nervously. "I think you've been at the ale again, old friend. Everyone knows that brute's been long dead. Don't tell me you're seeing ghosts, eh?" He teased, but from the reserved and suspicious countenance of John and Jack, he could sense something was awry.

"Wait," Robin interrupted, waving his hand. "You think you saw Gisborne?" His eyes stared hard at his comrade, who was then quite put on the spot.

"No, I... I merely thought this fellow resembled him a bit."

"*A bit?*" The old man squinted his eyes. "Not a minute ago, you said he could be the blackguard's very double."

"And why should that be of any concern if Gisborne is dead?" Alan scratched at his beard restlessly.

"Aye, we could easily brush it aside," Jack agreed, "though as no one has seen a body, nor witnessed any execution, can we ignore such a coincidence?"

"Now let's not fill our heads with some ridiculous conspiracy," John rebuked, "The man is dead, and that is that!" He determined, gripping his son's arm and giving him a warning glare.

"Oh... you- you're right, father," Jack sighed, nodding his head. "Will is probably just seeing things."

"Oh, would you all settle down! I wasn't claiming to have actually seen Gisborne, just that the farmer Hugo *looked like him*!" Will placed his fists against his hips, his cheeks flaring red.

"It's not important, Will, so shut up!" Little John snarled, pacing toward the man with a fury in his eye.

"Alright, that's enough!" Robin moved in between the men, "We need to make for Sherwood by noon, and we are running late as it is! So unless you would have us captured and tortured under the sheriff's hand, the quarrelling ends here."

"Aye, the master's right. We'll discuss this later," Tuck nodded, as the company shuffled about toward the road.

As the others moved forward, Robin remained behind a moment.

"Master, is everything alright?" Alan inquired.

"Yes, yes... I'm coming. Go on, I'll catch you up soon," he said, waiting as the outlaw walked ahead with the others, giving him leave to think.

Robin felt perturbed at this whole notion; the idea of a man who resembled Gisborne, calling himself by the name Hugo was quite enough to set his mind uneasy. For this was the very name of Gisborne's father; a name quite well known to the outlaw. For such a familiar name and a familiar face to reappear, was a mystifying thought indeed.

CHAPTER TEN

CURSE'S EVE

Bitterly, the aura of the night clung to the boughs of the trees.

Behind the mist, the moon concealed its light, and the stars hung shrouded. How the forest lay cloaked in darkness as a storm drew nearer, and the drums of the thunder haunted. Yet amidst the dreary night, a fire blazed warm and constant, the flames shining over Robin's stern face. By their master's side, Will and Alan remained, keeping the fire fed with what kindling they harboured in a small mound by their feet.

Staring into the golden firelight, Robin contemplated all he had heard but a few days ago, pondering whether his enemy was truly dead, or if such conspiring would lead him astray. As the three men sat in the stillness for a time, at last, Alan softly hummed a simple tune. While the melody unfurled in deep and solemn sway, something stirred in Robin's heart. A chord in his very being, which time allotted him to forget, had once more been plucked.

"I... I know this song," Robin whispered, his shoulders tensed, his curious eyes fixed on his comrade.

"Why of course you do master. It's the *Omen of the Forest*," A'Dale nodded.

"*Omen of the Forest*?" Will folded his arms over his chest. "What kind of nonsense is that? I've never heard of it."

"Come now," Alan chided, stretching his arms out before him, "It's been passed down for generations. Every woodsman knows it. Some say it's only a legend, others say it's real."

"But what's it about?" Scarlet wondered.

"It's an omen about the forest, you oaf!" Alan shook his head, smacking his hand against the back of Will's head. "It's a warning. A warning to all who dwell within the forest."

"Oh!" Will moaned, rubbing at his aching head. "No, that's not what I meant. What *kind* of omen? Is it meant to sound ghosty?"

"Does it sound like a jig to you?"

"I don't know for sure seeing as you've not sung one line of it! It certainly *sounds* ghosty."

"*Ghosty*?" Alan chuckled, his eyes merry.

"Oh, come along! You know what I mean! What about the words, then, eh? How's about you sing them for us?" Will leaned forward, his eyes eager. "A storm's on its way, a rather good night for a fright."

"Very well," A'Dale grinned.

Drawing a deep breath in and out again, the outlaw began to sing:

Upon thine shoulders, this thy portion,
Reconcile the vows left broken,
Beware, servant, lend ear to our call,
For if the children of Light should fall,
And the Forest fail his quest,
The earth shall lay forever in rest.
The lands laid waste under blackened seas,
The darkness of night shall never cease.
If one should succumb to death's dreaded gate,
The second shall fall, intertwined in death's fate;
The third shall remain only to breathe,
A final breath at the curse's eve.
O Lord of the Forest, cling to what is said,
For a moment unwatched shall bring forth the-

"Enough! Enough!" Robin shouted, his eyes wide as he gripped Alan's arm harshly.

"Aye, I've had quite enough as well!" Will jumped to his feet, "That is far too ghosty for me."

"What's wrong with you two?" Alan grumbled, shaking away Robin's grip. "It's only a song."

Suddenly, the earth trembled beneath them as a flash of lightning pierced through the heavens; the boisterous thunder following. At the roar of the storm, Robin fell to his knees, the veins in his forehead pulsing as his whole face went red. Clutching his chest, he panted and clenched his jaw in pain, as the earth rumbled greater and greater, still.

"Master!" Will shouted.

In an instant, the men knelt before their master who groaned all the more in agony.

"What is it? What's happening?" Alan questioned.

"Some madness has taken hold of him! He could be possessed by that witch's song!"

"You idiot, it's not a witch's song, and I'll have my ears cut from me before I hear anyone declare Robin possessed," he said.

"But what's to be done?"

"Tuck is a man of medicine, he'll know what to do," A'Dale thought, "Go fetch him here! Now!"

"Aye," Will tensed his upper lip, bounding away to find the old man and tumbling along the way as the forest quaked beneath his anxious feet.

Determined, Alan lifted Robin up to lean against the log they had sat upon. Moaning, Robin held fast to his chest, his hands shaking and his teeth grinding. Then, near as soon as the pain had come, it fled. The man lay breathless, staring out into the bleak forest as the rain began to pour.

"Master, what's happened?" Alan grasped the man's shoulders.

Robin could not speak a word but shook his head in dismay, his eyes betraying his fright.

"But whatever it was, it's gone, yes?"

Robin nodded. Then, just as his breath had calmed, his vision blurred. Looking down at his very hands, he could hardly distinguish it from the shadows of the night. "I... I..."

"Don't worry, Will's gone to fetch Tuck," Alan said, "They should be back any moment."

"I- I can't see, Alan!" Robin cried, blinking and rubbing at his eyes, "I can't see anything!"

The thunder rolled overhead once more, and the arms of the trees whipped ferociously under the wind's howling. Without restraint, the rain came down over the land, and in seconds the men were soaked through. In anguish, Robin bowed his head; the pain in his chest resurged.

"Help! Help us!" Alan called out, looking back and forth between his master and the faded path where his comrade had tread. "William!" He cried.

"Here! We're here!" Tuck answered as he and Will rushed across the way, the mud lapping up against their boots and the hems of their cloaks. "Stand aside!" He ordered.

Kneeling before Robin, Tuck shoved the others away, setting down his satchel and examining the man. Alan and Will could only stand back and watch under the reckless rain, as Robin lay wailing.

"Tuck, he said he couldn't see anything, as if he'd just gone blind in an instant!"

"Blind!" Will's brows flared. "Only an evil spirit could have done this. I told you it was that witch's song that made him go mad!"

"It wasn't a witch's song!" Alan argued.

"You two are wilder than a pair of wolves! He's neither mad or spirit-bound. It has passed," Tuck held up his hand, as Robin blinked wearily to discover his old friend before him. "You can see me, can't you?"

Panting nervously, Robin nodded, his whole body trembling. Tuck threw his own cloak about the man and retrieved a tonic from his satchel.

"Master, I fear you may have suffered a seizure. You are coming out of it," he muttered, "But here, take this."

"What is that?" Scarlet wondered.

"A tonic. It should help to stop the pain from worsening," Tuck held the vial up to the man's lips.

Robin swallowed the bitter tonic, clutching his chest again. Then, as he looked up, he saw something he did not expect. "No," Robin's green eyes burst out. Pointing his shaking finger toward a shadow passing through the trees, he shook his head.

At such a motion, the others turned their heads about to find what it was their master discovered. Yet the forest was only filled with the outpour of the tempest, and nothing more.

"There's nothing there," Will sighed. "Master, what did you see?" But the man could not produce an answer.

Glancing back at Alan and Tuck, Scarlet found they too hadn't seen anything, yet that which the outlaws could not perceive, Robin could. Behind the men, lingering in the fog of the forest, stood a grand figure, near as tall as the trees themselves. There, draped in mist, stood the white stag; his black eyes sharp and his words a whisper in Robin's mind:

Sleep, my son, sleep, for there may yet be time.

As the creature bowed its head, Robin felt such a strange sense of peace within him. Then, in a blink of his eye, the vision vanished, and nothing could be seen but the heavy rain.

"What is it?" Alan looked back and forth. "Tell us, what do you see?"

"It's gone," Robin sighed.

"It's a stormy night as it is… lots of shadows," Tuck said.

"No, it can't have been nothing," Alan insisted, kneeling before the man. "Please, can you tell us anything about it? What did you see?" He pressed.

But before the man could reply, his bearded chin slumped down to his chest, as the tonic took hold.

"Tuck, do you suppose he'll be alright?" Will darted his eyes between the two men.

"He should be," Tuck nodded, "That attack was severe… might've caused him to lose his senses a bit."

"A bit?" Will complained. "But do you not think it disturbing for him to be so thrown into such a fit? To go blind and then start seeing strange things?"

"What do you suppose started all this?" A'Dale asked.

"I don't know, lads," Tuck sighed, "By and by, the tonic will help him sleep, and we must all be sure to keep an eye on him. Now, this rain's something awful, it is. Let's be out of it or else we might catch whatever illness has befallen him."

"Aye, I'll take his arm," Alan said, as he and the old man and the copper-lock lifted Robin up.

"And we must take turns waking him every other hour or so," Tuck instructed.

"Every two hours?" Scarlet wondered. "What for?"

"To be sure he doesn't *stay* asleep," he answered.

"You mean, he could go unconscious?" Alan's brows raised.

"Not if we can help it. Now, come on," Tuck urged.

The three men worked in bringing Robin safely back to camp, laying him gently in the centre of the cots. And while Tuck and Alan were each eager enough to take the watch, Will insisted on being the first set for the task, and so sat by his master's side.

All night, Robin tossed and turned, his dreams a raging blur as if he were falling away into further and further nothingness.

Thankfully, the tonic proved strong enough to hinder any attacks, but it felt as if a battle of the will was taking hold.

Pale, the late morning light woke the outlaw.

Robin breathed in the cold, damp air, and his lungs ached. Rising up, he stretched his arms and scanned his eyes about the camp. Many of the trees had fallen in the throes of the storm, the roaring night's dreaded footprints not so easily concealed.

Finding the man had woken, John, Jack, and Alan rushed to his side.

"You're awake!" Jack called, holding out his hand. "How are you feeling?"

"Better," Robin mumbled, drawn to his feet.

"I'm glad of it," Alan said, "That storm was mad, madder than any I've ever seen."

"Don't," Little John chided, shaking his head.

"No, he's right. It was mad," Robin nodded as his eyes shone deep and dismal. "All the same, I think it was meant to happen."

"Meant to happen?" John's grey brows rose up.

"What I saw…" the outlaw began. Lifting his hand to his temple, he shut his eyes a moment to recall his vision. "There was a figure; a white stag. He… spoke to me."

"A white stag?" Jack's eyes went wide. "I thought they were just a legend."

"So you saw a mythic creature in the woods last night, and it spoke with you?" John tensed his lip.

"Well, yes, and no," Robin whispered.

"Forgive me, but the thought of talking beasts seems far madder than some storm," John grumbled, folding his arms across his chest.

"I believe you saw it," A'Dale stepped forth, "But neither Tuck, nor Will, nor I saw or heard anything. So whatever was spoken, its words only fell on your ears."

"Then, what did the creature say?" Jack wondered.

"He said: *Sleep, my son, for there may yet be time.* But I don't know his meaning," Robin sighed.

"That's it. I've had quite enough of this *ghosts and goblins* business," John complained, "You're working yourself to the bone, master. And… and that's what set you off seeing white stags and talking with beasts like a right old… Talk amongst yourselves, but as for me, I am done," he declared, stomping away from the others.

"Father," Jack sighed, nodding disappointedly to the men before he followed after.

Robin's shoulders fell in discouragement. "Alan, you're not patronising me... you believe me, do you not?"

The outlaw thought for a moment, staring down at his feet, then drew his eyes up once more.

"You know I do. But you must take care. The others might not understand, and they'll think you've lost your wits," Alan answered. "Howbeit, I have known you for many a year, and I know you would not speak such things out of deceit. If you claim to have seen the white stag, and it spoke with you, then I cannot deny you my trust, though such a thing would test me."

"Thank you," Robin grinned; comforted. "Still, I would know what it meant."

"Master," Alan sighed, "Please don't take me a fool for thinking this, but do you suppose it could have had something to do with that song?"

"The omen you sang?"

A'Dale nodded.

Robin looked about him, and as no one else was in sight, he felt free to speak his mind a little more.

"Just as you had begun to sing, that was when the pain in my chest started," he whispered. "That was the reason I cried out. As you kept on singing, the pain kept growing worse and worse."

"You think it could be... real? The curse?" Alan's brow raised, now considering so much, his eyes shifting from a gaze of speculation to understanding.

"It could be... but is that so entirely foolish? Does it make any sense?" Robin looked away into the grey of the morn, then back to A'Dale and observed the light behind his friend's eye. "Alan," Robin lowered his head, trying to regain his attention. "What do you know?"

The outlaw drew a step back, darting his eyes away from Robin. "I... it's nothing," Alan waved his hand.

Yet Robin wouldn't be persuaded otherwise and so gripped the man by the shoulders, his eyes fixed on Alan's.

"Tell me what you know," he said.

"I know nothing!" Alan shouted. "I'm only trying to make sense of everything... and yes, perhaps you are right. Perhaps it is folly!"

Roughly, he shoved Robin back, marching off into the woods. Robin remained a while, sifting over everything that had transpired. Although his companions would think otherwise, in his heart, the master outlaw would heed the words spoken unto him, for he esteemed the strange and wild stag trustworthy.

***

Days had passed.

Still, there was no improvement in Múriel's condition.

Her fever was severe and raging on in spite of the medicine. She hardly ate or drank for sleeping, and waking her proved more and more a toilsome feat; though in the moments she did wake, the talking helped to prolong it, if only for a few minutes.

All the while, Guy had scarcely slept, dutiful in caring for her.

That morning, the earth was not awakened to hopeful dawn, but to bleakness. No sunlight graced the heavens, for nought but a foreboding gloom filled the void. Lifting his head, the man gazed out the chamber window into the muted atmosphere. Taking to his feet, he withdrew from the chair to the pane, staring out; his fingertips pressed against the glass and his once bright blue eyes now cast into the hues of a storm-tossed sea. And in such troubled waters, a growing fear; knowing much and knowing little, and ever patient as it waited in the deep. Then his eyes fell on her and what grey light shone over her.

Pouring a cup of water, he returned to her side and sat upon the bed, and wrapping his right arm around her waist, he lifted her up, hoping she might waken.

Without a word, she took in a startled breath and stared up at him.

"Múriel, you must drink something," he coaxed, lifting the cup to her lips.

Nodding gently, she drank what little she could manage. Resting her head upon his chest, the lady drifted in and out of sleep, as Guy drew the blanket over her shoulders.

"I only need work a little while. I'll come straight up when I've finished," he promised.

Holding onto her, he remained for a time in the silence, not wishing to let go. In his arms, Múriel soon succumbed to sleep again, and gently, Guy laid her down and set to work.

Out into the barn, he went, and let loose the palfrey to gallop freely over the shadowed field and to eat what grass it may. While the horse trotted here and there upon the green, the man went out into the garden and worked what bit of stubborn earth could distract him well enough from his doubt, yet no task could truly guide him from it.

Ruthlessly, he rebuked himself for not having gone with her or else not having forced her to stay that day, then she would not have been stranded in the rain, wandering home in the cold and darkness. How guilt overshadowed him such that he could not dispel it. As the foretelling of the storm sung high above him, the man led the horse back to the barn, brought into the cottage whatever was yielded from the garden and washed his hands. For a breath's measure, he watched as the last clouded light peered through the window into the kitchen, filling up each drop of water that ran over his fingers. How rough and sore his hands grew from working, but it was good work.

Quickly, he prepared a simple porridge supper, and as the scents of herbs filled his lungs, he had not noticed how his stomach ached. All the same, he thought on the lady, hoping she might eat for she had eaten nothing for two days.

Returning to the bedchamber with a bowl of porridge in hand, the man sat by the maiden's side. So gently he tried to stir her from her slumber, as a thousand times before, yet she did not answer him nor even open her eyes. He could not bring himself to any other means of persuasion, and so finally, he went to the chair and took the bowl in his hands; staring at it, his mouth watered. He longed to satisfy his hunger but felt such shame all the more when he took the first bite.

She should be eating this, he thought, *how dare I eat when she is starving.*

He could not eat another morsel, and so he set the bowl down. Hungry and sullen and haggard.

For endless hours, he watched as she slept. By her bed, he remained, fighting away sleep so as not to lose one minute. Upon the table by the window, the faint light from a candle burned low, the wax dripping down onto the wood. Faithful, the candle kept its flame. Sitting in the silence, he thought and thought; his back bent, his elbows upon his knees, and his hands brought up together in one whole fist under his bearded chin.

Suddenly, shattering the quiet, the rain had come; the symphony of the tempest engulfing. Bright flashes of lightning shone bursting through the panes, and the thunder rang as a battle cry against the walls. And it was enough to wake her. Turning her head, Múriel opened her eyes to see Guy sit before her, his head hung low as he held the bridge of his nose.

"You look tired," she whispered.

"You're awake!" He called, such relief in his eyes as he drew to her bedside, and held her hand. "How are you?"

"The same," she sighed; though her eyes seemed brighter. "But you look exhausted. Have you had any rest?"

"I'm not tired," he answered, drawing his hand to her forehead; still hot. Dropping his shoulders, he brushed away a lock of her hair. "It is my fault all this has happened."

"Your fault?"

"If only I had gone with you…"

"It was meant to happen," she said, letting loose a grin.

"It's not what I would wish," he said, "I keep thinking about that day, wishing there was some way I could have prevented this."

"Oh, Guy," she sighed, taking in a deep breath; her voice so faint, "I would not have prevented it, because out of it, I've come to see your heart," she grinned. "I had not known how empty my life was before you. To spend time with you, to dwell with you, it has made each day a treasure," Múriel beamed up at him.

Holding her face tenderly in his hand, Guy smiled and hardly knew what to say. Then taking his hand, the lady held it against her heart as she closed her eyes.

"Here you will stay, in my heart, forever," she whispered.

"I will always be here, my darling," he promised, leaving a kiss on her cheek. "But if you are to get better, you must try to eat."

Glancing back at the cold bowl of porridge left on the table, Guy shook his head and gazed back on Múriel.

"I'll try," she answered; her eyes still closed.

"Good," he sighed, "I shall fetch you a fresh bowl of hot porridge and some bread. I won't be long," he smiled, kissing her hand.

Retreating from the bedchamber, he leapt down the stairs into the kitchen and prepared another pot of porridge. Hopeful, he wasted little time preparing the food, and while he cooked, he even took up some bread for himself, satisfying what pangs of hunger he felt. For he must keep up his own strength, for her sake. Working by the fire, his heart was quelled in her words, and how he thought on them over and over again; enraptured. When the meal was made ready, Guy bounded up the stairs, entered the bedchamber, and set the food on the table. Outside, the storm roared all the fiercer against the little house, as the rain leaked from the thatched roof, spattering and spluttering on the floor. Sitting down beside the lady, the man softly shook her shoulders to wake her.

Then, all colour ran from his face.

How quiet she lay.

Swift, he pressed his ear against her chest, waiting; listening for what sound might break his doubt, yet found it not. Clutching her cold hand, it fell limp under his touch. Frantic, he drew his hand

upward. Up and up her arm, he moved his hand. Ripping the sheets away from the maiden, he felt her feet; her legs.
Cold.
Cold as stone.

BOOK TWO
MOON

CHAPTER ELEVEN

PROPOSITION

Sheltered well within his home, Aldred lay in his bed, restless as the tempest poured over the forest and wailed against the cottage. Here and there, a crack of thunder jostled him, and then the rain resounded as he fought to gain what little sleep could be rendered. For a bewildering nightmare took hold of him.

Suddenly, amidst the rhythm of the rain, the old man awoke terrified. Breathless, he drew his shaking hand to his brow and sat at the edge of his bed, his bare feet touching the cold floor. But before he could make sense of his dream, he heard a strange noise breaking through the storm.

A knocking on the door.

Quickening, the old man bolted from his bed toward the door and took up his staff, for the evening had long passed and no midnight visitor could easily be welcomed. Then, for a minute, the noise halted.

Pressing his ear up against the wood, he listened.

Once again, someone knocked, now pounding out in great urgency. "Open up!" A muffled voice called.

"Who goes there?" Aldred said, holding fast his weapon.

"Who do you think? Open the door or else I'll knock it over your empty head!"

Peevish, Aldred muttered an ill-tempered word under his breath. Nevertheless, he set down his staff by the frame, lifted the latch, and opened the door. There, Winifred stood, quite vexed. Her deep brown eyes shone scornful under furrowed brows, her greying hair hardly concealed beneath her hood, and her arms folded tight across her chest.

"Woman, have you no knowledge of the hour?" Aldred huffed, his moustache curling in contempt. "I had thought you sensible enough not to go wandering about the forest at night, let alone, not to wander about in this blasted storm. No madman would do half as such for a kingdom."

"Oh, hang it, you mossy hermit! 'Tis not yet a quarter past midnight and a little rain won't send me to the grave," she quarrelled, "I've had a long day delivering a baby, and this was my only chance to call on you."

"And what could have been so urgent that you wake me thus?"

"Múriel," she answered, "I fear something's wrong."

"Oh," he sighed.

"Now, shall you call me in or would you have me stand in this rain all night?" Winifred complained.

"Oh, very well, then. Come in, come in," he said, motioning for the woman to enter the home. Having fetched a blanket, he placed it about her shoulders, and while she sat, he knelt by the hearth to start a fire. And from the instant the door was shut, Winifred's mouth was open.

"Now, before you start, I'll hear none of your lengthy tales nor will I tolerate any gentler verse on the subject, for I've come for answers and nothing less, even if it must wound me."

"*Lengthy tales*?" Aldred glared, "If my tales are as such to you, I'll give you two words together you might stomach, and you may be freed from such tedious company-"

"Tell me plainly," she pressed, "Where is she?"

"Múriel?"

"Yes, you goat! Do you know where she is?"

"Winifred, you and I both know the answer to that question. Please, I beg of you, for your own sake, let this not be the reason you've disturbed me."

"You don't understand," she shook her head, "I've not seen Múriel for weeks, nor has my Catherine heard any word from her. Just up and disappears! Seeing as she has no family, well, save you, I'm worried she might have gotten herself into some trouble. What do you suppose is going on?"

"Weeks? Surely, you're mistaken," he stroked his beard. "She brings food from her garden to my door once a week. Not a single week has passed that I haven't received a basket."

"Oh," Winifred raised her brows. "Well, what has she said to you, then? Has she told you of some resentment she holds against me? Or any cause why she would go into hiding?"

"But I still don't understand why you think her whereabouts such a mystery," Aldred said, as he stood away from the hearth, the firelight glowing in his eyes. "Surely, she is at her cottage. This is hardly worth such a fuss-"

Setting her hands firm upon her hips, Winifred sighed. "Does she mean nothing to you? She's been as kin to far too many. Moreover, she's been good enough to partner with me in my work, but since she's disappeared, I've received no herbs. No herbs, no medicines. And that's a good portion of my livelihood, and the health of Nottinghamshire, gone down the river!"

"Well go up to the cottage yourself tomorrow morning and ask what you may!" Aldred huffed.

"You know her cottage is near a two hour's walk from my home," the woman said, "It's already over an hour's walk just to get here, and I'm not so young as I used to be; walking for miles here and there takes a toll on my ankles. Now, what has she told you?"

"Well," he began, "to be frank, for the past week or so, I've not actually seen her."

"You've not seen her either?"

"I awoke in the morning, and the basket of food was there by my door. I simply assumed she had tried to come in the evening but was unable to gain my attention, and so left it," he answered.

"Wait," the woman said, lifting her hand, "So, neither you nor I have seen Múriel for weeks, and neither of us has had any word from her whatsoever."

Aldred's eyes grew heavy. "That is a troublesome thought... but have you sought her out? Have you called on her?"

"I haven't the time," the old woman grumbled. "I've helped to deliver two babies this week and in Locksley alone, never mind those who've been ill or injured. As it is, your home is nearer hers than mine. If anyone should call on her, it should be you."

"Very well," he said, "I shall go and seek her out."

"But it must be tonight!"

"Confounded woman... aye, I'll go tonight," he sighed, "I'm sure she is in her own bed, resting comfortably, and well enough indeed," he said, as he reached for his staff and his cloak.

Observing his calm and steady expression, the woman deemed it odd he did not consider the matter so urgent, yet being as he was, she knew something was withheld.

"Aldred," Winifred said, "Is there... is there anything I should know?"

The old man hesitated for a moment, as the entire matter was rather delicate. But as Winifred was an old friend, who was more than trustworthy, he felt no apprehension in sharing a little of his intelligence.

"Yes," he admitted. "Not long ago when Múriel had come to bring her weekly basket of provisions, she arrived on horseback with a man. Hugo, he called himself."

"Hugo?" She wondered.

"A traveller; he had come across Múriel and took to lodging in her barn and paying his way by working the land," the old man said.

Then, Winifred's eyes widened with discovery. "Aldred, not two weeks ago, I sold a tincture to a man called Hugo," she said, "I couldn't get a good look at his face. By and by, he claimed his wife was ill but hadn't enough money for the medicine. Of course, that roistering tree-rat, Scarlet, made a whole scene and paid for it. Do you suppose it could be the same man? Do you think Múriel would... oh! Oh, good gracious, she could be ill!"

"She could be, she could be," Aldred thought, stroking at his beard and rattling his brain of what to do, for the old woman was growing impatient.

"Then what are doing here? Go now! Go call upon her at the cottage and make certain she's alright!" She ordered, "I don't want to assume the worst, but what if this Hugo... what if he's dangerous?"

"Don't worry. I know him well," the man simply stated. "He is not dangerous, but this circumstance may very well be."

"You know him? How?" The old woman tensed her upper lip.

"Winifred, stay here and keep warm until the fire dies down, and when you are ready to depart, take the blanket home with you," the old man set his hand upon her shoulder comfortingly. "If there is any cause for greater alarm, I shall call upon you." He smiled gently, and she nodded in acceptance.

Into the night and the storm, the two neighbours parted. One, returning to her home; the other, in pursuit of the maiden.

***

Approaching the cottage, and now quite drenched, Aldred could still perceive smoke rising from the chimney and a faint light coming from an upstairs window.

Calmly and quietly, he opened the door. Nothing but the sound of the crackling fire could be heard in the open room. In the stillness of the night, he searched the kitchens, and though he found the home in disarray, he did not find the maiden. Now, he must try upstairs. Making each step light and agile, he climbed the stairs and made his journey down the hall. Drawing nearer and nearer the bedchamber, he heard that which he did not expect.

A man, weeping bitterly.

Silently, Aldred peered through the crack in the door, to find Gisborne, hovering beside Múriel's bed; his head buried low, his shoulders shaking. Her form lay still.

Then, through his tears and his shaken voice, the man faintly sang:

Where have you gone, my dear?
So far away from here,
O maiden where, where have you gone-

As swiftly as it came, the melody ceased, a wave breaking upon the shoreline.

"What's happened?" Aldred's voice boomed, as he flung the door open.

Startled, Guy whipped his head round in the direction of the door. What met the old man's stare were a pair of hopeless eyes; replete with such lament. "She... she is dead."

"Dead?" Aldred whispered, fearing what words came from his lips. Such anger ablaze within him, he marched across the room, rough and raging. Gripping Gisborne by the shoulders, the old man knocked him hard against the wall.

"What have you done to her?" He shouted. "Do you not know the consequences that bechance her death? How your fate is fixed with hers? What have you done? Speak!"

"I... I've done nothing-"

"Swear it! Swear by Rohkan that you've not fixed her end!" He cried, knocking Gisborne against the wall once more; the whites of his knuckles bursting.

"I'll swear by any name, I have done her no harm!"

"Ignorant man, he is a spirit," Aldred mumbled. "Now, what happened?"

"Over a week ago, she became very ill with a fever. It kept growing worse and worse, and so I went into the village to get medicine," Guy shook his head in such shame, "I did everything I could, but I... I've failed her. She did everything to save me and I couldn't..." His tears poured forth without restraint.

Shoving him aside, Aldred approached the bed and examined the body. Moment by moment, his scorn tempered into compassion, as he looked to Guy in hopeful astonishment.

"I believe you," he declared, as the weary man stared back in a puzzled expression. "And you have not lost her yet."

"What!"

"There is yet breath in her lungs, and a strong heart with a will of iron," he nodded, "Come!"

Rushing to her side, the tears upon his face, the man pressed his ear against her chest, clinging to her with trembling hands. Waiting, he listened. And though the faintest of hearts, it still beat within her. Relieved, the man sunk to his knees, his head hanging down as he brought his shaking hands up to his face, and wiped away his tears.

"My son, your fatigue has clouded your judgement. Múriel is not dead, but she is fading fast. If we do not act in haste, so will you."

"Me?" He asked, "I don't understand-"

"Now, why did you not seek me when she fell ill?" The old man questioned.

"Forgive me, I hadn't thought to do so," Guy said, "but do you have any knowledge of medicine?"

"I have been a sage, all my life," he answered, "Perhaps all would have fared better if you had come to me directly," he said. Observing a vial upon the table by the window, Aldred took it up in his hand. "Quickly, what medicine did Winifred give you?"

"The physician? I do not know," the man sighed. "I only told her of Múriel's fever, and she prescribed this, though she did say it was strong medicine. Could this have worsened her condition?"

Lifting the little vial, the old man uncorked it, dripped the liquid onto his finger, and brought the medicine to his lips.

"Oh Winifred," Aldred sighed, as he set the vial down.

"What? What is it?"

"Peppermint, boneset, elderflowers, and yarrow. It's a tincture for fevers, but this is no common fever. I can only guess she's remained in bed this entire time, hardly waking from sleep? And the fever has been as fearsome as the day it began?"

"Yes! The day before, she was ever as she always has been," Guy sat at the maiden's beside, taking her hand in his. "The following day, she was determined to deliver provisions though a storm was coming; she was out in the storm for hours and returned very late. That next morning, she fell very ill. She's not left this chamber since."

"Precisely as I had feared," the healer nodded. "This is Noctis Mortem, the Sleeping Death. It appears with much the same symptoms as an ordinary fever, but it is a condition which raises the temperature beyond what the body can handle, inducing an endless sleep. Eventually, it renders the victim unconscious. Few are drawn from their sleep, for it is a sleep unto death," he said. "But you believed her to be truly dead, for how long?"

"Not yet half an hour. I've not been able to wake her... but tell me, what can be done?"

"She needs night nettle," Aldred said.

"Night nettle?"

"Aye, a rare flowering plant; it blooms only in the moonlight. I've no doubt Winifred should have it. It is said, a tonic made from its leaves can wake the victim and cure the illness within a matter of days. In all my practice, I've never been driven to use it, and I do not know for certain it will..." the sage paused, gathering his thoughts, "There is a chance, it could work. A small chance."

"Then, I must fetch the physician here at once," Guy sprinted to his feet, grasping at his cloak which hung over the chair and draping it over his shoulders. "Where does she live?"

"My son," Aldred placed his hand upon Gisborne's shoulder. "You're pale as a ghost. Have you had any sleep all this while? Anything to eat?"

"That does not matter," the man resolved, taking up what supplies he needed. "Tell me, where does the physician live?"

"In the cottage nearest Locksley manor; she has a substantial garden that lies on the east of the house," he said, "But you are worn ragged. You should stay here while I call on her. Eat something and wait for my return."

Guy shook his head. "Let me not satisfy hunger, or quench any thirst, nor know sleep again save she wakens."

"Surely you cannot make such haste on foot in this storm. It is madness!"

"I will take the horse," he said, "and while I am gone, do whatever is necessary to sustain her." Firmly, he clutched the old man's arm, his eyes restless, "I cannot lose her."

Aldred let out a sigh and nodded in accord. "Very well, I shall remain here and do all that can be done, but there is one more thing," the sage hesitated, a question lingering on his lips,

"Winifred informed me, she had sold a vial to a man whose wife was ill. Are you-"

"No, we are not married. But I hoped, *still* hope to…" he sighed.

"I know, Gisborne," the healer smiled.

Bewildered, the man gazed upon the sage.

"Fly!" Aldred commanded.

Shaking aside his doubt with a determined glance to bid a hopeful farewell, the man vanished off into the night.

Instantly, he mounted the horse, the rain beating against him with no respite as he rode through the forest; quick and sharp and keen. Journeying amidst the maddening tempest, nagging in the back of his mind, Guy wondered at how the old man knew his name and why he had so readily accepted the false name. Yet time would prove of little benefit if he did not use it wisely, and so did he put all other thoughts to rest. He must cling to what passion fueled his fight.

There in the forest, the storm unleashed its impetuous voice; the blustering winds tearing through the branches as the howling thunder shook the very earth beneath the horse's tramping hoofs.

Suddenly, before them, a spear of the raging skies struck the earth, a mighty tree defeated under its wrathful blow. The horse staggered, its nostrils flaring as it squealed, drawing up its front legs. The man wrestled with calming the horse and press on toward Locksley, yet, as he continued on, suddenly he felt an unnatural pain in his chest as if a hand wrung at his heart from within. For a moment, he faltered, his vision failing.

Then the pain stopped.

Setting his mind to his mission once more, he cast aside the strange moment. Then it came upon him once more. The pain so intense, he moaned in agony. It felt as if his heart would give way, and for a moment he was blinded to all about him. Terrified he cried out, then the pain disappeared, and his sight returned.

He knew not what to make of this, yet he would fight it. He would press on for Múriel.

Finally, reaching the edge of the forest, he galloped down into the village through the thick of the mud on the road. At the very end of the houses, stood the physician's cottage. The shadows of a large garden teemed at the east of it and the warmth of firelight shone from within.

Reaching the home, Guy dismounted, panting hard and soaked to the bone. Incessant and savage, he pounded his fist upon the door, louder and louder, until it seemed he might have beat the door down altogether if not for an answer.

The door swiftly swung open as Winifred stood aghast at such a display and at the strange face which greeted her. Frightened indeed, she paced back from the frame.

"She is dying!" The man cried, his lips trembling from the bitter cold, and the rain dripping down his face. "Please, Aldred said you would have night nettle."

"Aldred?" The woman brought her hand to her temple. "He sent you?"

"Do you have it?" He begged.

"I don't know," Winifred shook her head in fear, "Wait here a moment."

There he remained at the door; his chest tense and aching, as he fought back his own pain. Soon enough, Winifred returned with a plethora of supplies and the night nettle. Without any delay, she fled with the man, back into the dark and danger of Sherwood, with little but a thread of hope to drive them.

***

Near the second hour, the man returned with the physician, and together, they went with all speed up to the chamber.

Deliberate, Winifred rushed in and stood beside the bed as she examined the maiden.

While Guy remained at the entrance of the bedchamber, watching as the physician and the sage whispered and worked, such a strange emptiness stirred within him. He longed to be near Múriel, to know what was spoken and what could be done; and how foreign it felt to be far from her touch.

Wearily, the man shut his eyes tight as he clutched his chest; the pain returning.

"Please," he muttered through strained breath, "What more is there to be done?"

"No, no. You've done all you can. Take your ease a moment, Winifred is sure to cure the lass," Aldred chided. Then noticing the man's stance, his brows furrowed. "You're in pain... when did this start?"

"It doesn't matter," the man tensed his jaw, "What more is there to be done?"

"You are in no state to be doing anything. You must go and rest," Aldred persisted.

"Set me to work!" Guy wrenched at the collar of the sage's tunic, his eyes wild with fear. As he could suppress it no longer, he let go

163

of Aldred and fell to his knees, groaning viciously as the pain resurged.

"Gisborne, if we do not treat her quickly, we will lose her! And if we lose her, then we shall lose you, also," Aldred reasoned, "Do you not yet understand?"

"Gisborne!" The old woman turned with a furious glare.

"Winifred, please, let me handle this," Aldred halted her steps with a hand upon her shoulder. Slapping his hand away, she marched toward the man.

"I knew I'd seen that face before. Your damned corpse should be rotting in a prison cell!" She growled; her eyes narrowing. "I don't know how you came to this place or how you seduced this innocent young lady into fraternising with the likes of you but mark my words, you've no business staying here any longer."

Panting and weary, he stared up at the woman, his anger boiling over. "Seduced her?" He rose, unsteady, grasping the frame of the door. "I've never tempted her with word or deed."

"Oh, you think such a forked tongue will fool me? I know your kind," she said.

"You do not know me at all," he said, "If such condemnations are drawn from my past, then you must know I am not as I have been."

"And though a snake may shed its skin, it bears, all the same, its venom. Múriel deserves better than some savage murderer."

"Watch your mouth, old woman."

"Burn, you Norman pig!"

"Enough!" Aldred cried, standing between the two; his eyes stern as steel. "We must put an end to this bickering! Now Gisborne, you must wait it out, and heed my warning; if you so much as challenge *anything* I put to you, you will be sorry you ever once drew breath."

"But I cannot abandon her," the man protested.

"You know right well that is not what I ask of you," the old man sighed, his hands set upon the man's shoulders. "You have done nobly, now please, go and rest. Winifred and I shall tend to Múriel and wake you when we have any news."

"I cannot leave her," Guy shook his head, his eyes brimming with tears.

"My son," Aldred resolved unwaveringly, "Winifred is a skilled healer. If you hold any desire to see Múriel safely through this, you must trust her. You must trust *me*."

The man's tired eyes darted between Aldred and Winifred, and then to Múriel. Letting out a deep breath, he departed from the chamber; and the door was closed behind him.

All the hours beyond, Guy did not rest but sat writhing; such pain as if the very hand of death were upon him. The pain resurged stronger and stronger, as his sight fled from him and returned at its own tormented will. Hours passed with no deliverance. Then suddenly, the pain stopped altogether.

His hands trembled, his raw lungs slowly found their rhythm once more, and his eyes saw what dim light was cast over the corridor. He could still hear the storm; unyielding. As he regained what strength he needed, he returned to the door of the bedchamber.

Peering in, he watched the candle's flame flickered into oblivion. Beside the table, the old man worked with the mortar and pestle, grinding more nettles, as the physician stood beside the bed; both speaking harshly between each other.

"She is not waking," Winifred said.

"Then we must try again," Aldred ordered. "She may simply need more of the nettle."

"This herb holds no use," she shook her head. "We must bleed her, to be free of the evil humours-"

"No, I'll never consent to it," he protested, "Life is in the blood. I'll not take one drop from her."

"Then, we must prepare ourselves, or call on our stars for a miracle," she whispered.

For a moment, Aldred stood silent; thinking. Then, turning to the physician, he drew the hood of his cloak over his head.

"What are you doing?" The woman pressed.

"There is one more thing that can be done," he said.

"You mean to leave us?"

"Wait here."

Not a moment passed before the old man burst forth from the chamber in great haste. He ran down the corridor, down the steps, and swinging back the door, he went out unto the unforgiving storm. How the wild thunder resounded through the dark, little home. Curious, the man listened, and amidst the tempest, he could hear Aldred's voice; strong and mighty and deep. No other voice answered back, save the cry of the heavens, though there was no doubt; the old man called out to someone.

Soon, Gisborne heard the door shut out the storm again and the thump of the old man's footsteps; the wood creaking as he climbed the stairs. All the healer carried in his weathered hands was a basin of rainwater. Nothing more. As he passed by the man, he did not look on him, not for an instant. Now Guy could bear it no longer. Reaching out, he grasped the sage's cloak.

"Please... what is happening?"

"If you do not let me go, I'll not be able to save her-"

"Let me help!" He implored, "Let me do something... anything!"

"No, you must wait," Aldred shook his head. "Trust me," he said, a look of understanding resonating in his eyes. Then, he closed the door behind him, leaving Guy in the corridor, alone.

With no occupation given him, the man remained there, guarding the bedchamber. His head leaned against the wall, his eyes were dark and his heart heavy. Staring aimlessly at the door before him, whether by his understanding or not, he perceived that the door vanished, giving way to a vast, untethered field of tall, green grass as he finally submitted to sleep. It was not a peaceful sleep, nor a restful one, but enough to still his restless heart.

***

Slowly but surely, the storm faded, falling away beyond the horizon as the dawn rode across the heavens. The light shone warm and gentle through the windows of the bedchamber, and over the slumbering maiden. Within the golden light, Múriel drew in a breath, as she lay in the early morning quiet; waking. Feeling a slight chill, she looked down, and saw the poultice bound around her chest; her arms and shoulders bare. Though her body ached, she carefully turned to her side and saw Winifred who remained fast asleep on a chair in the corner of the chamber. And then, her eyes met Aldred's, and what colour glimmered beneath his thick, grew brow.

"Where is he? Where is Guy?" She whispered, looking about the chamber as if it were wholly empty.

"Shh," Aldred soothed, as he came to her bedside, "You had us all worried, my dear. All will be explained in due course. But I will go and fetch the man. He will be anxious to see you are better."

"Wait," she said, reaching out to hold the old man's hand. "Merci por tout."

Beaming down at the sweet young lady, and in such tenderness, he placed a kiss upon the crown of her head. "All is as it was meant to be," he smiled. Relinquishing her hand, he departed from the chamber. While he was absent, Múriel sat up in the bed, listening to all that was spoken and to the voice she longed to hear.

"Gisborne! Gisborne wake up!"

"Please, let there be good news..."

"She is out of danger, my son."
"Truly?"
"Go and see her; she is awake."

Altogether, the sounds of bustling feet and muffled conversation ceased when Guy stood before the entrance. How his eyes did stare; first in disbelief and in bewilderment; but finally, in such pure and joyous wonder.

"Until tomorrow?" Múriel smiled.

The man could not bring himself to utter a single word, yet with tears in his eyes, he ran to her side, wrapping his arms about her; his hands caressing her locks, as her fingers entangled his raven waves. And so embraced, neither was willing to part. It seemed an age and a moment, holding her in his arms; the burdens of his heart mended.

"I thought I had lost you," he said.

"I promised I would always return. And a promise I make, is a promise kept," she smiled, the silvery glow in her eyes returning, as she brushed away his tear.

Beaming, the man swept aside a lock of her hair; his heart filled with such peace, he could not speak.

"Gisborne," Aldred said. "As we are all much in need of a hearty meal, would you care to help me prepare some food?" The sage fixed his hand upon the man's shoulder.

Though loathing the very thought of leaving her side, the man nodded in acceptance. Removed from the chamber, Aldred stood in the corridor, waiting for the man to join him.

"I'll return, my darling," Guy whispered, his lips gently brushing against her ear. Placing a kiss upon her cheek, he then stood and made his way to the corridor.

As the men ventured down into the kitchen, the healer began to search about for this and that. It was not yet the sixth hour of the morn, and about this time, the land was to be tended. Per his practice, Gisborne donned his cloak and made ready to start the morning chores.

"What are you doing?" Aldred questioned curiously, as he lit the kindling in the fireplace.

"Forgive me, but I must leave you to prepare the food alone," he said. "Please, be sure Múriel eats well. Much as I want to eat beside her, there is far too much work I've neglected, and I know she will need to rest soon enough."

"You'll not eat something now? Not even a piece of bread?" The old man wondered.

"I cannot ignore my duties for my own comfort."

Aldred nodded, his eyes squinted as he glanced at the fire. Then a curious thought reappeared in his vision; his brows raised. Gisborne stood still, awaiting Aldred's words.

"Then... then, it was you? You were the one who brought the provisions to my home? To the Smith family?"

"I confess I did," he nodded.

"But... why?"

"I know well what is it to hunger and thirst," he said, "Thus, I could not think of others being left uncared for with no hint of an excuse. And I had no wish for anyone to think ill of Múriel on account of her absence. So in her stead, I delivered the provisions, but only when I thought it would be safe to leave her to rest. I did not part from her any longer than was necessary."

Puzzled and impressed, the old man stared. "You're a better man than I had estimated," Aldred nodded, a smile broadening under his white beard. "Well," the healer began afresh, "when you have finished your duties, breakfast will be waiting."

The man bowed his head in thanks and set out into the dewy air of the autumn morning.

Near two hours had passed before he returned to the warmth of the cottage; quite famished. Upon removing his cloak and his muddied boots, he saw Aldred seated at the head of the table and all the food laid out before him.

"Has she eaten?"

"Aye, she has. Don't worry," the healer answered kindly. "She's resting for now, and Winifred likewise ate and has taken her ease."

"Good," he grinned, standing nervously.

"Come along, you've earned it. Sit," the old man urged him.

Instantly, Guy took his place at the table, and for the first time in what seemed ages, he sat down to a full meal. There was a hot pot of barley porridge seasoned with all manner of herbs, a pitcher of ale, and a whole loaf of rye bread. It was more than enough to satisfy his pangs, and could easily have been shared amongst two or three, but he felt not the least bit inhibited to take up every morsel he could. Ravenous, he took up the porridge, the rim of the bowl almost touching his nose as he ate spoonful after spoonful before he set it hard against the wood, poured the ale, and drank from the cup. Watching how the man devoured the food, Aldred looked on him, perturbed.

"When last did you eat?"

"Day before yesterday," he mumbled, tearing off another piece of bread and dipping it in the ale. "Now, I must ask you something."

"Oh," Aldred said, "Well, whatever you're pondering, I'll hear it."

"How is it that you knew my name?"

At this, the old man smirked under his wild beard, "You were once a noble in these lands, one of ill fame, but a noble nonetheless. I may be a hermit, but I'm not so wholly uninformed."

"But when I gave you the name *Hugo*, you accepted it. If you've known all this while, why didn't you-"

"You gave your father's name. He was a good man; a good friend," Aldred nodded, "And I knew you could be trusted."

"You knew I was trustworthy when I gave you a false name?" Guy wondered. "And you knew my father?"

"Gisborne, I know you of old, as I knew your father before you. Your manner and your intent were not so hidden from me. Therefore, I concealed my understanding," he answered.

Thinking on the healer's words, the man grew astounded, for he remembered such words spoken not so very long ago.

"It was *you*?" He whispered, "You were the one who sent her?"

Without a word, the sage brought a cup to his lips and glanced back at the man, and while nought was spoken, his eyes spoke truly.

"But why? Why would you do such a thing?" Guy questioned, "Why would you send a young maiden to my cell? You may not be so oblivious to those in power, but you sent her into a snare."

"Did you die there, Gisborne?" Aldred asked.

"No, I-"

"Are you glad to be freed from such an end? And that Múriel is alive and well?"

"Yes, of course, but I still think-"

"Then do not question it," the old man said.

As the two men sat a while in the silence, taking up morsels of food here and there, and drinking, the man couldn't contain his further pondering any more.

"I do have other questions to ask of you," he said.

"There is more you wish to know? Does your mind know no rest?" Aldred sighed, "Oh, go on." He waved his hand.

"I want to know how you knew my father and how you think you know me of old, for I've never seen your face in all my life," he began, "And how did you know where to send Múriel, or know that she might help me escape? And how is it that you knew Múriel was in danger when-"

"Steady on!" The healer raised his hand, "With such questions as these, one requires far too many tales, one is far too long a tale to tell, and one, not so worth the telling."

"But you'll still hear my questions?"

"It is not my obligation to give you any answers," he said.

"Then what can you tell me?" Guy pressed.

Setting his empty bowl aside, the old man propped his elbows on the table. Sweeping away the crumbs, he brought his rough and weathered hands together.

"Long ago, I swore an oath to my master. For this reason, I am here and doing his bidding."

"Those are the very words you bid Múriel speak to me," the man rested his arms upon the table, leaning in closer. "Do you think me simple?"

"Perhaps."

"If you have a master also, then are you a slave?"

"Slave? Oh, no," Aldred said. "A servant; and so have I been all my days."

"Is he a good master, the one you serve?"

"That is not for me to judge," he answered, "but, I suppose if I must satisfy your thought, then yes. Yes, he is good. Now," he straightened his shoulders, "you know of the children of the Sun and the Moon, yes? Of the Valtan king and his bride?"

Gisborne only shook his head in confusion, "No, I have never heard of it. Is it some faerie tale?"

"*Faerie tale!*" The old man wrinkled his brow, "If you must belittle it so, do have the decency to call it a legend. Let it not be counted with the stories those creatures tell, as to children in the eve."

"But I don't understand," the man said, "You'll ignore all my questions to tell me of some simple legend?"

"My son, you are a regrettably ignorant man. Ignorant of who you really are," Aldred sighed; his tone calm, yet disappointed. "You must remember."

This, in turn, was only met by the man's confused expression. "And what is it that you would have me recall so I might gain what insight you assume is lacking? Must you speak in such riddles that I am left with more questions than answers?"

"If you had taken some pains to study such *riddles*, perhaps you would not speak so as you do," Aldred chided.

Dropping his shoulders, Gisborne let out a frustrated sigh. "Then, could you find some means of speaking plainly?"

"Very well, if I must," he grumbled. Drinking from the cup, he peered over the rim at the man's face. "No doubt, you know of your birthright? And of your wealth?"

"I was given all that was my father's at his death, and I gained Locksley Manor after the Lord of Locksley denounced it," he sighed, looking down into his own empty cup. "But to what use, now…"

"No, no, no," the old man rubbed at his temple, "I speak of the golden brooch, wrought by the Ironstriker himself in the deeps of Mount Andír. Crafted with a ray of purest sunlight. Doubtless, your father must have given it to you before his passing and told you of your lineage. Its worth is far greater than all of England."

"Yes, my father owned a golden brooch, but *crafted with* a *ray of sunlight?*" The man chuckled, shaking his head lightly. "If there is one thing for certain, it is that you have been hermitting in the woods for far too many winters."

"Aye, many winters have I seen, yet would I have seen such things and lived to tell of it, if I lacked discernment?" He said, "Do not be so quick to dismiss my word. For it may be what your ears need most to hear."

"Then if you are a man of such years and wise thoughts, lend me such wisdom. Tell me what words you intend for my ears," Guy entreated. "What is the point of all this?"

"Do you truly love her, Gisborne?"

"Of course," he answered, "She is everything to me."

"Then have you told her the truth?"

Reclining in his chair, the man gazed, perplexed. "The truth?"

"Does Múriel know of your past?"

"Yes… she already knew of my crimes, and she spoke of it herself when she had come to see me. She knows everything-"

"*Everything?*" Now Guy's guilt deepened at Aldred's inquiry, as he stared nervously at the empty cup in his hand. "You know I am speaking of the Lady Marian," Aldred said.

"Whatever you know, I confessed to her of my past with Marian, and of her death-"

"Her death and that of her unborn child were sealed under the fate of your hand."

Now the man lost all concealment, and the colour drained away from his face. "How could you know that?" He whispered.

"I know many things," the old man answered. "Still, what is known to me is troubling."

"I..." his lips trembled. "I cannot deny, Marian had confided in me the morning before her arrest, that she was with child. But I begged her to flee. To return to Sherwood before it was too late. I had no wish to see her risk any more than she had already-" he shook his head. "What I did, what I was forced to do... the sheriff had threatened me with death if I dared defend her."

"The fact remains, such injustice was exacted under your hand," Aldred sighed. "Did you value your life so above Marian's that you were swayed by Rothgar's threat?"

"I alone was not threatened with death," Guy said. "The death of every man, woman, and child under my rule was at stake. Locksley would have stood as a graveyard that day if I had not yielded... I was threatened to follow orders, or suffer the consequences. Rothgar wanted nothing less than bloodshed."

"Yet none of this would have happened if you had not acted when you could have," the old man said, "Murdering the sheriff after her death was nothing but petty revenge. Be careful, Gisborne. You realise I am not doing this out of any fondness for the matter. I must do what is required of me," he sighed.

"Please," Guy said. "Múriel cannot know this."

"You don't think she deserves to know?"

"What good would it do if she knew?" The man stood up from the table. "And do you not know the depths of suffering I have felt at the folly of my own hands? How I've borne the chains of guilt as my portion? Would that I had given my soul to prevent it! Already, Múriel has seen me at my darkest hour. I can sink no lower. I..." Guy paused, breathless in his tortured rant, slamming his fist against the grain of the table, as he leaned forward. "I have been a worthless fool... Múriel saw that well enough," he said; his head hung low. Ashamed by his own reflections, he brought a hand up to cover his face.

The old man nodded, "Then, you will not tell her?"

"She already has every cause to despise me," he sat once more, his eyes heavy. "Being here, with her, this is a new chance, for a new life. I must cling to what hope I have left."

Aldred searched the man's eyes and sighed deeply. After a stretch of silence, he finally spoke.

"If you say you love her, and despite all your history, she has stayed by your side, then you should have nothing to fear," the sage reasoned, and feeling pity towards the man, he set his hand upon Gisborne's shoulder in assurance. "You must tell her the truth."

"And what if she hates me for it?"

"Do you not know her?" Aldred said. "Has she not proven her heart? And if you say you desire a new beginning, then you must cultivate it. Seek truth and honour; be noble and steadfast; lay down your life for her. Love her as she ought to be loved. Promise me you will do this."

"You have my word," the man declared, determined in every breath.

"Good, good..." Aldred brought his hand back to his cup. "You know, Gisborne, I am your ally in more ways than you may understand. And so, if you swear to do all this, here is what else I must put to you: wait until she is fully recovered before anything is said or done. Show your affection for her. Care for her, be dutiful. Then, when the time is right, you may reveal your love for her. And if she loves you in return, then ask for her hand, and I will give you my blessing. But trust that she has the strength to stand beside you."

CHAPTER TWELVE

ELEANOR

The passing months felt as and age, and all the while Eleanor's mind never strayed from her love. Over and over, she thought on their parting; how so long ago on that bitter night, he had bid her flee the perils of Nottingham castle.

Don't tempt the hour, he had said, *Find safety for my sake, and I shall wait for you.*

How his words resounded in her mind. She wondered if he would keep his word, if he would wait as he so fervently promised, and if he thought on her as she did think on him. Nestled under the very boughs of Sherwood once more, the pangs of her heart could not be tempered, for it was not her love who called her hence, but for the sake of her mother's grave. It was her mother's dying wish to be buried in Locksley, where she had spent her happiest days, and Eleanor could not slight such a task.

On the following morning, the old woman was buried in the field beside her fallen kin. With a heavy heart, Eleanor bid farewell to her mother one final time, though she toiled so to save face. When the rites were given, and the people departed, the young lady stood alone in solemn reflection. Nought but the whistling breeze through her long dark hair and the rustling of the early autumn leaves could be heard. When she could bear the weight no longer, she fell to her knees beside the stone and shed tears. Then, a kind hand rested upon her shoulder, as a soft, familiar voice greeted her.

"Oh, Eleanor," the old man comforted, "Do not weep without hope, for you shall see her again."

"It is not only for her loss that I weep," she confessed, brushing away her tears with her ivory hand.

"What else troubles you?" He knelt beside her.

Gazing back at the old man and his tender eyes, Eleanor sighed, the tears falling down her cheek.

"I feel as though I am a wandering soul, with neither name nor home to sustain me," she whispered.

Kneeling side by side, the two fell silent, and as the lady could not keep from her lamenting, the old man remained unmoved. Then, once again, the old man spoke in all gentleness.

"How can you think you are so without aid?" The old man asked, "Certainly, you have been well looked after by the Smiths."

"I cannot depend on them forever," she said, "I've no other family, no reasons to return to hiding, and nowhere to go. And all the same, who would take me in, and for how long before I was cast out? What should I do? Where can I go?"

With doubting eyes, the lady looked at the old man, wishing he might allay her fears. Bringing his hand to his chin, he thought, considering the circumstance in full.

"Would you so detest the thought of remaining here?" He wondered.

"No," the lady replied, "There is someone here I've longed to see again, and perhaps if I were to stay-"

"Perhaps you might see *him* again?" Aldred grinned, as a shimmer of something sweet and unquenchable shone in the young lady's eye.

"Do you suppose he still thinks on me?"

"I've no doubt, whatever time has passed, he has thought of none else save you, though you'll not know if you depart," Aldred said. Reaching into the grass, he took up a little acorn and held it out in his palm. "If a seed was planted long ago, and perhaps forgotten for a time, how will you know if a tree might be standing there this day, where that very seed was once sewn if you never return to it? And if the tree remains, ought you not to find it before you take to the roadside? I do not believe you would sew such seeds in idleness."

Taking to his feet, the old man held out his other hand to draw the young lady up, and in her hand, he placed the seed of the oak and smiled. At this, the young lady's complexion lightened as she swept away the tears from her face.

"You know of whom I seek?"

"Stay," he said, "take lodging with your friends, mourn for a time as you must, but there is a position to be taken at Locksley Manor if you would wish it; keeper of the manor; and I'll wager you would do splendidly," the healer nodded with a cheerful expression, just as he turned to leave the lady. As he walked farther and farther away, the lady held fast the seed in her palm, and in bewilderment looked onward.

"Wait!" The lady called, "But you've not answered my question!"

With a final glance, the old man turned about. "The tree remains," he answered, and as he withdrew into the forest, Eleanor stood alone.

While she grieved her mother, she swore she would shed no more tears beyond that day. No, the lass was not so wholly disheartened as when she had first come, for she believed most earnestly that she would find her love again. All that night, under the starlit skies of the wildwood, Eleanor dreamt of it.

***

Brisk and bright the morning rose, and eagerly, the lass made ready to venture into Locksley and inquire after the position at the manor. She knew not what to expect nor what mistress would await her. From the testimony of her friends, she did not doubt this to be a wholesome opportunity. Still, a strange air of doubt hung as a cloud over her thoughts.

Walking along the quiet path, she approached the edge of the woods and perceived the village before her. The soft morning light shone across the rows of thatched roofs, and at the very end of all the quaint little homes did she find a grand manor, standing bold at the crest of a broad green field. The manor itself was taller than he had remembered; its walls of stone, well weathered, and the three large arched windows at the face of it seemed to stare down at her, portentous. For but a moment she faltered, though her feet would not give heed to her warning mind, and were quick to bring her all the way to the manor's guarded entrance. Before her, there stood two guards, fully armed and suited. As towers of metal, so were they fixed, and what light that caught their eyes was not enough to make them appear any more human. Nonetheless, the young lady daren't turn back now.

"Who are you, and what is your business?" The first guard questioned; his voice firm and coarse.

"I... I am Eleanor," she said, "I am come to inquire after the position at this manor-"

"What position?" The man stepped forth, his hand upon the hilt.

"I was told the Lady of Locksley was in need of a keeper of the manor," she fumbled, "I only wish to seek employment."

"Wait here," the man held up his hand. Turning about, he entered the manor, as the second guard remained motionless.

Minutes passed, and the first guard had not returned. Eleanor grew worried. She began to doubt that she would ever be admitted into the manor, that she might not be given a chance to make a new life for herself and that her very presence before those doors was in vain. With such a hinderance afflicting her thoughts, and the empty minutes creeping by, she thought to depart altogether. Then, finally, the doors opened, and the first guard held out his arm to direct her.

"The sheriff awaits you in the hall," he said.

"Thank you," the lady said, bowing before her feet crossed over the stone.

Gazing up, she took in the sight of it. The home was large indeed, rich with all the furnishings and comforts any noble could possess. Tapestries were draped upon the walls; mounted shields and swords hung boldly; and everywhere, it seemed, the whole of the manor was lit with ornamented candles. At the end of the grand hall, was a magnificent fireplace, of which the mantle was most extravagantly carved with images of flowers, and vines, and deer with great, swirling antlers. On each side of the fireplace were two windows, overlooking gardens and permitting the early light shine through in such quiet splendour. By all accounts, it appeared so expense had been spared and the home was handsomely kept. Eleanor only hoped to discover a gracious master who presided over it.

Her gaze drawn down, the young lady's eye settled on a long table to the left of the fireplace, stretching nearly from one wall to the other. At the west end, sat the Lady Claudia herself, in all her elegance. Her gown was delicately embroidered about the hem and the edge of the sleeves and the neckline. Her hair was braided back in golden clasps, and her slender fingers were adorned with precious stones and metals.

And as she looked on the young lady, Claudia's expression fared friendly and curious.

"Ah! So you are the one who wishes to speak with me. Please, do be seated," she said. With such graceful composure, she gestured for the young lady to sit beside her.

Humbly, Eleanor bowed. Lifting her head once more, she took her place beside the woman, and for a moment, let her dark brown eyes wander about the manor.

"Now, I must ask, how did you come to know of the vacancy for this position? I've only just sent out inquiries three days ago."

Something behind the sheriff's eyes made Eleanor feel somewhat uneasy, but before she could conjure an answer, the woman continued.

"I must admit, I'm rather intrigued to find such a hasty response."

"Oh, well," Eleanor began, "An old friend was gracious enough to direct me hence."

"Hmm," Claudia thought, tilting her head as she considered the lady's words. "You look so young," she said. "Pray, have you any understanding of the position? Any knowledge of the duties and standards you will be held to?"

"Indeed, your grace," Eleanor said, straightening her posture, "For a time, I worked as the head maid to the Lady of Wirksworth, and soon was made apprentice under the keeper of the manor. I understand there is much work to be done in keeping an estate, and I have been well trained."

"That is rather impressive," Claudia said. "I've never been to the Wirksworth estate, but do know the Lord and Lady of the estate are loyal allies," she nodded. "May I ask, why is it you left to seek employment here?"

Eleanor bit her lip, fearing to reveal too much all at once, and so she let out a sigh, devising what words to speak. "I... I was content with my position, then upon accompanying my mistress to the courts of Nottingham for a council of the nobles, the sheriff Rothgar thought I might be offered a position at his castle. At the time, I had no reason not to accept, and so came to work there. Yet, after a time, and due to the declining health of my mother, I felt it was no longer suitable to remain."

"I knew Rothgar well... very well," Claudia sighed. "He died but a season ago, and I was made sheriff shortly after. How long ago did you depart from Nottingham?"

Stiffening her back so it would not touch the chair, Eleanor kept her eyes away from the woman. "Not a year ago," she mumbled.

"Curious," the woman said, her eyes narrowing. "But why come to Locksley? Why not return to your former mistress?"

"Locksley… is my home, your grace," she answered. "It is where I was raised, and where so many pleasant memories were made… I've been away from home far too long. And it always has been, or rather, always was a precious place to my mother. Now that she has passed, I would have no other wish than to honour her memory by making a life for myself in this very place."

Glancing back at the sheriff, Eleanor was surprised to find something gentle behind the woman's gaze. With all apprehension dispelled, Claudia outstretched her arm toward the young lady and took her hand.

"How noble of you, that you would honour her memory in such a way," she praised, "Perhaps it may be against my better judgement, but the position is yours!"

"Truly?" Eleanor's eyes widened. As the woman released her hand, both stood from the table.

"Why of course," she said, "I am certain you shall prove a trustworthy keeper, and I shall rest easy tonight knowing my estate is in such capable hands."

"Thank you so much, my lady! Thank you!" The young lady bowed again. "Forgive me, but when may I begin?"

"This very day! I shall have my head maidservant escort you to your quarters and inform you of all the details."

"Oh, but I shall need time to collect my things-"

"No need. I can send one of my servants to the inn to fetch your belongings."

"But I did not take lodging at the inn," Eleanor said, "I was staying with kin, the Smith family. Their cottage is near a mile outside of the village, in Sherwood."

"You mean to say, they reside *in* the forest?"

"Yes, your grace."

"Ah," Claudia tensed her lip. "And their names?"

"Cedric and Catherine, your grace. They have a lovely little cottage and-"

"Well, I shall see to it that your possessions are collected and your hosts are thanked for their generous hospitality."

At this, Eleanor sighed cheerfully, as if a weight had been lifted off her shoulders.

As all of this was settled, Claudia called upon one of her table servants to fetch the head maidservant at once and usher her into the hall. No sooner had she sent the lad on his way through the manor, than the woman appeared. A short, older woman of a full figure and a jolly complexion, came forth from the kitchens and stood before the grand table. Her eyes were soft, her curly grey hair bounced about her cheeks, and her expression fared blithe and amiable. Upon seeing her mistress's waving hand, she scurried over to the table.

"Yes, m' lady?" The old woman bowed, "You called for me?"

"Nan, allow me the pleasure of introducing you to Eleanor, our new keeper of the manor. You'll need to show her around the estate and escort her to her quarters by even fall. Oh, and send Gerald to fetch her belongings. She lodged at a cottage just beyond the village. The hosts go by the name of Smith. And do be sure they are thanked for hosting such a lovely guest."

"Of course, your grace," Nan bowed, her sweet voice echoing throughout the room. "Delighted to meet you, Eleanor. Come along, I'll show you around."

The young lady bowed before the sheriff one final time and excitedly followed the maidservant, leaving Claudia seated at the table behind her.

"Quickly, now! You must learn to hasten those feet," Nan said. "And you'll have to pardon me but a moment while I go and have a word with the head manservant. Grumpy old griffle-grim. He's always in one of those *moods*, but you'll find your way around all that soon enough. He's rather good-natured if one can find the time to see it. Now, hurry along!" Nan waved, as Eleanor was practically sprinting just to catch her up.

The two ladies hustled about the manor until Nan finally found the man. The woman spoke with such pithy vivacity it nearly gave the lass a headache. The old manservant only squinted his eyes under his heavy brow, huffed, and finally nodded as Nan concluded her list of instructions to retrieve Eleanor's belongings and deliver a basket of food to the Smith family.

Once the man had been given his orders, the ladies continued on their expedition. Endlessly, Nan chattered on about every minute detail of the up-keep. Eleanor was readily skilled and understood much of the simple tasks to be done, but Nan somehow found a way to dramatise every situation imaginable. And in some instances, the young lady found herself rather bored, not being able to pay the least bit of attention to another tedious word out of the old woman's mouth.

"And that is why he can *never* dust the tapestries. Understood?"

"Oh, yes! Yes of course," she nodded, her hands laced behind her back. She couldn't muster any other response, as she had lost all track of the monologue, and hoped the simple *yes* would suffice.

"Now, the bedchambers need the linens cleaned every week. We usually send it down for washing on Wednesdays. See to it that all the linens are brought to Beth, and she'll take care of the rest. Mind, we cannot have any delay in our routine. There was a dreadful misunderstanding a few months back... a maid flat out forgot to bring the sheets down to wash. When the ladyship discovered as much, poor lass was turned out before she could blink an eye."

Halting in her steps, Eleanor lowered her chin and stared. "That's rather harsh."

"Aye, 'twas a right shame, so I think. By and by, the ladyship shouldn't have to stand for nonsense," Nan shook her finger. Then, she let out a great sigh as she fit her hands upon her hips. "There now, that seems to be it. Anything else you wish to know?"

"Well, now that you ask, I do have something to ask you," Eleanor said, "How you do like working at the manor?"

"How do you mean?"

"Forgive me, I only mean to ask, is the Lady Claudia a fair mistress?"

"Shh," Nan brought her finger up to her lips. Pausing for a moment, she peered this way and that, making sure none else were present. Pulling Eleanor aside, Nan rushed her through to the end of the corridor.

Lowering her chin, she whispered, "If you want to know the truth, I'll tell you... the sheriff is a *mad* woman, she is."

"A mad woman?" Eleanor gasped.

"She's not here often, but when she is, there is nothing but trouble going about. Yelling at us servants, making a fuss over every little thing. 'Tis such a shame; for her fair face and her airs, you'd think she might be married off by now if not for her temper."

"If I'd known as much, I never would have come here!" Eleanor said. "This was a terrible mistake."

"Now don't go getting all upset, dearie. So long as you do as your told, and mind your own, you'll do just fine," Nan encouraged, nodding and patting the young lady's shoulder. "Moreover, the pay is good; better than most other nobles would be willing to pay, that is."

"But, what if I make a mistake and she turns me out? If she is so wholly unreasonable-"

"Don't fret," Nan said, "It'll do everyone good having someone sensible about the manor. Honest, she's not here more than once in a fortnight. High-strung as she is, we all know it right well."

Nan started giggling, which set Eleanor's nerves at ease. The two ladies laughed a little, peeking around the corridor again and snickering all the more.

"Well, I suppose I could stay," Eleanor nodded with a gentle smile.

"Good, and if ever you should need help, I'll be sure to lend a hand," Nan said.

As they made their way down the corridor, and down into the great hall, Lady Claudia had vanished.

"The bat's flown from the cave I suppose."

"Nan!" Eleanor tried to mask her laugh. "What if someone hears you?"

"Oh, pish! Now, come along, let me show you to your quarters," Nan said.

As Eleanor followed behind, Nan led her through the kitchens. The kitchens were a merry place, and the larder neatly stocked. As they whisked through, how the scents of so many new and exciting spices rose in the air, and the symphony of sizzling meats and the bubbling of pottage, sung all at once.

Beyond the kitchens were the doors leading out to the garden, and just ahead, a flight of stairs. Up and up they climbed, the winding staircase barely lit by what sunlight could come through the narrow windows dispersed along the walls of stone as the ladies ascended. Finally, as they reached the top, before them was a narrow corridor with several doors on either side. Halting at the first door to the right, Nan opened the door to what would be Eleanor's bedchamber.

A simple chamber, indeed, with nought but a bed, a small table, and an old chest remained inside. But for its bare and lonely state, all this was soon mended, in that the little window overlooked the forest.

Magnificent, each tree stood, and every branch bending under the breath of the wind; donned in vibrant hues. Breathing deep the sweet morning air, and looking upon a place she loved so well, Eleanor's hope was evermore renewed, for in these very woods did her darling outlaw roam, and her eyes searched out eagerly for a banner of copper hair that might perchance wave so boldly through those very trees.

CHAPTER THIRTEEN

PROPENSITY AND PERSPECTIVE

A week had passed since Guy had spoken with Aldred.

All the while, the physician and the sage had stayed to nurse Múriel back to health. Initially, what was meant to lighten the burden for Gisborne served only to divert the burden. For it was not the maiden's condition which pained him so much as it was Winifred's brandished intolerance of his very presence, as she made good on every opportunity to speak whatever foul, conceited judgement could be contrived. The little cottage was growing littler and littler, and there was no respite to be had.

Yet, to the allayment of all, the young lady was swift to heal. Each day she gained strength, and by the third morning, she had will enough to come down the stairs and take a mild stroll through the garden. Most fortuitous the seventh day came, and late that very afternoon, the cottage would happily bid farewell to its guests. Drawing out of doors, Gisborne was quick enough to wish the old man a safe journey and to give a sharp and silent nod to the physician before he set for the edge of the forest to continue his work, chopping wood. Gentle as ever, the maiden remained by

Aldred and Winifred at the door; her bright complexion returned and her grey eyes shining.

"It is grand seeing you well again. I swear nothing else shall dampen my spirits, least not for the whole week to come," the woman smiled.

"Thank you, Winifred, for all your kindness," Múriel embraced her, "I don't know how I can ever thank you enough."

"You're a sweet lass," she said. "Just be sure to keep out of trouble, mind."

"I will," Múriel sighed.

As the old woman stepped aside, Aldred embraced the maiden, his full and wild beard tickling her cheek.

"Farewell, dear," he grinned, "If ever you or Gisborne should be in need of help, please don't hesitate to call on me."

"Well now, she might keep him on if she likes," Winifred interrupted, "but if that good-for-nothing steps so much as one foot out of place-"

"Oh, be sensible," Aldred grumbled, "Here stands a trustworthy young lady as ever has been. And surely we can *both* agree Gisborne's proven himself an honourable man. Now, it's high time we return to our own homes."

Reluctant, Winifred pursed her lips, for she had not prepared a rebuttal and coveted the final say. Still, she complied and followed the sage, though she took the extra measure of glaring through narrow eyes at Gisborne before turning about in the direction of the forest.

"Farewell!" Múriel called, watching as they walked across the field and then disappeared beyond the elder trees.

A few moments of peace settled sweetly over the field; the trees crowned in their warmer hues shed their leaves. Of sunset reds and earthy browns, of glimmering golds and butter yellows, each leaf soared overhead and then softly glided down to the grass. The maiden remained a while, drinking deep of the rolling breeze and smiling to herself as the man she looked on came bounding to her side. His waves of dark hair flowed in the wind's breath, and his eyes, as the ocean's tide, called unto her.

"Would it be dreadful to say I am glad they've gone?" He smirked.

"Guy!" She said, holding back a little laugh. "They were more than helpful, and I was quite ill... but, perhaps it wouldn't be quite so dreadful to say you're glad *Winifred* is gone."

"Perhaps," he grinned, "Howbeit, it's grand to have the cottage back to ourselves again."

"It is," she sighed.

Rolling up his sleeves, Guy turned about, marching back toward the forest. The maiden's eyes followed, standing so still and unsure of whether she should ask him what had been on her mind. And just as he had taken up the axe again, she found the courage to speak.

"Wait!" She called.

"Yes?" He answered, facing her once more.

"Forgive me, I wanted to ask something of you," she said, as she swept her hair over her shoulder, avoiding his eyes cautiously. "Do you... do you still have it?"

"Have what?"

"The brooch?"

"Oh! Of course, yes," he replied. Reaching his hand into his pocket, he revealed the gift she had so lovingly bestowed. "I am never without it," he beamed down at her.

"Bien," she smiled.

Tucking a lock of hair behind her ear, she gazed shyly and fondly all the same at his endearing expression. Then, he took her hand in his.

"Múriel," he said, "I'm sorry we've hardly spoken much these past few days. I can only imagine all the thoughts you have, and I have much of my own. But one thought has not given me a moment's peace and it has been restrained long enough. I must confess it now."

Nervous, she nodded, and though her heart beat so fiercely, she looked up at him and listened.

"What you said, the words you spoke when..." he paused, composing his words. "Did you truly mean it?"

The maiden's face flushed crimson as her lips fell silent. At the time she had spoken those words, she truly believed it was her only chance to tell him. Fear had driven her to profess such affection, yet now, it was her timid spirit which held her tongue. Suddenly, she discovered something she had nearly forgotten; a temporary escape presented itself.

"Today is Monday, oui?" She asked, stepping backwards.

"Yes, it's Monday," he answered, his brows furrowed as her hand fell away from his touch.

"Then there are provisions to deliver," she said.

"Provisions?"

"We should have left this morning," she shook her head. "I will finish my work in the kitchen and prepare the baskets. Then we ought to make our way before sundown." She turned about, drawing all her hair together and braiding it hastily, as she marched away towards the cottage.

"But Múriel-"

"Would you prepare the horse when you are finished with the firewood? Merci!" She called back as she entered the cottage, and shut the door fast behind her.

Guy stood dumbfounded.

Why is she so afraid? He thought. *What have I done to make her afraid?*

The hours beyond soon faded, and with it, much of the evening light. As the maiden returned to the entrance of the barn, the man set the baskets about the horse and helped her mount, yet he spoke not, and kept his eyes away from her. Taking his place in front of her, she drew her arms about him.

"Are you certain you don't mind coming with me?" She said. "I could go alone if-"

"I want to be sure you are protected," he replied; his voice sharp and stern. "It is my duty."

"Only if you wish it to be," Múriel dropped her shoulders. "Is everything alright?"

As she struck the chord, the man snapped the reins under his grip and kicked the horse's side with his heel. The creature galloped madly across the field such that Múriel held on tighter and hid her face in the man's cloak. Fleet and fierce, the riders drove into the forest, the sun's last rays departing from the heavens. Finally, as the moon assumed her place in the sky, they arrived at the Smith's cottage.

Entangled amongst the trees laid a home of very modest means. Behind the dwelling was a small garden with a simple fence about it, and leaning up against the outer wall stood a mountain of kindling. Smoke from the chimney rose up in great swirling puffs, and through the window, such light and warmth could be seen. Though they were at a distance from the little house, the walls could hardly contain the sound of merry conversation and laughter.

Halting a few yards from the cottage, Guy leapt down from the horse and aided the maiden down beside him. Still, he kept his eyes away from her; his jaw tense and his brows low.

"How long do you suppose this will take?" He asked.

"I'll only be a few minutes at most, then we can return home," she said, trying to meet his gaze.

Without a word, he nodded and fixed his eyes upon the reins; Múriel could only stand and stare, loathing the errand which staid her, and the courage she did lack. Yet, for the time being, she must set her heart aside. They had made it this far, it would be foolish to turn back. Therefore, unto the door of the cottage, she walked, her grey cape fluttered in the chill autumn winds, and the crunching of her steps over the leaf-laden ground drew her closer to the little house. Further away from him.

Gently, she knocked upon the door, and before another second could be given leave to pass, the door swung open. The cosy light from the fire gleamed through, as a tall woman greeted her. Her chestnut hair was braided up as a crown around her head, and her deep brown eyes mirthful.

"Múriel! It's grand to see you!" The woman embraced her.

"Catherine, please, forgive me... I know it's been far too long since I've come; I had fallen ill. Please, don't think I have forgotten you."

"I don't understand," Catherine said. "What do you mean you were ill?" She wondered, her expression far more intrigued than disgruntled.

"I had fallen ill a few weeks ago, very ill, and thus I wasn't able to bring provisions," she said, "I hope you've not thought me heartless. Please, forgive me."

"But I don't understand, we *did* receive provisions," Catherine nodded.

"Truly?"

"Yes, we've received your basket at each turn," she said. "We didn't see you, and that seemed a bit odd, but I assumed you had your reasons and would soon come round. I had no idea you were ill! But it's good to see you are well again."

Múriel stood in thought. Her eyes went wide at Catherine's word, but soon the maiden's expression changed when she understood.

"Guy," she whispered with a blushing smile.

"Who?"

"Hugo. I meant Hugo," she mumbled, "He is the one who must have brought the food, though he didn't say anything."

"I suppose you mean *him*?" Catherine pointed to the tall man, standing by the horse. "How did you come to know him?"

"He is a friend... a dear friend," she smiled.

"A *dear friend*? Oh, you'll have to do better than that," the woman winked. "Well, tell him to come in. Perhaps you might join us for supper? We have a guest staying with us, and I'm certain you'll never guess who."

"Don't make me guess, Cate," she rolled her eyes playfully, "Who is it?"

"I'll just go and fetch her," the woman smiled as she turned into the cottage. "She's talked of little else save you and her outlaw since she came back!" She called.

The maiden was given no time to make any answer before an old friend appeared before the door. Her dark locks hung over her shoulders, and her smile brimmed with delight.

"You're here!" Eleanor threw her arms around the lady, and the two embraced sweetly. "It's been so long! You still remember me, don't you?"

"Of course I remember you," she laughed. "Now why is it you've returned to Locksley? I thought you meant to travel for a year or so."

At this, Eleanor's lively expression suddenly withdrew into sobriety. "My mother... she passed away. We held a service for her this morning. She had wished to see Locksley again before she died."

"Oh... I'm so sorry," the maiden embraced her friend once more, pulling back as she looked into such deep eyes. "How are you?"

"Well enough, given the circumstances," the lady nodded. "It was her time. But there is so much to tell you. Would you stay? Catherine says your friend is welcome also." Peering through the doorway, she glanced at Guy. "He looks rather serious. Is he always so?"

"He, well... *we've* had a long day. I must admit, I would love to stay," Múriel sighed disappointedly, "but we really ought to be getting back."

"Nonsense," Catherine interjected, taking her place with the other ladies in the doorway. "We've all been much deprived of each other's company, I shan't hear of you leaving so soon."

"But, Hugo and I are quite tired-"

"And now those dainty fingers of yours need not scrub a single pot or pan. You're welcome." Catherine winked, determined to encourage her friend and the man. "Hugo!" She called out, "We're all having supper, why don't you come in and make yourself at home?"

At first, his frustration with Múriel, mingled with the possibility of being recognised, delayed him. Then at last, when he found no alternative, he walked forward, leading the horse toward the cottage. Nearing the entrance, Catherine instructed him to secure the horse on the edge of the fence nearest the door.

Entering the home, Múriel instantly disappeared off into the corner to chat with Eleanor, leaving Guy to stand and greet the Smith's alone, and feeling somewhat awkward, he stood in the shadows. But such devices would not so easily conceal him. For a man of unsurpassable stature approached him with a friendly handshake. His thick, reddish hair was something wild, his beard was long, and his eyes were blue and merry.

"The name's Cedric," he began, his grip quite firm and tough, "I hear you are a friend of Múriel's?"

"I am," Guy answered, apprehensive.

"And your name?"

"Hugo," he said.

"Well welcome to my home. You know, I've a cousin called Hugo! A blacksmith. He lives quite far north these days; thinks Sherwood isn't quite untamed as he would have it and I'll not disagree. There's nothing better than good quiet country," he said. "By and by, having a Hugo about again is luck indeed, isn't it Catherine?"

"Honestly, if I hear one more word of your cousin," the woman jestfully rolled her eyes, as she brought a large pot of stew to the crowded table. "Never mind him, Hugo, he only wants to tell his tale of how his cousin can sharpen an axe such that one could fell trees with one swing," she teased.

"But he can! It's incredible. Come along," he waved his hand. Without another word, Cedric removed his axe from above the mantle and held it out to Guy. "Go on, I'll wager you've never seen anything like it."

Guy took hold of the tool, admiring the brilliance of the reflection as he ran his finger along the grind, only to accidentally nick his fingertip. Quickly, he licked the cut and returned the axe to Cedric.

"I'll admit, it is rather impressive," he nodded. "How long has it held its edge?"

"If you'll believe me, since last season," the gentleman grinned proudly.

"Now, can we have one evening where weapons aren't discussed at the table?" Catherine smirked at her husband, as she let out a little laugh.

"It's only a weapon if you use it as such," he said.

"La," she rolled her eyes.

Suddenly, three children came bounding into the kitchen, running about in between the two men, shouting and playing, their smiles broad and their freckled cheeks glowing. With all the noise, Catherine's brows flew; one hand firmly planted on her hip and a wooden spoon in the other.

"Ahem," she gently scolded, as the children halted in their footsteps before her. "You can't go mucking about when supper's set, and we've a guest in the house. Now, Hugo," she said, "these are my children. This is Odette, my eldest, only just turned six, and Godric-"

"I'm five!" The little boy smiled up at the man, raising his hand to show his five stubby fingers.

"And this here's our Oliver, not quite three yet," Catherine smiled. Then her eyes grew as a thought emerged. "Múriel," she called across the room, "Would you do the honours? We really haven't had a proper introduction."

A little embarrassed, Múriel found she had left Guy to fend for himself. Presently, she made her way to his side, and thoughtlessly, she took his hand in hers.

"Well, everyone, this is Hugo. And Hugo, as you've already met everyone else, *this* is Eleanor."

"Pleasure to meet you," the man bowed his head, but the lady's expression shone analytical, as she studied his face.

"Delighted," Eleanor muttered, bowing her head slightly.

Then, he remembered. He knew that lass, and how often he had seen her in Nottingham. For the rest of the evening, he made every attempt to avoid any conversation with her. But keeping his thought on Múriel, he wondered how he might gain her confidence again.

Observing her way of telling tales and recalling memories of long ago; her warmth and tenderness toward the children and her willingness to listen to their little stories. It seemed she would never cease to enchant him, yet it was her laugh which delighted his heart most. And how he wished to know her more.

Then, his mind attended the talk about him, stepping back from his secret world, and taking in what words were spoken.

"And it was the first day of warm weather, we couldn't let it go to waste. So, the three of us went round to fetch her, and found she was in the barn milking the cow," Catherine said. "So that's when Robin thought we could catch her by surprise."

"By surprise?" Múriel protested. "You nearly scared me half to death!"

"Oh, 'twas only a bit of fun," Eleanor giggled. "Go on, go on!" She encouraged.

"Right," Catherine continued, "We were all in agreement. Eleanor and I took up some sticks from the edge of the woods and started scraping them along the barn walls, making growling noises while Robin rubbed his face with dirt and tousled his wild hair til it stuck up every which way."

"And that's when he made the signal, and we pushed the barn doors open, and Robin pounced in on all fours growling like a hideous wolf! Grr!" Eleanor bore her teeth as she tickled the children.

"Ah!" Odette shouted and laughed amidst the tickling. "Stop it!"

"But Robin frightened Múriel such that she screamed and startled the cow!" Catherine laughed. "Poor old thing ran straight through the barn, knocking Múriel over the milking stool, the pail of milk spilling everywhere, and she kicked Robin flat on his back!"

"Well, serves him right for being an impish little snot," Múriel chuckled.

"Oh, but you've forgiven us all, haven't you?" Eleanor smiled.

"I suppose I must," she answered jestfully, nudging Eleanor with her elbow.

"Is that why you have a barn? You had a cow?" Guy wondered.

"Well, yes," Múriel began. "We had a cow and calf, and a few goats not so long ago."

"Then, what happened?" He wondered.

"One by one, they were taken away," she said. "When we couldn't meet the sheriff's demands…"

"But Robin bided the sheriff a while, and let us all live free. Good friend, he was," Catherine said, comforting the young lady with a gentle smile.

"I did not know you were acquainted with the Rebel," Guy sighed, staring at Múriel. "You never mentioned it before."

"We were children together," Múriel admitted shyly, "and even that instance was the last I remember of seeing him before he went to war. We all had to grow up sooner or later."

"All of us knew him well," Cedric began, "A good friend he was, no doubt, but if memory serves me right, you weren't spending so much time with him as you were with-" Cedric paused under Múriel's warning glare. Clearing his throat, he started once more. "But, em, we've been laughing over that vinegar story for years. And I'm sure Robin still thinks on it now and then." He leaned back in his chair, stretching his arms up behind his head.

"Robin is everyone's favourite," Odette chimed in cheerfully. "I'm sure you and Robin would make good friends."

Guy's eyes grew heavy. "I doubt that," he murmured.

"Well, bringing those provisions to us, caring for Múriel when she was ill, those are the sorts of things Robin would do," Cedric patted Gisborne on the shoulder.

"That's not the way I see it," he shook his head.

"What do you mean?" Cedric lowered his chin.

"He's nothing more than a common outlaw. Thieving from people with power and property, people of nobility. Stealing away someone's birthright in the name of justice isn't what this country needs."

"And precisely how did you come to these conclusions?" Eleanor glared. "How could you possibly know anything about him?"

"I know he's far too willing to leave people defenceless in dangerous circumstances," he said. "That outlaw is nothing but trouble."

"That's not fair!" Godric pounded his fist upon the table. "You don't know anything about Robin!" His little eyes welled with angry tears.

"Young man, that is no way to speak to a guest," Catherine darted warning eyes toward the lad.

"But he can't say that! Robin's not an outlaw. He's a hero!" Godric stood abruptly, and stomped away from the table, down the corridor.

Catherine only sighed and shook her head. "Suppose I should go after him?"

"Let him alone, Cate. He needs a moment to settle down," Cedric nodded, his elbows propped up on the table. "Now, friend, I'm not sure what you have heard about Robin, but he has done much good," he said; his eyes calm. "You might not know this, but Robin used to be a lord, the Lord of Locksley. He had great power over these lands. Even then, he was humble, and looked after us all, like kin."

"Never proud, never selfish," Catherine whispered.

"When the king went to war in the east, taking our fathers, our brothers, our sons, Robin went, too," Cedric continued. "With so many fighting for king and country, we were left, forgotten. I'm certain you know that well enough. We've all been taxed beyond our means; our lands, our homes, our families, taken... we've had very little to keep us going. Then, Robin returned, and gave up all his glory and riches, for us. Just by his being here, we have hope."

"But leaving all that privilege, to fight another man's battle, he returns and then chooses the life of a criminal? Giving scraps to the poor; looting; thieving... you think that's giving anyone hope?" Guy furrowed his brow.

"If Robin hadn't chosen that life, we would be on the streets," Catherine leaned forward; her eyes intense.

"What do you mean?" Guy wondered.

"This home lies only a mile from Locksley. It's far more a part of the woods than it is a part of the village. Nevertheless, before we lived here, we had a little farm in Locksley. Wasn't much, but just enough to start a family and make an honest living. Then came a day when the sheriff made a dispute against us," Cedric sighed. "Said his new tax collector, who was to take over the manor and all the land after Robin left, would *need* our land. We were forced out of our home, and the sheriff had everything burned down right in front of us. The cottage, the barn, all the crops. Gone. We had nowhere else to turn, and Odette was just an infant at the time. But it was Robin who found us and gave us shelter. Helped me build this very cottage with his bare hands, he did; gave my family food when we had none. We owe Robin everything."

Gisborne sat bewildered, parting his lips a moment as if to respond, yet he could conjure nothing and brought his hand to his temple. All those years, he never understood the damage he created. The Saxons seemed only that; petty commoners who always had an excuse for their empty pockets. Now the very people who had so little gave so freely. And while they were robbed of their home, they were abundant with joy. Guy felt ashamed, and the pang of guilt was difficult to bury.

"Forgive me... I," he gazed downward, shaking his head. "I had no idea."

"Well, if only every village in England had a Robin Hood," Cedric nodded. "And I'd near forgotten how long ago all that was," he smiled at Catherine and took her hand in his.

"Papa, I was a baby when Robin rescued us?" Odette's eyes shone brightly.

"That you were, my little half pint," the gentleman beamed at his daughter.

"You were the tiniest, sweetest little one," Catherine nodded.

"Pff! The tiniest, *loudest* littl'n who never let us sleep!" Cedric's brows raised as he let out a laugh.

At length, the night slowly drew to an end. Guy and Múriel made ready to say their goodbyes, donning their cloaks, and making their farewells to their neighbours.

"Psst," Odette tugged at her cloak. As the maiden knelt down to the little girl's height, Odette whispered something in her ear.

"Go ask your mother," Múriel nodded sweetly.

Gleeful, the little girl ran up to her mother and whispered the same question in her ear. "Of course, love, go on," Catherine said.

As Odette to return to the door, she paused directly before Guy. Quite with the same strong-willed nature of her mother, she placed her hands on her hips, and lowered her chin, her big brown eyes commanding his attention.

"Kneel, please," she instructed. Thus the man obliged and knelt down before her. The little girl then held his face in her hands and placed a kiss on the tip of his nose. "Thank you for bringing the food when Múriel was ill."

"Oh, em," Guy smiled as he stood once more, "You're welcome."

"Bonne nuit, tout le monde. Good night!" The maiden waved, as she and the man departed. "And Eleanor, I hope all goes well at the manor tomorrow."

"Thank you. Farewell!" Eleanor waved, still eyeing Gisborne suspiciously.

Having mounted the horse once more, the man and the maiden journeyed deep into the forest once more; bound for home.

***

Once the children had gone to bed, and Cedric had set off for bed as well, Catherine and Eleanor remained in the kitchen a while, and made a spot of tea.

"You've been rather quiet tonight," Catherine said, "Is everything alright?"

The lady stared down a moment, finding what words to say. "No," she said, "there's something I don't quite like about Hugo. I fear he's not to be trusted."

"Now if this is for his first comment about Robin, you ought to show him some grace," the woman said. "He couldn't have known that Robin isn't the ruffian the rest of England makes him out to be. He's only just arrived."

"But arrived from where? All Múriel said is that he is a traveller from the north," Eleanor said.

"And why should that trouble you? Be he as northern as you like, I found him quite agreeable," the woman answered.

"I found him secretive," Eleanor grumbled, setting her cup down firmly upon the table. "He's no history, no connections save Aldred... you cannot deny, that is quite odd."

"He met Aldred?" Catherine wondered, "Did Múriel tell you what his thoughts were on the man?"

"Only they got on well," the lady said.

"Then if the old sage has already judged his character in good light, so should we," Catherine resolved. "Think, he brought provisions to a strange family in the woods while Múriel had fallen ill, even cared for her until she was recovered. If that's odd, then I'll not dare think what you judge as normal."

"Acts of kindness are all very well, but there's something about him... he seems familiar, and not in a good way."

"You think him to be some outlaw? One of ill repute?"

"He certainly resembles someone of ill repute."

"Who then?"

"Sir Guy of Gisborne."

A chill air filled the room.

"Him?" Catherine whispered, glancing behind her to be sure none could hear her. "Hugo looks nothing like that blackguard. And even if he reminds you of the Norman, let's not pit one devilish man's sins against him, only because he resembles the former."

"No, no, you don't understand," Eleanor shook her head, "I don't feel so uneasy about him because he *resembles* Sir Guy."

"Then what?"

Eleanor said nothing, but with her dark eyes did stare back at the woman, and Catherine knew her thought.

"How can you think such a horrid thing?" She frowned.

"Cate, I served at the castle, under Rothgar. And Sir Guy was always present at court. It might have been near a year ago, but I couldn't forget that face or that voice."

"And though its been years, I've not forgotten the face of the man who took our home from us, be certain of that," Catherine said. "And despite all your assumptions, it's impossible. That beast was thrown in prison, and pronounced dead by Lady Claudia months ago."

"Truly?" Eleanor's brows raised in disbelief. "Why?"

Catherine nodded solemnly, "He was sentenced to starve to death in the prisons for murdering the sheriff, long before you returned."

"He murdered the sheriff?"

"Shocked all of us," the woman drank from the cup. "Perhaps, only a *very little*, I can see how you might think Hugo resembles Sir Guy... but that is no reason to accuse him of anything. We might not know the whole story, but Múriel does. And if we know anything of our dear friend, she would never keep company with some bloodthirsty Norman. We're terrible friends to speak like this, anyhow."

"I suppose you're right," Eleanor sighed, staring at the steam rising from the cup in her hand.

The two women sat a while in silence, watching the fire blaze on, the crackling of the wood bursting, and little embers like starlight blinking.

Though not another word on the subject was spoken, Eleanor still harboured a warning feeling and a secret dread.

CHAPTER FOURTEEN

PERSEVERANCE

Glistening, the stars twinkled high above the quiet cottage, and the radiant moon softly lit the tips of every blade of grass across the field.

How gently the breeze stirred the branches, how pleasant the refrain of the night, and how cool the air sang about them, as the man and the maiden ventured homeward. While the world about them felt so tranquil and free, their journey fared a little less than civil. For neither one had spoken a single word, though each had their share of things to say; not withholding in anger but in worry.

Approaching the barn, Múriel dismounted immediately. Landing with a thud on the ground, she quickly pulled at the edge of her hood to hide her face and kept her back turned to the man. Without so much as a word or a glance, she began to walk toward the cottage.

"Múriel?" Guy called, leading the horse into the barn. "Until tomorrow?"

Looking back, she only nodded in response. Then, turning away again, she hastened her pace toward the door. Yet before her fingers could touch the handle, Guy's hand gripped her arm.

"You'll not bid me *goodnight*?" He sighed.

"The hour is late and-"

"Will you not spend a while with me? Even a little while?" He wondered; his eyes set on her hand as his breath tensed.

Silent and stern, Múriel remained; her hand clenched into a fist at her side. Then, dropping her shoulders, she sighed and let her fingers fall. "Bien," she replied. "A little while."

Gently taking her hand in his, Guy led her back to the garden, and released her touch as she followed. The harvest moon sailed overhead in the clear autumn night, its light cascading over them and making shadows as they passed. Standing by the well, he waited for her, and timid as she was, the lady took her place beside him. For a moment, the two stood in the stillness, listening to the symphony of the woodland eve. Then, finally, the man spoke.

"Are you angry with me?" He said, his hands set on the edge of the well.

"How can you think I am angry with you?"

"I've asked something of you, something important... yet you have given me no answer," he said. "Now, returning home, you cast me out again."

"I've not cast you out," she shook her head.

"Tell me once and for all, what have I done that you spurn my regard? That you wound me thus?"

"Wound you? But I... please, if anything I've done has caused you to feel as if that is my intention, I beg your forgiveness. I've many things to consider, many thoughts weighing on my mind-"

"And I cannot know them unless you tell me," he said, taking her hands in his and glancing down at her once more. "Please, tell me."

Turning her face away, Múriel stared over the garden as the wind whipped the strands of her hair across her cheek. Gathering her words together, she slowly drew her gaze back up at him. His eyes like the frosted skies of a winter morning; cold and craving.

"Guy, there is something you need to understand, something I've not spoken of to anyone," she said.

"What is it?"

"Long ago... a very long time ago, I fell in love," she sighed. "He was kind and brave, a good friend and a fighter," the maiden smiled contemplatively. "He had my heart, though he didn't know it. One night, I went to see him. He was making ready to leave his home, to... well, he was leaving for his own reasons. I couldn't bear the thought of him leaving and did plead with him not to; even more so, I couldn't bear the thought of him not knowing. When I finally found the courage to tell him how I felt, he told me England was his only love, and there was no place in his heart for me. The next day, he had gone."

"But this man, he, encouraged you?"

"No, not really. Or, at least, he had not meant to," she said.

The man ran his fingers through his hair, as he thought, and let out a deep breath. "A'Dale."

Múriel's face went pale. "How did you-"

"Why else would you have gone to him for help?" He shook his head, a flame of anger and betrayal in his eyes. "Why else would he have been so willing?"

"*He* discovered me that night! *He* was the one who had followed me, for his own reasons, and if there was any chance of saving you-"

"Do you still love him?"

"No! No, that was so long ago," she answered.

"Then why tell me any of this?"

"Because you need to see why I must guard my heart-"

"Guard your heart? Have I given you any reason to doubt my sincerity? Are any of my words or deeds cheapened by some infidelity?"

"No," she said. "If I've failed to speak my mind, then pardon me, and know now that I hold you in the highest regard."

"Múriel, I have toiled so to prove myself. I am not a perfect man and have confessed to you of my past. Even still, there is more I would confess, but I fear you will never accept it if you have already rejected me," he said.

"I would never reject you," she said, placing her hand on his arm. "You know how I care for you, such that you need not indulge any ceremony and speak freely whatever you wish."

"How can I when you have lost faith in me?"

"But I've not lost any faith in you," she insisted.

"Then why must you torment me? If I've done nothing to make you angry with me and your heart does not belong to another, will you give me no answer?" Guy grasped the lady's shoulders, staring hard at her silver eyes. "I believed you had died in my arms. Can you yet comprehend what I've faced?" He choked back his tears.

Though Múriel's heart pounded within her, through trembling lips she spoke, "You must understand, I declared my love to someone who turned me away. I admitted my feelings to myself, and to him, at the wrong time. I loved too much, and by such was my heart taken from me!"

"I would never turn you away. And I would never take from you anything that I would not be willing to give of myself," Guy resolved. "Do you not know that you already have my heart?"

"And if you had my heart... what would you do with it?"

"I would cherish it as my very own," he proclaimed; his eyes so earnest as he held her face. "But I'll not take it, nor look on it, save you offer it to me of your own desire."

"But... I must be certain of my feelings," she pressed her hand over her heart. "All I ask of you is that you give me the time I need."

As he held her face, he closed his eyes, resting his forehead against hers. "Yes, I'll wait," he promised.

They remained a time, their foreheads touching as he brushed away a tear upon her cheek. Tenderly, he laid a kiss on the crown of her head. Then, a gentle hand took hold of his, as the maiden's eyes gazed upward.

"Come," she said, drawing him away from the well, down upon the green. As he sat beside her, she swept away a lock of his hair. "Close your eyes," she whispered.

While he felt unsure, he closed his eyes and waited. Gently, the maiden placed a kiss upon his bearded cheek; her touch so lovely, he loathed the parting. Yet, a hopefulness contented his zealous heart. He would not command the rose to bloom but would wait eagerly ere the sun's rising would soon call it to waken.

Returning to the door of the cottage, hand in hand, he gazed into her bright grey eyes once more.

"Múriel, I still need to know. When you were... when you said that I would always be in your heart, did you truly mean it?"

"Oui," the lady glanced up at him. "I meant every word."

Guy beamed down at her, the breeze rustling through his dark waves. Bringing his hand up to her cheek, he drew his thumb down her jawline, and resting his hand under her chin, he beheld her beauty.

"Until tomorrow, my darling."

"Jusqu'à demain," Múriel smiled, as she closed the door behind her.

Withdrawing to the barn, the man resented laying in the loft. How strange it felt. He had grown so accustomed to sleeping by her side, yet, while he had the brooch in his possession, he held it longingly against his heart; a heart that in every way belonged to her.

As Múriel retreated to her bedchamber, she felt such an unquenchable yearning for his presence. The chamber felt quite empty, and all that night, she thought on what words she had spoken, and if only she had the courage to say more. All she desired was to be with him. Looking out through her window, she perceived him resting in the hayloft; his arms folded behind his head, and his legs stretched before him.

Múriel wished with all her might to fly across the night to his side, yet to watch him sleep so peacefully was enough in that moment. For in her dreaming, she was not so far from his touch.

***

Days had passed.

As the weather grew colder, the sun hung shrouded behind grey skies. Winter was fast approaching. Still, there was warmth to be had, for each evening, Múriel started the fire a little sooner and fed the flames a little longer, so Guy would linger until the final embers faded. Only the height of the moon harkened him back to the barn. All the while, he knew the maiden's thought in her subtle suggestions to stay by the fire, and how his heart was allayed, for she did wish for his company as he did long for hers. And he knew, whatever befall, her heart would not stray from him.

Late one evening, when all daylight had vanished behind the forest, and the work of the day was finished, Guy remained in the barn, brushing the horse's coat; thinking. For something grave was on his mind, biting at his conscience. Over and over, he knew he must say something; and night after night the man had let it pass and forgotten until he lay his head down to rest. Again, the thought came, and would not loosen its harrowing grip. Once spoken, he would be free of it. He dare not let it wait.

Suddenly, the barn door creaked open; there the maiden stood with blankets piled in her arms, breathing out in vapours against the chill night air. "I thought you might need these," Múriel smiled, as she hung the blankets one by one over the rungs of the ladder. "I'll set them here for now, and perhaps if you're settled, would you care to warm up by the fire a bit?" She wondered.

He made no answer.

Guy could hardly look at her, but staring at the brush in his hand he paused in his work, as the maiden drew nearer.

"What's the matter?" She asked, pulling her shawl tighter about her shoulders. "Guy, what's wrong?"

After a moment of silence, the man could no longer contain himself. "There was a child," he whispered; his jaw tense.

"I don't understand," the lady said as her eyes grew heavy.

"I've not told you everything," he said, gripping the brush firmly in his hand until his knuckles shone white. "I've not been honest about my past with Marian."

The maiden's face flushed pale, and her heart raced within her, fearing to hear his words. "You... you mean to say you seduced her?"

"No, I never knew her. Let me explain," he shook his head, setting down the brush. "When I told you of my past with Marian, I did not... when she was sentenced to death, it was in part for her treason, for her alliance with the Rebel," he paused, rubbing at the bridge of his nose.

"And what of this *child*?" Múriel pressed, her breath hastening.

"She had wed the outlaw, and at length, she had confided in me of their circumstances," he sighed. "She told me of the child the morning before her fate was sealed."

In silence, the maiden stood; her brows furrowed as she stared back at the man. "And still, you willingly condemned her and her child to death? Have you no heart?"

"Múriel, please," Guy sighed, drawing near her, though she stepped back from him. "I had no choice."

"Why do you tell me this now?" Her eyes stared fierce. "Why did you not confess it all when I had met with you in the dungeons?"

"Do you not remember how you found me? I feared you would only despise me further," he said, "but you taught me that what I once was, is finished; I need no longer bear the weight of it. You gave me this hope. Therefore, I only wish now to begin anew with everything, and have given my word to Aldred that I'll keep no secrets from you-"

"Aldred knew of this?" Her eyes widened. "All this time you've been here, you did not think to tell me, but you would first speak with some old man?"

"He had confronted me the morning you were healed and bid me tell you."

"So you confess this now because you have been threatened," she grumbled. "Did you ever think to tell me this of your own accord? If Aldred had not spoken with you, would you have ever come to me?"

Silent, he stared, then lowered his eyes. "Múriel," he sighed, "trusting in what we have been and how... how I care for you, I thought-"

"What other secrets have you kept from me? How many more were slain by your hand?"

"I've kept nothing from you save this, I swear," he petitioned. "You know of my past, in full. And you know of who I am now."

"No," she whispered, "no, I do not know who you are."

Dismayed, her eyes brimmed as she stepped farther and farther away, until her back hit against the barn door, and she fled into the night.

"Múriel! Wait!" He called, but just as he neared the entrance, his feet pounding against the earth, the maiden had vanished into the cottage.

And the door slammed shut.

***

The cold dawn shone thin through the cracks of the wall, its pale hues waking the man from his reckless sleep.

Breathing deep the frosty air, he descended from the hayloft, lifting the hood of his cloak as he paced across the way. Opening the barn door, he resolved to speak with the maiden, for his heart ached at her disdain, and he could not bear that she thought so ill of him. Gazing out, the man saw smoke swirling up from the chimney and a soft glow from within glimmering through the panes. But when he had approached the cottage, there at the threshold was a bowl of cold porridge, a simple wooden spoon, and a cup of water.

"Múriel," he called as he tapped his knuckles against the door. "Please... will you not let me in? Will you not speak with me?"

Waiting, he listened.

Nothing.

He could hear no crackling of the fire, nor any evidence of her, yet he felt her presence; and how it pained him. There he remained for a time, staring at the door. And when his stomach demanded that he give in, so he did. Taking up the food, he ate until his hunger was satisfied. Then, drawing to the garden, he took up water from the well, cleaned the cup and the bowl and the wooden spoon, and set them all neatly back at the threshold where he had found them.

All day he chopped firewood as he let the horse roam free across the field, and all day it seemed the maiden kept to the house. Every so often, he thought he heard a door open, and surely, the sound of footsteps thudding toward the hen house. Then he stopped to listen and stare but found nothing. Again, he returned to his work, with numbing fingers, and a weary heart. At even-fall, he piled the kindling up in the barn and led the horse inside, and the whole of the day felt as a void.

Howling, the winds blew across the forest, and cut through what linens he wore. Even the woollen cloak did not break the wind's harsh cries. Shivering, he went to the door of the cottage again. Yet before his rough hands could knock against the door, he looked down at the threshold and found his supper; peas pottage, a small loaf of bread, and a cup of cold ale.

Crestfallen, the man lifted his hand as if to knock and found no strength to do it. And what hunger he had felt, he had no wish to satisfy, though his stomach wailed against him. Still, he must try. Sitting by the door, he pressed his back up against the wood and felt some warmth, though it was little. In the unforgiving solitude, he ate every morsel, and when he had finished, he trudged back to the well. Again he washed the bowl and the spoon and the cup, but his fingers were raw and his palms sore. Tearing away at the corner of his tunic, he took the strips of cloth and bound it around his hands. Returning to the cottage, he set the dishes at the threshold, and could not bear parting from that door. Again he stood, his breath as mist before his face, his feet firmly planted, and his eyes strained as he waited.

Then, when it had seemed much of the night had yet passed, and the cold must drive him back to the barn, the door opened. Múriel stood with her cloak about her shoulders and a lantern in her hand, startled as her eyes met his. Moments passed as she stared at the dark cloaked figure before her; his eyes which caught the moonlight, glowing dim and hollow.

"I know I deserve nothing," he whispered. "But can I not beg your forgiveness?"

Finally, and without a word, the maiden set down the lantern and embraced him, her head pressed against his chest as he held her.

"You've not wronged me," she whispered, stepping back to look up at him.

"But I have caused you to find a grievous fault in me such that you think me heartless and have scorned me. That I cannot endure," he said. "Please, grant me a moment by your side, that I might restore my honour."

Nodding, the maiden led him into the cottage, and there they remained by the fire, watching the flames dance and the kindling burn. The little house was quiet and calm and still, but the man's mind would give him no rest. And at length, he revealed what thought he could lend, and all his lament over the fate of the lady.

"It was then, I knew nothing would not free me of it," he said; his eyes upon the fire. "I remember when they took her body down, and I saw her face…" Covering his own face in his hand, he closed his eyes.

Gently, Múriel took his right hand in hers, and held it fast; her eyes full of sorrow. "Forgive me, I did not know," she whispered. "Je suis désolé."

"Comprenez vous? Voulez-vous me faire confiance à nouveau?" He entreated, turning to look on her with such despair. "Avez-vous perdu vos soins pour moi?"

"I know your heart," she answered. "And I will always hold it dear."

Without another word, she threw her arms about his neck; his heart pounding as he held her. For a time, they simply held on to each other, and what tears he let fall in silence, the maiden felt them on her shoulder. And when all had seemed mended, and she brushed away his tears, the maiden encouraged him to stay a while longer, by the fire. And he accepted.

They spoke of their day apart from each other, and the emptiness of it. And how each had waited and even sought to find the other, and how each was too complacent to break any door down, though each felt such want for it. Only when the final embers had died did the man bid her goodnight according to their fashion, and she, in turn, spoke the words he craved to hear, that he would surely see her tomorrow. For both had firmly agreed, such a day as this would never be let passed again.

***

At length, autumn drew to an end.

The trees once adorned with vibrant leaves shed its hues to reveal bare branches. No snow had graced the world below, yet the icy air foretold of the frosted days to come.

Guy and Múriel continued on, caring for the cottage and for each other, and there was still much to be done in preparation for winter. Though he insisted other measures be taken, the chickens were most unfortunately returned to the barn, and so every morning he awoke to all their irksome cries. Still, he managed. And each day, Guy set out hunting what game was left to find while Múriel worked in the garden and the kitchen, gathering what little food could still be gleaned from the cold earth and preparing everything for the larder.

Early that morning, when breakfast was finished, Guy took up a warmer cloak, and the brooch the lady had given him lay clasped at his shoulder. As the young lady waved farewell from the kitchens, the man marched toward the door, ready to begin the day's work. Standing in the entrance, he halted, the door barely shut behind him. There he lingered, and as the maiden thought he'd gone, she began to hum a merry tune and twirled about the kitchen. Graceful, her locks swayed about her, and her soothing voice warmed the whole home. Even in the smallest moments, the simplest moments, he was enthralled by her spirit.

Reluctant, Guy quietly closed the door and awaited the chilling realm beyond. With supplies in his pack and an axe in hand, he set off into the forest. For hours, he gathered wood, binding the kindling together with lengths of twine and leaving portions at the ends so he might sling the bundles over his shoulder. By and by, the sun began to set, and the man was swift to gather together everything he had. As he walked through the shadowing woods, he stopped and hid the bundles of firewood beneath a pile of fallen leaves. He was careful to cover everything and mark the spot by placing three stones before the mound. Seizing his opportunity, he departed from Sherwood, ever onward toward the road, and so sought to carry out his secret errand.

It was dark when he had completed his quest.

By moonlight and the luck of his step, he returned to the mound. Having gathered the firewood, he ventured home. Along the winding way, he scolded himself for not having brought the horse, and so resolved that on any subsequent expeditions, he would be certain to take it. High above the forest, the stars did shine as the man passed through the elder trees. All the while, he thought on the roaring fire, the good food, and the lovely maiden who waited patiently for him. As he finished storing the firewood in the barn, he walked briskly toward the cottage. His fingers bitterly cold, and almost numb.

Suddenly, Múriel burst forth, with freshly laundered blankets in her arms.

"You've come home!" She gave him a look of surprise and relief, "I thought you would be back by supper."

"Oh, forgive me, em, I lost track of the hour," he fumbled, rubbing at the back of his neck.

"C'est bon," the lady sighed. "There's some pottage left for you; it should still be warm. Go inside and eat! I've only to cover the horse and leave some blankets in the hayloft. I'll not have you going cold."

"No indeed," he grinned. "But you've done so much as it is; allow me."

"Merci, but I've already eaten, and I'll be quick enough. Go in, go in!" The lady insisted as she continued toward the barn.

"Very well. I'll see you inside then," he nodded.

Entering the cottage, the scents of thyme and rosemary and sage filled his lungs and made his mouth water. Presently, he removed his cloak, took up a bowl, and served himself from whatever was kept out. At the table, there was a loaf of bread before him and a cup of hot ale. After a while of satisfying his raging hunger and thirst, he noticed something.

The stillness.

In that very instant, he heard her scream.

Vigilant, Guy leapt to his feet and swung the door open to find Múriel by the entrance of the barn, her simple dagger in hand against a pack of wolves who bore their fangs, snarling as they corned her. From where the man stood, he saw five in all. Four fared near three feet tall, and the fifth, a gruesome grey brute who stood above the rest. A glint of moonlight reflected on their jagged teeth, and their breath whirled as smoke out of their hungry mouths. Múriel stepped farther away, finally hitting her back against the barn door. Thinking quickly, the man took up a torch and staff, then marched forth; ready.

"Whoa!" He shouted, gaining the packs' attention as he drew closer. "Múriel, get inside," he said.

"But I-"

"When you have a clear path, get inside."

Guy kept his eyes on the wolves, moving closer and rounding about to deflect their attention from the maiden so she could escape. "Now!" He cried.

She could hardly move for fright, but as she attempted to retreat, a wolf had marked her and dashed in her direction. Suddenly the wolf was upon her, its large jaw snapping. But regaining her stance, Múriel threw her fist against the wretched creature's snout and cut across its ear with her dagger. Whimpering, the hound comforted its injury with a thin paw, as it retreated.

Eager to ambush the man, the rest of the pack had advanced. Pacing farther and farther across the field, Guy lured the wolves away from Múriel, and every hair on his head stood on end with each step taken. As each made its attempt to bite, he wielded the staff, hitting one in the snout then turning about to face another with the flames of the torch. Persistent, the wolves growled and grunted as they began to circle about the man; their green eyes grim as they followed. The beasts were tireless in their raid, each making a strike against him. Then, the leader of the pack seized his moment, and lunged forward; his sharp claws stretched and his ravenous mouthing gaping.

"No!" Múriel cried, as the hound bit into Guy's left arm.

Groaning, the man faltered, yet he was determined to protect Múriel at any cost. Retrieving the dagger from his side, he stabbed the wretched creature's eye, the fearsome leader now loosening its grip and howling in pain. Resolute, the maiden ran after Guy. Picking up the staff once more, she fought against the wolves, as the man regained his footing and wielded his dagger against their foes. Finally, the pack whimpered in defeat, running back bloody and breathless into the thickness of the night, as the sound of their cries all but faded into the silence. Panting and bleeding in the bitter cold, the man knelt, grasping his left arm as the blood trickled over his rough fingers.

"We need to get inside," Múriel said, aiding him up.

Though the walk was slow, they finally returned to the safety of the cottage. Guy lumbered to the table, the blood dripping across the floor.

"Rest here," she said.

Múriel flew into the kitchen and in a few short moments returned with some clean cloths and some herbs. A pot of water was quickly hung over the fire, and she made use of it as soon as she could.

"The wounds must be cleaned before I can create a poultice," she said. "Remove your tunic."

The man stood, attempting with one arm to remove it, though he only winced in pain, and mumbled something harsh under his breath.

"Here, let me help you," the lady assured.

Cautiously, she guided his arms out of the sleeves and brought the garment over his head, and lay the bloodstained tunic on the table. For just a moment, Múriel took in the shock of his wounds. He was covered in blood, with a savage bite mark on his forearm; countless gashes and scrapes scattered across his chest, back, and shoulder. Quickly, the lady dipped a cloth in the warm water and carefully pressed them against the wounds. Guy held his breath at each touch, trying to hold back from the pain.

"I'm so sorry," the lady sighed. "This is all my fault."

"No. It's not your- Ah!" He cried as she cleaned the wound on his arm.

"I'm sorry!"

"No, you have to do it, just be quick," he said; his eyes tightly shut, and his fists clenched. Opening his eyes briefly, he discovered a cut across her cheek, and the blood falling down her face. "Múriel," he managed, "You're hurt."

"I know. Shh," she scolded, using the hem of her sleeves to wipe away the blood on her face. "It's only a scratch, I'll be alright," she nodded, as she delicately applied a salve to the wounds on his chest and shoulder.

"Must you use this?" He winced.

"This is the only way to ensure the wounds heal properly."

"Very well, if you must," Guy acquiesced, taking in a deep breath before she began again; his temper growing unsteady. Though he had restrained himself thus far, finally, he could bear it no more.

"Enough woman!" He roared savagely, clenching her arm tight in his right hand, and his eyes something fierce, and wild, and fiery. Then returning to his true self, his eyes went from fury to shame, releasing her and realising how frightened she was.

Her anxious eyes stared hard at him, as she stepped back, "I'm only trying to help."

"Forgive me," he dropped his shoulders. "I should not have shouted at you."

The lady nodded and let out a sigh. "Then, may I continue?"

"Of course," he said, as she drew near him once more. Tightly shutting his eyes with tensed breath, he waited, as Múriel applied the herbs to his arm. "Oh, would that the damned thing had no fangs at all!" He grumbled, throwing his head back so that the tendons of his throat stood out. Lowering his head down again, he took in another deep breath.

"Would that none of them had come in the first place," she added, "But, you are not angry with me, are you?"

"I'm angry because I should have brought the blankets to the barn in your stead, and spared you from any of this," he said, as she bound the cloth around his forearm. "It was foolishness on my part, and I've paid for it."

"What you did was courageous, and I'll never forget it," she encouraged. "When I needed you, you came, just as when you needed me, so I came. You must see that we *both* are in need of each other."

Guy thought on her words and nodded in agreement.

"You're right. I need you just as you need me," he said, permitting a little smile while she finished binding his arm in the long strip of cloth. Gazing upon her with such longing, he brought his right hand to her chin, lifting her face to meet his, "But I'd not be able to live with myself if any harm came to you," he said. "I love you too dearly."

"What," Múriel whispered. Her eyes glanced up in amazement, her face blushing madly as her heart raced within her.

"Forgive me, I know you wished for more time, but I cannot wait another minute," he admitted. Though still in great pain, gallantly he moved to kneel before her. "Múriel," he said, "I was consumed by the darkness of my life, by such emptiness. Yet you were brave enough to find me and give me hope. I never thought I would come to know such love, or kindness, or compassion, as you have so lavished upon me," he paused, taking another breath to retreat from the pain. Revealing a ring from his pocket, he held it before her. "Will you be my wife?"

Astonishment halted her words, and all she could manage in that moment was a bright smile, as blissful tears welled in her moon grey eyes.

"Je t'aime de tout mon coeur... Oui! Yes!"

As they stood, he wrapped his right arm tightly around her waist, the maiden clasping his endearing face in her hands. Overjoyed, he pressed his lips against hers. It was a kiss, unlike any other kiss. A kiss as to surpass all others.

Resting his forehead against hers, he sighed in such pleasure, his smile broad, and his heart so full. "I was wishing you would say yes," he whispered.

"I could never refuse you," Múriel said as she kissed him once more, her fingers entangled in his locks. Pulling back, Guy placed the ring upon her finger; a silver band engraved with intricate floral etchings.

"This was my mother's ring," he held her hand, gazing upon her so affectionately. "It suits you perfectly, my darling."

"It's beautiful," she smiled, admiring the ring.

It was then that Múriel saw out of the corner of her eye, his clenched fist trembling. His knuckles white, and the tendons of his hands raised. "Guy, are you alright?"

"Well, I'm still in pain," he answered, "but that doesn't matter now."

The maiden saw how he tried to compose himself, yet his affliction was evident.

"Perhaps, you can sleep here tonight," she thought. "Stay here by the fire. I want to be sure you'll be alright."

The man nodded in acceptance and smiled.

"I'll just go fetch some more blankets, and a clean tunic," she grinned, retreating up the stairs.

There, he awaited her, before the blazing fire. The crackling of the wood, the red flames rising, and the faint music of the night filled the room with such peacefulness. As she returned to his side, she laid the blankets upon the floor, and in her hands, she held up a tunic, of simple, light blue linen.

"Come," she said.

Lovingly, the man gazed upon her, as she drew the garment over his form. "What do you think?" He asked, standing back with playful brows raised.

"Very handsome," Múriel sweetly concluded, laughing a little. "The colour makes your eyes look... enchanting."

Guy stepped forward, and brought his finger under her chin, "*Your* eyes are enchanting," he whispered in her ear; his lips brushing against her skin and his hand in hers, as he laid a kiss upon her cheek.

Múriel stood besotted. His words so sincere, and his touch so inviting. Blushing, she tucked a lock of hair behind her ear, trying desperately to find her mind again.

"We- we should retire for the night," she began. "It is growing late."

"Very well, my darling," he brought her hand to his lips, placing a kiss upon it. "But please, stay with me a little while longer?" His eyes begged.

"A little while," she sighed, her mind chiding her passionate heart.

Pacing backwards, he grinned, leading her with him to lounge upon the floor. As he lay down, the lady remained by his side.

"Múriel, you have made me the happiest man," he sighed, drawing her near to kiss her lips once more.

The maiden brought her arms about his neck, drawing him deeper into their kiss. Pulling back, she caressed his bearded cheek as they laughed softly.

"When was it that you first loved me?" She wondered.

"When you sang to me. When you sang *with* me," the man sweetly closed his eyes a moment, remembering. "That was when I first loved you," he said. His eyes drew her in with such affection, her heart nearly burst for joy. Gazing upon her beauty, he stroked her long hair, a question lingering upon his lips. "Would you..." he began, "Would you sing to me, as you did so long ago?"

"Of course, my love," she smiled in response.

Her eyes as purest silver shone and her voice as the melodies of the clearest waters poured forth as she sang to him. While she sang and stroked his hair, all his cares melted away, falling under her spell into the realm of sleep; though as he slept, his dream was of something wild and waring.

> Under restless waves of the sea, he was tossed,
> drowning in the deeps of a storm.
> What sky his eyes could perceive hung dark, and grim, and grey;
> the rain and thunder, baleful and foreboding. Then, as he cried out
> below the waves, someone heeded his call and lifted him from the
> depths. Suddenly, Guy was on the shore; the storm ceaseless.
> Before him, stood a man of great stature, donned in a dark cloak,
> and fastened at the neck of the cloak, was a golden brooch.
> Guy could not see the man's face clearly, for his eyes were
> shrouded under his hood; only the end of his nose and jaw could
> be seen. Drawing nearer the cloaked man, Guy sought to discover
> what face lay beneath it. As he lifted the hood, he uncovered the
> face of a man with long, golden hair; his grieving eyes a piercing
> blue. For but a moment the face remained, a face he knew not, and
> yet somehow found it familiar. Then as Guy blinked, the man's face
> vanished entirely and took the face of his observer. Shuttering in
> fear and bewilderment, he stepped back, as the haunting of his
> very own face upon the figure stared hard at him. Then, as it
> placed a hand upon his shoulder, the phantom whispered,
> "Remember, my son. Remember."

Breathless, Guy awoke.

His heart pounded madly beneath his chest, as he sat straight up, panting. Searching about, Múriel was nowhere to be found; nought but the low burning embers of the fire were there to console him, for she must have retired long before. As he sat, staring at the embers, he knew not what to make of this nightmare and thought back to his encounter with the white stag, for it too implored him to remember.

What must I remember? What have I forgotten? He thought.

Unravelling every detail of his dream, he could not help but let his thoughts run ever after his darling Múriel. Craving her presence, he wished to hold up in his hand her brooch, to admire it as he did so many nights before. Yet, his pocket was empty.

Where is it? Where did I- oh! The cloak! He recalled.

There, his own cloak hung upon the wall, yet he searched the garment to no avail. The brooch was not there. Frantic, he pushed himself, though his arm was still in considerable pain, searching every avenue where the brooch could have fallen. He swept across the floor, retraced all his previous steps; he rattled his mind over and over again. A sudden creak from upstairs startled him, halting his mission as he paused in his pursuit; the lady could not know. When no further sound was made, he began pacing back and forth, back and forth.

It was there as I went to the woods, and there as I finished my work, and there as I... wait... that noise.
Claudia!

CHAPTER FIFTEEN

AN UNEXPECTED TREASURE

Contented, Eleanor concluded her tasks for the day.

Every chamber was empty, every cupboard was closed, and she alone ensured all was in order as the day drew to an end. All work about the manor felt free and easy when Lady Claudia had departed for Nottingham, for she did endlessly demand whatever her mind fancied and did so most unreasonably. And this was the final night of ease, as the woman was due to arrive by the morning. All the same, the lass made use of her time, enjoying the stillness of the night. As she passed down the quieted corridors, a single candle within her hand against the darkness, she stopped amidst her steps for she heard something peculiar. A quick and heavy thud echoed from Lady Claudia's bedchamber.

Eleanor turned about and stood motionless. her ears discerning everything and her breath steady. Harrowing, other strange sounds followed, as she heard the creaking of a door opening and then shutting abruptly.

Resolved and irrefutably bold, the lady moved steadily back towards the bedchamber. Observing a decorative spear hanging upon the wall, and cunning as she was, the lady took it down, now armed to face the blackguard. Nearer and nearer the chamber she drew, the candle set on the floor as she let her senses lead her through the darkness. How the sense of danger, the thought of the unknown excited her.

At the door she paused, calculating how she would hold the upper hand and overcome the thief. Without any warning, the lass then kicked open the door; spear in hand.

Roaring madly, she sprinted with all speed and vigour into the chamber. During her raid, something weighty fell to the ground; clanking. She stopped. Though she saw no one, the lady could sense a presence.

"Listen well," she called, her heart pounding fast, "I know you're here. There's no use hiding!"

No answer.

Only the whisper of the wind through the open window met her ears. As the lady searched about the chamber, there was no sign of an intruder. No furniture unturned and seemingly nothing out of place save an open chest and a box left on the floor amongst the scattered jewellery. This kept the young lady distracted long enough for the thief, who hid well, to sprint toward the open window. Instantly, what caught Eleanor's eye was the waving of his cloak and his considerable stature, as he withdrew and fled from the manor.

"Stop, thief!" She cried.

Yet as she reached the window, throwing back the drapes, the thief had vanished out into the night, and she could not see where the man had gone. Moreover, no guards were present to hear her calls for aid. Turning back into the dark room, she huffed angrily.

Returning to the corridor to regain her candle, she replaced the spear, and upon retrieving the candle, she turned into the chamber again to search about for what may have been stolen. As she stepped through, she then discovered what had made that odd noise when she had first entered the chamber. There, upon the floor, by the foot of the bed, was a silver brooch.

The lady took up the peculiar trinket, then upon a better view under the light of the candle, she immediately recognised it.

Múriel... but why? She thought.
Surely no, the thief couldn't have been...
too broad-shouldered; too lofty; a man undoubtedly.

As the lady pondered all this, suddenly a familiar voice boomed from the doorway.

"Eleanor!" Nan called, bustling into the chamber with a candle in hand, donned in her simple night apparel and cap. "I heard a cry such that set death to my eyes! What's the matter?"

The young lady made no answer but hastily tucked the treasure in her sleeve before she faced the old woman.

"A thief broke in. I couldn't catch him-"

"A thief! Oh, bless, and you thought you would catch him! That's a bit of thick-thinking if you ask me. What if he had a weapon and attacked you? Good gracious," the old woman shuttered.

"I'm quite fine, Nan," the lady comforted. "But we must make certain nothing's missing."

"Oh, very well, very well," Nan mumbled, rolling up one sleeve after the other. "Mind, I'll not have you do something so rash again!" She shook her finger. "No lass in this manor should face some bleeding burglar when we've enough guards to fell a lion."

"Let's get to work, then?" Eleanor asked.

"Aye, let's," the old woman said. Squinting her eyes, she began inspecting the chamber.

"Now, all that was left open was this one chest of garments, but I think our thief was after the jewellery. Look," Eleanor pointed to the treasures haphazardly strewn upon the floor.

"The scoundrel! Didn't you call down to the guards to stop him?"

"Of course, but none of them marked me," the lady replied. "But the blackguard couldn't have made away with much, do you think?"

"I do hope you're right," Nan sighed. "But, we must check everything. I'll wager the contemptible raggabrash was at least half clever. Them's the ones that get you; the clever ones you weren't expecting to be clever," Nan pursed her lips.

The two ladies sought through every inch of the chamber. The chest, the armoire, the cupboards; nothing was neglected. Anything a thief could wish to pinch was taken into account, and finally, when all seemed quite sorted, everything was set back in its proper place. It appeared to them, every tempting thing imaginable was still there. As the final piece of jewellery was returned to the box, Nan let out a sigh of relief.

"Well, 'tis good to know nothing of value has been taken. Well done, lass!" She grinned, "I think your shooing away was enough for that pansy," she said, patting the young lady on the shoulder. "Come along, we've quite the day ahead of us tomorrow. Her ladyship will be here with the cockerel's crow, and then all this quiet will be a far off dream."

The old woman smiled cheerfully, leading the way back down the corridor, while Eleanor followed behind.

When the lady reached her quarters and bid the old woman goodnight, she sat upon her bed and took out the brooch once more, considering every circumstance that would bring such a thing to the manor. Perhaps, the next chance she was afforded, she would seek out Múriel.

***

"Is it such an impossible request to be given breakfast when I have returned to my own home?" Lady Claudia complained, sitting impatiently in the great hall of the manor, and tapping her long, ivory fingers tapped incessantly upon the arm of the chair.

"Here, m'lady," Nan said, bundling into the hall with a tray and hastily setting the food upon the table.

"You've kept me waiting a full hour," Claudia pursed her lips, "Look, I can see the sun over the gardens as we speak. It must be the eighth hour already. Have you any excuse?"

"Forgive me, your ladyship," Nan bowed her head. "It shan't ever happen again."

"Indeed, it will not," the woman said. "You know I am to host the prince shortly. If you cannot serve my meals at the appropriate hour, how can I possibly allow you to manage anything else? Do you not know you risk my reputation?"

The old woman could only nod in response, feeling rather miffed and not in the least bit intimidated by the sheriff, for years of such impudence did lend her some sturdiness of will. Stepping back, she took her place as Eleanor came through the kitchens into the great hall.

"Ah, Eleanor! I trust we shall work to review the preparations for the prince's arrival?" The sheriff feigned a cheery disposition.

"Yes, your grace. Nan and I have completed nearly all the preparations," Eleanor smiled sweetly.

"And the menu's all set," Nan added unsuccessfully, as Claudia rolled her eyes in disinterest.

"Very well," Claudia said. "And how has the manor been kept in my absence?"

"Everything's been kept just as you please, your ladyship," Nan continued, "All's gone well, except for that horrid robbery last night. Gave me a good fright, so it did!"

"A robbery? You allowed a simple thief to slip past undetected?" The sheriff's brows flew up. "What happened?"

Eleanor's face went pale; her stomach sank inside her so she could hardly speak up. "I, em, well-"

"Well, what?" Claudia lowered her chin as she leaned forward.

"Your grace," Eleanor began, "I had completed all my work for the day and took a stroll through the upstairs corridors, to be sure all was ready for your arrival this morning. That is when I heard strange noises coming from your bedchamber."

"From *my* chamber?" Claudia's eyes narrowed in curiosity.

"Yes, your grace," she nodded nervously. "I couldn't stand idle and let the fool do as he pleased. So, I took down the spear from the hall and ran into the bedchamber to confront him. But when I entered, there was no one to be found, and most of the chamber was left untouched. Then, in a blink, the thief came out from his hiding and fled out the window. Looking out, I couldn't see where he'd gone. That is when Nan came in."

"Oh, I was frightened something awful!" Nan shook her head.

"We noticed the burglar had searched through the jewels," Eleanor continued. "We placed each piece back, to make certain nothing was missing. And nothing's gone missing, your grace. Whatever his intentions, he was prevented."

"So, let me see if I understand this correctly," the sheriff straightened her posture as she stared at Eleanor. "You *alone* were the one to hear and witness the thief?"

The young lady nodded.

"And when Nan had finally arrived, the blackguard had fled without any evidence of his devious end met?" Claudia asked.

The young lady nodded once more, unsure of whether to speak up.

"Nothing else transpired?" Claudia pressed.

"That is all, my lady," Eleanor bowed her head, anxious to hear the woman's conclusions.

Taking a deep breath, the woman composed herself, and continued, "Then, I thank you," she said. "As you've enough stomach for a fight, I should sooner promote you to head of the guards than waste such tenacity. Those blundering idiots wouldn't be able to catch a fly if it were drenched in honey. And mark my words, I will speak to them about improving their tactics."

"Thank you, your grace," Eleanor sighed. "I'm only relieved nothing was taken."

"Yes, yes," the sheriff waved her hand. "Go and fetch all the plans for the feast. I should review them now while I may."

"Indeed, m'lady," Eleanor answered.

The ladies bowed before returning to their servant's quarters to fetch what parchments they needed. Once they had departed from the hall, the sheriff motioned for a guard to come near.

"Did you hear any of this nonsense about a burglary attempt last night?"

"No, my lady," the man said. "Forgive me, it was not brought to my attention."

"What about strange noises? Anything that would persuade you there could be something amiss?"

"None, my lady."

"Thank you, that is all," she said.

The guard bowed as the woman motioned for him to leave her, and there Claudia remained; her mind digging deep into suspicion and all the conjuring of mischief.

***

Far and away under the boughs of Sherwood, Robin and his men remained.

A day of hunting and delivering provisions to the poor had ended just as the frosty air beckoned them back to their camp. And Will quickly set to work on supper. Casually, he took his place at the fire, stirring a sizable iron pot, and every so often, casting more of this and that into it.

"What are you cooking?" Jack asked as he peered over the man's shoulder, inhaling the aroma. "Smells delicious!"

"Thank you kindly," Will nodded cheerfully. "It's a simple rabbit stew. Finally, the weather's good and cold, and it is now stew season."

"*Stew season?*" Jack laughed.

"Aye. Stew season," Scarlet said, puffing up his chest defensively.

"I can't be much mistaken, but I believe there are only *four* seasons, Will," Alan snickered, standing quite near the fire. "And not a one is *stew season.*"

"I know that. Still, when the winter sets in, it is stew season," the man insisted. "You cannot have a stew in the summer when it is hot out. You might sweat to death," he paused to take a sip of the brew, "But this, my friends, this is *peak* stew season," he grinned; quite satisfied.

"*Peak* stew season?" Jack mocked, trying to maintain a sense of composure. "How on earth do you know when it is peak stew season?"

"It comes just at the end of November right into the second week of December, without fail," he answered. "Before that, 'tis a bit too early for stew. At length, stew season lasts only until March."

"Ah! So, I've been much very mistaken, indeed," Jack smiled, seeking to fuel the flames of amusement. "This is a technique, a science if you will, of a learned man. Pray, tell us Master William, Knight of Scarlet, as spring comes we aren't to have any stew?"

"But that simply cannot be, Sir Jack, son of John, for I've certainly had stew in April, at least once," Alan said. "So, if we approach the matter scientifically, spring must needs be part of stew season." At this, Alan made a playful punch against Will's arm.

"Oh, come off it. I know what you're doing," the outlaw grumbled, as he rubbed his sore upper arm and stirred the pot carelessly.

"Doing what?" Jack laughed, raising his brows behind his messy hair.

"What is it this time, lads?" Old Tuck questioned, his dark cloak swaying as he approached the fire.

"I've only marked that it is stew season, which *it is*, and these two simpletons are turning it into some fun, funny fun-fest of fun!" Will replied, growing quite aggravated and even more so at his inability to insult them at the moment.

Giving a warning glance under his thick dark brow, Tuck eyed Alan and Jack keenly.

"Lads?" He began, "I'm surprised at you, behaving as children. I'll have you know, a man of education can only be pushed so far!" With a hearty smile, Tuck released a full-bellied laugh, as the others joined in the merriment.

"Clodpolls, the lot of you," Will huffed.

"Well, my son, as we've no bonny lasses about to cheer our humours, we must stick by our means," the old man winked.

With such words spoken, the laughter began to settle; the outlaws staring at the fire in thought. Much time had passed since any fair maiden had graced the eaves of Sherwood, with song or dance. And for such a time did all their hearts weigh heavy over the loss of Sherwood's lady.

"Where's that lovely Marian, with a melody?" Tuck shook his head, as he sat before the fire.

"Would she was here now," Alan smiled soberly.

"Would that Robin had not let her do as she pleased, no matter how bold her blood," the old man whispered; a shadow in his eyes. "Shame, it is."

"Aye," Alan brought his hand upon Tuck's shoulder.

"By and by, Robin did love her as none of us," Will sighed, "and, while Marian has all our hearts, the all of my heart is for another."

"Who?" Jack wondered.

"Eleanor," Will sighed, dropping his shoulders. "It was always Eleanor... always *is*," he said

"What happened?" The lad asked.

"She worked for a time in Nottingham castle," Scarlet began. "After what had happened to Marian, I bid her flee, and so she did. If such a thing could happen to Marian, over Robin, what was preventing it happening to her? She knew us all. She and I were... and I couldn't risk..." Turning his gaze downward he halted his words as if by leaving his mouth, they hurt him. Then, he shook his head to be rid of such a heavy thought. "Been near a year since we've seen each other, but I know she must be somewhere out there; living well and doing who knows what." Into the night sky, his gaze wandered; a hopeful gleam in his eye.

"I had no idea," Alan thought aloud; his expression pensive, as he brought a hand to his chin.

Nodding, the copper-haired outlaw brushed aside his feelings, as Robin and Little John drew near the fire.

Robin smiled cunningly, standing so near the fire that his eyes were alit with winsome mischief. His arms rested upon his knee, as he bent closer to the flames, looking at his men before him, and eager to share his thought.

"Comrades," he said, "Prince John and several nobles are now travelling on to Nottingham for the festival on Saturday, and after the feast, the prince and his most loyal allies shall remain at Locksley Manor. There will be many of noble blood bearing far too many treasures to honour the prince. I fear they will be far too greatly burdened."

Old Tuck smirked, anticipating some of Robin's mind. "Well, we must find some means of lightening such burdens, should we not?"

"Oh yes," Robin said, as he winked and gave a dashing smile. "I've quite the plan in mind. Trouble is, we need a clever distraction, or at least, someone who would be willing to *be* the distraction."

***

Obstreperous, Lady Claudia came raging down the corridor of the manor. Her dress hung loosely about her frame, her blonde locks left long and wild, and her eyes, something venomous. "I'll have her hanged for this!" She shrieked.

The servants and guards were left horrified by such an unfounded display, as they witnessed their sheriff fly out into the great hall.

"Guards!" She cried.

Nervously, two guards marched behind the lady, following her up the winding stair to the servant's quarters; the scorching fury and the heavy footsteps pounding.

There, Eleanor sat within her chamber, contemplating all she had witnessed as she held onto the silver brooch. With such a shock as could shoot a bird out of the air, her door was kicked open, as Claudia burst in, followed by the guards.

"You've stolen my ring, you rotting snipe!"

Claudia could no more control her anger than Eleanor could control the circumstances. For without warning, the sheriff clasped the lady's face in her ivory hand, the nails digging into her cheek.

"M'lady, I don't understand," the lady protested; her eyes full of fright. "I've stolen nothing!"

"I'll hear none of your lies," the sheriff snarled viciously, her grip tightening upon the lass, as she forced her back up against the wall of the room. "Search everything!" She ordered.

The guards overturned everything. The whole bed was upturned, the chest was emptied, and whatever possessions found belonging to the lady were strewn on the floor, for they knew well enough, Claudia desired no less than to create a spectacle.

"Your grace," the sound lady said, "How can you think I've stolen anything from you?"

"Oh, you do not fool me," the woman hissed through gritted teeth. "I didn't believe a single word about that attempt of theft. My ring is missing, and neither guard nor servant saw any sign of a thief. I know it was you who came into my bedchamber and helped yourself to my possessions!"

"But I did no such thing!"

"No ring, sheriff," the man remarked.

As the guards had finished, and the commotion halted, Claudia let go of Eleanor. Upon her release, the lady brought her trembling hand up to her cheek, only to bring it down once more to discover the blood on her fingers.

"Ah, but what is this?" The sheriff wondered, for out of the corner of her eye, she saw a shining trinket on the floor just beneath the window.

As she picked up the brooch, her countenance shifted from a sinister air to something quite curious. She took a moment to think, and regaining her presentness of mind, she set aside those curiosities.

"Here; unequivocal proof you've stolen from me!" She made to persuade the guards of the lady's guilt.

"No! Please, that is my-"

"Arrest her!" The sheriff cried, pointing with her white finger at the lady.

"Please have mercy!" Eleanor protested, as the guards roughly took hold of her, leading her out of the chamber. "I swear I stole nothing!"

"See that she is put in the stocks," the woman ordered.

As the noise of the riot fled down the corridor, Claudia paused a while, admiring the clasp and rummaging through the wiles of her mind.

I've seen this before, but where? She thought.

Swiftly, she fled from the servant's quarters and returned to her own bedchamber. With a devilish eye, and the brooch still in hand, she closed the chamber door behind her.

Presently, the woman moved to the wall behind the bed canopy. Pulling back the fabric, she revealed a secret vault. The key to it, she always kept in a little drawer hidden amongst the carvings of the bedpost. Each of the bedposts was expertly engraved with all manner of lovely things, but in this one particular place on the first bedpost, a rose was carved and wreathed with a delicate frame. This was the hidden drawer. Having retrieved the little key, the woman cautiously opened the vault and removed from it a delicate wooden box, ornamented with a golden lock, and within, laid a golden brooch. It was of similar design to the silver brooch, yet this was quite its own. As the woman held the two, she brought them together, the two connecting to form one masterpiece as if they were crafted for each other. The moon, calming a glittering sea, and the sun, guiding the forest.

Puzzled by such a discovery, Claudia wondered how this silver brooch could have appeared here, and how Eleanor could have come by it, yet here it fit so perfectly with the golden treasure she had in her possession. Then, something strange met her eye. For but a moment, she perceived a figure in the window, and then it suddenly vanished. The woman shook her head in disbelief, yet she could not dismiss the thought of an intruder. Drawing a dagger from her side, she leapt up, facing the window. Yet, there was no one to be seen.

Quickly, she placed both brooches in the box and secured her treasure in the vault once more. She would think more on the matter later, for there were other circumstances to address at present. Though she left her chamber, the nagging curiosity would linger in her mind, pecking at her every waking thought; ceaseless.

***

When all was quiet, and still, the figure reappeared in the window of the bedchamber. With a whisper resounding as the symphonies of a summer breeze, the figure entered. Majestic, he stood, cloaked in emerald light; his face hidden beneath his hood. Lifting his hand before the canopy, he spoke ancient words, so the fabric was swept aside.

The vault was opened.

CHAPTER SIXTEEN

DIVERSION AND DISCOVERY

Word of the prince's arrival rung in every ear, on the day of Winter's Feast.

Across the whole of Nottingham, bright banners flew unfurled and garlands hung, and the castle was bursting with servants, and maids, and guards, all making ready for the celebrations. By and by, the weather did not greet Eleanor so kindly, nor herald any merriment; for she had been kept in the stocks by the entrance of Locksley village for a full day.

As dawn drew on a new morning, she found some comfort in the sun's rays, though her hands and feet were raw from the frost of the night; her neck sore and her wrists aching. When the lass opened her weary eyes to the quiet world about her, she instantly perceived a long red hair waving in the wind, and a familiar face approaching.

"Eleanor!" Catherine cried.

Rushing forward, the woman set down her belongings and stood before the stocks; her eyes heavy with fright. Quickly, she brought her hand to Eleanor's face.

"What's happened? Who's done this to you?"

"Lady Claudia," the lady sighed. "She has accused me of stealing one of her possessions."

"And did you steal it?"

"No! Of course not!"

"Then, what will this accomplish?" Catherine stood back, her arms folded across her chest as her eyes grew stern.

"The sheriff intends for me to remains in the stocks until I make my confession of guilt. Only *then* will she decide my punishment."

"The loathsome woman," Catherine muttered, "Forcing a young lady into the stocks... abominable by all accounts, regardless of what she thinks you've done," she said. Kneeling down, she retrieved a flask of water from her basket. "Here, please drink something."

"Thank you," Eleanor managed a smile, and drank enough to wet her palate.

"Why does she think you've stolen from her?" The woman wondered.

"A few nights ago, a thief broke in," the lady began. "I had finished my work for the day and heard strange noises coming from the sheriff's chambers. I took up a weapon, to defend myself and entered the chamber-"

"You would defend yourself single-handedly against a burglar?" Catherine scolded, "Are you mad?"

"Would you please listen?" Eleanor raised her voice. "I didn't actually *see* the thief," she explained. "And whoever he was, he fled before I could make any confrontation. But there was clear evidence of the thief's searching about for something. No one else saw or heard anything, so Lady Claudia believes that I have concocted the whole lot to cover for my actions."

"That's dreadful," Catherine sighed. "But what did he steal?"

"A ring supposedly, though I searched the whole chamber and nothing was missing. I fear Claudia devised much of that accusation," she shook her head, "But Cate, there is something I must tell you, lest I forget. When I entered the chamber, the thief dropped something, just before he leapt out of the window. Something that didn't belong to Claudia."

"Dropped something? What do you mean?"

"When I first entered, I heard a clanking sound of some metal thing hitting the floor. I looked down, and... it was Múriel's brooch."

"You found her brooch in Lady Claudia's chamber?" Catherine's mouth hung open. "But, you are not accusing Múriel of being the burglar, are you? She couldn't possibly-"

"No, no," Eleanor reassured, "Of course not. Múriel would never... and it was most certainly a man."

"Hmm... and you found Múriel's brooch, which you believe the burglar was in possession of?" Catherine brought her hand to her chin; her eyes searching; thinking.

"Well, I've had no word from Múriel, but perhaps this thief has been helping himself to the trinkets of more than just the sheriff. We ought to consider it. Who knows how many he's stolen from."

"Eleanor," the woman started, hesitant to share her thoughts. She opened her mouth to speak, then closed it before any portion of that particular thought could meet the lady's ear.

"What? What is it?"

"There's no time now," the woman shook her head. "We'll speak of this later. What we must do is find a way to get you out of here!"

"Shouldn't we worry about proving my innocence so the sheriff may release me?"

"This is hardly a time to become fixated on your reputation, especially when such a witch as that blasted Lady Claudia doesn't think twice before putting an innocent woman in the stocks!" Catherine said. Removing her shawl, she placed it over her the lady's shoulders. "Now, I shall go straight home. Cedric should have finished his hunting trip and should return within the hour. He will know what to do. But Eleanor, I do have a half-penny loaf in my basket. Please eat first, then I shall go and fetch my husband."

At length, Eleanor ate, and Catherine departed with a promise to return swiftly.

As the young lady waited, the morning light drew many from the warmth of their homes unto the work of the day. Several villagers walked by and spat at the lady, shouting curses at her. As the hour drew on, there was still no sign of Catherine or of Cedric, and the lady grew anxious. The shawl her friend had given her fared better than nothing but was still no match for the winter winds.

Suddenly, two burly men appeared, walking past the stocks, and took notice when the wind blew the shawl off of Eleanor's shoulders. Revealing their jagged teeth, the men sneered as their sinister eyes set upon the lady.

The first man moved to retrieve the shawl, and returning to the second man, they stood for a moment, making gestures with smirks and squinted eyes.

"Seems you dropped something, pretty lass," the first man said, walking towards her as he held out the shawl.

Eleanor hardened her expression and didn't make any answer.

"Oh, a shy little thing, isn't she?"

"Right shame, it is. She's not like to stay warm that way," the second man teased.

"You want the shawl back, sweetheart?" The first man leaned over his knee and mockingly waved the shawl around her face.

"Stop! Stop it!" Eleanor turned her head away, as her hands grew to fists.

"Well, how's about this, then," the man said, leaning so close the lady could smell his foul breath, "I'll give you the shawl back for a little kiss, eh?"

The men laughed snidely.

"Oh, come along," the man grabbed Eleanor's face with a firm grip, "Just one kiss."

Before the man could make another move, an arrow shot right by his head and stuck fast in the wood before his face. Turning about, the man drew from his side a simple dagger.

"Who shot that arrow?" He called. "Come on, then! Who done it?"

"You'll find I don't take kindly to men who behave in such a manner towards a lady," a voice answered; strong and steady. "Leave now, and I will not harm you." A man, cloaked with a hood over his eyes approached the stocks. A quiver at his back, and a bow in his hand.

"And what scruffy rat is like to challenge us, all by his lonesome?" The second man threatened. Tilting his head this way and that, he puffed out his chest and sniffed the air coarsely, as his comrade stood beside him, eager for the fight.

At this, the man with the bow removed his hood, whilst three other men gathered behind him. The first man wielded a sword and shield, the second, a sword of his own, and the third held an axe in each hand.

"I never said I was alone," the archer warned with a playful smirk.

The ruffian looked about at the other men behind the bow master, and though for a moment his eyes betrayed his fear, he refused to submit to sound reason.

Together, the brutes made themselves ready, and the fight was on.

Of course, no man was a match for Robin Hood. He wielded his bow and arrow as an extension of himself. Cedric swung each mighty axe fleetly, and Little John was apt with his sword.

As the men brawled, Will knelt with his shield above him, deflecting a blow from the second man who only carried a club. Yet at that moment amidst the attack, he took notice of the young woman who was set up in the stocks.

"Eleanor?" Will whispered; wholly bewildered. For such a time his heart ached for her, and now, finding her once again fueled his fight all the greater.

Rising up, he struck his enemy square in the nose with his shield, the man falling flat on his back. With the accomplice dispensed, the first man who had started the commotion stood surrounded. Blustering, he swung his dagger in hand, though he suffered scrapes and bruises enough to render retribution. With little patience left for the man, John conked him on the head, the man joining his comrade; flat on his back.

"If you dare come within a mile of this village again, be sure you won't have so much as two legs to stand on!" John warned as he stood hovering over the wretched men.

The two men ached and moaned in pain. The first man taking the second man's hand, they aided one another up and headed back towards the road.

Robin's men watched for a moment as the savages hobbled away, then suddenly realised Will was not amongst them.

Approaching the lady cautiously, he knelt before her; his eyes filled with wonder. "You've come back," he whispered.

"Yes, I've come home," she sighed. Though she tried to look into his eyes, she wished with all her might she could hide. Yet, it seemed her state was no offence to him whatsoever; in fact, he beamed at her so tenderly.

"I had no idea you returned, and forgive me, I should have looked for you sooner," Will fumbled, scratching at the back of his neck. "But Cedric was the one who called on us, to come and help you, though he didn't say it was you, only that his friend was in trouble and, well, I… I'm sorry Claudia did this to you."

Eleanor took a breath, gathering her words before she spoke them.

"It will take much indeed to regain my name in her eyes," she said.

"Are you mad? You're not going back there again!" He insisted with such conviction. "I promise to get you out of here, and you never need worry over Claudia so long as you live."

Clumsily, he laid a kiss upon her hand.

At this, the young lady smiled, "You are too kind to me. Strange though, this will be the *second* time you've rescued me from the fate of a sheriff."

"I'll rescue you a hundred times, from a hundred sheriffs," Will smiled.

As the others took their time in following, they soon approached the stocks.

"Robin!" Eleanor called. "I can't thank you enough-"

"No need," Robin said. "Now, we still need to find a way to free you."

"Well, why are we waiting?" Cedric questioned with an artful look in his eye. "Let's free her now!"

At this, the man raised his axe above his flaming red hair, ready to strike the lock.

"Wait," Robin halted him, grasping Cedric's arm with such a grip the man could not refuse his warning.

"What do you mean *wait*? Poor lass has been stuck here for near two days. We can't just leave her here."

"No, indeed," Robin acknowledged.

The others stared at the man, anticipating his thought. There he stood still for a time, stroking his beard with one hand, his bow held fast in the other hand.

"You know," he continued, "We're still in need of a distraction for later." The outlaw's eyes met John's in perfect understanding.

"For *later*? What are you suggesting?" Cedric lowered his axe.

"Smith, would you be willing to take part in our quest?" Robin offered. "There's some risk, but if accomplished, it can benefit all the poor in Nottingham. Will you come?"

"Perhaps," the man thought for a moment, his eyes squinted. "Would this quest involve taking revenge upon the sheriff in some way?"

"It might," Robin answered.

"Right," Cedric grinned broadly, "I'll come. Only we mustn't let Catherine know."

"Agreed," the outlaws remarked in unison, while the lady rolled her eyes.

"But, Eleanor, if we are to succeed, we will need your help," Robin addressed the lady.

"Me?" The lady raised her brows in confusion. "But I'm locked up. How on earth could I be of any help?"

***

Later that very day, carriage after carriage rode through the streets of Nottingham, each retreating from the castle, towards Locksley Manor.

On the first day of Winter's Feast, the celebration was held in Nottingham castle, but on the second day, there were some elite guests, the prince and those of his inner circle, who ventured to seek the esteemed hospitality of Lady Claudia.

One by one, each carriage drew before the lavish estate; nobles exiting the coaches, whilst an entourage of servants hauled trunks, and chests, and cases of all sorts into the manor. Each guest was heartily greeted by the sheriff, and escorted by servants to their designated chambers. The final carriage to arrive, and by far the most exquisite of them all was that of his royal majesty, Prince John. Luckily, the prince was in good spirits, though he secretly anticipated any news of Robin Hood's capture. As his carriage halted, four men came rushing towards the door of the coach. The first man unrolled a length of perfumed fabric before the foot of the carriage; the second and third stood together at the end of the length of cloth, to herald their sovereign's arrival; and finally, the fourth man was tasked with opening the door of the carriage.

Resplendent, the prince descended; donned in costly raiment. He wore a vibrant red cape, lined with miniver. A sword within a gilded sheath remained at his side and his stance was everything bold and magnificent.

"Your highness," Claudia bowed gracefully before him. "Welcome to Locksley Manor!"

The prince smiled broadly as he held out his hand, implying her duty to kiss his ring before he made any remark.

"I'm rather impressed, sheriff. Everything looks positively exquisite," he commented, looking behind her at the decorated manor, and grinning from ear to ear. "You've done rather well."

"I only wish I could do more, sire," the woman smiled. "Come, let us dine."

As the two entered the manor, the feast commenced at the prince's announcement. Before the great hall, stretched lengthy tables, teaming with food and drink. How the fire roared and mingled with the jolly music of the minstrels. Some nobles lounged, enjoying light conversation and the comforts afforded them, while others felt the call of the dance; and so the whole manor was bursting with laughter and merry sound.

Suddenly, amidst the feast, three guards hastily made their way into the hall; urgency driving their heels. The first guard made a motion to gain Claudia's attention, calling her away from her guests. With no intention of causing alarm, she smiled and laughed with her guests as she slowly found her way to the entrance of the hall, where she pulled the guards aside to discover their need.

"Do you not see I have a feast to attend to, and that I am hosting the Prince of England?" She whispered most begrudgingly; her shoulders stiffened In perfect posture, with her folded hands before her.

"Forgive us, your grace," the guard bowed, "We've a pressing matter to bring before you," the man said, looking around in search of any undesired eavesdroppers.

"Yes, yes, yes," she whispered anxiously, "My guests are growing impatient, *as am I*."

"The matter is of the servant lass. She's escaped," he said.

"What? Who was it?" Now the sheriff's stance became rough, with her arms folded across her chest, as she shrugged her shoulders.

"The lass called Eleanor," the guard continued, reluctantly, "She escaped from the stocks. It seems one of the Rebel's men helped her."

All Claudia could manage with such an audience behind her was a coarse sniff as she glared. Lowering her head, so that one could barely see anything but the whites of her eyes bulging beneath her brow, she finally spoke.

"She escaped?" Claudia whispered hotly. Now the guards shuddered, as she spoke. "If you do not catch her this instant, I'll make certain your head is set on a platter at the centre of my dining table, with an apple in it. Now go!" She hissed.

Turning about to the guests, she masked her frustrations with an exaggerated smile, regaining her place beside the prince once more.

***

Quickly, Will took Eleanor's hand in his and ran.

Will and Cedric had waited until the guards were present to witness their use of the axe to free Eleanor so they might make a dash for it. The outlaw and the lady would keep to running about and taunting the guards as long as possible, for Robin's sake. And of course, they intended for their centre stage, the very green of Locksley Manor. Buzzing about like two mischievous bees, they flew this way and that, and no guard was able to catch them.

"You'll never catch us, you clay-brained congers!" Eleanor called as she swung free around the edge of the village.

"Watch your tongue!" A guard shouted.

Suddenly, as the guards drew too close, Will grabbed her hand again and bounded away with her. Once they reached the estate, the whole charade became quite the spectacle, for half a dozen guards went running after the outlaw and his lass, who escaped their advance at every turn; climbing up over stone walls, diving through the hedgerows, and curving around the garden gate.

As they continued on, the lady perceived Jack, who openly carried away a hoard of loot into the forest. Keen as ever, she and the outlaw diverted the attention of the guards to the opposite side of the manor. Presently, this gained the attention of the guests, who could hear the rattling of the guard's armour and all the shouting.

"What on earth is that racket?" The prince squinted his eyes as he rose from his chair.

"I can't imagine what you mean, sire," Claudia said, "I'm rather enjoying the music! Aren't these minstrels... delightful?" She raised her brows in faceted enthusiasm, taking a cup to her lips.

"Yes, yes, they're very amusing, but-"

"Surely you are tired, my lord, from your travels. Come, take your ease! Would you care for some more wine?"

"Oh, hush!" He rolled his eyes. "Can't you hear it? Shouting, and... and those strange noises?"

At the prince's words, the other nobles fell silent, watching and whispering over what the prince was doing. Pausing in silence, he then lifted up a finger to his lips, and slowly turned his head in the direction of the door.

"It's coming from outside," he said, hurrying towards the entrance and making no acknowledgement whatsoever of Claudia's diversions.

"You know, your highness," she scurried after him, "Perhaps, you should retire for the evening, and we may continue the festivities tomorrow."

"Oh, would you let me alone, you silly woman," he grumbled.

"Your highness, I did not mean-"

"Be quiet!" He roared.

Audacious, the woman thrust herself between the prince and the entrance, her back pressed against the doors, barring it with outstretched arms.

"Your majesty!" Claudia cried. "No strange noises are coming from anywhere, and no noises worth the pursuit. Surely, you are in need of rest!"

"I beg your pardon," Prince John's eyes were ablaze, quite insulted. "You dare insinuate that your sovereign has lost his senses?"

Shoving the woman aside, he flung the doors open; the entire commotion revealed.

The outlaw and the lady rushed about wildly, using every object imaginable to prevent the guards from reaching them. Across the green were strewn various garments, crates of food, and all manner of animals were running free. The manor was in such disarray, the guards no longer chased after the outlaw and the lady, for there were goats and chickens and sheep scattered about that none could scarcely reach the two without tripping over a lamb or being pecked at by a flock of frightened hens.

The two imps, who had caused the riot, returned to their comrades at the edge of the woods. With the company all assembled, the Rebel alone stood forth from the shadows.

"Good day, your majesty!" He called cheerfully, as he bowed. A loose crown sat tilted upon his head, and luxurious jewels were draped about his shoulders. The prince's mouth was left agape; horrified at such a gesture. "On behalf of the poor, I wish to give you my most humble thanks for your unmatched generosity!" Robin smiled broadly, as he tipped the crown toward the prince. "What do you think, sire? Befitting a king, is it not?" He mocked with a wink.

"Blasted swine, you shall hang for this!" The prince barked, his whole face flushing crimson as he bore his teeth. "Guards, arrest that man!"

Much to the prince's disappointment, the disoriented guards failed to assemble and reach the thief before he slipped away into the deeps of the forest. All the while, the entire party of nobles had witnessed the whole ordeal. Several of them laughed at Claudia's expense, then, upon realizing the outlaw had burgled the manor, each went scrambling back in pursuit of their bedchambers, to be certain none of their precious belongings were stolen.

Through the doors, they rushed, and the staircase was soon bombarded with their trampling feet, the halls resounding with the uproar. One by one, each noble shrieked and cursed and scowled for they had every one of them been robbed. Every chamber was left ransacked, and not a single chest was left with so much as a farthing. Of course, the prince, along with two guards, made for his chambers, yet his majesty was no more fortunate than his fellows.

There, amongst all the commotion, Claudia followed the prince to his chamber.

"Your grace, I can explain," she stammered; terrified.

Removing a leather glove from his belt, Prince John stomped towards the woman, and with a sharp sting, he slapped the glove across her face. She winced but a moment, yet held her stance, trying desperately to hold come shred of countenance.

"Lady Claudia," he towered over the woman, "By my sovereign word, you are hereby stripped of all your claims to Nottingham and your titles-"

"My lord," Claudia trembled, kneeling at his feet. "I beg of you, please! Don't do this!"

"Silence!" He barked. "You are now stripped of all your titles, including your acting title as sheriff over Nottingham. You may remain at the Locksley estate until other arrangements can be made. If you attempt any challenge on this judgement, you will be hanged by the neck until dead, as penalty for treason against your lord and master!"

Gazing up at him with frightened eyes, and a shaking voice, the woman spoke. "But sire, have I not been a faithful servant? Have I not proven myself loyal again and again? I beg of you, have mercy!"

"You would dare compose such pitiful excuses?" He scoffed. "I single you out as my future queen, I give you power at your fingertips, and you allow the most wretched outlaw of all England to swindle my treasures? The very one who with every coin taken wages war against me?"

"I have arranged plans to capture him if only you would allow me-"

"I need subjects I can trust without hesitation; a queen who can obey my every command. I've given you ample opportunity to demonstrate such loyalty, and you have failed me," the prince said. "As for the dread Rebel, I shall leave his fate in the capable hands of my newly appointed sheriff; Victor of Levisham."

Prince John immediately strode off into the corridor, toward an older man who remained at the top of the stairway. The old man was not of any notable stature, nor of any markable features, save his grey beard and long grey hair. He and the prince shook hands firmly and chatted a moment. Aghast, Claudia stood and turned with wide eyes; her sharp ears enrapt. For she remembered that very name, given her by a cousin, not so long ago.

Fearless, the woman marched towards them. "Sire," Claudia approached with cringing lip, "You would have such a scoundrel as my substitute?"

"How dare you!" The man puffed up his chest, stepping towards the woman. "And what reputation could precede me to invoke such disdain from so foul a woman?" His nostrils flared.

"Your majesty, this man has done great wrong against his wife in squandering their wealth-"

"Hold your tongue before it is cut out of your head!" The prince held up his hand. "Woman, you have tested my patience at every turn, and now you conjure such accusations against the earl?"

"Your majesty, his wife told me of it herself, and in her words was no deceit," Claudia protested, directing her eyes away from the prince, and towards the earl. "Jacqueline spared no detail of your odious repute before she fled for France."

"Impossible! My wife has been dead these five years," Victor testified. "Are you so addled that you accuse me thus?"

"Vile woman, someone was set upon dripping venom in your ear, and you should have known well enough to ignore it!" The prince glared.

How perplexed, she stood. Her breath quickened, as she thought and thought, searching for the answer to all the strange happenings of that very day; of that moment with that young woman; of the brooch. In an instant, all the pieces fit together. "The brooch," she whispered, looking back towards her chamber.

"The what?" The prince echoed.

Claudia swallowed nervously, for though she was inwardly furious, she was compelled to keep the matter concealed. "Forgive me, your majesty," she mumbled; her voice tempered as she bowed. "If by your mercy, you let me live, then please, let me return your favour, and give you the Rebel. Let it be my final gift to you, that you may yet pardon my actions and permit me to keep Locksley."

At length, the prince nodded in acceptance, though still appalled at the woman's ghastly behaviour.

"Very well. I shall show you this mercy," the prince stared down at her. "But do not let me catch a glimpse of your pathetic existence until the deed is done."

"Yes, sire," she said.

"Oh, and Lady Claudia," the prince addressed, towering over her once more, before he whispered in her ear. "My patience is wearing thin."

Finally, the whole assembly departed in outrage. Every noble, every servant, every guard who accompanied their master, every empty chest and case, all withdrew to the carriages. For none could stand to remain a minute longer.

When all had left, and the manor was left quiet, Claudia leapt back to her own bedchamber to seek out the hidden treasure. It was clear the Rebel, and his band of outlaws made no effort to conceal their theft, and everything was strewn about the chamber. Still, the woman hoped the brooches were concealed well enough. Moving aside the canopy and opening the vault, she discovered that the box which had held her treasures was gone.

First, she felt a wave of horror, her heart racing fiercely, her breath hastening, and her blood boiling so that she could not contain her fury any longer.

"Damn you, Robin Hood! Damn you!"

Taking hold of any object within her reach, she threw each piece across the room. Breaking bottles of perfume and oils, smashing her mirror, shredding pillows as feathers flew about the chamber. Suddenly, amidst her fit of hysteria, she paused. Rattling her brains, she paced back and forth, back and forth, muttering to herself.

She must know who the brooch belongs to… but if she is out of my grasp, Claudia thought; her fingers entangling her golden hair. *Oh!* She wrung her hands. *That family in the woods!*

***

Safe at last in Sherwood, the company laid aside most of their loot for the night and lounged quite comfortably around the heat of the campfire to celebrate.

"To a quest well done!" Tuck raised a cup, bearing a jolly grin.

"Here, here!" The comrades echoed, raising up their goblets, and chalices, and whatever other trinkets they had obtained that night.

"And to our newest, bonny outlaw, Eleanor; well done indeed!" Robin smiled merrily as he presented the young lady with a dagger in a decorated scabbard.

"Thank you, Robin," she smiled, as she received the token. "It is an honour."

"Now, I'll ask what none else are brave enough to ask," Alan moved to kneel before the lady. "Would you sing us a song?"

Sweetly, the lady blushed, "Oh, I'm not so sure my voice is for the singing."

"Nonsense! I've heard that voice in song and 'tis fairer than any I have ever heard," Will insisted, coaxing the lady as he held her hand.

"Aye! Go on, sing for us," Jack encouraged with a smile. "Sing of the Ironstriker!"

"No, sing of *Videreth and the Star*!" Old Tuck said.

"Lads, let the lady sing a song of her own choosing," Scarlet petitioned; his voice gentle as he calmed the company. "What shall you sing for us?" He wondered sweetly.

For a moment, the lady thought, and then with a gleam of the firelight in her eye, she knew. "*The Prince and the Fieldmaiden*," she answered. The men sat listening to what melodies rose from her heart unto the night, and how her song enchanted them:

Long ago, a prince did come,
from the mountain o'er the field,
Through the waving grass, he called to me,
Eyes shining as the stars.

'Young maiden, do you know a place
where I might sleep this night?
I've travelled far that I might rest
my heart from the fight.'

And I bid him stay awhile with me,
and take comfort in my song,
Thus he promised he would love none else.
For I, his only one.

Oh, how he told me of the war,
of his fallen kingdom's cry,
His people fettered, broken, lost;
The good king left to die.

'Sweet maiden, my home is far gone,
I've no place to dwell,
My people suffer for their fate,
and I, forsaken still.'

And I held him fast against my heart,
and held him through the storm,
'This your kingdom, my sweet Prince, is here;
These arms ever your home.'

When morning shone, he must away,
to rise against the foe,
To reconcile the kingdom ere
the warrior take his throne.

'Dear maiden, I must ride this day,
far beyond the hills,
The great halls of the mountains wild,
I must redeem again.'

And I let him go, as he did swear,
with tears upon his face,
He'd return to me, save when he,
Victorious king ascend.

Oh, how the seasons shifted by,
and winter grew to spring,
And years went passing far from me,
with no hope of him.

But then one day, I saw a man
descending o'er the field,
Through the waving grass, he called to me;
The crown upon his brow.

'O my darling, how I've longed for this,
and how I've loved thee still,
Come, my darling, to the mountains wild!
In my heart ever dwell!'

Then bounding through the autumn wind,
o'er the waving fields of green,
With eyes like shining stars that sing,
the child smiled up at him.

The king, with such joy on his lips,
did beam across the way.
He reached his arms out wide and held,
the precious son, his own.

And we looked upon our kingdom well,
the people all made free,
Oh, for all the treasures he restored,
none so grand as this.

And I held him fast against my heart,
and held him through the age,
This your kingdom, my sweet King, is here;
These arms ever your home.

Song after song, the men begged, and song after song, she yielded. Yet, for all their basking in her delightful presence, the men's rumbling stomachs would not go easily ignored.

Over the fire hung a pot of stew, and some rabbit roasted upon a spit. While the warmth of the flame, and the revelling of the merry men lingered in the air, Will and Eleanor soon found their moment to steal away, into the stillness of the night.

When it seemed no one would notice, the outlaw took up some blankets and motioned for the lass to follow him. Leading her to a clearing, where the light of the full moon greeted them, there the man beckoned her, and there they remained for a time; the blanket wrapped about their shoulders, so close their hands were almost touching. And then, when she felt leave to do so, Eleanor took hold his hand, fixing her gaze back up to the stars.

Grinning, Scarlet sighed, lacing his fingers with hers. Then, as their eyes met, swiftly, the outlaw seized his moment and placed a sweet kiss upon her lips. Pulling away for just a moment, she blushed as he smiled at her.

"Forgive me, I-"

"Kiss me, William."

Though time had staid their love, it could not undo it; for beneath the wintery starlight, the rugged outlaw and the lady found what was never truly lost.

CHAPTER SEVENTEEN

AN OATH FULFILLED

Deep within the forest, stood an ancient oak.

It was said, in many tales of old, this was the first tree sprung from England's soil. Not a one could tell the age of it, for as the seasons shifted onward, so the generations came and passed away, and there it stood as ever, at the very heart of Sherwood.

There, beneath such boughs, the man did wait so patiently. His stature draped in a dark cloak, cascading to the earth; his dark hair hung down to his shoulders, and his eyes shone soft in the moon's glow. Gazing upward, he perceived the moon over the forest and beheld its quiet strength. How far away it hung in the heavens, and yet in some bewildering sense, he felt its call. Then, laying his hand upon the bark of the tree, he felt such life and ageless wisdom beneath his fingertips. Beyond understanding, it felt as if he had done all this before as if a memory lingered in the hollows of his mind which he could not fathom. A memory faded yet present; foreign and familiar.

Breathing in the winter wind, he suddenly felt something new; an essence of something far grander washed over his mind. Turning his eyes westward, he stepped away from the tree; searching.

And there, in the distance, he saw... her.

How her long hair caught what starlight glimmered through the branches, and her expression; sweet and soulful and sublime. So enraptured, the man drew unto her and held her face in his tender hand.

"What name has such a maid as this? Surely, the lily white is fair, but my darling is fairer still," he sighed. "And, for all your loveliness, not one name could dismiss it from you. Thus, shall I ever call you *lily*, for you are the purest beauty."

"And what shall I call you? Far more than your name is well known to me," she said, "and how this heart has been remade. Your name was once sorrow, yet before me now, your name is valour, and you, the very crown. If you shall call me *lily*, then shall I call you *king*. For what gift could a simple maid offer such a king, but the fair blossom?"

There they lingered but a moment and took no notice of the old man approaching beneath the mighty tree. With a broad grin under his wild beard, he smiled and softly called to them. Taking hold of his maiden's gentle hand, the man guided her. Standing before them, with eyes of a kinder green, a green that had known and seen so many things, the old man spoke.

"A mystery profound, that two souls so come to be in want of the other, yet herein is found such peace and each wholly mended," the old man said. "My son, as you take this maid, will you bind yourself to her, in truth and in honour, and love her well as ever you both shall live?"

"I will," he said.

"And you, my daughter," the old man said, "as you take this man, will you bind yourself to him, and so love him as ever you both shall live?"

"I will," she said, "With all my heart, I will."

"Finally, with these promises you hold, tonight and ever, as one," the old man concluded.

The maiden let a single tear fall, though the man was swift to brush it away. And as the sage stepped aside, the man embraced his wife.

"Have I now your heart, my darling?" The man whispered.

"Always," she smiled, "As I bear it unto you, it is yours to hold."

"Then fear not," he said, "I shall never do it harm, for as you have borne your most precious heart to me, I will cherish it."

And so it passed, under that ancient tree, a love so sweet was forged, and their kiss, the very seal of it.

"So ends my journey," the old man whispered quietly to himself.

Steadily, what wintry winds had sighed smoothly through the eaves grew colder and stronger, and all the wilder still, such that a great and terrible gale stirred about them. The earth beneath them trembled, the very trees of the forest swayed and bowed and creaked under the mighty rushing wind, and in such breaths, strange starlight mingled with it; mists of golden light in ribbons swirled and filled the air so that all about them was as a mystic tempest.

Bursting through the night sky, a song alike of thunder resounded, and the heavens blazed as though the rising of the sun broke upon the land. Then amidst such lighted skies and the roaring winds, figures of light descended.

Terrifying and beautiful beyond comprehension, they appeared; and their faces, shrouded in purest glory. The first, crowned with rays of sunlight; his shoulders broad, his stature matchless, and his robes of glistening gold. The second, with waves of silver hair as a waterfall about her, so adorned in threads of woven starlight. Lofty, they stood upon the earth, as great pillars of light.

But as the man held fast his wife, shielding her from the fearsome beings before them, he looked to find the old man was unafraid. His countenance was quiet, his expression calm, and when the old man met his glance, how his eyes were full at peace.

"Aldred, how can you be still? How can you endure?" Guy called, lifting his arm to cover his eyes from the brilliant light. "Do you fear nothing?"

"He has no cause to fear us, for he knows his Masters well," the first Spirit returned, his voice booming deep and fiery. "You fear us in that you do not remember."

"What must I remember?" He cried. "Why must you haunt me?"

Under the shadow of his arm, Guy opened his eyes again, clutching Múriel against him as she hid her face in his chest. As he looked on Aldred, he perceived how the old man's eyes so brightly gleamed under his white brow; eyes so vibrant and so very young; and how he smiled beneath his white beard.

Then, as he spoke, Guy found his eyes did not ache so as they first did before the spirits' light. In wonder, he brought down his arm and loosed his hold about his wife, little by little. As she knew his mind, so too did Múriel turn her glance unto the old sage, for she still feared to gaze upon the spirits.

"Do you not yet know of who I am?" The old man spoke.

"Surely, you are Aldred, as you ever have been," Múriel reasoned. "You are the Aldred of my childhood, and the Aldred as I grew, and as I have seen your crown of silver turn to white, so shall you always be my Aldred."

"Fair daughter, I was not always he," the old man said. "You knew me by that name for a time, yet that life and that name must pass."

"I don't understand," the maiden said.

"To many, I am known as the Lord of the Forest; the Guardian of the Wood," his voice rung smooth, like a flowing river. "All the earth is my forest, though not every forest is mine to tend."

Drawing near the mighty oak, the old man set his hand upon the bark, and with his touch, all the branches which had hung barren began to bloom, swift and teeming as in the spring; its boughs adorned as never before.

With widened eyes, the man stared, "Surely, this cannot be," he whispered.

"Ah, but there is much you have not seen or understood," the old man said.

"Then can you tell me what all the beings of this world would have me know?" Guy begged. "Why I have been so tormented?"

"Long ago, your ancestors, the children of my Masters who were once bound to each other in love, were torn apart by a malicious war; their union destroyed by the greed of man," he said. "Therefore, the Great Spirit of the Rising Sun and the Spirit of the Fair Moon entrusted me with this quest; to redeem the vows of Auringon and Kuun; to redeem their love at the appointed time ere they set their curse upon the land. You are the descendant of the Rising Sun. And this, your maiden, the descendant of the Moon. You were destined to be hers, and she yours, from the first ages of this world."

"How can we have come from the spirits? We are of this world! Surely, we cannot be made of earth and spirit," Guy shook his head.

"It was out of ancient magic that the souls of Auringon and Kuun came into being and of our very essence with which we had fashioned them," the second Spirit spoke; her voice a calming melody. "As you so stand before us, there is ancient magic in you. And now, our dear servant's quest is complete," she spoke. "We have come to free him of his bond, for he was faithful to keep it."

"Complete… but why? Where are you going?" The man wondered as he looked on the old sage.

"You shall not see me as I am again, and few have seen my true form," he answered. "Where I venture, you cannot go, but in a little while, you will come to the land where I once dwelled, though you will not find me there."

"You are leaving us?" Múriel's eyes grew saddened, as she let a tear fall down her face.

"But you cannot leave!" Guy implored.

"I must, for it is my time. But before I leave you, I wish to bestow a gift," the old man smiled, as he revealed something precious from the sleeve of his cloak. In his weathered hands, he held out a gilded box.

Graciously, the man retrieved the gift and opened it. Inside, set together, were the brooches of the sun over the forest, and the moon over the sea.

"Then it is true? The golden brooch... I thought it only a simple trinket from my father," the man said.

"Oh, Auringon, such a gift was crafted from my magic," the Great Spirit spoke, "and the other, from the magic of the Moon, each forged by the hands of Vasar under our command, as a symbol of such a union."

"The brooches," Múriel whispered in wonderment. "Guy, I thought you had lost my gift."

"Forgive me, but I must confess I did," the man admitted. "That day I went out into the woods, I set out to retrieve my mother's ring for you. That is why I returned so late, but I thought I had lost your gift. How... how did you find it?" The man fixed his eyes upon the sage in astonishment.

"Not all tales are worth the telling, though here are both, safe and in your keeping," he smiled, as he fastened each brooch at their shoulders. "Thus, it is time my Masters bestow their blessing. For sealed in magic must this union be."

Together, the man and his wife bowed before the Spirits, as the old man bowed his head in turn.

The Great Spirits drew forth their mighty hands, and lifted up their hallowed voices; a song so full of life upon their lips. Such aged words did they pour over their descendants, words beyond all time and memory, though somehow the lovers understood it:

> *O Children, of Resplendent Light,*
> *Drawn so deep into the night,*
> *Thine souls reforged, anew the union made,*
> *This love untouched by earthen age.*

Long years of life we give to thee,
Joy and peace, thine unwavering tree,
An endless love held ever in time,
O Children of the Light, arise!

Alit with the purest flame, the man and the maiden's eyes shone; clear and bright and glorious; teeming with the brilliance of the Spirits before them. As the light softly faded, and as the lovers gazed upon each other, unfathomable magic reawakened within them. Their love, far stronger than they had yet unveiled.

"Farewell, precious children," the Spirits whispered, as they drifted away in the wind's tide, and all starlight and sunlight drifted away in the twinkling of an eye, as gentle as a vision's end. Then, when his Masters had departed, the old man turned toward the ones he had guarded.

"Must you go?" Guy asked. "How can we ever thank you, for all you've done?"

"Go now, and live," he smiled warmly.

Before them, in the simplest, smallest breeze, his form began to fade as fallen leaves scattered in the wind. One by one, each leaf sailed away into the shadows of the wood, until his kind face was gone, and in a moment, he vanished altogether, as if he had never stood in that place, nor had ever dwelt in that vast forest.

In the stillness of the night, the man and the maiden stood sheltered beneath the blooming boughs of the oak; full of awe, and bewilderment, and a lingering sadness. Yet, as they looked on each other, each took comfort in that they were not alone as they had once been, and what love they held could not be shaken. Silent and sweet and unexpected, twinkling all about them snowflakes fell as stardust falling upon the forest.

"The first snow," the maiden whispered, glancing up at the skies. Turning into her husband's arms, he held her close.

"The first of all good things," he whispered in her ear.

Then, out of the forest, came their horse, galloping towards them and neighing, casting the length of its mane into the frosted air. And for such a sight, Guy and Múriel did laugh.

"Shall we venture home?" He asked.

"Oui," she replied, "Take me home, my love."

Swift, they leapt through the snow-laden forest, snowflakes flying past them as shooting stars. It was not long before they strode before the three elder trees, and finally onto the field before the cottage. There the little cottage remained, as always, with smoke coming up the chimney and the warmth of firelight awaiting them.

As the horse halted at the path, Guy helped Múriel dismount and laid a tender kiss upon her cheek before bringing the horse back to the barn. There, at the door, she waited for him. When he returned, he swept her up in his strong arms, his smile captivating her.

"Do you realise we need never say '*Until tomorrow*'?"

"Yes," she acknowledged, draping her arms about his neck. "Then must we design something else to say every night. Something just as wonderful."

Gazing upon her with such longing, the man sighed. Words which could not fall upon his lips, resonated in his eyes, and she understood them.

Nodding in response, he then took her across the threshold of their home. Eagerly, he carried her up the steps, and down the corridor to their bedchamber.

As they entered, the crackling fire blazed, and across from it, the bed lay draped with ivory linens. Setting her down, the man watched as she moved before the fire, staring into it, as he stared at her.

How her beauty was unmatched. Her long hair flowed down her back like the waves of the sea. Untamed and dauntless. As she turned toward her lover, her eyes glistened as pure as the moon itself. Delicately, she held out her hand towards him, drawing him in like the endless rhythm of the tide. Taking her hand, the two stood facing each other, their hearts racing wildly within them. He perceived her enchanting smile and her radiance, her figure touched by the firelight, and he yearned for her with such affection. Slowly, she brought her hands up to his cloak, and unclasped it, letting it fall to the floor. Guy remained motionless, breathless, watching as she unclasped her cloak, the garment falling behind her. Not for a single moment did she take her eyes away from his. Resting her hands upon his chest, she slowly brushed her fingertips down, grasping the hem of his tunic, and with his heart pounding, the garment drew over his head, revealing his muscular form.

Turning about, sweeping all her hair to the side, the lady waited. With tender fingers, he unlaced the gown, revealing her back as the dress hung loose about her bare shoulders. Running his fingers across her shoulder, he traced down the length of her back. Leaning in, with his left arm wrapped around her, he drew kisses across her shoulder, his lips sweeping over her smooth skin.

Gallant, he lifted her up in his arms once more and brought her to the bed. Laying her down upon the linens, he hovered above her. His breath hastened; his body tense. His fierce blue eyes shone through the locks of dark hair that hung over his face. Zealous, he kissed her, and Múriel could not but fall under the spell of his passions, and let her lips dance with his. Pulling back, he gazed into her eyes.

"You are my treasure," he whispered, so assuredly.

Beaming up at him, she brought her arms about his neck, weaving his locks in her fingers. Fervent, he embraced her and kissed her neck.

"Mon tresor c'est vous," she whispered, drawing him up again to kiss her lips.

All that night, he knew her as she knew him, in such beauty, and passion, and tenderness. At long last, the lover had found his darling.

BOOK THREE
SUN

CHAPTER EIGHTEEN

THE GIFT AND THE WARNING

All winter, the man and his wife spent their days dwelling in their secret haven, hidden well behind the veil of glistening frosted trees. And every once in a while, when the bitter winds settled, they would venture off into the thick of the forest and visit their friends. There they shared good food and song and told tales of old, and when evening fell and bid them return home, a gentle fire was swift to fill the whole cottage with light and warmth again. Never had the man estimated that such a simple life could yield such richness, yet it was truly this untamed spirit, his darling, who made each moment so precious. It was in her kindness of heart where he found such comfort; and she in him, such strength.

Though the harsh of winter had faded, spring was yet to come. It was then, when the trees and fields did slumber, the man awoke to the song of a swallow; its melody ringing out so sweetly as the pale light of dawn shone through the pane and over the linens of the bed. There he lay beside her, his right arm embracing her as the cool morning light cascaded over her form. How her silken locks brushed softly against his cheek, delighting his besotted heart.

As the two laid together, in the quiet of the early morn, the man thought on his land and what was to be done that day to care for it; some trees had fallen onto the field during the winter, scattered here and there, along the way. While the snow had concealed them, surely now it was time indeed to remove them. Letting such thoughts settle, he returned his mind to the present moment, holding his wife as she rested. But as he listened to her breath, it grew tense, and her expression of calm had vanished. Suddenly leaving his embrace, Múriel sat up, bringing her hand to her forehead; her eyes clenched shut.

"What's the matter, love?" He wondered.

"Nothing," she whispered. "I... I thought to begin working in the garden a little earlier today is all. We should have begun planting last week." Casting away the linens, she set her feet on the cold floor.

"Come, rest a while with me," he coaxed, as he held her hand, "We'll tend the garden soon enough."

"Mon Dieu, I cannot stay in bed all day," she persisted, relinquishing her hand with such haste as she departed from the bed to be dressed.

Puzzled, the man lay staring, as the lady rushed about the chamber, and kept her gaze downward. Removing from the bed, Guy followed, throwing his tunic over his head as she headed toward the door. "Múriel, we have time. What's really troubling you?"

As the lady stood silent before the door, the man observed her; how pale her complexion, how her eyes shone, holding such a bewildering light behind them, and how quiet her step as she moved away from his touch. Then as she glanced up at him, her expression softened.

"I must deliver food to the Smiths today, and I must bring herbs to Winifred," she began. "If I am idle and do not tend the garden now, there will be no time to reach them and return home before sunset."

"Very well, then let me help you in the gardens, and we may ride together straight away," he grinned, caressing her face in his hand.

"*Together*?" Múriel gulped.

At this Guy tilted his head, his eyes growing dark. "Are you so opposed to the idea?"

"I'm not opposed," she shook her head. "Only, if we ride together, the horse will grow weary, and there will be no one here to work the land. Surely that would not be wise. If you remained, I could deliver provisions to the Smiths on my journey to Winifred, and I wouldn't be more than three hours at most." Finishing her thought, she closed her eyes and set a tight fist against the frame of the door as she breathed deep.

"Darling, are you certain you'll be well enough to ride?"

"Of course, I'm only a little tired. But the sunshine will do me good," she forced a smile. "I promise I'll not be long."

"Very well," he nodded, "after breakfast, we'll set to work then."

"Merci," the lady said. But just as the man had kissed her lips, she quickly fled down the corridor.

Standing in the empty doorway, the man remained; thinking. It seemed strange she would wish to ride alone, and in his heart, Guy felt uneasy at this. Turning back into the chamber, he paced across the way and glanced out the window; how cheerfully the sun beamed over the white-laced field, as patches of grass peeked through the melting snow. Certainly, she would be in no danger of being caught in a storm; indeed, he had nothing to fear in her riding alone, he reasoned.

At length, the man and his wife worked well in their garden, so that much of the planting was finished before the ninth hour, and Múriel made ready to ride. Bidding her husband farewell, the lady mounted the horse and strode across the open field.

Anxious, the man watched as she disappeared amongst the trees.

All the while as he wielded his axe against the fallen trees, working in the warmth of the sun, the thought of her journey weighed upon his mind. It was not so long ago that he had tasted the bitter emptiness of a fate which felt so fixed. The more he thought on it, the more he felt foolish letting her ride out alone. It was not the trusting her which troubled him, for she was neither lacking in either sincerity of character or cleverness of mind. Rather, it was the uncertainty of her being found in any pressing circumstance; far from his aid. Clinging to the assurance of her word, he resolved to see her on that horse, crossing over the field ere the golden light of midday shine.

***

Along the path, as she strode, Múriel kept her hood far over her face as she tried to shield her eyes from the sun; her trembling hands gripping the reins as she winced in pain. Here and there, for but a moment, she closed her eyes altogether, but then the pounding, pounding, pounding of the hoofs felt as war drums resounding in her ear. Opening her eyes again, she could return her mind to the road, as she inhaled the fresh air. Then, not so far from the way, she caught a glimpse of smoke rising up into the air; the Smith's cottage.

Please, be here, she thought.

Neither she nor Guy had seen the Smith family for near two months. While the lady had come faithfully to supply provisions, in each turn, she only met a silent home and a door shut fast. It seemed a strange circumstance indeed, for it was quite unlike Catherine or Cedric to be forgetful, or at the worst, discourteous to such dear friends. Still, as slighted as she felt, Múriel believed there must be reason enough for all of this.

Swiftly, she arrived at the cottage, and while she might have dismounted at that instance, she could not bring herself to it, and so remained for a time motionless before it. Arduous, the journey already proved unwise, though she could not falter now. Faint, she rested her weary head against the horse, her eyes shut tight and her hand drawn to her temple as she breathed, hoping to regain her strength.

"Je vous demande pardon. Une minute," she whispered.

As the pain declined, giving her some respite, the lady removed from the saddle and took up the basket of provisions. Suddenly in the distant wood, she heard the crunch of leaves beneath agile feet. Her keen ears found the noise drawing nearer from behind the cottage. Holding her breath she waited, and at length, as the forest lay still once more, she stepped lightly toward the home. Upon approaching the door, she gave three heavy knocks; and how the noise was unbearable. Patient, she stood, listening as strange whispers echoed from within. Then, a tense voice called forth.

"Catherine? Cedric?" The lady called, "Is anyone home?"

"Who goes there?" The woman's muffled voice called out.

"It's only me. It's Múriel," the lady returned. "I am come to bring provisions and see that you are all well."

Frantic, Catherine found open the door, grasping Múriel by the arm and pulling her inside as the door was shut behind them, and locked. The woman's eyes shifted about, as she moved away from her friend to steal a glance out a nearby window, pulling just an inch of the curtain away, but briefly. "Forgive me, I had to be certain of who it was," Catherine explained nervously. Turning around, she found her children peering around from behind the table. "Odette, shouldn't you be helping Godric with his chores? And take Ollie with you, please?"

"But can't we stay with you and Múriel?" The little girl begged sweetly.

"As soon as you're finished. We need only speak a few moments, is all," Catherine nodded. "Now, go on!"

As the children chased each other back towards their bedchamber, chattering and making mischief, Múriel finally felt leave to speak. "Catherine, what's the matter?"

The woman's expression fared rather anxious; her dark brown eyes intense. Lowering her head, she spoke. "It's that Lady Claudia and her henchmen," she whispered, sitting down at the table.

"Lady Claudia!"

"Shh! We must keep our voices down lest the children hear, or anyone else for that matter."

"What's happened? What's she done?" The lady sat beside her friend. "And where is Cedric?"

"He's gone hunting. I wager he'll not be back until nightfall."

"Then what of Claudia?"

"Two months ago, she came here with an entourage of her guards," the woman whispered. "She smiled and gave compliments and made every attempt to draw out whatever information we could lend her, though we'd have none of her wiling words and she discovered as much. Since that day, men have been coming; disguised as woodsmen; hiding all about our home; spying on us."

"Why would the sheriff wish to question you?"

"Oh, you've not heard how she was stripped of her title as sheriff? By the prince and at Locksley manor, if you can stomach the thought."

"No, I didn't know," the lady confessed. "But Cate, what information was she trying to gain from you? And if she is no longer sheriff, then under what authority could she question you?"

"By all rights, she is still Lady of Locksley, and in her eyes, we owe her taxes just as any. But it was after that whole dreadful episode with Eleanor that Lady Claudia came looking for answers. I'm sure Eleanor's spoken with you of it, yes?"

"I only know she was accused of thievery and was thrown in the stocks, though Will was swift to rescue her; but no more," the lady sighed. "I believe Eleanor's been keeping much from me... perhaps as she rather disapproves my marriage, she disapproves my friendship."

Setting her hand on Múriel's shoulder, Catherine's eyes shone understanding and sincere. "I know she's not been so fond of Hugo as the rest of us, but she'll come round, don't you worry. Just give it some time," she smiled. "By and by, if that's all she's told you, then I'll warn you not to mention to her anything of what I'm about to tell you." Befittingly, the woman related to her friend of all that had transpired according to Eleanor, and how Lady Claudia had come to find a silver brooch.

To Claudia's misfortune, it was the infamous Rebel who had stolen the piece from her; and though the woman was deprived of such indisputable evidence, she not only remembered the piece, but also the very lass to whom it belonged. Moreover, she warned Catherine and Cedric that the lass in question might be offering shelter to a criminal; one who matched Guy's description entirely. With such knowledge at her disposal, Lady Claudia gave all power to discover them.

"She gave her word she would reward anyone who could capture the lass and the fugitive with a good sum of gold."

"And what of her intentions for the lass and the outlaw?" The lady asked.

The woman's eyes shone fearful, as she shook her head. Horrified, Múriel's face flushed pale, and her stomach churned. Of course, now she understood everything.

"I'm relieved Robin found the thing and returned it to you," the woman sighed, "Or else who knows what Claudia might have done with it."

"Oui, bien parle," the lady nodded, as she lowered her eyes. Then looking back up at her friend, Múriel grew faint; she had glanced up too quickly, and so brought her hand to her face a moment. Thankfully, the woman didn't take notice.

"Don't worry," Catherine continued whispering, "I swear I've not given her your name, or Hugo's, and I'd sooner spit in her face than tell her where you live. And now you see why we've been so cautious. Still... and please, forgive me for doubting you in any light, but why would Claudia wish to seek you out?"

Petrified, Múriel could hardly conjure a single word but stared at the floor; pensive. Catherine leaned nearer the young lady, attempting to regain her attention.

"Tell me once and for all," she gripped the lady's shoulders. "Why is she looking for you?"

"It is a very long story. If I were to tell it, I fear for putting you in greater danger," she whispered.

"Listen well. I've known you long enough to know with all confidence that you are no fool. But what manner of danger is this in which you have found yourself? Is Hugo really some brutish outlaw? Do you know at all if he has committed any crimes?"

"I hardly know what to tell you… I've done nothing but follow my heart, to do what I judged to be right in the face of injustice," Múriel resolved.

"Then it is true? He is an outlaw?" Catherine's eyes widened. "Can you not confide in me, even in some small way?"

The woman's eyes shone gentle, yet the lady knew it would be exhaustive to indulge in her request, and no matter the evidence or cause presented, her case would not be so wholly accepted or understood. Guy would always be judged in ill-favour and to tell of his escape now would only serve to exacerbate the circumstances at hand. No, she could not confess a word of it, and at length, she spoke what little she could, though it could never appease the woman's doubts.

"Perhaps it was right of you to be so guarded as you have been," Múriel said, taking her friend's hands in hers. "I am so sorry… for all of this, for all your family has endured on my account. I hope you will forgive me."

"No, it is not your fault," the woman insisted.

"It is," the lady concluded. "If Claudia is searching for us and questioning villagers, then all that is left for us to do is make certain your family is safe… safe from us."

"But you are not the threat! It is Claudia who has threatened us all! My only wish is for *your* safety," Catherine's eyes grew sombre.

"If she has gone this far already, who knows what more she might do if you are seen with me. We don't know if one of her men could be in these woods at this very moment. I cannot stay a moment longer."

"Aye, you're right," the woman nodded. "I know you must go, and go you should, but… will we ever see each other again?"

The two fell silent, their eyes speaking far louder than their lips; and what bittersweetness in this, that such a thing could part such old friends. Mournful, the two embraced.

"Kiss the children for me, and tell Cedric I've said farewell," Múriel whispered.

"I will," Catherine held back her tears. "Do what you must, and mind, if you are ever in need-"

"I shall call on you," the lady answered. "Now, I must ride out to your mother."

"Surely, let me go to her in your stead. It would be mad to set for Locksley."

"Merci ma soeur, but you don't understand. I've been... I need to discuss something important with her. I fear this may be my only chance."

"You headstrong lass," she scolded. "Then fly!"

Departing from the cottage, the lady mounted the horse as her friend cautiously remained behind to wave farewell. Soberly, the woman stood; her long auburn locks caught up in the wind as the lady travelled on through the forest in pursuit of Locksley. And as the lady had vanished amidst the thick of the wood, the woman closed the door.

Again the journey had taken its toll on Múriel; her eyes tired and heavy, and her whole form yearning for rest. Nearing the town, she dismounted and fastened the horse to a tree, just at the edge of the woods. From where she stood, five guards could be spotted about the village, and close enough to set some fear ablaze within her. When she looked down at the clasp of her cloak, she breathed a sigh of relief, remembering she had fortunately forgotten to wear the brooch, as her mind was quite unravelled.

Discreet and cunning, the lady made her way to the healer's cottage. As it was not so far from the manor, the lady took further caution, approaching the home from the thick of the woods behind it. There, the lady heard that familiar voice; the old woman calling out to a bristly old man, as he hurried on and away from the cottage. The woman remained for a moment, calm in all her cares until her eyes fell on Múriel.

The moment she noticed the young lady, the old woman's brows raised in warning. Daunting and direful, two guards proceeded down the road before her home. Luckily, Winifred didn't call out the lady's name, nor did she make any friendly eye at her, but as the guards had passed on, hastily, the lady and the physician withdrew into the cottage. With the door shut fast behind them, the two were finally free to speak.

"What on this green earth are you doing here?" She whispered rather crossly. "Have you lost all your senses? There are guards enough in this village such that a whole army wouldn't dare step near it."

"Quick, I've brought some herbs for you; here, take it," the lady said, removing the contents of her satchel upon the table.

"You're here to bring me herbs? You're as mad as they come, dear," Winifred scolded. "Do you not know Lady Claudia has been searching for you day and night? She knows right well you and Gisborne aren't so far from her clutches, and she's sure to have hatched some scheme to draw you out. I swear you marrying that scoundrel and living out in the middle of nowhere isn't doing you any favours. It won't be long until she unearths you, and-"

"Winifred, please," the lady stared sternly. "I'll not have you speak of Guy in that manner. He has been so kind to me, to all of us! I had hoped you would have forgiven him by now. And I thought you had, seeing as you've not told Catherine anything."

"La. 'Tis not my business to tell," Winifred sighed, folding her arms across her chest, "Howbeit, it would do more harm than good."

As the physician spoke, the lady faltered in her step, her breath uneasy as she fell to her knees, and held her forehead.

"Good gracious, what's the matter?" The old woman rushed to her side, and lifting the lady's chin she found such weak eyes. "You look as if you've seen a ghost."

"I would not come, save it was imperative," she whispered.

"Then, tell me, what's happened?"

"I've had headaches for weeks now," she said.

"You've let this continue on for *weeks* before you call on me?" Winifred huffed indignantly, pursing her lips.

"I had no wish to cause any trouble. But, they've been growing worse."

"And your husband, he knows of this? He willingly let you ride alone into the pit of war when you can hardly stand?"

"Guy only know what I've told him."

"And what have you told him, then?"

"Nothing," she answered. "I feared if he knew I was in any pain... I couldn't bear to see him... but there is no end to the pain. The headaches began at night and would subside by the afternoon. Now, they persist a full day or two, then stop, and begin again for another two days. I hardly sleep, I can hardly work my own land, and no matter the remedy, the pain does not leave me."

"You stubborn mule, suffering all this time," Winifred sighed. "Why did you not call on me sooner and have done with all this misery?"

"I thought if I let it alone, it would sort itself. And I didn't want to be a bother," she said.

"No lass, this seems rather something to bother about. Come along, sit." Nothing in Winifred's tone gave Múriel any encouragement. As the lady sat down, she waited while the physician fumbled about retrieving this and that from her cupboard. When she had found all she needed, she returned to the table and without a word, laid out her supplies.

"You don't think it could be something serious, do you?"

Winifred made no answer.

"Please, I need to know," the lady begged, gazing up at the woman with weary eyes.

"I'll not lie to you. Headaches as you've described them, continuing on for weeks and the pain only increasing... it can be something serious, though let's not entertain any fates until I've examined you."

Múriel nodded, with a lump in her throat. She only hoped the old woman could discover the truth behind all of this, and quickly. The journey home wouldn't prove any easier with ill news, still, the sooner she fled, the better.

***

Working about the cottage, Guy took every opportunity at keeping busy and keeping distracted, until Múriel's return. A pot of stew hung cooking over the hearth, as he loomed above it; worried. Every other minute, he stole a glance through the windows, though at each instance, he found nothing.

Dimly, the light of the sun faded low behind the trees, the snow-laden world quieting as the moon rose high. Still, the lady had not returned, though the forest grew dark and quiet and hollow. Suddenly, his ears pricked up as he heard the faint echo of hoofs fast approaching. Following in time, the sound of gravel crunching beneath those hoofs set his anxious heart at ease. At the creaking of the heavy door, the lady entered their quaint little corner of the world. There she stood, something hidden behind her expression.

"Múriel, you've been gone for hours. I thought you would be back long before sunset," he scolded.

"Forgive me, that was my intention," she began, "I took a while longer than expected when I visited Catherine. She and Cedric and the children are all well-"

"Oh," he said. "But you did go to Winifred, yes?"

"I did... I saw Winifred," she whispered.

Lowering her gaze, she let loose a tear and lifted her hand to cover her face. Indeed, there was so much to tell, for all that day was so burdened with news it was entirely too much. Ultimately, there was only one piece of news which held the most significance, and she must be brave enough to tell it, and nothing else. With such wistful endearment, Guy took to her side, holding her close his arms.

"What's wrong?" his voice cracked as he pulled back. "Are you in any danger?"

"No," she shook her head, reassuring him as she caressed his bearded cheek.

Relieved, he sighed, closing his eyes. Then opening them once more, his pale eyes shone beneath his furrowed brow.

"Then, what's wrong?"

"Nothing's wrong."

"Nothing?" His brows furrowed. "But, you've been unwell. Surely Winifred couldn't have dismissed your need so leniently."

"You knew?"

"Of course I knew. Or rather, at least, I feared it," Guy said, "but you've said nothing all this while. Are you ill?"

"Well, not exactly," she sighed.

"What do you mean?" He grasped her shoulders. "Please, tell me precisely, what did she say?"

"My headaches should go away soon enough. She gave me some herbs to help with the pain and... it won't harm the child," she smiled.

"Child?" He whispered; his eyes wide as he stared in awe.

"You're not upset, are you?"

"No, no. I," the man mumbled, searching for what words to say, yet as no words could match what his ever-broadening smile could tell, he brought his hand to his heart. For all-encompassing within, this, her happy instance, and for him, an age.

With eyes brimming, the man beamed at her. "I am to be a father?"

"The noblest and kindest of fathers," she grinned.

Into his arms, Guy held her close as his lips met hers; her arms draped about his shoulders. Resting his forehead against hers, he remained, smiling all the more.

"My darling, how is it that you have so quenched the longings of my heart," he sighed, drinking in her beauty and the secret light behind her eyes.

Lifting her hand to his bearded cheek, she smiled sweetly, "But of all you have longed for, it is I who have been given beyond what could be comprehended. For having you, I have everything."

There the man embraced her once more, his arms cloaked about her, and his heart so full.

"But when will the child come? Did she say?"

"Some time at the end of the summer solstice, perhaps September. But, there's something else I-"

"No, don't worry about anything. Whatever your need, lay it on me, and rest," he smiled down at her,

"Darling, whatever we are given, a son or a daughter, I only hope the child might have your fearless heart," he sighed, leaning down to place a tender kiss upon her lips.

Sweetly, the lady blushed, and with this, the man with all joy in his eyes sat beside her before their hearth and began to eat and drink.

All night, they spoke of the child, yet persisting in the hidden eaves of her mind, the lady knew she must tell her husband the truth.

Out of optimism or brash confidence, she did not fully believe Claudia would find them, yet beyond that shadowing threat, what might happen? Abominable as it was for that foul woman to send out scouts day after day, searching, Múriel hoped it would not prolong; if they could remain hidden until the summer, the villain might withdraw, her fire for revenge burnt out.

No, the lady could not burden her husband now, for his heart was merry, and it appeared there was no choice but to conceal the matter, until another hour.

CHAPTER NINETEEN

A LITTLE GOLD, A LITTLE GAIN

The hour had grown late.

Awaiting word from her spies, Claudia lingered before the hearth of the great hall, her eyes marked upon the flame; callous and hollow. The night afforded no moon, nor stars, so all was as endless darkness about the quiet world. As night had not yet fled altogether, the woman tempted not a wink of sleep for she daren't be left to her nightmares. At length, the doors of the manor were opened, as only one man came forward; clothed in simple apparel. His shoes were muddied from his journey, and his cloak frayed at the hem.

Approaching his mistress in the great hall, the man bowed low. "My lady," he said.

"What news have you?" The woman questioned; her eyes unmoved from the fires. "And why have the others not come?"

"Your grace, we must have men keep watch at all times," he said, rising to his feet one more. "We cannot risk our absence."

"Howbeit, have you found anything?"

"No, your grace," he returned. "Only, there was one young lass who came on horseback not three days ago, but she departed rather hastily."

Embittered, the woman slowly turned her attention toward the man. "A young woman came to the cottage on horseback, and she was given leave to depart?"

"My men informed me she did not bear the silver brooch," he answered. "Surely, she is not the one we seek."

"Very well," the woman sighed. "Be sure they're flogged in the village tomorrow. I'll not have anyone of any consequence be given leniency."

"But my lady-"

The stillness broken, a sudden trumpet's call blared from outside the hall.

"Make way!" A man's voice cried out.
"Make way for the herald of the prince!"

Anxious, Claudia leapt up and bounded across the hall unto the entrance. The doors swung open, and there she saw the man, mounted on a white horse, carrying the royal banner, and so adorned in scarlet, as his sovereign. As the herald approached the woman, he bowed humbly, then standing up again, his eyes shone keen.

"Lady Claudia, I have come with a message from His Majesty, the prince of England. He bids me speak this: *These words I send forth, borne of my sovereign mind, spoken by my sovereign tongue, and sealed by my sovereign hand. Lady of Locksley, heed well these words, for the hand which writ them holds fast the hilt.*" Revealing a roll of parchment from his satchel, the herald placed it in the woman's ivory hand. "Pray, forgive me, your grace, as I must beg your hospitality that I might lodge here tonight. My horse is weary, and we shall depart at first light."

"Yes, of course," she nodded, her lips trembling as she clutched the parchment against her chest. "Should you wish food or drink or any means of comfort, it shall be granted." At this, the woman called for her servants to attend the herald and lead his horse to the stables.

Retreating into the great hall, the woman paced across the floor, waiting until all had settled silent once more. When all was quiet, and the herald had gone to his bedchamber, the woman broke the seal upon the parchment. Her face flushed pale as she had come to know the prince's thought; she sat down, staring hopelessly into the fire as she let the parchment fall to the floor.

Watching as she had let it slip from her hand, Dumont came forth from the shadows and knelt beside her.

"Your grace, what troubles you? What news from the prince?" He wondered.

"Read it," she whispered; petrified.

As the man took up the parchment and stood near the flames to gain better light, he read what words he dare not know, and now he faced his mistress; his eyes full of fear. "What do you require of me, my lady?"

"I do not yet know," she answered.

"Surely, you must have some intention to act?" He pressed, still she gave no answer.

At length, when the silence had choked her well enough, the woman stood. "At first light, we make for Nottingham castle."

"The castle? Your grace, the sheriff may not-"

"Dumont, I am left with no alternative. You know this," she concluded.

Bowing his head, the man took his leave and made ready the carriage and the horses, and called together the guards for dawn crept over the skies.

***

By daybreak, she departed.

Robed in velvet and costly silks, Claudia fared a magnificent beauty as she rode in her carriage, sifting through the village streets on towards the daunting castle. With her, she brought a chest of treasures, teeming with gold and silver, precious gems and jewels, and every kind of luxury she could afford. It was by all accounts a gift most worthy of being presented to his grace.

Clever and cunning, the woman was convinced she could twist the sheriff's arm to meet her ends, and it seemed her gift would be enough to sweeten his palate.

Through the narrow streets and into the courtyard, the carriage finally halted. At the steps of the court, the Lady of Locksley was ushered up to await her lord. Pompous and unyielding, Victor descended from the castle; his eyes were of an unfriendly light and his countenance of odious conceit towered above the woman.

"Lady Claudia," his voice boomed. "I had not anticipated your presence. Still, you are welcome all the same."

"Thank you for receiving me, your grace," she bowed; a fraudulent smile fixed on her bonny face and the silks of her gown draping over the edge of the steps.

"Come, let us to the hall," he said, offering his arm.

Indignant as she was, the woman took his arm and followed as he, along with several guards, escorted them into the great hall. Pale and thin, the morning light shone through the high windows, muting the hues of the banners which hung high above, and the stillness of the hall could scarce be matched.

The long table which stretched before her stood bare, yet the sheriff was quick to call upon his servants. In a matter of moments, a tablecloth was set, along with plates and goblets and bowls of silver, and all manner of foodstuffs and drink were set before them at the clap of Victor's hand. Seated at the long table, now as a guest, the woman restrained her disgruntlement, now invoking her keen and enticing tactics.

Victor reclined quite comfortably in his seat, his long grey hair resting upon his shoulders, sweeping over his garments of black damask and golden threads. His elbows resting upon the arms of his chair, his fingertips met with open palms at the centre.

"Come, fair lady, what brings you to my halls? Are you yet willing to show your allegiance?" His brow raised in curiosity.

"Indeed, your grace," she said, "I am come to wish you wealth and prosperity in your new position and to demonstrate my unswerving devotion under your rule. Surely, I've no wish for you to harbour any guilt for what pangs might have been felt at your succession, for I've none to claim against you. It is for this reason, I have brought you a gift."

As Claudia called her guards forth, the men presented her gift, though they did so with more brawn than delicacy; for in bestowing the chest of treasures, they set it rough upon the dining table so that it upset much of the tableware. Given that it was of such substance, this was not an extraordinary result. Thus, it only served to amplify the woman's generosity.

"A gift to be sure. This is quite elaborate for a simple Lady of Locksley," Victor said, curiously eyeing the chest as he spoke. "May I?" He wondered, and swift, the lady nodded.

Upon opening the chest, he looked upon the luxurious trinkets with a satisfactory gaze; the sunlight glittering over the riches and casting lights of every colour upon his face. As he seemed rather pleased with the token of good will, he closed the chest and motioned to his attendants, as three men came forward.

"Bring this to my chambers at once," he commanded.

Heaving the chest off the table, the men carried it up to the flight of stairs in the destination of the sheriff's private chambers. Returning to his former position, Victor drew a goblet to his lips.

"I am surprised, my lady. I assumed Robin Hood had relieved you of such earthly burdens?

"Robin Hood may be a devilish outlaw, but he could no more rob me of my wealth than could a rat deprive a household its bread," she pursed her lips. "And, I had assumed a man of your consequence should expect nothing less than what I bestow unto you. A true ally is known by their deeds of loyalty, and an offering yielded by their own will, loyalty's confirmation."

"Well said," he acknowledged. "Yet, I suspect you have come for more than neighbourly banter?"

"Indeed, you are a man of insight," she said, as the corner of her lip curled. "Yes my lord, I would speak with you of some business."

"What business, fair lady?" He brought his fingers to his bearded chin.

"That of the infamous outlaw," she began, plucking a grape from a cluster before her. "He has been a blight on our kind for far too long. Everything we stand for, everything that makes us what we are, he would see us demolished, all in the forsaken name of *the poor*, as if they are free from the law. He is the king's fool alone and makes every attempt to thwart our plans for a new government under a new king. His thieving is contemptible, but his persistence is waring on the prince. Now, Prince John has expressly tasked me with discovering the outlaw; to once and for all put an end to him. He must be finished," she said, crushing the grape in her fingertips.

"Yes, I believe those loyal to the prince would readily condemn him, as you would. But why do you come to me?"

"I propose we strike an accord. I have come to seek your aid in abolishing the outlaw and all of his accomplices. Ridding the men of their leader, only provokes a new master to stand. If we are to be rid of the Rebel, we must be rid of his men."

"Undoubtedly, but why not carry out this mission yourself? Surely, the *rat* and his rodentious comrades can be easily caught?"

"Sheriff, I believe we may both benefit from eliminating the threat together. It would allow the people of Nottingham to see their new sheriff in all his glory, willing and ready to work alongside other nobles to defeat the outlaw. Moreover, would it not demonstrate your ambition to restore peace to England under our new king? Under King John's rule?"

Narrowing his eyes, Victor studied the woman, before the grin upon his face grew so that a laugh emerged from his lips.

"Oh, Claudia," he shook his head, staring at her under the ridge of his brow. "I will say, I've been most impressed by your charade. By and by, we both know Prince John would never give you such an office after demoting you so dishonourably. You forget I was there when you begged on your knees before him. In fact, I know precisely why you are here."

"I don't understand," she sat back, her gaze nervous.

"No doubt, you have received the message, detailing the prince's ultimatum? I had the privilege of advising the prince upon it, myself," Victor smiled, raising his brow before he took another sip from his goblet; watching as the woman's eyes widened in fright.

Claudia could hardly respond, for there were no other means of masking her defeat. Still, there was hate enough in her to retaliate. "You blackguard," she whispered.

"Ah, now don't be hasty," the sheriff wagged his finger, "You also know I am your only recourse in capturing the outlaw before the end of the summer, for if you should fail, your head will be rolling off the chopping block before you can cry out for mercy," he said. Moving to stand behind her, Victor placed his hands on her shoulders, pinning her where she sat. "Naturally, it is befitting that you come so to beg my assistance but you know I am by no means a man of charity," he continued; his hands still heavy upon her shoulders. "What did you wish to glean from this interlude? Did you presume I would be swayed by your flattery?"

The woman could hardly swallow.

Cautiously, she made her request. "In exchange for a division of fifty mercenaries, I am prepared to give you one-third of my wealth."

"One-third of your wealth in exchange for a division of mercenaries?" He scoffed, now pacing away from her, as he dragged his fingertips over the length of the table; his voice echoing throughout the hall. "And what precisely were you intending to accomplish with such a division?"

"I would have them scour Sherwood Forest until the Rebel is found and captured. Certainly, no outlaw could arise against such a force. Anyone found to aid the outlaws would be put to death, as an example."

"Hmm," Victor paced around the opposite side of the table, "This scheme of yours may not prove entirely useless. Yet, I will be deprived of my mercenaries. You offer only one-third of your wealth?"

"Yes, if it would satisfy you," Claudia confessed so reluctantly as she stared forward into nothingness. Once again, the sheriff paused, gripping the back of her chair.

"Fair lady, you know I cannot be bought with simple riches. While I am Sheriff of Nottingham, I still hold the title as Earl of Levisham, and the entire estate and its fortune are still in my possession. I am far wealthier than you may comprehend. I've no need of your pennies."

"My lord, if one-third of my wealth will not content you... to offer you any more of my wealth-"

"I am in no need of your money, you impudent fool," he rolled his eyes. "I am interested in the acquisition of more land. With more land, comes more titles. More titles, more power. And the prince will be in want of powerful allies and advisors when he is crowned king. If you hold any desire to find the dread outlaw, then you will give me Locksley."

"You go too far," she hissed. "How dare you demand my estate!"

"You will give it to me," he said. "The entire estate; the title, the rights to the inheritance, and the rights to the lady of the manor," Victor demanded, as he took up a lock of her hair and breathed deep its scent. "Despite your folly, you are quite the captivating beauty, and I would as soon give you anything your heart desired, save you obey your master," he whispered in her ear. "And consider, after your disgrace before the prince, I am the only man of noble blood willing to take your hand. That is my price."

Warring against herself, the woman knew she must capture and kill the Rebel or face the penalty for high treason. She was but a pawn in the sheriff's hand, and they needed to use each other. At last, after a moment of troubled silence, the woman lowered her head and spoke.

"Very well, your grace, I acquiesce," she said, turning her disgusted gaze toward the man. "I shall pay your price in exchange for your aid in capturing the outlaw. When, and only when the outlaw is well and truly dead shall you take up your end of the bargain."

"Excellent. I believe we have struck a most pleasurable accord," he grinned. "Let us retire to my study. My scribe shall detail our agreement in full," he said, motioning for a guard to come forward.

"Ah yes, would you please bring the Lady Claudia to my study? I'll be there shortly."

The guard bowed, as Claudia turned to follow, though not without shooting a hateful glance at the sheriff. Once the hall was absent of the lady, Victor called forth three guards, while he stood at the base of the stairs.

"All is going according to plan," he whispered through his grey whiskers. "The Lady Claudia has given her consent; she will sign the document detailing our bargain. Then, when Robin Hood and his men have been captured, kill her," he ordered.

In such lucid disdain, the woman signed the papers according to the sheriff's terms, gaining a division of fifty mercenaries to use at her disposal, all of whom would be instructed to rampage the forests in search of the notorious Rebel. Seemingly, it would not be long before the outlaw was drawn out, like venom from a wound, for no sooner were the papers signed than the mercenaries arrived at Nottingham castle.

CHAPTER TWENTY

PREMONITION

As the golden dawn shone through, leaving its footprints over the hills and valleys of the bed, it bid the lady waken. Soft was its glow, as a river of light, and the whole room teeming.

Though the day came so gently, the lady's mind was astir in unbridled thought. Presently, a full week had passed, and still, Múriel had not yet told Guy of what threat may lie beyond. For she feared to utter a word of it lest she might break what peace had sustained them in their quiet world. Nonetheless, the matter could not be concealed without end, and though all would be at peace, to ignore such a shadow would be their undoing. Turning to her side, she made to wake her sleeping husband, and lend him all her thought, but as she opened her eyes, she found him not. The linens of the bed were cast aside, his garments were gone, and the door was left open.

"Guy?" She called. "Guy, where are you?"

No answer.

Retreating from the bed, the lady fled down the corridor, down the stairs, and found nothing but an empty home. Faint, the pounding of the horse's hoofs echoed, the rhythm drumming farther and farther away. Swift, her heart racing madly, the lady hastened to the field, her bare feet greeting the cool of the grass at the very moment the man rode fiercely over it and into the forest; a quiver of arrows at his back, and a bow in his hand.

Guard him, she thought. *Guard his very footsteps.*

Gazing up at the brilliant dawn, the sky so clear and free, she wished with all her might he would return safely from the hunt. The fleeting peace could not match his very life, though her heart ached for both in equal measure. And yet, where fear to speak had restrained her, fear for him now bolstered conviction. Resolute, she would speak ere he returned.

***

In the dark and stillness of the forest, Guy sat perched high in the boughs of a tree; his watchful eyes surveying the moonlit wilderness. At length, the woods stood silent, save only the evening song of the wind and the echoing owl calling forth the creatures of the night. As the man remained, suddenly, he heard the snapping of a twig. Pricking his ears up, he listened as the crunching noise came nearer the tree. Calm and steady, he waited; ready. His eyes searched, and still, nothing could be seen for the pace was even and light.

With an arrow taut against the bow, a glint of starlight against the iron, he searched, and then, his eyes suddenly fell on a figure, cloaked in black, his own bow ready. And as he neared the tree, he spoke.

"Loose your arrow, and you shall fall at these feet," the figure began, "Indeed, 'tis strange to see a dead man ride amid the forest."

"Who are you?" Guy wondered, his voice unshaken, his grip firm.

"To such a loathsome beast as yourself, I am but the final hour," the figure returned. At this, he loosed his arrow at Guy, grazing his cheek, just as the hunter loosed his own arrow, though the stranger was quick to dodge it. As the iron stuck fast in the earth, the adversary readied his bow again, but in the very moment he did so, another strange figure stepped forth, a sword drawn in his hand.

Setting the edge of the blade against the archer's throat the stranger spoke, "Loose your arrow, and by the Spirits, I shall slay you where you stand," he said.

"You know not my office, outlaw," the man grumbled coarsely, "You've no more cause to defend the man than you do in defending your keep."

"Mark my warning, Norman. I'll not show mercy," he answered.

Yet, the first man was of such foolish blood, and so did loose his arrow against Guy once more. Such was the feat his downfall, for the swordsman made good on his word and cut the man's throat. There, in the darkness, the archer lay slain, and the earth drank of his blood. But as the hunter remained high above, he loosed another arrow against the blade bearer, but the man was too keen of eye, and so deflected the attack with his very blade. Dauntless, the man peered up through the branches, perceiving a pair of eyes he knew right well. Throwing back his hood, he called out to the man. "Gisborne?"

"A'Dale!" The man called, leaning forward into the starlight.

"Why did you shoot at me? Did I not prove my standing?"

"Forgive me, I could not be sure if you were friend or foe."

"Friend or foe? You blind idiot," the outlaw shook his head. "I could have lost a toe. Or my whole foot with that shot!"

"Enough shouting," Guy ordered, "If an enemy appeared in the stillness, then our bickering should soon call others hence. I'm coming down." Casting down the bulk of his supplies, the man climbed down from the boughs to greet the familiar outlaw. As the two met, they shook hands heartily.

"It is luck indeed I recognised you. But what are you doing?" The outlaw looked over his shoulder, lowering his voice. "I thought for certain you would wish to stay hidden from Claudia's sight as long as possible."

"What do you mean?"

"That man was one of her spies. Do you not know?"

Disquieted, Guy gripped the outlaw's shoulders. "Why would Claudia send spies into Sherwood?"

"Here," the outlaw revealed a bit of parchment from his jacket and held it forward.

As the man took the parchment in his hand, his gaze grew all the more troubled. A bounty of two hundred crowns was offered for anyone who might capture the mysterious fugitives and deliver them to the Lady of Locksley. Dead or alive. The names of the criminals were not given, but there was enough description that there could be no mistake.

"How... how could she know we would be in Sherwood? How could she know of the silver brooch?" Guy questioned.

"Do you recall a young woman by the name of Eleanor? A servant to Rothgar."

"Yes, I confess I do," he sighed. "I knew of her then, but she is also a friend to my wife. For fear of being discovered, I am known to her by a different name, although I believe she suspects the truth. But how have you come to know her?"

"She's been a sweetheart to one of the company for a time. Not long ago, she had worked at Locksley manor and witnessed an intruder; one who left behind a silver brooch."

"But what does this have to do with Claudia sending out spies?" Gisborne squinted his eyes.

"You don't understand," Alan said. "Eleanor was accused of stealing. When the thief came and left the trinket, she took it with her, knowing to whom it belonged. When she was arrested, it was found in her servants quarters, and Claudia came to possess it for a time."

"And Eleanor gave you this account?"

"Aye, and she's no fool; she knows 'twas you who came that night to the manor. Only you would have had the brooch, and it isn't hard to imagine Múriel would have given it to you."

"You've not confirmed this to the others, have you?"

"No! None are inclined to believe you may yet live, nor would Robin tolerate any speculation. It was damn near impossible persuading Eleanor she was mad for having formed such a conclusion. As it is, you and Múriel are in far too much danger remaining," the outlaw continued, setting his hand on the man's shoulder. "The sooner you have fled, the better."

"But she is expecting a child and has not the strength for such a feat. Not yet," Guy said.

"A child?" Alan's eyes widened. "Then for the sake of your family, you must go, and leave no foothold to the tempest."

For a moment, Gisborne closed his eyes to compose his thought and breathed out a heavy sigh. Opening his eyes once more, he stared hard at the outlaw.

"A'Dale," he said, "I know we've asked much of you, and why you are so willing to concede I'll never know, but you are the only one who knows our secret, and who has been a true confidant indeed to keep it. If anything were to happen to me, can I trust you to keep Múriel safe?"

"Aye, you have my word," he nodded. "But sure as death, I'll not let anyone wrong you, or your family."

"Thank you, friend," Guy said.

"Still, if we are comrades, heed my advice. The woods have grown too perilous for you to come here, even to hunt. You should return home this very moment, and ride not a moment later."

"I would, but we've had no meat in the cottage for weeks. I cannot return with nothing."

Alan stood for a time, rubbing his dark bearded chin and thinking. At length, he held out his hand.

"Aye, then we must be quick. To the hunt," the outlaw determined, as he and Gisborne turned further into the forest.

Ominous, a sudden rustle of leaves and the pounding of heavy footsteps echoed in the distance.

"What was that?" Guy whispered.

"Shh!" Alan chided.

The man and the outlaw halted a moment, their feet still and firmly set upon the ground. Holding their breath, they cautiously turned about as their anxious eyes searched for any sign of an adversary. The bleak of the forest engulfed them; their lungs pained for want of respite. By and by, nothing more was seen or heard, though the lingering suspicion of a presence haunted them.

Resolved, the men continued on to the hunt, and with every other step they peered over their shoulders, their eyes gazing far behind, their ears sharp; knowing, and yet not knowing, that someone was there. With dawn steadily sweeping over the horizon, and a doe felled under the skilful arrow, Gisborne and A'Dale parted ways beneath the eaves of the forest. The first, steadily onward toward his home; and the second, to his brothers.

As Alan wandered through the trees, his thick dark hair swayed in the warming breeze; his dark eyes shining. Whistling a merry sort of tune, he kicked his feet up, here and there along the hidden path, for he was through and through a mirthful spirit, and whatever danger lay ahead was but a trouble for which he was well fitted to face. Ever clinging to cunning, his mastery was of the discerning eye. There, amongst the trees, was his very heart, and his heart beat ever for those woods. Along the path, as the whisper of a phantom, he heard heavy thudding footsteps again, crunching behind. Following.

A moment he stirred, and his song faltered. Turning about this way and that, he set his hand upon the hilt of his sword, though he was only met by the foreboding stillness of the forest. Guardedly, he returned to his song and the path his feet remembered. Again, the drumming steps followed behind. But a few paces onward, he heard the sound, until at last, the man could stomach no more of it.

Fearless, Alan turned and drew his sword, when he met someone familiar. "Little John!" He rolled his eyes, lowering his weapon. "I thought you were one of Claudia's men. A simple greeting would suffice."

The man's breath was heavy, his blue eyes staring indignant, at the outlaw. "You traitor," he mumbled.

"Traitor? What do you- Whoa!" Alan had not one instance to speak his mind before John grabbed him by the collar and held a dagger at his throat.

"All this while, you were fraternising with the enemy?" He shouted; his nostrils flaring. "Make not to appease the offence, lest I make your end!"

"I swear, I do not know who you mean!"

"Oh, you know well of what I speak," he huffed. Hurling Alan to the ground, John paced before the man; his long grey locks waving behind him. "It was you who helped that murderer escape after all. Jack was right, I should have listened long ago. How have you the gall to do it? To lie to Robin, to all of us?"

"I'll not deny it," Alan sat up, his hand upon his chest. "Gisborne is alive, and I did help him escape, but I am no less myself for it, nor am I any less your devoted brother."

"Have you been plotting with him against Robin?"

"Never!"

"Then why did you do it? Why free him?"

"John," Alan sighed. "My reasons are my own. But you must believe me, he's not so villainous as we had condemned him to be."

"Marian's blood is on his hands! The blood of countless people is on his hands, all for the crimes of their poverty. If for no other evil than for killing Marian, he has merited death. A life for a life. And if you cared anything for our master, you would feel no different."

"You would think me so without loyalty?" Alan finally took hold of John, gripping his arm. "Have we not all suffered her loss? She was one of us! And Robin is as much my kinsman as yours. Gisborne has paid the price for his deeds, well enough. We must let it be."

"To let evil be is to let it fester," John snarled. Now with lofty gaze, he towered over the young man. "You have taken pity on a devil, and it has addled your reason. The truth will out, and Robin must know of it, once and for all!"

"Have you no sense?" Alan cried, scrambling to chase after his hasty comrade. "You can't tell him now! What'll that solve?"

John's grey brows raised, as he stood with clenched fists at his side. "His grief has been sustained with a lie. A treacherous lie! And lies cannot comfort a man forever. Robin will accept no excuse as you've kept the truth from him all this while."

"Then what would you tell him? If you truly believed me a false friend, you would have confronted me; you would have rebuked me. You would have brought all your suspicions before the rest of the lads, and you would have had me stand trial. Yet, you knew if any of it were true, that I must have had my reasons. You know I can be trusted. And now you and Jack, as you say, having kept your suspicions to yourselves for so long, only sets you as guilty as I. You said it yourself, Robin will not accept any excuses."

Setting his fists at his hips, John fixed his doleful eyes upon the ground.

"Please think on it, lest you act in haste and undo us all," Alan said, placing his hand upon John's shoulder.

"Our master ought to know," John said. "He deserves no less."

"If Robin knew, he would stop at nothing for the sake of his revenge when a far greater threat has been set at our very feet. Claudia's alliance with Victor cannot be discounted. What benefit is there to our division? Would you have us quarrel amongst each other? Would you have those who depend on us become endangered by our negligence? My friend, we must let the matter be."

Staring off into the tangled woods, Little John stood motionless; thinking. Then after a heavy sigh, he nodded. "Very well," he grumbled. "If we must conceal the matter for a time, then so be it, only so long as Gisborne keeps to himself. But be sure of this, if he poses any threat whatsoever to my master, I swear his blood shall stain my very blade!"

***

As the golden rays of the rising sun shone over the swaying field, the man returned to his precious home. The sweet smelling grass and the cool of the morning dew filled his lungs. Just above the cottage, two sparrows flew, chasing each other as their little wings beat fast. Observing their flight, Guy remained silent, his eyes following as one sung forth his song and the other answered back with her own song; their voices cheery and bright. How it warmed his heart to see such beauty, even in the simplest moment, and it set all his thought on Múriel. She, who waited for him.

Then, as he turned to glance at the woods behind him, dark clouds lingered far away at the shallows of the horizon. A storm, coming.

Facing the cottage once more, now with his hand upon the door, he hesitated.

How can I tell her? He thought.

Firm and steadfast, he opened the door, and there the lady stood. Allayed by his very presence, she flung her arms around his neck and placed a kiss upon his bearded cheek.

"Dieu merci, you're home! I was so worried-"

"I promised I wouldn't be long," he gave a gentle smile.

"May I please speak with you now?"

"My love, whatever it is, forgive me, but it must wait. What I have to tell you, I cannot restrain it a moment longer," he said; his gaze met with hers in such earnest. "Please, let me speak, and then you may lend me all your thought."

"Bien," she obliged, though quite reluctantly.

In much haste, the door was shut fast behind them. Heedlessly, Guy paced back and forth before the hearth, expounding upon his encounter with A'Dale in the forest, and all the outlaw had related to him of Claudia's endeavours. Though he spoke with such severity, the lady's expression somehow shone less and less troubled, and all the more relieved.

"You know," Múriel sighed.

"What do you mean? You... you knew about this?"

"This is precisely what I had wished to tell you all this while," she confessed. "When I had gone to call on Catherine, she told me of how she had been threatened directly; how men were sent out to spy on her home should we appear. I intended to speak of it sooner, but when you had departed yesterday, then I feared you might not return."

"Why did you not tell me this before? If I had known as much, I would have taken more precautions when I left."

"I tried to tell you," she whispered. "But you were so preoccupied and too delighted hearing about the child. I had no wish to upset you. I should have been more forward and made you listen, but I wasn't sure how to tell you... forgive me."

The man's gaze fell in embarrassment, having realised the countless times she had attempted to speak with him of something, though he so thoughtlessly dismissed it. Taking her hands in his, he comforted her.

"No, I should have been more attentive. I never want you to feel that you must keep anything from me," the man dropped his shoulders, "but if Claudia is searching for us, then you must see we have no other choice." Still holding her hands so faithfully, he sighed; his eyes a troubled tempest.

"No choice, but what? I don't understand," she said.

"We must leave."

"Leave?" Múriel shook her head. "You are so determined that you will not consider my thoughts?"

"It's far too dangerous for us to stay as it is," he resolved. "It won't be long before she finds us out. Such a day would come upon us without any warning."

"But it would be near impossible for her to find us. Hardly anyone knows where we live-"

"And who does know where we live? Winifred, Cedric and Catherine, and Eleanor. Already, several people could be forced to reveal our whereabouts."

"Guy, they would never betray us. Surely you know that!"

"No. I do not know that, and neither do you!" He shouted; his eyes fervent and his jaw tensed. "Do not entertain the thought that Claudia would not harm them. I'll not risk their safety any more than I'll risk losing my family, all for being careless!"

Now with tears in her eyes, the lady set her hand upon her heart. "You think it is careless to stay hidden? That it is best for us to abandon our home?"

"I think it's careless for us to be sitting targets!"

"We are not sitting targets. We are in the middle of the wilderness, where few hardly dare to venture! And do you not trust that we are guarded? Unless Claudia is a keen woodsman, she would be hard pressed to find us, indeed. No, we cannot leave our home. This is where we should be raising our child, where we should grow old together."

"Múriel, do you think I make this decision lightly?" The man sighed, sitting down at the table as he rubbed his the bridge of his nose. "I take no pleasure in leaving our home, but the threat is greater than you suspect. If not for A'Dale who came to my aid... I cannot think what anyone might do if they found you."

"But, this is our home. *Our* home," she said, drawing her hand over her mouth.

Tenderly, Guy stood and held her in his arms, as a tear fell down her face. "It is," he sighed. "It was."

"Where would we go?" She whispered.

"I... I don't know."

"Please, can we not take time to think on this?" Múriel entreated. "Let us weigh every course at our disposal; whether we leave or remain. And if we must leave, we cannot wander aimlessly. Promise me, we will not do anything until we've given everything its due thought?"

Closing his eyes a moment, he thought. In truth she was right, they couldn't be so brash, considering the danger that lingered beyond their home. If they were to flee, they must know which road to take. And as he thought better of it, he knew it would be wiser for them to remain hidden for a time, at the very least, until Múriel felt strong enough to travel.

"Very well, my darling," he acknowledged. "You have my word."

***

Abandoned in the midst of a desert, the man stood, the wind howling around him and the sands beneath his feet, blazing and insufferable. As he surveyed the landscape, he found nought but the rolling hills of sand, shifting and changing and shifting again. Fast approaching from the great expanse, a terrible storm turned over the land, the golden sands glistening in the sunlight. East and west, north and south, all at once encircling, and he could not find his way. Under the torrid sun, the man wandered, his vexing thirst could not be quenched. Listless, he fell to his knees, drawing his hands over his face as the sanded winds whipped around him. Doubtless, this would be his end, and none would know of it, save the silent heavens. When the end seemed so sure, suddenly, the winds of sand were held suspended in the air. Looking down at the ground before him, there he saw his own golden brooch and its silver mate beside it. Bringing them up, he held the two and fit them together, so they formed one piece.

As he did so, the engravings of the sun and moon illuminated with such brilliant light. Round and round the lights spun, faster and faster, shining as one, directing him to the far north. Drawing his eyes upward, the man found he was no longer in the harrowing wilderness of the desert, but upon a shoreline; his feet greeted by the cool of the foaming tide, the deep waters, beckoning him. Dauntless, he followed the light, deeper and deeper into the waves of the ocean, never once looking back. Where the light was drawing him, he could not tell, yet all at once, he trusted. His eyes at first upon the waters, then lifting up his gaze, he now stood in a grand hall. A hall of kings.

The walls stood high about him, the arch of the ceiling as high as the heavens, fashioned of oak, and inlaid with strands of gold and silver. Great shields hung upon the walls, and high above, caressed in the gentle breeze, banners of rich and vivid hues hung aloft. His

feet guided him, slowly toward the great light shining over the
throne; a masterpiece a thousand craftsmen could not form.
And there, upon the crest, he found words he did not know,
and yet understood them all at once,
as a voice ever echoing in the depths of him.
Remember, my son.
***

Guy awoke to the music of the rain pitter-pattering on the rooftop, and the brisk morning air reaching through the cracks of the window pane. Setting his hand upon his heart, he panted, casting aside his cares, for he knew it was all but a dream, and he was not so abandoned to foreign lands as he had for a moment believed.

And sweeping through the mists, the rain brought with it the scents of a warm and wakened earth. The garden flowers bloomed once more and the air teemed with such pure fragrance.

Turning over in their bed, the man drew his eyes to Múriel, sleeping peacefully; her long waves glistening in the gentle light, her face glowing. So enchanted by her radiant beauty, he dare not wake her, though tenderly, he smoothed his hand over her, as the child quickened beneath his fingertips.

"Good morning little one," he whispered. Beaming with joy, he laid a kiss upon her belly, and the child kicked again in response, knowing well his deep and steady voice.

Softly, the man drew the covers over the lady's shoulders and kissed her cheek. Retreating from the warmth of their bed, he made ready to begin the work which belonged to that day. As the showers and storm clouds cleared away, he ventured out into the barn and freed the horse to roam the field before the cottage.

So majestic and free, the horse galloped through the emerald deep; his coat of amber shining, his mane waving as a valiant banner, heralding every wild thing to waken. A creature of such strength, such beauty; how nothing in all the world could drive from him his stalwart spirit.

There in the quiet of the garden, the man set to his work, and his mind found such peace in it. The sun only shone here and there upon the land, its rays enough to promise the end of the rain, for a time. Stilling his breath, the man could hear the song of the morning humming its pleasant melody, and drifting overhead; the birds singing forth and the wind welcoming their eager wings. When the morning work was finished, the man returned to the cottage to fix breakfast, determined to surprise Múriel, who still lay fast asleep. Quietly, the man entered the bedchamber with a tray of food in hand and set it on the nightstand beside her.

"Darling," he whispered as he sat by her side, stroking her silken locks, watching as she stirred.

"Bonjour, amour," she grinned contentedly, her grey eyes gazing up at him. Then slowly bringing her hands down to her growing belly, she smiled so blissfully, "Bonjour mon doux petit," she whispered. "Oh, won't it be grand when he's finally here?"

"*He?*" Guy lowered his chin, "Not two weeks ago, you were determined to have a daughter," he smirked.

"Well, now I am quite certain. We are having a son," she nodded cheerfully as she sat up.

"How do you know?"

"My heart tells me so," Múriel smiled. Drawing her hand up to her husband's face, she perceived something dark which lingered behind his eyes. "What's wrong?"

Lowering his head, he removed from the bed; pacing. Stern, he stood, glancing out the window; his finger tracing down the pane, as he looked out upon their waving field of green.

"How... how are you feeling?" He muttered.

"Well, indeed," she answered. Taking to the man's side, she held his face once more, though his gaze was hesitant to meet hers. "What is it? What are you not saying?"

"If you are feeling better, then, it is time," he resolved. "We must make ready this day and then, we shall depart tomorrow, at first light."

With tears in her eyes, Múriel's gaze fell as she backed away. Hardly a word could rise from her lips, and she searched so ardently for the words to say, for her heart was aching. "Must we leave?" She whispered.

Compassionate, Guy drew her into his arms, embracing her with such tenderness. "We must," he said. "Though time will never draw breath and though our feet must wander many miles, we shall never forget this place. And far from it as we may be, we will find new joy in what lays beyond. You, ever in my arms, and I, ever in your heart... in such a treasure as this, there is always hope," he promised.

While sorrow held fast her spirit, Múriel took comfort in his words.

All that day they made ready, gathering together what could be taken and silently bidding farewell to the home they would never see again.

As the evening sun hung low in the sky, Múriel ventured out into the garden to collect herbs. With her basket and knife in hand, she knelt down to begin her work, the darkness of the world closing in as the sun sunk behind the trees. It seemed a shadow grew ever more in her mind; a shadow and a doubt, though she repressed it. Go they must, and there would be no turning back. Then, in the distance, she heard hastening footsteps, drawing nearer and nearer.

"Guy?" She called out, peering around as she rose to her feet; listening. There the empty forest stared; haunting.

No answer.

Gradually she knelt down, only pretending to set to work again; the knife held firm in her grip; her ears sharp. Again she heard the footsteps; measured and cautious. Ominous, the weighted feeling of two eyes watching her set her heart pounding. Still, she remained; still as stone. Then, a voice called out from the forest.

"Múriel! Psst! Múriel!"

Beyond the well, she searched until her eyes fell on a figure moving through the trees. Startled, she let out a cry, but as she soon recognised that face, she lowered the blade, relieved.

"Eleanor!" She called, as the young lady cautiously descended into the garden. "Mon Dieu, I've not seen you in so long," Múriel said, as she embraced her friend. "What are you doing here? Is everything alright?"

"I wanted to be certain you were safe and to give you a message," Eleanor whispered. Warily, she backed away, observing the lady's figure. "He... he has done this to you?"

"You mean my husband?"

"I mean Gisborne," Eleanor returned.

Nervous, Múriel brought a hand over her belly. "How long have you known?"

"Long enough," the lady answered, setting her hand on her friend's shoulder in earnest. "My friend, you've no reason to conceal anything from me. Tell me truly... has he forced your hand in any way? Has he threatened you such that-"

"He has done all that is good and honourable. He is a good man, Eleanor. A kind man," Múriel said.

"You would stand by him so willingly?" The young lady wondered. "Have not his crimes proved his heart?"

"His heart is much changed from when we had once judged it."

Eleanor's eyes shone discontented at these words; her dark locks blowing in the breeze as she stood silent. Then, with breath afresh within her lungs, she spoke once more. "You know I can never accept the path you've chosen, but I must know once and for all, why?"

"I love him," she said. "Cannot love conquer darkness?"

Bewildered, the lady stared, for she could not spar with such a friend over such a thing, though she wished to in her heart, for her loathing of the man. "You forget why I've come," she said. "Doubtless, you know Claudia has been searching for you, yes?"

"Oui, I know this," Múriel nodded. "That is why we-"

"Please, listen. There is something more that I fear you may not know," the lady bit her lip, hesitant. "Claudia has made a deal with Sheriff Victor that he might supply her with a dispatch of mercenaries to capture and kill the Rebel and his company."

"How many mercenaries?"

"Fifty, though there is talk there may be more," she answered. "She will not be so idle with such a force and her time is choked well enough, for the prince has demanded she bring him Robin by the end of the summer, or he shall have her hung as a traitor."

"Then, I must tell Guy we should flee tonight while she is so occupied. If she is so bent on discovering Robin, she will not care if we should-"

"No! I've come to warn you to stay hidden as long as ever you can," the young lady urged. "Her men are well informed of the criminals to be sought after, including you and Gisborne. Now there are camps of soldiers spreading all across the forest, such that I've risked my own life coming here to tell you this."

"Merci, pour tout," Múriel whispered. "But what of Robin and his men? Are they safe?"

"Aye, we've already taken precautions to ward off any soldiers, and have set some traps. But I beg of you to stay here. Claudia will not find you, I am sure, and the end of summer is not so far from our reach."

Faint and far off, Múriel heard Guy's voice, calling out to her.

"I must go. I should return to the camp before dark," Eleanor said.

"But will you be safe remaining amongst the company?" The lady wondered.

"Múriel?" Guy called once more, his voice drawing closer.

As Eleanor peered around the cottage, she found him close in view and whispered in great haste. "I shall try to call on you again when I am free to do so, though that may not be for some time."

"Please, promise me you will be careful," the lady sighed.

"I will," she nodded.

Embracing, the two bid farewell to each other. Múriel stood resolute, watching as the lady disappeared amongst the woods behind the garden. Breathless, the man paused at the entrance of the garden gate, finding his wife standing in silence, facing the woods.

"I thought I heard you scream," he said, "Is everything alright?"

As she glanced back at her husband, her eyes shone dark. "Amor, there is much to tell you."

CHAPTER TWENTY-ONE

SILENCE

Pale, the morning light cascaded into the great hall of Locksley.

Much of the manor was quiet as Claudia descended from her bedchamber; her golden hair loosely flowed behind her, bright against the dark blues of her silk gown. With light and measured step, she reached the centre of the hall and stood before the arched window at the left of the fireplace. Slowly, her eyes looked out unto the dawn of a late summer morning; her ivory hands resting gently at the window ledge.

Breathing deep the quiet moment, she remained.

Suddenly, all calm was broken, for just as she heard the pounding of horse's hoofs and men's voices bustling, the doors to the manor were opened, and there, standing in the entrance with all fire behind his eyes; the sheriff.

"Claudia!" He called, marching forth. "How many men were given you?"

Astonished, the woman's heart raced within her; her eyes wide with fright. "My lord," she fumbled, as she bowed, "I don't understand-"

"Fifty, I had given you! Gracious and trusting, I gave them you!" He snarled. "Now, I am told men have been leaving their office."

"Your grace, that cannot be," the woman said.

"*That cannot be,* so you say? Have you not spoken with the captain?" Victor pressed.

"No, not since the orders were given to search for the outlaws. I instructed him not to return to me until the deed was done," she returned. "How many of my men have fled?"

"No," Victor shook his head, "Of *my* men, seventeen altogether have returned wounded; several caught up in what traps have been laid all across the forest by those reckless outlaws, and two are yet being held ransom. One hundred crowns per man, the Rebels have demanded!"

"And you'll heed their demands?" Claudia wondered.

"Yes! If nearly twenty men are decommissioned thus far, would not abandoning two more to an outlaw's judgement cause the men to despise the one who sends them?" He replied. "On behalf of the men I so generously bestowed, you shall meet the outlaw's demands."

"Me? Give my money to the Rebel for some meaningless soldiers?" She scoffed. "They'll not get a penny."

"Oh, yes they will," he demanded. "For I've suffered pains enough in assuming the daftest, most incompetent woman of all England could complete a simple feat such as capturing a ruddy band of outlaws whose concealment is nought but leaves and twigs!" He roared. Taking up a chair from the table, he hurled it across the hall. "You are finished, woman!"

"Finished?" She gulped. "What do you mean *finished*? Have I not been loyal to you, my lord?" She begged at his feet.

"Get up!"

"But what of the prince's demands? Summer is nearly gone, and I must have the outlaw!"

"Would that you could think for the sake of your own head," Victor muttered under his grey whiskers. "I shall resume command of the task since you are so inept. You shall ready the ransom money for my soldiers at once, and after, the real work begins."

"What do you mean?" She asked as she rose to her feet.

"The mercenaries will begin taking in witnesses for questioning today, and you shall make the announcement," he said. "For any who have ties with the outlaws, any of the outlaws, they shall be brought to the Nottingham dungeons."

"And what if they divulge nothing of the rebels?" She wondered. "What then?"

"Don't worry," he said, "we'll find ways of making them talk."

***

"Why can't I go to her?" Eleanor complained. "Please, I gave her my word I would call on her as soon as possible."

"Will you be gathering supplies?" Robin questioned.

"Well, no."

"Or delivering food to the needy?"

"No, but-"

"Then you already know my answer," Robin said. "John and Tuck are to take the soldiers safely to Locksley and glean the ransom. When they have made the exchange, they must go on to give the money to the people and finally, return to the camp. While they are away, Jack and I shall work to devise another decoy camp to the east. Only Alan and Will are left here, to tend the camp and-"

"And watch the helpless lass sit all day as an idle stump?" She folded her arms across her chest.

"Eleanor, this is not a question of your skill, but of your safety. It would be wrong to let you go off into the forest defenceless."

"Do you think me so entirely helpless?" She asked. "I am capable of defending myself if need be, and I know these woods, the mercenaries do not!"

"They are well trained and armed for combat," Robin reasoned. "You are a good fighter, but you are no soldier."

"Could not Will escort me there?" She wondered.

"Two together at all times. You know the rule," he sighed. "Many against one is an ambush. Many against two is a battle. And two can easily overpower a dispatch if they work together. Alan cannot be left to defend the camp alone."

"Then I must go back on my word to Múriel?" She petitioned. "I must be made a liar?"

Without another word or glance, Robin took up his bow and quiver of arrows and walked away from the fire pit toward Jack. As he reached the lad, the two set off to the east of their dwelling, and Eleanor was left with her clenched fists at her side, and her dark eyes stern.

How the heat of the sun beamed down through the boughs overhead, as blossoms of light scattered here and there across the forest, illuminating her form. As she stood, quiet footsteps drew near her, and a hand took hold of hers.

"Come," Will smiled softly. "Help me gather firewood."

"He thinks I'm a child," she said. "He thinks I'm useless."

"You don't believe that," Will answered.

"Why else would he have me trapped in the camp like this?" She muttered.

Sweeping a lock of her dark hair away from her sullen face, the outlaw gazed down on her with understanding. "You are quick-witted and loyal and stouthearted, as no other lass I've ever known. All of us know your strengths, right well. Master Robin is merely doing what is best for all of us, as befits our circumstances. Surely, you know this."

"But for months I've been made to wait behind, every day, while the rest of you may be put to good work! Fashioning traps and false camps, and warring against soldiers. And I've not grumbled over my lot. I've done my duties, here at the camp, and haven't strayed. But now, I am denied leave to call on my friend, when she is in just as much danger as we? It is not fair."

Letting out a deep sigh, Will brought his arms about the lass and held her fast. "In times of trouble, each of us is called to make sacrifices, and none escape the necessity of it. To ignore it, one loses all, but to accept it, one may lose but little and come to realise it was a small thing to let go of all along," he said. "But risking your life is not the sacrifice I ever wish to make." Pulling back, he stared into her dark eyes.

Nodding, she understood the man and embraced him. Still, in her heart, she loathed this constant feeling, this state of uselessness. When the day had ended, the soldiers returned to their captain, the ransom given in secret to the poor of Locksley, and every outlaw had come home to the quiet of Sherwood again, Eleanor sat determined. She spoke no other word against Robin, but in her mind devised her way.

By nightfall, when all the men had gone to sleep, she lay staring up at the starlit skies. Breathing in the cool of the late summer air, the scent of the fire swirled in her lungs. She could feel its warmth at her feet, and the glow of its light spread over her face. The forest stood calm all about the camp, as the men each slept in their cots. Peeking cautiously, the lady looked on at Will to her right and the steady movement of his shoulders as he breathed; sound asleep. What copper strands of his hair caught up in the breeze shone brilliantly in the firelight, and the ends of his beard glistened as red flame. When she felt safe to do it, she opened her eyes completely and stared down past her feet. Jack was still keeping watch by the fire. Thus, it was only the second hour; Tuck would not take up the watch until the fourth hour. Indeed, by the fourth hour, the forest would not be so full of shadows.

Stay awake, Eleanor thought. *Only two more hours. Stay awake.*

As she lay there, worn from the length of the night, she gripped tight the dagger at her side, and slowly, to keep Jack from any suspicion, she reached one arm down under her cot to pull out her boots. To the edge, and no farther, she pulled them, and let the corner of her blanket cover them.

Finally, as those hours crept by, Eleanor watched with eager eye and strained breath as Jack stood up and stretched his arms. With a crunching of leaves under each step, the lad made his way back to the cots and stopped.

"Tuck," he whispered, nudging the old man's shoulder. "Tuck, to the watch."

"Aye," the man grumbled, bringing each foot down to the earth, as he sat up. "Go on, get some sleep then."

With a pat on the shoulder, Jack nodded at the old man, and went off toward his own bunk and settled in it. Drowsily, Tuck departed from the warmth of his blankets and turned toward the fire. His step was slow and his eyes weary. Eleanor's heart pounded in her chest, for she knew it was nearly time; she could hear the early song of the birds echoing in the trees, and admittedly, as the old man sat by the fire, its flames did not blaze so strikingly against a dark forest for all about was waking.

Turning her head to the left, the young lady examined the row of other men. Closest to her was Alan, then beyond him, Robin, John, and just before Tuck's cot, was Jack. All laid still and sound.

Now was her chance.

Heart racing, her breath shallow, she let one foot down, then the other. Tuck's back was turned to the camp, and so he would not see, but she feared his hearing. With both feet down, she slowly slipped them into her boots and fastened the leather strings tightly. Then, lifting her hood, her satchel strung across her shoulder, Eleanor backed away from the camp, step by step, and when she was far enough that the flames of the fire looked no bigger than the nail of her finger, she ran.

Onward, she journeyed, toward the path.

I must reach the cottage by dawn, she thought.

Along the way, as she drew nearer and nearer to the elder trees, she suddenly heard a rustling sound come from behind her. Halting in her step, she held her breath and peered around.

Nothing.

A few more paces, she strolled, and soon heard the rustling again, no longer from behind her, but coming from her left and from her right. Once more, she stood still; listening. Turning her head this way and that, her eyes fell on nothing, though her heart warned her fiercely.

Then, just as she made to step forward, a hand reached out from behind her and covered her mouth.

***

Seated at a table, in the dark of the dungeon chamber, Victor waited.

Two guards stood at either side of him, as he scribbled away on a bit of parchment. The light of the room was dim, as only one torch hung from the damp stone wall. The sounds of muffled cries and the heavy thudding of the guards echoed from beyond the chamber, and suddenly, a knock came heavy upon the door.

"Enter!" The sheriff called. As the door opened, Victor's gaze fell on the young lady who wrestled against the soldiers.

"No!" She protested, "Let go of me!"

Inexorable, the two men ushered the captive in, casting her to the floor; the chains which bound her hands rattling, and scraping against her wrists.

"So, a comrade of Robin Hood. A bonny maid to be sure," the sheriff remarked, eying the prisoner with devilish pleasure. "Here are my terms; if you tell me what I wish to know, I will show mercy. Lie, and you shall know the pain of consequence. Now, tell me, where is the rebel camp?"

Intrepid, the young woman rose to her feet and spat at the man, her hair hanging in front of her face. "I will die first!"

"You might," the man returned, as he wiped the saliva from his cheek. Deliberate, he advanced toward the lady, clutching her jaw with his bony fingers. "How was she discovered?" He called to the guards behind her.

"We caught sight of her wandering the forest before daybreak; it would seem, from other sources, she was once a servant to Lady Claudia and an accomplice to the robbery of the manor."

Upon hearing such a report, the man raised his brows and curled his lips. As he leaned close to the prisoner, the man's breath could be felt on her cheek.

"Ah, how fitting," he sneered mockingly. "Well, you might prove a difficult horse to break, but when I'm finished with you, you'll be broken, indeed."

***

Restless, the men waited for the return of their comrades, as the darkness of night engulfed them. Caged within their dwelling, Robin worked, preparing more and more arrows, along with Alan and John, as Tuck busied himself with other tasks. Not a one spoke a word, for the silent dread haunted them; not knowing whether Will and Jack would return.

Then, three sharp whistles resounded through the eaves; the call of the outlaws. They had returned! With eager footsteps, the men bounded toward the edge of the camp, finding Jack and Will panting, and alone.

"Jack!" John called, "Have you any news?"

"No, father," the lad sighed, removing the hood of his cloak. "There's no sign of where she went."

Downcast, Will's eyes welled with tears, "We searched as far as Locksley. We questioned everyone we could... none have seen her."

"Do not lose hope," Robin consoled, "We will find Eleanor."

"And what if she's been captured?" Will cried, gripping his comrade's collar. "It has been three days, Robin. Three days and no sign of her! She is out there somewhere, waiting for me to come and find her, the very one who should have protected her... this is my fault, and I have failed her." Falling to his knees, the man brought his hands to his face.

"No, you've not failed her, and we will not abandon her to any harm," Robin insisted, setting his hands firm on the man's shoulders. "My brother, she will not be lost from us forever; we will search again tomorrow, I swear it. But for now, we must rest. The hour grows late."

The man nodded, comforted by his master's counsel, though his worry would give him no rest that night.

As the men ate and soon set to sleep, Robin and Jack were the first to keep watch by the fire, watching as the swirls of smoke rose high in the midnight air, blotting out the stars. There was no wind to give them music, and the woods lay far too still, and silent, and empty, but for the crackling of the fire.

"Master, is it right that we should only venture out for such a short time? Could we not search longer?" Jack whispered, his soft eyes reflective.

"It's too dangerous," the outlaw stroked his beard. "Evil days have been set hard upon us. This is precisely why I had established the curfew, to prevent such things as someone disappearing. We cannot risk more than we can lose."

"I do not contend with you on this reasoning, but all the same, we cannot pretend she is not in grave danger. And we cannot patronise Will."

"The matter cannot be diluted, but he must keep his wits about him if we are to find the lass. If I give my kinsman any confidence with my words, it is kindly meant. I know all too well what brash, witless anger does to a man... what loss does to a man," he paused, gazing off into the woods as he reflected.

"Oh," Jack mumbled, fidgeting with the edge of his sleeve, as a question on his mind pounded and pounded within his head until finally, his mouth could detain it no longer. "Master," he hesitated, "what truly happened, to Lady Marian?"

Forlorn, Robin sighed, twisting the ring about his finger as he shut his eyes a moment, contriving his answer, or what answer his barred heart could surrender. For a moment he remained silent, and Jack began to fear for finding his feet wandering on sacred ground. "Forgive me, I-"

"It's alright," the man reassured. "It's been so long since I've spoken of her, I hardly know where to begin."

Another moment of silence lingered in the air. Jack's mind ever curious, and Robin's heart heavy laden.

"What happened? What was she like?" The lad coaxed once more, still lacking in learning his place, yet the outlaw was both patient and gracious to accept him.

"She was the boldest, most fearless woman I'd ever known," he smiled. "Kindhearted through and through, and my heart trusted in her as none else. But, I could not tame her, nor persuade her to still her wild spirit. And I was an idle husband. She should have remained with me in the forest, but I let her do as she wished. Marian was adamant, believing it would be easier to keep the marriage hidden whilst she remained in Nottingham; and being the king's niece, she could lend us aid if ever we needed it."

Pausing a moment, Robin stared back at the fire, unsure of how he could continue, for his own conscience bid him suffer. Then he spoke, "Not long before her arrest, she found she was with child, and still like a blind fool I let her go back. I indulged her far too willingly. Somehow, Gisborne discovered her, and I was too late. It was my fault she met such an end," bowing his head in shame, the man brought his hand over his face.

"No," the lad shook his head, "no, master, surely you cannot blame yourself! Sir Guy is the one whose hands are stained with their blood! He is the villain!"

"Aye, 'twas his hands that spilt such innocent blood and as long as I live I'll never forgive him; but all the same, it was my folly," the man confessed. "I fear for William. I have borne this guilt as no man ever should, and I would not wish it upon any man; to lose what is so precious in neglecting diligence, and duty, and care. You see, Jack, he may be anxious to save the lass, but I am anxious to spare him such lament as has befallen upon my own spirit."

Jack could scarce manage any answer but stared at the man; astounded.

For such long years, the name of Robin Hood had stirred up such courage and passion within him. A man who sacrificed all for the benefit of his people, in the face of an evil rule. Yet here, in such a moment as this, seeing him and knowing him, knowing him and revering him; how impartially the lad felt such pity and such pride. For though this man before him was so stricken, his perseverance proved all the more his worthiness.

"Robin," the lad whispered, setting his hand firm upon the man's shoulder, "if ever a man has lived well enough to be given honour, it is you."

Rising to his feet, the lad bowed his head and retreated from the fire. Although the lad's words passed in such fleeting measure, Robin remained before the fire, meditating upon them; and wept.

***

Alone, Eleanor stood chained to the wall of the cell, each hand shackled above her.

No light could comfort her, for the dark was as a thick abyss before her tired eyes; ominous and cold, the damp cell snuffed out all hope. Weary from sleeplessness, the young lady let her head hang; her eyes closed only to shut herself within her own mind. Her whole being ached and the wounds from her beatings were raw. Her side bled, and the pangs of hunger were unbearable.

Why has he not come? She thought. *Oh please, please come.*

Suddenly, the creaking of the iron bars startled her. Jolting her head back up, and shivering, she watched as a light from a single torch blazed before her, and two figures approached.

"It appears we have the perfect suspect. A member of the Rebel's elusive company, and the former keeper of Locksley Manor,"

Victor's daunting voice resounded against the stone walls. "You, my dear, have been withholding crucial information from your sovereign," he scolded, drawing nearer. "Now, I am prepared to show mercy if you are willing to cooperate, but I only give you this final chance to redeem yourself. Tell us plainly, where is Robin Hood?"

The young lady made no answer, yet kept to hanging her head low. After a moment of silence, she slowly brought her gaze up to the villains and spat at them.

"I will not betray my conscience or my kin," she said, a fire lit in her eyes as she made her final resolve.

Enraged and untamed, Claudia slapped Eleanor across her cheek and clutched the young lady's face in her hand.

"Confess, you repugnant whore!" The woman shrieked madly; her nostrils flaring. "I am sick of your games! Where is the Rebel? Where are Sir Guy and the lass with the silver brooch? Confess it! Confess it all this instant or I shall have your vile head hanged!"

"*Sir Guy?*" Victor's brows raised, indignant. Forcing the woman against the wall, he gripped his hand around her neck, the veins in her face pulsing. "He lives?"

"A minor indiscretion, my lord," she panted.

"You dare manipulate your superior!" Throwing her to the ground, the woman trembled, drawing a hand up to her throat. "I shall determine your fate in due course. As for you," the man returned to the captive, "If you are so determined to be a stubborn wretch, then I have no choice. At dawn, you shall be hung by the neck until dead."

"No, my lord!" Claudia begged. "She knows too much! Can we not detain her a day longer? Hold her for ransom? Surely, the outlaw Scarlet would-"

"It has been near a week, and we've gained nothing! She has outlived her usefulness!" He howled, his dark eyes narrowing. "If we are to capture the Rebel successfully, and any remaining traitors to the crown, we must make an example of her. Anyone who harbours or aids a fugitive must be tried to the fullest extent of the law. No measure of treason will be tolerated!"

What words that followed, Eleanor could not comprehend, for fear struck her very heart, and there was no respite.

Haunting, the dim light of dawn came.

Bound and gagged, she stood at the gallows as crowds of people gathered; a sea of strange faces, who would forget her at the foreboding end. In her frightened and breaking heart, she knew there would be no rescue. Her mind raced, terrified. Her hands shook, and every bone in her body bid her flee, but where?

Then, a strong and unwavering spirit of bravery stirred up within her, as she thought on her love, knowing she had prevailed. With her feet firmly set upon the ground, she would face death. She could face this final curse for the glory of that great dawn approaching. For freedom, and the future it would gift this broken land.

The judgement was all a mist of a man's hateful voice and a crowd of the ignorant chanting; all was as a blur in Eleanor's mind.

Then, the moment came; linen as white as snow came over her eyes, and the rope clung fast around her neck. Death was a bitter cup to bear, yet beyond, it was not the end.

CHAPTER TWENTY-TWO

OF SORROW AND SEEKING

Summer was swiftly hastening on, as autumn drew fast on its heels.

The trees stood clad in bright green leaves, as the sun cast brilliant hues of light like the dappling of fairy dust across the beaten path. Though nature would have them comforted, the looming shadow that lay beyond bid their eyes and ears be vigilant.

The sun began to set upon the seventh day of Eleanor's disappearance.

Scarlet ventured out every day, searching and searching, as each of his comrades took their turn in accompanying him. Door after door they passed, and still no word. No one had seen her, and many who knew the outlaws feared to answer, for the whole village was teeming with soldiers whose ravenous ears were eager for any mention of the rebels.

For days, Scarlet scarcely ate or slept for worry, and what faint and fragile light of hope he had so faithfully clung to was all but snuffed out.

As evening fell, the company set off to sleep while A'Dale took the first watch. There he sat alone before the fading fire, its embers growing dim. High above the forest, the sky hung thick and dark and hollow. Neither moon nor star could aid the night, for a tempestuous call resounded through the wood, its threat growing nearer. By and by, the man remained; his breath ever steady. No sound of the night, nor the heralding thunder could deter him from his thought. Suddenly, that which he could not see or hear cautioned him; a sense of something lost.

As the outlaw rose and turned to face the camp behind him, Will was gone; his cot found bare of all his belongings, save the bed coverings. Not knowing which way the man went, Alan clung again to his senses. He closed his eyes and waited; trusting.

East, he thought. *But, the men*

The outlaw stood fixed, conflicted as he looked upon his kinsmen.

There is no time, he resolved.

He could not chance to wake them, for if more than two had advanced to reach Will, it would draw too much attention to them; and Tuck was not set to keep watch until the second hour. Thus, Alan determined to risk time and trouble for the sake of his brother. His feet far more driven than his reason, the man lifted his hood, and sprinted through the wood, in search of Scarlet.

At length, Alan observed a figure not so far ahead upon the path. Fastidious in his stealth, the figure paced ever forward; the sway and rhythm of his step, Alan knew right well. Undoubtedly, it was Scarlet, yet the outlaw could not cry out to his comrade. He daren't. There was no telling what blades or bows hid amidst the shadows. Beneath the wave of the thunder's brawling, Alan made good on his intent and hastened onward towards the man. Impetuous and steadfast. Despite such delay, the man panted not a few paces from his comrade. But, keen as a hawk, Will spun around with his sword at Alan's neck.

"Wait!" The outlaw gulped, his hands raised up. "It's only me!"

Letting out a deep breath, the man lowered his sword and kept silent, as his gaze revealed such sullen preoccupation.

"I know you're worried, Will, but you cannot abandon the company like this. It's far too dangerous," he said. "We can search again tomorrow-"

"I must find her," Scarlet whispered, "I will not rest until she is found. Go back to the camp," he ordered. "Leave me be."

"No," the outlaw grasped his arm. As he scanned the forest about them, he lowered his chin and whispered, "This is foolishness... let me come with you."

As Will gazed out unto the road that stretched before him, he thought; his arms folded across his chest.

"Very well," he permitted. "You may come, but you must promise not to speak a word of this to Robin."

"As it is, we've only a few hours before Tuck is set to keep watch, and then Robin will surely know. If we are to search, we must make haste," Alan insisted.

At this, the two men dashed through the forest, with an air of sanguine ardour. A'Dale and Scarlet ventured tirelessly in their pursuit of Eleanor and made for Locksley once more. Perhaps those with words to speak might find some reassurance in the night's concealment. Heavy-hearted, the men drew upon the village. The storm overhead afforded little ease as the rain descended upon the world below. As they passed on the way, they perceived three soldiers not far beyond them. One was of considerable height, the other fared quite stocky, and the third had a long, dark beard. Though the soldiers did not mark the outlaws, all three came marching in their direction, and they were not likely to let them pass.

"Quick, over here!" Alan whispered as he and his comrade hid behind a bale of hay.

"Why did you do that?" Will complained in a harsh whisper, "We could easily question those men as anyone else-"

"Are you mad? There are three of them and only two of us!"

"You think we are no match for them?"

"I think we've no idea if they could be of any aid at all, and we'd do better not to test it. Wait," Alan held up his hand, bringing a finger to his lips. For just as the rebels had knelt down and were given a moment to bicker, the soldiers drew closer. A'Dale and Scarlet steadied their breaths, fixing themselves as still as statues, their sharp ears listening, as the others continued talking.

"This morning?" The bearded fellow questioned.

"Aye. The sheriff wouldn't tolerate it any further," the burly man sighed. "Shame it is; the maid couldn't have been more than nineteen-"

"Well, serves her right, for fraternising with those outlaws," the tall man said. "If you ask me, they should have done her in long before."

"True enough," the burly man said. "And mind, if only she had confessed of the outlaws' camp, and of the maid with the silver trinket, we might all be free of this madness!"

No, Will whispered. *They cannot mean-*

Shh! Alan chided, holding his comrade back.

"That lass knew of the matter?" The bearded man questioned.

"Indeed," the burly man confirmed. "She knew enough of every sort of criminal, so they say, and there was evidence enough against her for having been one of the Rebel's allies. When at first they could not persuade her to confess, they gave her over to the sheriff himself. Still, she kept silent."

"Damn the lot," the bearded fellow shuttered. "They didn't hang her for sport so much as to put her out of her misery, I'd wager."

"Aye, a gruesome fate all the same, though perhaps the villagers will be more pressed to finally give up the bloody Rebel and put us all out of our misery," the tall man concluded.

Will could scarcely draw breath for he knew of whom they spoke; his face flushed white, and his very heart ached. Wrestling against Alan's hold, his distress boiled into rage. The man could not hold back his brother any longer.

Bursting forth, Scarlet ambushed the soldiers and drew his sword. Clutching the collar of the burly man's tunic, the copper-haired outlaw held the blade against the soldier's pale and pulsing throat; his eyes something savage, as he confronted the man.

"No! Stop!" Alan cried, drawing forth his own blade, as the other soldiers stood ready for the fight. "What are you doing?"

"Tell me it was not her!" Will snarled. "Tell me it was not Eleanor!"

"You are not in your right mind! Come away!" Alan called out, though Will would not heed his words.

"I do not know of whom you speak!" The man trembled.

"The lass who hung, what was her name? Tell me her name!" Will urged the soldier, pressing the blade against his skin so that it drew blood. "Answer me!"

"I swear, I heard no mention of her name!" The man begged, "Only that a maid with dark hair hung this morning, and she, an intimate of the Rebel's men!"

"Wait a minute," the lofty man tilted his head as he stared at Alan. "I know you! They're the Rebel's men, lads! Sound the alarm!"

Unhinged from all restraint, Will thrust his sword through the soldier's side and sent him to the muddy ground.

With not a moment to lose, the other soldiers fought hard against their foes. Swords were raised high in the throes of the storm, and the mud beneath their stamping feet sloshed and spattered. Finally, though the outlaws could hardly render justice for it, the soldiers were felled under their very blades. As the angered voices and the sound of the rain beating against their weapons drifted away, Alan shook his head.

"Will," he sighed, wiping the blood from his brow, "You should have listened to me. This was wrong."

"I did what was necessary."

"Necessary?" Alan said. "*Never shed innocent blood.* Are those not words we swore by?"

"Do not speak to me of the oaths-"

"But you have not marked them! Brother, these men did not deserve to die!"

"They did not deserve to die?" Will's vengeful eyes brimmed, grasping his comrade by the shoulders. "Eleanor did not deserve to die!"

"But they did not kill her!"

"No... no, I did," Will panted, his eyes downcast. "I was not there. I was not there to protect her, and now she is gone from me." Bringing his hands up to his face, he fell to his knees and wept bitterly.

With his hand laid upon his own heart, Alan could find no words to comfort his kinsman, for he too was grieved in his spirit. Staring hard with woeful eyes, he could hardly keep back his own tears and held fast to his brother.

***

As the weary men returned, sore and soaked to the bone, the rain had finally passed, though the night was far from over.

Bewildered and perturbed, the rest of the company sat about the freshly lit fire, arguing; the flames illuminating their anxious faces. Yet, as Tuck caught the phantom comrades in his view, he sprinted toward them.

"You reckless fools!" He scolded, his grey brows furrowed. "You're right lucky to be standing here alive! But sure as the halls of Vorík, I'll have you two dead at my feet if you don't explain yourselves! Where were you?"

"Oh, for good and all, we know where they ventured," John huffed, as his moustache curled.

"Not now, John," Robin marched forward, his green eyes heavy. "Men, have you anything to say for yourselves?"

The comrades stood silent, their gaze cast downward. They could not speak, for what words could be said? Yet as Will's eyes met his master's, in them was all the answer Robin needed; and he understood.

At length, the rest of the men were given the account and were sorely grieved for the loss of Eleanor, but of the fallen soldiers, Robin saw fit to let the matter be, for though he was angered, nought else could be reconciled now.

Before the first light of dawn could cast its fragile glow upon the world, the men sought to honour the death of so brave and faithful a maid. Together, in the waning darkness, the men journeyed through the forest to the great oak. Ever it stood, unwavering in its ageless wisdom and constant above all else. It was there, in such a sacred place, that the men brought forth stone after stone and built a cenotaph. Upon it did they fix a sign which read, *The Golden Sacrifice*. There, William bid farewell to his love, though in his heart he trusted he would see her again, for in the very moment the sunlight broke across the skies, he felt her presence beside him.

***

Days passed, and though the man could not set aside his sorrow, he felt such an inescapable urge as a thought ever broadened in his mind.

As night fell, Scarlet kept the first watch, for he insisted, though his comrades considered him. Howbeit, he was adamant, and so the men obliged him. At length, when all the world was quiet, and the men lay fast asleep, he took up his belongings and made ready to flee the camp. For his feet would not permit him to be idle and his mind would give him no rest, for the question that nagged him. As he stepped lightly away, suddenly a hand fell on his shoulder.

"Will," Robin's steady voice whispered, "Where are you going?" The outlaw paused in his steps, and turning to face his master, he sighed. "You are not abandoning us, are you?" Robin questioned.

"No," Scarlet shook his head, his eyes saddened. "No, master, never. Forgive me, I took no pleasure in deceiving you, even in the smallest measure. But... I must find the lass."

"What lass?"

"Eleanor did not face death merely for our sake, but also for the sake of the lass with the silver brooch. I should have believed her; we all should have heeded her words when she spoke of her friend."

"I remember that maiden and am confident she could never be capable of any evil. But you are not suggesting that Gisborne is truly alive?" Robin lowered his chin.

"No… perhaps… I cannot tell," the man closed his eyes. "It's only rumoured this lass is harbouring a criminal, but all the uncertainties aside, I need to know why Eleanor would die for her," Will begged.

"Would you not die for your kinsman?"

"Master, I believe there is more to it than the simple bonds of fellowship," he sighed. "Do you recall her name?"

"Múriel," Robin said. "But this seems to me, a fool's errand," he shook his head disapprovingly. "We should not be divided in this hour."

"We are not divided, master," the outlaw answered. "Eleanor thought this worth dying for, and that cannot be discredited."

"But, what about the rest of the men? What would you have me tell them?"

"Tell them whatever you judge to be right," he nodded, "but certainly, tell them I'll return."

"Very well, but you must swear to return in three days," Robin challenged.

"You have my word," Scarlet promised. "If I've not returned by then, count me as lost, and do what must be done for the good of the company."

"Oh, Will," Robin sighed, "Do not esteem yourself so low. If you are lost, then surely we shall seek you. Good luck."

"Thank you," Will nodded. As he bid his master farewell, he turned to face the path ahead, and so followed it.

***

Two days had gone, and still, no answers.

Embittered, Will toiled to find the lass with the silver brooch, yet the journey was bringing him round and round again in hopeless circles. None knew of who she was and those who gave any hint of understanding were far too quick to turn the man away; for they had already been taunted enough by this very inquiry, and it seemed this mysterious maiden was becoming an ill-favoured household name. Despite all this, the man resolved to make one final inquiry before returning to his kinsmen.

As the crimson hues of the sunset washed over the tops of the trees and the rows of thatched roofs, the third day drew to an end. Every villager retreated into their home, and high above the village, as one great puff of cloud hung in the atmosphere the smoke from their chimneys. All the savoury scents of herbs and stews cooking filled the air, and Will's stomach grumbled. He had only taken a few provisions with him to keep his load light and had hoped to gain some hospitality on his quest, but there was no such door to welcome him in. With a deep breath and the weight of the world upon his shoulders, the man marched to the entrance of an old, reliable healer. Surely some answers and a bit of wisdom could be found therein. As he reached the cottage, he rapped his knuckles three times against the door and waited.

"Winifred? Are you home? It's Will," the man called. "I'm here on urgent business."

Suddenly the door swung open, as the woman appeared somewhat begrudgingly in the entrance, holding one hand on the door and the other fixed upon her hip.

"Will the Scarlet?" She whispered as her eyes widened. "What on earth are you doing here? And you've scarce a hood enough to keep your face hidden!"

"I need to ask something of you; about Eleanor, and a lass with a silver brooch," the man admitted, lowering his head as he whispered.

Winifred stood motionless for a moment. Then, she nodded and let the man in. Hastily, she closed the door behind her, as the outlaw took a seat by the fire.

"Knave, indeed. You ought to take more care in asking about such things. I've been expecting a visit from you. There's been little talk save what conjurable complaints arise from my neighbours of your rabble-rousing," she scolded, pursing her lips. "Why have you been meddling about, alone, over all of this nonsense?"

"Robin gave me leave to search as I may, though I am to return tonight, and therefore am anxious to find even the smallest answer," he sighed. "When Eleanor... when the sheriff and Lady Claudia had..." the man paused, leaning back in the chair as he thought, "That is, what I mean to say is that Eleanor concealed all information regarding the company and regarding the matter of the lass called Múriel. I need to know why she would have done this."

"What happened to Eleanor chills my very core, and I can hardly imagine your heartache for it. She was a strong young woman," Winifred consoled, placing her hand upon the man's shoulder as he stared into the fire. "But this is dangerous business, asking questions. Do you not know how people have suffered enough? How Victor's men have taken more villagers to the dungeons for questioning? Few have returned, Will."

"All of England has been driven to madness," he said. "But you must understand, I cannot have peace in my heart until the matter is settled," the man urged. As he turned his gaze up at the woman, his eyes shone heavy. "Do you know anything? Any idea where I could find such a maid?"

"Don't ask me such things," the woman said. As she paced away, she set her hand on her hip and held tight a pendant which hung around her neck.

"Please," the man entreated. "Surely, if you've had days to meditate on it, can you not lend me aid? I need to know why Eleanor would have gone to such lengths to protect her. She would not have done so without great cause," he leaned forward, his gaze tilted up at the healer.

Pacing back and forth before the fire, the woman folded her arms across her chest, then halted. Shaking her head, she glanced back at Will. "I'll only tell you what I am at liberty to say. Understood?"

"Aye," he nodded.

"Very well," she began, "Now, Eleanor, Múriel, and my Catherine had all grown together for the better part of twelve years. I'm more than certain Robin has made mention of her, perhaps even in passing, as they knew each other for a time. Not so long ago, it was brought to my attention that Múriel had wed a man called Hugo-"

"Aye!" Scarlet recalled, "That man who needed to buy medicine from you! Though you were causing enough trouble for him until I arrived," he scoffed.

"Oh let it be, you imp," Winifred rolled her eyes. "As it is, that is all I will speak on the subject. I'm sure if Eleanor had any reason for her silence, it was no less than her unswerving devotion to her kin."

Confident, the man stood up, his eyes bright with understanding and his own reasoning upon his tongue. "So, it is true then... Múriel *did* steal from Claudia after all!"

"How do you suppose that to be certain?"

"Eleanor claimed that a man had come and dropped the brooch, presuming it was Hugo, who resembled Gisborne - which is the very distinction I had made in the village - but perhaps Eleanor fabricated her account of the incident to protect her friend? Múriel, the true thief who stole from Locksley manor... and not wishing her friend be put to shame, Eleanor concealed it?"

"I... I don't know about all that," the physician muttered nervously, darting her eyes away.

"You think it impossible?"

"Well Múriel, she," the woman paused, her mouth hanging open, yet the words resisting, "I don't know anything about her thieving from Claudia. I think you're mistaken."

"No," Will sat, as he continued rambling. "No, but... I thought it only a rumour but as this strange fellow who resembles Gisborne appears from nowhere... and Eleanor would not lie; would *never* lie," he thought.

"Will," Winifred said, "You're making a right lot of nonsense. As I've nothing more to say, you ought to return to the men while you can."

"There wasn't a body, no true evidence... and something about his countenance and his voice," he thought. "Winifred!" He sprinted to his feet, standing face to face with the woman; his light eyes staring honest and raw. "Winifred, tell me, is it Gisborne? Is he truly alive?"

The woman's gut wrenched as she stood fixed in place; her expression hard as steel though her mind was in such heated conflict. Her jaw clenched, she locked her eyes upon the young man. "No," she said at last. "That blackguard was brought to justice, long ago."

Releasing a sigh of vexation, Will glided away from the woman, only to slump back in the chair as before. In his core, the man would not accept her words, weighing the account a little longer in his thoughts.

"You must understand, I have risked much to find answers, not to wander aimlessly for the sake of an endless riddle," he declared. "Am I only to be left with the assurance that this woman exists? Tell me, where does she live?"

"That I will not tell you. And I think you've asked quite enough of me this evening," the healer replied, her expression cold and unyielding.

In her heart, there was no commendation regarding the prospect of such a lovely woman having been wed to a Norman so abominable as Gisborne, but if Robin were to discover the circumstance, it would end in unpredictable madness for them all. Thus, she concealed it. As she marched towards the door, the woman placed her hand upon the lever, only to be halted by the outlaw.

"Please, tell me," he implored.

Avoiding his glance, she walked away from the door and back to the fire. "I've said too much, as it is. I will not be held responsible for endangering others. This is most likely why Eleanor wouldn't speak a word to the sheriff or Lady Claudia. To protect lives that would otherwise fall into the pit of chaos."

"And yet you are withholding what I need to know most of all!"

"And you are testing my patience!" She protested.

Shaking his head in frustration, the man stormed out of the cottage, slamming the door hard behind him.

CHAPTER TWENTY-THREE

THE HUNT

Dispirited, Scarlet returned to the forest.

As the evening sky shadowed the land, he hiked through the long and winding paths of the wild. Then, far beyond him, he saw a faint golden light painted across the branches and dimpled bark of the trees, brightening their outstretched arms as they bent and swayed in the calm and gentle breeze. Drawing nearer, he inhaled the rich scent of the smoke rising from the bonfire, now meeting the faces of his companions.

"Scarlet!" Alan's eyes gleamed with excitement as he raced toward his comrade. The others, in turn, leapt up to find a copper banner approaching, and all leapt up together to greet him.

"Welcome back," Robin smiled, placing a firm hand upon the man's shoulder. "Sherwood has not been the same without you."

"Have you any news?" Tuck asked.

Looking about the men, as they all watched with eager eyes, Will searched for what words he might say, yet found none that would suffice. Pacing away from the men, he went to his place amongst the cots and cast off his belongings. For a moment, the men stood together in silence, for it was not like Will to keep to himself, not for the world, and not for such a quest as this. Then, with little thought to heed him, Jack followed, letting the soft earth touch his bare feet as he sought the outlaw; though as the lad approached, the man did not mark him.

"Did you find her? The French lass?" Jack wondered. "Did she say anything to you of Eleanor?"

Glancing downward, the man made no answer, but kept to unpacking his belongings, and turned his back to the young comrade.

"Where's your head, lad?" Little John reproved as he approached his son. "If he found anyone, there wouldn't be enough restraint in all of England to keep him from telling the tale, and surely, none would hear the end of it."

"Are you so quick to judge my sufferance?" Scarlet questioned. Turning about, he faced the man with a cold, inexorable glare.

"I'll judge what I please, as you've wasted three days to rove the riddle-road while we've faced foes enough for your sake. Howbeit, for all that gallivanting, we've no compensation by your ramblings to justify the folly of it."

"You think it folly to seek out someone whose very name was guarded by the blood of another?"

"I think it folly to lose one's mind as you have over Eleanor, and she who was buried, and all about us is becoming as a battlefield," John quarrelled. "Speak, and settle the debt for our forbearance."

"I'll speak as I may when I have the mind to do it!" Hurling the rest of his supplies against the ground, Will let out an angered grunt, and so marched away from the camp, leaving the others behind; dumbfounded.

"Master, will you not reproach him?" John questioned, his arms folded across his chest. "Again he deserts us."

"Perhaps careless words were spoken that gave him need to retreat," Robin said, looking back at John sternly. "For the now, if he wishes to be left alone, we'll not disturb him."

This resolve satisfied most of the company, though Alan and Little John felt a growing doubt. As each pondered such a thought, they eyed each other; knowing.

***

At length, Will returned to his cot.

He neither came towards the fire nor ate a morsel of food, not for all the howling of his stomach, but as he lay down, he brought his hood up over his face and spoke not. As the night drew on, and the others had gone to sleep, Little John and Alan met in the woods, a wise distance from any undesirable listeners.

"Have you told him anything?" Little John whispered.

"No, of course not," Alan shook his head. "Doubtless, he discovered nothing."

"But how can we be certain until he speaks? Do you suppose he knows of Gisborne?" John lowered his chin.

"To my knowledge, none else could possibly know. And surely, Robin does not know," A'Dale peered back toward the fire-lit camp. "As long as we are faithful to conceal it, we've nothing to fear."

"Well, I'll do as I must, to keep the peace and protect my son," John said.

"Protect him?" Alan squinted his eyes, "I thought he knew very little of the matter."

Glancing back at his comrade, Alan noted how a moment of reserve kept John from confessing; his grey moustache curled over his lip and his brow furrowed. But the young man would not accept it.

"If he knows anything, then we must both be on our guard," he continued. "You see how he yet acts and says whatever he might."

"He means no harm to anyone," John said. "He is a youth, but he is no fool."

"Aye, and all of us see that right well. But if Jack harbours any intelligence, he need only let slip one word, and thus all is undone. What has he told you?" The outlaw pressed.

Disgruntled, the man hesitated, and then, he spoke. "The night he first came to the camp, he confided in me of how he saw the savage at the castle, being brought out to some young lady in the courtyard. Moreover, he recalled seeing a man who resembled you entirely, aiding in the escape."

All colour drained from Alan's face as he looked back at the man with wide eyes. "He knew I had gone?"

"No," John returned. "He suspected as much, though I assured him he was mistaken. I take no liking to any of this; still, you are my kin."

"Thank you," Alan sighed, rubbing at the back of his neck. "So, Jack will keep silent?"

"I think so. Still, I fear what Scarlet has concluded... it may not be long before he begins to fill the void."

"Aye," the outlaw acknowledged, "and yet, even if he were to arrive at such a conclusion, it's doubtful anyone would find Gisborne or Múriel."

"Hasn't Gisborne told you of his lodging?"

"He didn't say much, only that his home lay deep in the woods somewhere or other," Alan said.

Shifting his gaze to the ground, Little John thought. "Then a grave decision remains. If Will has discovered the truth, should we persuade him otherwise? Should we make him out to be mad?"

"I hadn't thought of that," Alan shrugged his shoulders, "No... I don't think I could do it, John."

Breaking through the stillness of the forest, the sound of a rustling bush and hasty footsteps rushed past them.

Without a moment's thought, both men raced after the scoundrel. The chase was on.

Following the thudding and crunching that went weaving about the forest, the outlaws began to gain on their adversary. Not so far beyond them, they perceived the cloaked figure. The man peered his face around the edge of his hood, only to view his pursuers before returning his gaze to the road once more. John's feet could not carry him fast enough nor were his eyes so sharp as they had once been. Sprinting all that way in the dark, he failed to see a large tree root that curved up in the path; thus it entrapped his foot, sending him to the ground. Not far behind him, Alan came bounding up the road, but just as John had fallen, the young outlaw tripped over the very same root, and down he tumbled. Looking up, they found that the cloaked man had escaped far into the night.

"Damn!" John threw his fist against the ground.

"Who was that?" Alan slowly sat up, rubbing his aches and bruises. "Oh, my head-"

"Never mind your head. You haven't got one to begin with seeing as we had a spy in our midst, all this while, and you've given him a torch enough to burn the whole forest!" John snarled, standing up as he stretched his sore limbs.

"Don't go blaming the sheep for the open fence! Each of us had ample word to speak, and neither of us could have known he was there," Alan huffed, as he held out his hand to his comrade. Though he rolled his eyes a moment, John finally took the fellow's hand and aided him to his feet.

"Did you catch any sight of the bloke?" Alan glanced down the path.

"No, no I didn't."

"What do we do now?"

"I don't know."

***

Seven days, she had; a mere seven days to capture the Rebel and appease the prince.

As the night wore thin, Claudia's mind was wrought with fear, for such days as these rendered little sleep. Mad as a caged creature, she paced back and forth before the hearth of the great hall, its embers burning low, and the warmth of it, fading. Muttering words here and there under her breath, she thought; her eyes, jolting about at the slightest sound.

Amidst the emptiness, a sudden cry came forth. "M'lady! M'lady!" A man called out as he sprinted frantically into the hall.

Gripping the poking iron from the side of the mantle, the woman drew it forth against the man; the sharp tip pressed against his throat.

"If you dare bring me ill news, Dumont, you will regret it," she whispered; her nostrils flaring.

"Please, your grace," the man begged, raising his hands. Cautiously, he drew back his hood, revealing his grey and weathered face. "I bring good news," he said. "I've discovered the rebel camp-"

"Do you not know how many men have come into this very hall with such news? You imbecile!" She shrieked.

"No, my lady!" He twitched. "I saw the outlaws with my very eyes! The camp was not abandoned as the others!"

"You found him? You've found the Rebel?"

"I overheard what was spoken between two of the company. They stood far off from the camp, where I lay hid," he said.

"And why did you not follow them directly to the camp?" She asked.

"Your grace, the men were speaking of a very delicate matter."

"Of what then?" She pressed.

"Of Sir Guy," he answered. "He is in Sherwood! They have seen him, and the younger of the two men who spoke knew him well."

"They know where he is?" Claudia raised her brows. "Can they lead us to him?"

"No," Dumont reluctantly shook his head. "But, they mentioned a lady's name. She'll certainly know where to find him."

Lowering the iron, the woman drew closer, staring hard into the man's eyes. "What name, Dumont?"

"The name of that young maiden who had aided in his escape; the one with the silver clasp," he sighed. "Her name is Múriel."

Tilting her head, the woman glanced back at the dying embers, her mind chasing after the thought; the name.

"What would you have me do, your grace?" The man drew forward, his hands behind his back.

"Gather together two elite troupes. Be discreet; we've no need for the sheriff to interfere," she said. "The first is to return with you to the location nearest the outlaw's camp. Be ready to ambush them."

"And the second troupe?"

"Send them to the cottage of Catherine Smith. Have them question her about the maiden Múriel. Under no circumstances will you let her refuse to give an answer. Use whatever means necessary."

"Yes, my lady," he answered.

As he departed from the hall, the woman stood alone once more, grinning.

***

Catherine had neither seen nor heard from Múriel in months and did not know whether her friend remained or had departed altogether. In her mind, she persuaded herself that Múriel and her new husband had fled the forest, far and away beyond any danger.

In the warmth of the afternoon, her long, red hair danced in the breeze catching copper sparks of sunlight. Dutifully, she tended the garden, gleaning what little harvest she had, and every other moment, did she look up, brushing her wrist against her brow, as her children skipped in and out of the shadows of the trees overhead. How quiet, how unconfined, how free; and all easiness was her contentment.

Then, as she looked up from her work again, the children halted in their play. The three stood perfectly still, their faces pale, and their eyes pinned to something behind their mother. Odette grabbed Godric's hand, and Oliver, who remained a distance behind the two, carefully moved to hide behind his elder sister.

Quickly, their mother shot up, wiping the dirt from her hands with the corner of her apron.

"Children, what's wrong? What are you staring at?" Her brows furrowed as she turned about.

"Mummy! No!" Odette screamed.

In an instant, thick, dark fabric came over the woman's head. Rough hands took hold of her arms and tied her hands behind her back. These very hands pulled at her arm, dragging her across the forest floor. By the sound of the creaking door, she was forced into the cottage, the children's cries a piercing echo amidst Catherine's pleas for help.

Vigilant, she wrestled against the aggressors, yet as they tied her down to a chair, her will to fight proved useless against the strength of the men. With the ropes bound tight around her, she was helpless.

As the hood was removed from her head, she saw before her, the three children; gagged and bound. Behind each one, stood a man in a black cloak.

"Let us go, you devils!" Catherine howled, her dark eyes raging. Shaking the chair from side to side, she fought to free herself; her locks, hanging over her face, as she snarled.

"Oh, Catherine," a man from behind her placed his hands upon her shoulders. "You're rather a wild creature, aren't you?" His voice whispered in her ear.

Quick-witted as ever, she threw her head to the side, knocking it fast against the man's temple. "Wild indeed!" She shouted as the man fumbled forward, rubbing at his injury.

She could now see he wore a black cloak similar to the others, yet his face was visible. His hair was a mingled grey and rusted brown, and every line on his face drew him to be quite an older man.

"You stubborn whore!" The man grumbled. Raising his fist, he struck the woman's cheek.

With her mouth full of blood, she spat it at his face. "I may be stubborn, but you'll not bark at me with such foul words in my own home!" She scolded, as the man wiped the sprinkled blood off his face.

"I'll say all I please," he insisted, as he towered above the woman. "Now, I've only to ask you a few, simple questions. If you cooperate, you and your little runts shall be left unharmed."

"What do you want?" Catherine questioned, her eyes fixed on her wimping children.

"It has come to my attention that you are well acquainted with a young maiden called Múriel," he said. "Tell me plainly, where does she live?"

"I know none by that name," she answered.

"Very well. I presumed you might not cooperate," the man turned about, pacing towards the children. "'Tis a shame you're willing to speak lies in front of your own children."

"I swear I've never heard that name!"

"He'll do," the man said, taking Oliver up by the collar; the lad squirming in fright. "Dreadfully scrawny lad, isn't he? Don't you feed him?"

"Don't you dare lay a finger on him!" The woman begged. Her heart sank into her gut, as the man drew forth a dagger, and gripping the boy's shaking hand, laid it upon the table. "No! Please don't hurt him!" She cried.

"Let's try this once more," he continued, "Where does Múriel live?"

Finally, she could restrain herself no longer. Bursting into tears, Catherine hung her head low.

CHAPTER TWENTY-FOUR

THE LONGEST NIGHT - PART I

August had come to its final days.

Under the full and warm and pleasant light of the morning, Guy made ready to hunt again.

While Alan had given him warning enough in the thick of the wood, and while the imminent threat of soldiers haunted every shadow, go he must; for their little home had once more been without meat for quite some time, and the journey must be made before the child came.

Standing in the heat of the barn, he fastened his belongings beside the horse's saddle. It had been a long while since the creature had been taken out, deep into the forest, and how eager it was to roam amidst such green.

"You fancy a ride in the wild country?" Guy whispered, stroking the horse's mane as it whinnied in response.

Then softly, the sound of footsteps came padding across the way, and the man smiled to himself; knowing.

"Amour?" Múriel called out sweetly, as she approached and stood before the entrance.

Gazing back, the man took in her gentle beauty. Her long hair glistened in the golden light, and her eyes shone a bright and brilliant hue, as a great wave crashing against an expanse of grey, pebbled shores. How lovely she was, and ever his delight.

"I shall miss you... *we* shall miss you," she admitted. Glancing down she sighed, drawing her hand tenderly over her womb as the child quickened beneath her palm.

Taking to her side, Guy brought his hand beneath her chin, so her eyes met his. "And I shall miss you both," he smiled. "I won't be long, darling," he promised, placing a kiss upon her lips.

"One day, oui?" She whispered.

"One day," he said. "I shall return tomorrow morning."

Silent, the lady nodded. Mounting the horse, Guy looked down on her, and what disquiet he beheld in her; how she gripped the reins, how her eyes did fix upon the forest beyond, how she stood so still. "Guy," she began, staring up at him with sober eyes, "Fais attention... "

"Vous avez ma parole," he nodded. "Je reviendrai."

Swift, he departed, galloping away over the open field and under the boughs of the forest. With all restraint, the lady remained; watching. Though she had trusted him to go, persuading herself most persistently that all would be well, in her heart, there lingered a warning, one which she could not so easily cast aside. Yet, when he had finally reached beyond her sight, she returned to the well.

There, she readied a large basin and drew from the well until it was filled, so she might launder the linens and what garments she intended for the child. And for all the work of her hands, she did not mind it, for the cold water felt good as she knelt under the sun's heat. When she had finished, she took all the linens to the clothesline, and one by one hung them up as banners waving in the gentle wind. What wealth, what reward, what sweetness she felt in lounging upon the green, as the breeze sung through the sheets and kissed her face with cool, refreshing melodies. Reclining in her quiet garden, she closed her eyes, and though she had not intended it, she drifted off to sleep.

Fortunately, when Múriel had awoken, the hour was no later than noon, and she had not lost the bulk of the day, much as she had on previous days. Thus, she retired into the cottage, eager to make the home ready. Beside the window of her bedchamber, a wooden cradle was set, of which Guy had fashioned himself. Along its sides were carved depictions of the sun and the moon shining together, and twinkling stars all about. Set beside the cradle stood a modest cupboard, filled with linens. Bringing out all these pieces, to fold, and fold once more, Múriel's heart teemed with joy. And then, only as she must, she rearranged the swaddling cloths and draped her favourite neatly over the end of the cradle.

As the last light of the sunset bid farewell through the open windows, the lady fixed a simple meal and sat at the table. In her solitude, the quiet of the empty cottage was not so welcome as it had been long ago. Those wistful moments left only to one's thoughts, so submerged in a river of reflection, how they were so precious. To retreat to such waters was a gift, but in feeling her darling's absence, there was no one to share in that great secret. For a moment, she must venture alone. And in this wandering, her mind did not stray far from her worries, from her fears for his return. Now, the food set before her could not be stomached, nor did her drink satisfy. All the same, she waited patiently, listening intently to the sounds of the atmosphere; the crackle of the wood in the fire and the whispering wind sweeping through every blade of grass. Suddenly, the sound of horse's hoofs thundered not far beyond. Yet, in such fleeting moments, she dismissed her doubt and rose.

Hastily, the lady drew to the windows overlooking the field, but her eyes did not find the one she sought. Instead, she looked out upon a sight which she had feared ever to behold. Seven riders clad in black; hooded and cloaked and well armed. Ruthless, they charged past the wall of elders, advancing toward the cottage.

Terrified, Múriel's heart pounded within her; her face felt hot, and her hands grew numb as she retreated from the window into the shadows. Quickly, she lowered the lever to lock the door, then stealing away to the hearth, doused the fire, and fled into the kitchen. Retrieving a small satchel, she took up her dagger, flint and steel, and at last, she took up her cloak which hung by the back door. Portentous, the galloping of the horses rumbled all the fiercer, all the nearer. She could hear the men and their horses halting just around the front of the cottage, and the stamping of their hoofs resounded as war drums.

"Don't just stand there, break the door down!" A man's voice shouted viciously.

And then came the noise of their battering against the door.

With no time to lose, Múriel dashed out through the back of the cottage; the door closed shut behind her. As she turned to run forward and into the garden, she stumbled, scraping her knees and the palms of her hands against the stone threshold. Sighing, she brought her hand to her side, relieved, for she thought of the child. Wiping the blood from her hands on her dress, she glanced back and discovered what had caused her to falter. The hem of her dress was stuck fast in the doorframe.

"Search the property!" The same man called. "We leave none alive!"

Wrenching harder and harder at the garment, it slowly began to tear, but she couldn't manage to get it out. There was still enough fabric left to hold her captive. Time was running out.

"Mon Dieu!" Múriel whispered, panting as she heard the sudden clank of the front door kick open, and slam up against the wall behind it.

In the distance, she could hear the noise of heavy footsteps sprinting nearer the garden. With shaking hands, she groped for the knife from her satchel and cut anxiously at the hem of her dress. Finally, the edge was cut, and she was free. As she rose again, she ran as fast as her feet would carry her, far beyond the garden and into the woods; and the loud and boisterous shouts of the men soon faded behind her. She daren't look back, not for a moment, but ran until her feet were raw, and her breath grew faint; still, she would not stop. At length, she fled so far into the woods, she didn't know where she was at all. No tree, no rock, no sound felt familiar, and the evening sky had long slipped away into the darkness. Under the stillness of the night, the world grew uncertain. Looking back, she could not tell the way she came, nor how she would ever find her way again. How ominous the forest stood; how hollow. The only comfort Múriel found was in a rolling stream not far beyond her.

Weary and sore, she knelt before it. Her mouth was parched, and each breath ached in her lungs. Her hands trembled; her mind was restless. As she bent low, she dipped her hands down into the flowing waters and drew up to her mouth the cold water. Drawing her gaze upward through the eaves of the wood, she looked upon the full moon; its soft and radiant glow, her solace.

Keep him safe, she thought. *Please, keep him safe.*

There, she determined to rest until the morning, for she had no strength left to go on, and laying beside the stream, she closed her eyes.

Just as her spirit grew calm and her mind was quieted, a sudden strain swept over her and remained. As quickly as it came, it soon retreated, and after a time it returned once more. Over and over again, deeper and deeper into the night, she found no respite. Fixing her mind on the rhythm of the stream, it guided her. Dauntless, she determined to face the coming tide.

***

Far and away in the woods, Guy halted.

The sunlight shone brightly through the branches of the trees, and the scents of the forest filled his lungs. Yet, for all its serenity, he could not give in to thoughtlessness. Watchful, he searched with all discretion until he had found a secluded place to set his camp before the hunt. Dismounting from the horse, he guided it through fern and gorse to a grove of pines, and taking the thick rope in his hand, he fastened it to a tree. The horse neighed and swayed his head from side to side, not enthused in the slightest at having been made to stand by. By and by, the creature soon found the green about him tempting enough to be persuaded.

Diligent and quick, the hunter laid out his supplies. In skilful manner, he fashioned a little camp in the grove. Not so far from where he stood, there was a grand tree; grand enough indeed for him to gain a befitting view of the forest, and watch for some game. With bow in hand and a quiver of arrows at his back, he sat perched far up in the heights of the tree such that he could observe the rolling waves of the bending, billowing branches that lay beyond. Some of the trees of that vast forest fared delightfully green in their youth, and some of wiser years bore a golden leaf, here and there, making ready for the coming season.

There, Guy waited; and all the long hours of silence did not deter him, as his contemplations wholly stayed upon his duty. He thought on Múriel, and on the child, wishing with all his heart to return safe and sound to his home and his darling. In the warmth that life had found fit to afford him, though he esteemed it unmeritable, it proved his most cherished wealth. For the purest of riches could not be won by his own hand; yet he, having been given this garden, was somehow deemed fit to tend it. An office he was proud to hold; a quest of the lightest burden. Contended with such a meditation, he smiled, knowing all the more, the depths of his blessed treasure. Morning fleeted, evening waned, and soon the moonlight beckoned the world to sleep, calling forth every creature of the night.

Then, fierce and unyielding, the sound of horses resounded beyond, amidst a cloud of muffled roars. Cautiously, Guy listened, his mind retreating to the battlements. In an instant, below the boughs of the tree, two men stood encircled by cloaked riders.

339

Wreaking of dread and fury, the riders in black appeared as an extension of the darkness.

The woodsmen who stood surrounded by the riders had their weapons ready; one wielding a sword, and the other a bow and arrow. Perceiving the soldiers below, the hunter readily understood their errand and from where they might have come. No, he could not keep idly by. By the light of the moon, he loosed his arrows and felled two of the riders.

"It's an ambush!" A rider shouted. "His men are here!"

Descending swiftly from the tree, Gisborne ran to the aid of the two men. Loosing another arrow, he shot the rider who had cried out. The swordsman glanced over his shoulder but a moment to see who had aided him and his comrade.

"Who are you?" He called.

"A friend," Gisborne nodded, readying another arrow as he and the two men advanced.

One of the riders dismounted, sprinting hard toward the man; his sword drawn. The rider raised up his weapon to strike a deadly blow, but the first woodsman blocked the sword with his own, though he fell to his knees forcing his enemy's weapon back.

Regaining his stance, he halted yet another blow with the edge of his sword against the rider's blade. As he lunged forward, the rider grazed the man's arm, but just as the rider had lost his focus, the woodsman took up his sword and hacked it into the base of the rider's neck, the flesh severed down to the bone. While the swordsman endured in the fight, Gisborne and the archer pivoted back to back, as the three other riders remained on their horses.

Tighter and tighter the riders drew them in, swinging their broad and heavy swords low, and sharp, and quick; there was no chance for the archer or the hunter to put their skills to any use. Relinquishing his bow, Gisborne took the reins of one horse. Wrestling, he clawed the sword out of the rider's hand and forced the blade through the man's gut. Bounding to the earthen floor again, the hunter struck the horse, sending it away as it wildly galloped into the deeps of the wood.

Amidst the brawl, but two riders remained to battle the archer. Dismounting, they made ready to attack. But the archer was agile, and so drew his own blade and sparred between the two; their swords flashing in the moonlight until a rider took a blow to the archer's side. The archer fell to his knees, crying out in agony, as the two soldiers towered above him, their swords inches from his head. Instinctive, Gisborne and the swordsman rushed to his aid.

Taking up his bow once more, the hunter loosed an arrow straight through the eye of the rider nearest the archer; all at once, felled; and the swordsman was swift to knock a heavy blow against the final rider, sending him flat upon his back. With their adversaries defeated, the men fell breathless.

"Master, you're wounded!" The swordsman cried, kneeling before his comrade, observing his injury and the blood. For his side had been gashed by one of the enemy's blades.

"I'll manage," the archer groaned, grasping his wound. "Go. Fetch John and Tuck."

"No, it's too dangerous to leave you here," he answered. "Hunter!" The swordsman called to Gisborne. "Come, we must get him to his feet."

Breathless, the man stood, distinguishing at once the faces of these woodsmen; faces he had taken such lengths to avoid. His heart pounded as never before, and there was no deliverance.

"Here, take his arm," Will said, directing the man to take hold of Robin's right arm, as the two brought the man to his feet. "We must get to safety."

Nodding, Gisborne simply followed his instructions, determined to make the journey and when the moment struck well in his favour, he would flee. Having met Robin once, long ago, there was still a chance the outlaw would not recognise him, and so much had changed since then. Surely, he could make his escape as soon as he found leave to do it.

Slowly, the men supported the outlaw, as all three trudged with tired limbs through the woods. Not a one spoke a word, for fear of drawing any more unwarranted attention, and this gave Gisborne some comfort. At length, a strange firelight could be seen across the way, as shadowed figures came bounding near.

"Scarlet!" Jack cried out, racing ahead of the others; a torch in his hand as his eyes searched about.

"Master Robin!" Tuck called, his breath heavy, and his feet, aching. "Where are you?"

"Don't call their names, you imbeciles!" Alan scolded, "Victor's men could yet be about." Just as the warning fell from his lips, the man heard a voice echo in the darkness.

"Over here!" Will cried, his voice weak, "We're over here!"

Cunning as a fox, Alan dashed through the trees and came upon the sight; the men walking side by side, and Robin limping. "What's happened?" He pressed.

"We were attacked by a league of riders. They had us surrounded," Will answered, his breath strained as he carried his master. "It was luck indeed that this hunter came to our aid," he panted.

Tense and anxious, Gisborne lowered his gaze to avoid the glance of a knowing eye. Much to his advantage, as they came unto the others, all were fixed upon Robin and his wound. While Tuck, Scarlet, and Robin still had no clear sight of the hunter, Little John, Jack, and Alan marked him instantly.

Alan looked sharp at the hunter, then at John. The outlaw's keen brown eyes then met Gisborne's as they exchanged a quick nod; at least the man could depend on A'Dale to keep quiet.

"Lay him here," Little John ordered, as Gisborne and Will set Robin down upon the mossy ground.

"Where's the wound?" Tuck knelt before Robin.

"My side-" Robin huffed, sitting up, though still in great pain.

"Let me examine it," the old man insisted. Pulling away at the cut of the man's tunic, he observed the severity of the injury. "Well, there's a good deal of bleeding, indeed, but the cut is not so deep at it seems. A few stitches should do the trick," he nodded, searching about in his satchel for supplies.

"You have what you need with you?" John asked.

"I've a needle and thread, yes, but nothing to cleanse the wound," the old man shook his head. "We must bring him back to the camp."

As the rest of the men hovered around Robin, Will stood far off. Aghast, he observed the hunter who began to step lightly away from the commotion, withdrawing into the shadow. But Scarlet was given light enough to find the man's face familiar.

"Gisborne," he uttered.

Then, the hunter's eyes betrayed him, for he looked back at the outlaw. Immediately and irrevocably, the outlaw knew. Turning to flee from the company, Guy sprinted as a madman, but Scarlet was too quick. With angered brows furrowed, he had already gripped the hilt of his blade and drew out the weapon as he advanced.

"It's him!" Scarlet cried.

Turning his gaze westward, Robin discovered what his mind could not accept. His pale green eyes went wide in disbelief, "Impossible..." he whispered.

Gisborne's blood ran cold, and he wished he had fled long before. But now it was too late.

"No!" Alan cried as he leapt past the company. Intercepting the advance, he stood before Gisborne so shielding him from Will's strike.

"What are you doing?" Will shook his head.

"Put down your sword," Alan returned.

"But it is him, you fool! Let me strike him where he stands!"

"I'll not let you do that," Alan answered, straining to keep his kinsman back.

Standing firm, Will's nostrils flared; his eyes, flustered. "Why do you hinder me? Why do you guard him thus?"

"You deceived me?" Robin cried. Finding the strength in his awe and fury to stand, he moved toward his comrade, with a fire in his eyes.

"Master, I can explain," Alan cautioned, though the outlaw shoved him harshly out of the way.

"You heartless villain," Robin snarled, hurling his fist square in the jaw of his adversary, sending him to the ground. "You should be dead! Dead!"

"And if I had not defended you against those riders, *you* would be dead this very minute!" Gisborne answered, wiping the blood from his mouth, as he looked up at the outlaw. "Did I not save your life?"

Bitter and provoked, the outlaw towered over the man; his breath heavy, his stare virulent and vengeful. Taking hold of Will's sword, he held the edge of it against Gisborne's neck.

"For too long, I believed there was justice. Too long, I clung to the comfort of your death. I should have slain you myself, long ago!" Robin's eyes narrowed as he pressed the blade harder against his enemy's throat, drawing blood.

"Please, can you show no mercy?" Guy threw up his hands, "A life for a life!"

"Mercy?" Robin gritted his teeth. "You, who did not heed the cries of the innocent! You, who slaughtered the poor for the avarice of a rebellious prince! And you would speak to me of mercy? Why should I spare you?"

"What you speak is true," Gisborne returned. "My hands are stained with much blood. I am not worthy to be spared."

"What…" the outlaw tilted his head in bewilderment.

"You are right to despise me. And of Marian," he sighed, "If I cannot yet petition your mercy over my life, I must beg your forgiveness for her death."

Now Robin could not contain his contempt any longer but gave way to all his malice and hatred.

"Do not speak her name! Don't you dare speak her name, you devil!" At this, he cast the sword aside and charged forward, gripping his hands tight around Gisborne's neck; strangling him and forcing him to the ground.

"Master, stop!" Alan entreated, doing all he could to get hold of Robin and unhinge his hands from Gisborne. "Is this what Marian would wish? Such revenge will not appease your burdens!"

"He must die!" Robin wrenched at the man's throat so that his knuckles went white, as Gisborne choked, desperate for respite. "He must suffer as she suffered. Let him gasp for breath as she had!"

"You don't know what you are doing!" Alan cried, battling against the man. At last, wedging his arms under Robin's, he pulled his kinsman's hands away from Gisborne; the man left gasping in a stupor.

At this, Robin thrust his fist against Alan's face, though the outlaw was quick to retaliate, with his own fist against his master.

"Listen to me!" Alan begged, wrestling against him as he made to pursue his enemy once more. "You cannot murder him! For the sake of his family!"

Indignant, Robin lunged out of his comrade's grip and clutched his sword once more, pressing the edge of the blade under his enemy's jaw. "Did not he take my family from me?" He roared. "And what grief could be felt for his conclusion? What family has he, that would be so robbed of his foul existence? What woman has he, that would weep o'er his end?"

"It is Múriel whom you would have weep! The very one who bears the silver brooch," A'Dale professed in great earnest as Robin searched his comrade's eyes. Despondent, as he saw the truth in them, he loosed his grasp. "She is his wife and carries his child. If you kill this man, you will create the very evil you have toiled so to prevent," Alan warned.

"No… it cannot be true," he shook his head.

"Aye, master, 'tis true," John confirmed. "She is the one who helped Gisborne escape and is the very one who Claudia is hunting."

"Eleanor was right all the while," Scarlet mumbled, his expression grave. "She died to protect Múriel… to protect Gisborne."

"Lies!" Robin barked, his eyes brimming. Wincing, he faltered and held his sore and bleeding side; his eyes woeful and weary and stricken. Altogether the men fell silent, for not one of them knew what to do, but prevent their master from falling. Though he kept the blade at Gisborne's throat, Robin lifted his eyes and spoke, "How many of you knew of this?"

As Tuck and Will searched about, three heads gazed downward in shame, and could not be brought to look back at their master.

"Why did you conceal it from me?" He sighed, glancing at the three. "Will you give no honest account?"

"Master, we did not know when or how to speak of it," John replied.

"Enough," Tuck interjected. "We could quarrel over this matter of knowing and not knowing for hours, but the question remains. What is to be done with the man?"

Raw in pain, Robin gave Tuck a stern glance. "Bind him," he commanded through gritted teeth. "We will hold him captive for one full day. If his tale proves false, then he must be put to death."

***

A mere three days remained for Claudia.

Anxiously, she awaited any word from her men, for news of the prince's journey to Nottingham had already reached her ears, and she must keep her neck. In the solitude of her bedchamber, the woman lay upon her bed. The night had overcome the world below, and a pebble of voracious hope lay dormant in the chasms of her mind. Dumont had sent out his troupes of assassins into the forests of Sherwood that very day; one to end the Rebel, and the other, to capture Gisborne and his accomplice. As her mind drifted off in silence, suddenly, there came a knocking at the entrance of the manor.

The clank of heavy metal hitting against the wood frame resounded through the hall; though with many a guard positioned all about the place, the woman would not trouble herself in discovering who it was that appeared at such an hour. Yet, as the visitor had most egregiously disrupted her crippling air of fictitious rest, curiosity would not preclude her. Slowing her breath, she listened. She could hear the grand doors creak open, and more clanking of metal, along with the voices of men, rumbling. Then, the racket came crawling nearer and nearer, only subsiding under the weight of a heavy knock upon her very door.

"Your grace, we've urgent news!" A guard called out.

Claudia's pulse hastened, as she threw a coverlet over her shoulders, and rushed to open the doors. "What is it?"

"It's Dumont, m'lady... he's returned," the guard bowed his head.

"I shall be down shortly," she nodded, closing the door behind her. With her robe fastened and her dishevelled hair cascading behind her, she descended down the flight of stairs and unto the great hall, restless to hear the whole account of Robin's death. There, before the fire, she found Dumont, and a maidservant attending to his wounded forehead.

"The deed is done, yes? Will the prince be satisfied? Oh, do not rebuff my inquiry, I want to hear every savage detail," Claudia hounded.

"Your grace, I am the only one of my assassins who has survived. My men were struck down like beasts," he replied, wincing as the maid pressed the wet cloth against his skin.

"I don't understand," the woman said, "Did you not find the Rebel? Did you not discover his camp?"

"Yes, your grace," Dumont managed, flinching as the maid applied a salve to the gash across his forehead.

"Oh, leave it you insolent wench! Go on!" Claudia shrieked at the maid, who hastened away in fright. Then, turning back to the man. "Where is he?" She snarled, leaning her hands on the arms of the chair, staring hard at the man.

"He was alone at first," the man swallowed nervously, "and then another fellow, a swordsman, came out of the woods and started running alongside him. My men and I followed them for a time. Finally, we had the two surrounded. Then out of nowhere, arrows came flying down, killing two of my men. The rebels must have expected us and had prepared a trap! My men and I, we did all we could, but that blackguard and his men proved too skilful-"

The veins throbbing in her neck, and her hands clawing at the chair, the woman stared with eyes ferocious and foreboding. "You had Robin Hood within your grasp, and you let him get away?"

Startled, the man shivered in his chair, his mouth trembling. Though it hung open, no words could be summoned forth.

"You witless worm!"

Driven mad beyond her means, Claudia turned, gripped the hot poker from the side of the mantle, and forced it through the stomach of the man, the blood dripping from his mouth as his eyes went still.

"Guards!" She cried out, through her clenched jaw. Without delay, two men approached.

"Yes, your grace," they answered.

"Remove this odious carcass from my hall at once!" She demanded, watching as the guards took the skewered body out from the hall. Seething, she stood before the fire. Boiling repugnance and malevolence consumed her, then welcomed the unquenchable fear.

CHAPTER TWENTY-FIVE

THE LONGEST NIGHT - PART II

Hours passed, and yet the troupe found no sign of Gisborne or Múriel at the cottage, and midnight was upon them. With nothing gained, and little to report, the assassins were most apprehensive in returning to Locksley Manor, yet they would have no other choice.

Amongst the upheaval of the home, the captain of the riders did come across a rather peculiar silver clasp, left on the dresser of the master chamber. But as he couldn't quite place whether it was a crucial element in their mission or not, he left it behind. Mounting their horses again, the soldiers rode out under the veil of night; their capes, like the wings of ravens, flying across the field; a plague through the wild.

As they reached the manor, the men dismounted and marched into the great hall. Claudia sat at the hearth, staring restlessly at the fire, watching obsessively as each flame licked and devoured the kindling into oblivion.

There the captain stood before her, austere and inexorable, though the woman neither acknowledged his presence nor that of his men. Their shoulders were broad, their hoods low, and their cloaks cascaded as waters down a mountainside, pouring over the earth about their feet. But still as statues, they waited; a harbinger of tribulation.

"Captain, have you any word of Sir Guy? Any news of the lass with the silver brooch?" She questioned, her eyes unmoved, her expression blank.

"Yes," the captain hissed, his voice sharp and clear. "We have found the cottage. It dwells beyond the village, deep in the forest, guarded by the three elder trees."

"Are they dead?" She whispered.

"We searched everywhere, though there were none to be found," he returned.

"Then why are you not waiting, hidden at the cottage this very minute?" She turned, her eyes a wicked hue and her expression wrenched. Rising to her feet, slowly she drew near the captain. "They may return, and you must put an end to them."

"Your grace, I mentioned the trees with good reason," he insisted. "Standing before the field, are the three elders; ancient trees of protection. The area of land surrounding them cannot be tainted by the shedding of human blood. If a man be slain on that land, and his spilt blood touches the earth, a curse will follow upon the one who felled the man. All his days, he will walk under the shadow of evil spirits."

"You do not wish to kill them on the land, all for the bounds of superstition?"

"We will not tempt the spirits," the captain answered, wholly resolute.

"You malingering heathens!" She cried as she struck the man across the face. "If they have not returned by morning, you will escort me to the cottage directly, and we shall have it burnt to the ground. If we cannot spill their blood, then we will snuff them out."

***

In the camp, Tuck tended to Robin's wound as Will and John bound the hunter to a tree, and gagged him, according to their master's instructions. The night waxed on, and dawn was hours away. Gisborne only hoped he could be proven true that he might return home, and all that while, he could not sleep but did listen impatiently for the conclusion of his fate. As the men sat together, they held counsel over the matter, weighing the extent of it with such vexation, for much had been withheld, and many had been deceived.

At length, A'Dale openly confessed to what part he had played in Gisborne's escape, and how Múriel had implored him to help her, as she, in turn, aided him in discovering a way in and out of Nottingham's dungeons. The outlaw remained adamant, unwaveringly justified in the exchange, as the company could not have afforded the loss of Jack; moreover, as Jack and Little John discovered Gisborne's circumstance and their comrade's supposed connection to it, they were only given leave to speculate based on what the lad had witnessed at Nottingham. Neither wishing to bolster a breach, they kept quiet. Yet, as time went on, the concealment of the matter grew all the more strenuous.

Still, there remained Eleanor's testimony, in which she implored the men fervently, though they had so passively brushed her conviction aside. And finally, Will's witness of the man in the village, seeking aid for his ill wife, and his strange account from Winifred, had driven the evidence to its fullest measure.

As each account was considered with all reverence and sobriety, Robin sat in silence and bid the men afford him time to think. But soon enough the men began to argue, heated in their ambivalence.

"Whether one has betrayed the company or not is another matter of scrutiny entirely!" Tuck contended. "What we are all hinged upon is whether this man has truly cast off his life of violence and oppression. If we set him free, will he continue in his wickedness? And what of his tale? How can we be sure any of this is true?"

"Your mind is weathering faster than your flesh, old man," Alan huffed. "Already I have borne witness! Surely, and if he were so vile to continue in what ways he had lived, would we not come to hear of it? I stand by him and Múriel. I've no doubt of her reason nor of his honour."

"But what proof have you? You plant your feet on what webs that man has laid before you. And you, not knowing dirt from deception, have called it earth indeed!" Tuck bickered, storming toward the man.

"Brothers!" Jack stepped forth, standing between the old man and the outlaw. "Quarreling will not supply our need! Altogether we should agree, there must be irrefutable evidence of his amendment, lest we slay a good man, or free a madman. If we could send someone to the cottage, to search for his wife and fetch her here, doubtless, she would give testimony of his character. And if she is not to be found, then the truth will out, yes?"

"Perhaps," Tuck grumbled, still eying Alan crossly.

"You would taunt such a thought, that Múriel has given herself to a fork-tongued snake?" Robin shook his head.

"Master, we must be sure of the truth before we make our judgement," Jack persisted. "Can we not try to discover the woman?"

"But who could I send?" Robin looked about the men. "Who amongst you is left that I can trust?"

"I'll go," Will stood. "You have my word, I will look on the task with an impartial eye."

Robin sniffed angrily, yet the sensible part of his spirit quietly called him to recount Scarlet's loyalty; ever honest and forthright, in all things. And the matter could not be left to fester.

"Very well, you may go," he acquiesced. "Still, another must go with you. As we have found this night, the woods are far too dangerous to wander alone."

"Then I shall go," John nodded, setting his hand on Scarlet's shoulder.

"Good," their master said. "Go. Scout the cottage for Múriel and make haste. Do not remain any longer than is necessary."

At this, Jack stepped toward the distant tree where they had bound up their hostage, and as he approached, he removed the gag, the captive's eyes, watchful and tormented.

"What are you doing?" John questioned.

"Father, both you and Scarlet need to know how to find the cottage. Only he can tell you," Jack advised the men as they drew near. "Sir Guy, if we are to test your word, we need to know where the cottage lies. Could you tell us the way?" The lad questioned.

"Why?" He said.

"Robin will not be satisfied unless he knows with utter certainty that you are telling the truth," Jack whispered. "If your wife is there, then she can confirm your story, and we shall have no choice but to let you go."

"Very well," the man sighed. "Back where your comrades and I were ambushed, I left all my supplies. Not a few yards from that point, my horse is secured. He will lead them back to the cottage."

"And how will we know the home is yours?" John asked, listening as he set his hand upon the hilt of his sword.

"You'll find three elder trees, lined beside one another; behind them stands the cottage," he answered.

"Men," Robin said, "Do not waste any time. Be quick, be safe," he cautioned them.

Valiant, Little John and Scarlet set off on their quest. It was not long before they happened upon the horse and whatever provisions the hunter had left behind. Into the night, the outlaws let the horse lead the way. Flying through the forest, like an arrow, the horse took them to a strange path which led to the three elder trees, just as the captive had told them. There was something wild and mystical about those trees, for as they passed and looked up, how the moon herself shone such light on every leaf, and what ancient strength they sensed in beholding them. For a moment, they tempered their pursuit, to gaze upon them. Then, through the trees, they came to the open field, and not so far in the distance, stood the cottage.

As they approached, an ominous feeling hung in the air. No light shone from within, and no smoke rose from the chimney. It seemed all that stirred was the sound of the waving blades of grass. The horse halted, and as the men dismounted, they drew near the door. Then, something caught John's attention.

"Look," he said, as he pushed the door open. "Now, what woman left all alone would leave her door open at night? Do you not think that odd?"

"With a property such as this, it may not be so odd," Will shrugged his shoulders, as he followed John into the cottage.

With flint and steel in hand, Scarlet lit a candle he found lying on the floor. And as it burned, he tore away at the hem of his cloak, and with the scrap of his garment, bound it round the candle, so the wax would not drip onto his hand. Though the light was faint, the damage of the home could be seen full well.

"What do you suppose happened here?" He whispered, as he stepped over bits of broken furniture and scattered shards of pottery.

"It looks as if this place was abandoned years ago," John said, wandering about aimlessly.

"Wait," Will called, as he knelt down beside the overturned table. "There is pottage left in this bowl, and still warm. And over there," he pointed, "a pitcher of water, spilt. Múriel was certainly here."

"I don't know about that," John rubbed at his grey-bearded chin. "We've come to find a woman, not the remnants of some peasant's supper, and mind, it may not have belonged to that lass at all. I'll keep searching down here. Why don't you venture upstairs?"

"But you've no light," he said.

"I'll manage. Go on," John returned.

Nodding, the outlaw then turned toward the staircase and climbed the creaking steps. As he made his way down the corridor, he cautiously opened the first door, and this, the bedchamber that had once belonged to the maiden's brother. Beyond the overturned furniture, it seemed rather plain and empty. Surveying the chamber, he observed there was no dust, nor any traces that time had ravaged this place. Returning to the corridor once more, he slowly paced to the second door. Múriel's previous chamber. Once again, no sign of a single soul, but every evidence that someone did live here, and quite recently. Finally, Will approached the entrance to the master bedchamber and opened the door. A large bed stood at the left of the chamber, though the linens were strewn about. To his right, there was an empty fireplace, and once again, furniture turned over this way and that. Yet, in the corner of the chamber, he saw something peculiar. Tilting up the strange wooden piece, he recognised it.

"A cradle," he whispered. "A cradle!"

Stirred with curiosity, he searched thoroughly about the chamber and out of the corner of his eye, he perceived something glittering. The light from the full moon shone through the window panes upon a small treasure of some kind, half hidden under a length of fabric. As Will lifted the garment, he discovered the most beautiful silver brooch he had ever seen. Picking it up, he studied its delicate engravings, of a full moon over a glistening sea.

"This has to be... must be," Will muttered. "John! John!" He called, as he bounded back down the corridor, down the flight of stairs, and unto his comrade. "The silver brooch! 'Tis Múriel's, undoubtedly," he said. "And there in the chamber also was a cradle. Gisborne has spoken the truth."

Stern and unyielding, the man did not glance for one moment at the clasp. "We are not here to look for shiny trinkets or pieces of furniture. We are here to look for a woman, and she is not here."

"But, we cannot ignore-"

"Ignore what?"

"This! This proof, right here!"

"Would that you might gain some sense," John grumbled, as he cuffed the treasure from Will's hand. "It proves nothing."

"But both Alan and Eleanor have testified of her silver brooch!" He argued, picking up the piece once more. "This is the very thing Claudia has used to track her down. Evidence, indeed!"

"Why are you so resolved to find Gisborne innocent?" John pressed. "Would you wish the scoundrel freed?"

"I only wish to discover the truth," he said.

"No, you are blinding yourself to the truth, all for Eleanor."

"Your words are too hasty, friend," Will said. "All this while, I have stood unbiased. As for Eleanor, though it has caused me such pain, I have accepted her death."

"You've not accepted anything," John rebutted. "You cannot accept that she is dead any more than you can accept Gisborne is lying, and all such ignorance is met right well because you'll not stomach the thought that her death was meaningless. You're obsessed with it, and it has blinded you!" As the man let the words fall from his lips, he regretted them, for his brash indictment had so pierced his brother.

"No," the man shook his head. "You are the one who is blind. Blind to the evidence because of your hatred for the man."

"Will," John sighed, "I didn't mean-"

"And you think I make to free myself of my burdens by vindicating a Norman?" Will questioned.

"I think it's time we return to the camp," he huffed, as he pushed past the man toward the door.

"Return? Do you not see the condition of this place? We cannot leave now," he said. "There may have been a raid and his wife may have been here this very evening."

"And yet, to the epiphany of all, there is no one here!" John shouted, his hands clenched into fists. "We have wasted time enough with this squabbling. We must return to the company."

"But we've not yet been here an hour. We must keep searching!"

"There is nothing more to search!" The man snarled. "This is utter folly. If you wish to remain here and continue searching like some common knave, then so be it! I shall return to the camp!" Fuming, the man stormed out of the cottage, took the horse, and galloped back into the forest.

"John! Stop!" Will called across the field, his voice echoing against the walls of the night and all for nought. For his kinsman had abandoned him. Furious, the outlaw marched back into the cottage.

Putting the brooch in his pocket, the man made his way to the kitchen, and as he searched, there, at the bottom edge of the back door, he found a swatch of fabric stuck fast in the frame. Kneeling down, he lifted the candle so he might see it better. Suddenly, he heard a quick thud as something weighty hit the floor behind him.

His hand upon the hilt, he rose and drew his sword, and turned back.

Nothing.

Retreating to the front of the cottage he looked about, and as the whole of it stood still and empty as ever, he returned his attention to the fabric caught in the back door. Slowly, he opened the door, and as the fabric came loose, he brought the piece under the candlelight and observed it. This was no simple scrap of linen. The material was strong and well stitched with exaggerated frays at the end that had been sticking out the back of the door. Then, at the threshold of the door, he saw speckles of blood, and the area of grass beyond it looked as if it had been trampled down. As he overlooked the garden, he noticed the mark of a footprint, and certainly small enough to be a woman's. Beyond it, was another and another, and so it went, leading out toward the woods. Extinguishing the candle, the man cast it to the ground and dashed forward, following the tracks deeper and deeper into the forest. At length, he had pursued the trail for over an hour, adamant that such a chase would not be in vain. As he continued on, he soon heard the rippling and rolling of a stream not far ahead. And the sounds of someone panting. Nearing the stream, he saw the woman.

"Múriel? Is that you?" Will approached cautiously. "You're... you're in labour!"

"Who are you? And how do you know my name?" She trembled, her silver eyes glistening in the moonlight as she stared, terrified. Clenching her eyes shut, she breathed deep once more.

"Don't be afraid. I am one of Robin Hood's men, Will the Scarlet. Your friend Eleanor, she spoke of you often," the man comforted. "But your husband, he..."

"Guy! You've seen him?" She managed through another surge. "Where is he? Is he safe?" Her soft eyes begged.

"Yes, I've seen him. He's safe," the man answered, "but he is far from here."

Nodding, she looked back up at the man with fearful eyes, for she understood. "Please, don't leave me," she whispered.

Smiling gently, the outlaw knelt before the lady. "No, I'll not leave you," he promised. Without a second thought, Will held out his hands as she took them, and breathed.

***

Sullen, the rebels waited.

Their eyes sought out every so often, hoping to see their comrades on the horizon yet all that could be found was the vast emptiness of a dolent wilderness. While the outlaws kept close by the campfire and shut their eyes only as they must, Gisborne fought hard to stay awake. His body ached, his heart was doubtful, and his eyes grew heavy. But he mustn't lose one minute, save any word came of his darling.

Thundering amidst the darkness, a horse came tramping through the camp.

"What news?" Tuck called from the fire. As he sprung to his feet, his expression hardening for he realised there was but one rider. "What's happened?"

John only shook his head, as he dismounted from the braying horse, and fastened it to a nearby tree, ignoring the others.

"Where is Will?" Robin questioned, his gaze narrowing.

"He did not wish to return," the man answered flatly.

"You left him behind?" Robin scolded, as he stood before the outlaw. "You were told to find the woman, not to desert your kinsman! How do you suppose he shall return? On foot, where any soldier can besiege him? Why did he not return with you?"

"He was determined to keep searching," John complained. "Haven't you taken notice? He's been far too willing to accept Gisborne's allegations. Well, let the fool search!"

"But father, why did you not remain with him?" Jack asked.

"There was no one there!" John answered, his grey hair flailing. "The entire cottage was left in shambles. There was no table left unturned, and the ground was littered with shards and fragments of every broken thing. We searched every corner, and the whole place was as empty as a tomb."

"So what you mean to say is, *you* thought it was a hopeless business, and fled," Robin said.

"What did Will think?" Tuck asked, tilting his chin downward.

"He believed someone may have broken in," John folded his arms over his chest. "But there was no proof of it, nor was there any proof that the cottage we found belonged to that wretch or his supposed family. It's indisputable, Gisborne's lying."

"John," Alan said, "has not Claudia been searching for Múriel and Guy?"

"Aye," he said.

"Do you not realise that she may have sent men to search for them, and so ransacked the place? That someone could have taken the lass?" Alan urged. "Did you even consider it?"

With his eyes cast downward, John grew ashamed.

Twisting the ring on his finger, Robin sighed and searched his comrade's face. "Was anything found that might give us clarity? Anything at all?"

"All we found of any significance was a cradle, and a silver brooch," the man answered begrudgingly.

"A silver brooch," Alan echoed, his dark eyes glistening. "Do you have it with you?"

"Will has it," he said. "I suppose, all that is left for us to do is wait for him to return," John sighed, running his fingers through his thick locks.

"No, surely one of us can ride out to retrieve him?" Tuck darted his eyes between the men. "He cannot be left there all night."

"But night is fading. Look," Robin whispered. Far beyond, a very dim, very pale light was growing. "At dawn, we shall retrieve him. By and by, none of us has slept a wink, and if we are to be of any aid to our brother, we must get some rest."

With these words spoken, Robin retreated to his cot and shut his eyes. As the others followed, Tuck remained to keep watch. Seated beside the campfire, the old man stared beyond him, as the light from the flames shone over the captive's afflicted expression.

All while the men spoke amongst themselves, Guy could not hear them well enough to understand why Múriel was not there, nor why Will had not returned. How any word would give him reprieve, though it would be hard to gain them, indeed, especially from Tuck. Acquiring the old man's gaze, he spoke up.

"Outlaw!" He whispered, "Water?"

Dropping his shoulders, the man slowly stood and made his way toward the captive, with a ladle of water. Having given the man something to drink, he turned to retreat back to the fire.

"Wait," Guy called, "Have you any news? Have your men spoken with my wife?"

Motionless, he stood; his back toward the captive as he contemplated his answer, for he still held doubts over the man's story. "No," he muttered.

"But why has your comrade returned alone? Where is the other?"

"You wish to pacify the disquiet of your mind?" Tuck faced the man once more, his keen eyes dauntless.

"I need to know that she is safe," he answered. "And if I will be set free."

"We shall see what the morning brings," Tuck said, bringing his hands behind his back as he retreated to the fire.

***

Hollow, the cottage stood, enveloped beneath the shroud of midnight. And through the shadowed realm, a dread assembly approached the secret place. How the ground was brutally trampled, tainted by the hoofs of revenge. In loathsome haste, the riders drove forth, with Lady Claudia leading the gruesome lot.

Halting before the empty home, the woman dismounted, and with a torch set ablaze in her hand, she cast it upon the threshold, watching as the flames licked the edge of the door, climbing higher and higher. With torches blazing, the other riders threw their flames upon the cottage. The thatched roof soon caught fire, and in every pane shone its consuming light. Such was its bitter end; a place of all peace and consolation, demolished.

Iron-hearted, Claudia then turned to face the riders, the large vein of her throat throbbing as she commanded the men to scour every tree and shrub. The fugitives must be found that very night.

Upon her dark stallion, the woman rode on ahead, as some riders followed close behind her, while the other five separated into the thick of the forest. One such soldier lingered a while by the cottage, watching as the flames grew to consume it. Then, a curious pattern in the grass caught his eye. It seemed there was a trodden path leading back into the woods from the garden of the home. With little but curiosity and the excuse of office to guide him, on he went, following the trail, confident the following it would lead to its own reward.

***

"La douleur est trop," Múriel pleaded, her hands trembling, her eyes weary, her body weak. "I can't do this," she groaned, gripping Will's arm. "I can't-"

"It's nearly dawn, and the night's almost behind us," he encouraged, though his voice betrayed his own exhaustion. "Don't give in, not for one moment."

"But I'm so tired… I'm not strong enough."

"No, you are strong enough," he soothed, "Trust it."

Her eyes clenched shut, she summoned all her courage to fight on. Will's face flushed white, in shock and excitement, her grip so tight on his arm as she pressed her forehead against his shoulder and cried out one final time.

At last, reaching down, she drew the child up into her arms, the infant's cry heralding the first light and the swift dawn stretching across the skies. Múriel held the child close, and as the tears fell down her face, she smiled so sweetly, caressing her little one so tenderly.

"A son," she whispered, her eyes radiant as the coming morning. Bending her head down, she placed the gentlest kiss upon the child's head. "Oh, how I wish your father were here, little one," she sighed, cradling the child in her arms as she gazed down upon him.

"That was the most terrifying, raw, most beautiful thing I have ever beheld," Will sighed, his smile bursting. "And he is perfect."

"He is," Múriel nodded. "Merci pour tout," she said, as she held out her hand towards Will, who grasped it firmly.

"Of course," he said, as he brushed away a tear. "What will you call him?"

"Guiscard," she said, gazing so fondly at her son. "The brave and wise one. For his brave father."

"And wise mother," Will tilted his head, grinning.

When both mother and child were settled as well as could be managed, gently, the lady held out the child and placed him in the man's arms. Never before had he esteemed how precious and fragile and sweet was such a life. For a moment, he thought of Eleanor, and what could have been, what was lost, and all that lay before him now. A road, quite uncertain. Howbeit, in some small measure, he was thankful for such an instant where he met a glimpse of hope, in the one he held.

At length, Will had prepared a little grove for Múriel and the child, to rest at the base of a willow that grew by the river. There, he removed any twigs or bristles, and laid out his cloak, before he guided them to it. As the lady lay down upon her side, she undid the lacing of her garment and brought the child to nurse at her breast, stroking his little arm to keep him awake. Then, as she looked up, the outlaw had begun pacing away.

"Where are you going?" Múriel wondered.

"I shall need to move you soon, but take some time to rest. I'll keep watch," Scarlet said, standing in the distance with his arms crossed over his chest.

"Merci, my friend," the lady whispered, as she closed her eyes, and let the stillness of the early hour sweep over her.

***

The black rider was not so far behind; following the track, deeper and deeper into the wild. Night was cast asunder, as the morning light enriched every hue of the earth beneath it, and made all the clearer the path to be followed.

Then, a soft sound greeted the rider's ears; the rolling of a stream's waters.

CHAPTER TWENTY-SIX

DAWN

Calm and contented, the lady rested a while; her mind drifting in and out of dreams.

Not so far beyond her, the outlaw kept watch. How quiet he stood as the wind whispered through the slender boughs of the willows, and the early light caught up in his long, flaming hair. Gently, the song of the wrens rose high above as they stretched their wings and descended from their nests. And the very air did teem with their melodies; free and merry and sublime. As the child lay sleeping in her arms, Múriel opened her tired eyes and gazed down upon him. How he took in a sudden breath, and for a moment, his eyelashes twitched and his little brow furrowed, then breathing out, he was at peace again. For his whole temperament was serene, safe in his mother's arms. Tight around her finger, the infant held fast, and though so small, his grip was strong. Dark was his hair, very like his father, and his chin was his father's altogether. Yet, his smile fared far calmer, and steadier, and quite his very own.

Where are you, my love? She thought. *Come, find me here.*
Suddenly, something shifted in the distance, not far from the grove.
As the lady glanced up, she found that Scarlet had sat down; his
back leaning up against a tree's trunk, and as he lounged, he carved
a bit of wood in his hand.

"Will?" She called out.

Presently, he turned his gaze to the side, hearing her voice. Rising
to his feet, he hurried to kneel before her.

"Yes? Is everything alright?" He looked down upon her in such
warmth and kindness.

"Could you fetch me some water?" Múriel sighed.

"Oh, here," he said. Removing the leather flask which hung across
his chest, he gave it to the lady. "Drink it all. I can refill it by the
stream. Forgive me, I should have offered you something earlier."

"C'est bon," she answered. Drawing the flask to her lips, she drank
until a few drops were left. "And is there anything to eat?"

"I've nothing with me," he said. "I could forage about the wood
and see if I might find something. I'll not be one minute," Will
nodded. Gallant, he leapt up and departed, but as he was not so
heedful, he strayed too far.

Soon, Múriel could no longer hear him; not a rustle of leaves, nor a
single twig snapping, nor any evidence of his presence. The
stillness of the wood felt unnatural. The sunlight which shone so
hopeful now hung veiled by cloud, and all about was as an endless
shadow. Nought but the faint rippling of the stream could be heard.
For the songs of the birds had now vanished, and the leaves of the
willow did not sway but hung lifeless.

"Will? Will!" She called, her keen eyes surveying the forest as she
stilled her breath and listened. Then, an ominous feeling engulfed
her, drawing nearer and nearer. She held the child close and
wrapped a corner of the cloak beneath about them. Pressing her
head down, she waited.

She could hear the muffled sound of a single horses' hoofs trotting
the ground and a snort from the creature's nostrils; the shadow of
fear crept closer. Shutting her eyes tight, Múriel fought to hold her
breath, though it pained her lungs. Her heart drummed all the
fiercer.

A sudden thud.

The soldier dismounted from his horse; his breath harsh and heavy,
and each step resounded, trampling the earth. She daren't open her
eyes.

She could sense it, how he stared. But she couldn't quite tell where he was, nor what she should do.

Though frightened beyond all measure, the lady cautiously opened her eyes, to discover by any means, who it was that had come. There, before her, stood a rider in black; hideous and fearsome, indeed. His hood hung such that it would seem no face would be found behind it. His cloak draped so that it trailed upon the ground, yet his armour beneath could be heard, clinking and clacking as he stepped closer. And yet, while the man stood directly before her, he could not see her, and staring hard at him, he took no notice of her.

As he paced this way and that, searching past the stream one way and then the other, it would seem his prey disappeared altogether. The tracks ended just before the edge of the rolling waters, with no other signs to direct him further. Outraged, he muttered curses under his breath, turned back to his beast, and hastened deep into the woods again. Her ears keen, the lady remained still until all traces of the soldier had well and truly disappeared, for she feared to make any movement or any sound lest she and the child be harmed. When all was quiet again, quiet as it should be, the songs of the birds softly echoed through the eaves, and the light of dawn shone fair once more. And what respite was to be had, for the breeze returned, and all the suspended arms of green bowed and swayed.

Amidst the repose, the lady's ears pricked up at the rhythm of twigs snapping, and grass crunching as someone drew unto her. Shifting her gaze, she made to follow with her eyes precisely where the sound resonated, for she was not so afraid as she had been before. But when she turned back to face the river, her eyes fell on something she had nearly forgotten.

"It is you?" She whispered, as her eyes widened in awe.

The white stag, graceful and magnificent descended from the other bank, his hoofs as mist, stepping through the waters unto the lady.

Now, grander than ever before, his horns as a gilded crown towered above the tops of the trees. His eyes shone as great orbs; bright and calm and pure. As he approached the lady, he bowed his head, then, kneeling before her and her child, the stag set his nose upon the infant's head. And the child did not cry, but stirred a little, and smiled under the creature's soft touch. Lifting his head, the stag locked his eyes upon the lady, his good nature lifting her spirits, and all at once soothing her heart, for he spoke to her innermost self.

"Do not be afraid," he whispered. *"No harm shall come to you, or your son. The heirs of the Kingdom of Light shall not be left unguarded."*

"Heirs?" The lady gazed in wonder. *"I don't understand."*

"Not far from you lies one of the Woodland Realm; a descendant from my bloodline and a guardian, though he knows it not. He has been appointed to bring the Sun and the Moon and their offspring to the shoreline, and their kingdom shall see the Age of Light reborn."

"But what realms, what kingdoms are these that you speak of?" She wondered.

But, before he made an answer, the stag rose up again and vanished.

Such a strange, bewildering feeling settled in the air as if that moment had taken place such long years before, and somehow, all at once, was new; a fresh and ancient memory. How it lingered in her mind.

Soon, Múriel heard the rhythm of the outlaw's step, and peering out unto the forest, she saw him coming forth. As Will returned, he knelt before the lady with a timid smile and a jolly complexion, as he laid out the provisions beside her. "I've found some mushrooms and berries, but I'm afraid there wasn't much else to be found... Múriel? Are you well? You look as if you've seen a ghost," he said, tilting his head as he looked on her.

"How... how long were you gone?" She asked, placing her hand upon his arm, and glancing up with such light in her silver eyes.

"No more than a few minutes. Why?"

"I cannot say," she brought her hand to her temple.

"Here," Will said, holding out a handful of berries. "Forgive me, but you must eat quickly. We cannot stay here much longer, and I cannot leave you and the child here, defenceless. I must bring you back to the cottage."

"No, we cannot go back! Those soldiers are sure to be there still!" Múriel insisted, the height of her tone waking the child. "Shh," she caressed the child as he cried.

"Then that is why the cottage..." Will thought aloud. Setting his hands upon her shoulders, he spoke. "Múriel, the riders, they appeared last night, didn't they? And that's why you came all the way out here? You and your husband did not abandon the cottage?"

"We would never abandon our home," she said. "He left yesterday morning to hunt, and at nightfall, the riders came. Please, take me to him. Where is he?"

"But you don't understand, the soldiers are not at the cottage any longer," the man said. "Before I was sent to search for you, my master and I had faced a troupe in the forest and had defeated them. It was after this that I was sent. Perhaps these men were searching for you, and having found nothing turned to the deeps and happened upon my master," Will reasoned. "Surely, whatever threat had come, it is ended. Howbeit, I must bring you both somewhere safe, that I might return to my kinsmen so my master may free your husband."

"Free him?" The lady stared. "You said he was safe. What have your men done to him? Tell me," she urged, gripping his arm firmly, her eyes fearful.

"There is no time to explain," he sighed. "The longer we remain, the longer it will take for me to get back to the camp. And I must return before they-" Will paused, lowering his head before he gazed back up at the lady; her face pale.

"Swear to me you will not let Robin harm him," she begged.

"I swear it."

Making herself ready, the lady invoked all her strength to stand and walk; the child held fast in her arms and the outlaw supporting her. As they journeyed back down the path towards the cottage, the closer they came to it, the stronger the scents and vapours of smoke filled the air. Quickly, the lady drew a corner of her cloak over the infant's nose to shield him from it.

"What is that?" She whispered.

"Stay back. And do not make a sound," the man instructed, as he aided her to sit down out of the smoke's range and darted ahead into the thick of it.

Approaching the edge of the wood, where the garden lay behind the cottage, how dark was the sight that met his eyes. For there was nought but a heap of rubble; the frame of the home crumbling in weakening flames before him. The man stood watching, as another piece of the structure fell down to the ashen ground so that large clouds of smoke rose up. How the layers of soot had settled on the land, and all about what burnt and hollow and dead.

Hastily, the man fled; his hand over his mouth as he coughed and the smoke burning his lungs. Panting, he sprinted back to the lady, half out of breath.

"What's wrong? What's happened?"

"The cottage... the whole cottage. They burnt it down," Will sighed. "I'm so sorry."

Múriel could only nod, as a lump swelled in her throat. A single tear rolled down her cheek, as she held her son close in her arms.

"Then where can we go?" She glanced up at the man, frightened. "Could you not take me to the camp? Let me speak with Robin and plea my husband's cause?"

"No, the camp is too far from here, and you cannot walk that distance," Will answered. "Let me bring you to Winifred. She is a skilled healer, and you must see a physician... you're still bleeding," he sighed.

So overwhelmed with fear and drive, the lady had not thought of her condition. "No, Winifred lives in Locksley, and we cannot risk Claudia's eye," she said. "But where is Eleanor? Is she at the camp with the others?"

"We must think on this need now, lest more danger follows," the man insisted.

"Wait," Múriel's eyes lightened. "I know of a place that is not far from here, and it is quiet and safe. A cottage which once belonged to an old friend. It is vacant, and no one will find us there."

"But you cannot be in this state for hours without a physician," he shook his head. "Bringing you to safety will mean nothing if you die there." Pacing, Will rubbed at the back of his head as he let out a great sigh. "Very well; I'll carry you."

"What! Surely, not all that way!" Múriel protested.

"First, I must get you to safety, then I shall call on Winifred as soon as you and the child are settled," Will resolved. "Now, direct me," he said, as he swept Múriel up in his arms with the infant clutched tight against her chest.

***

Soft, the morning light dashed over the skies, creating stripes of light across the camp and over the hands and faces of the men, as they readied their weapons. Swords and bows alike were eager for the fight, much as the ones who wielded them. For each sought to make their purpose, and bring about whatever end.

"We've delayed long enough. We must find Scarlet," Robin proposed, his green eyes fierce as he tightened his leather gauntlets. "John, what words did he speak before you departed?"

"I do not recall, yet he persisted we stay to survey the whole of the property," John said. "I've no doubt he stayed, indeed."

"Do you suppose Claudia could have captured him?" Jack added, his arms folded across his chest. "What if the riders found him? She could be holding him for ransom. What'll we do then?"

"We don't know he's been taken," John shook his head. "But master, can I not go with you?"

"Brother, I need you here," Robin sighed, as he shifted his eyes toward the captive.

"I must stay behind to guard *him*?" John snorted.

"You're the only one I can trust to do it, at least, to handle him if he starts any trouble," the outlaw said. Lowering his voice, he leaned closer toward his comrade, "Do not hesitate to end him if he challenges you."

"Master, surely you cannot mean that," Alan protested, his brown eyes bold and brazen. "You cannot have us bind him as an animal and kill him without a fair trial."

"Would you shut up!" John barked. "Already, we've given him ample time to prove himself, and nothing's come of it save more peril and misfortune. Given all this chaos with these foul soldiers, how do we know he's not working for Claudia?" John accused. "Perhaps he's made a deal with her. Capture the Rebel, win his freedom?"

"Are you mad?" the captive shouted. "How can you think I would strike any bargain with Claudia? I would not bend my knee to her for a kingdom."

"Aye, yet devils will only practice what is like to their nature," John huffed. "Strange it is, for just as the soldiers ambushed my master, you were there to intervene. Now, my kinsman is suddenly missing after we had ventured out to that damned cottage which you claimed to be your own. What more proof of plot? What more proof of your alliance with the woman?"

"I've taken no part in any of Claudia's dealings!" Gisborne proclaimed, his blue eyes raging. "She sentenced me to death and thought to make a profit in selling me as a slave. She has abused her servants and has openly demonstrated her callousness toward the people and their suffering. And now, she has threatened to slaughter my family and harm anyone who hinders her. If I be a devil for my past, what breed of devil is she for her present?"

"I'll hear none of it! Your words are but deception in its waking," John spat, his grey, wiry brows raised.

"Enough of this!" Robin cried out. "Our brother is gone. He could be in grave danger, and Gisborne is the only thorn in our side determined to see us quarrel amongst ourselves. Do not heed his words, whatever he speaks. Alan, Tuck, I shall need you two to scour the woods. If you must go into the village, do so with the utmost caution. Claudia has little time left before she owes Prince

John my head, and every one of us is marked. Jack, you'll come with me. We must go back to that cottage. Are we ready?"

"Aye," the men answered, as they withdrew, embarking on their quest.

"John, you have my word we won't be gone long," Robin placed his hand upon his kinsman's shoulder, quieting his voice. "I have a feeling we'll find him soon."

"But what if…" John whispered as he lowered his chin.

Robin shook his head and made no answer. Turning about, he mounted the horse with Jack, as the creature galloped back through the woods in pursuit of the cottage. Alan and Tuck sprinted off into the forest, their dark cloaks as great sails billowing behind them. And there, alone in the camp, Little John and Gisborne were left in the stillness of the morning air. Minutes passed with not a word spoke between them. At length, as the outlaw remained but a few yards from the captive, Gisborne's thirst could not be borne.

"Will you give me no water?" The captive called, finally breaking the silence.

Disgruntled, John rolled his eyes in response, as he grabbed a flask by his feet, and marched toward the man.

"Here," he said, tilting the flask as Gisborne quenched his thirst.

"Thank you," he nodded, watching as John silently returned to his post. "Whatever you think of me, I would never seek to put any of you in danger."

Little John only huffed, ignoring the man and keeping his eyes fixed on the piece of wood in his hand, as he whittled away at it. Pausing a while, the captive thought, remembering how the rebels had argued over something in the night, and he was given no answers from the old man. Perhaps, he could gain some knowledge from John, at least enough to ease his mind.

"I know you and your comrade were sent to the cottage. Why did you return alone?"

The outlaw continued to ignore the man, carving away in contempt and whittling roughly against the wood in his hand; the chips and curls and fragments, flying up and landing all about his feet.

"You refuse to answer me?"

Finally, drawing his eyes upward, the outlaw stared at the man. "I saw your deceptions clear as day. Thus I returned."

"But why has your kinsman not yet returned?"

"He stayed behind because that blasted shred of kindness left in him is determined to find some truth in your words," his nostrils flared. "He shall see soon enough there is no merit to them."

"You think him mad then?"

"Mad at worst," John muttered. "I think him foolhardy. A good comrade, but foolhardy."

"But when you went to the cottage, did you speak to Múriel about all this?"

"We found no one, Gisborne," the man replied. "That pit of a cottage looked more weather-beaten than your own face. Looked as if a pack of wild beasts was set loose upon it, or else it must've been abandoned long ago."

"What do you mean? Then, where is she?" Gisborne urged as he struggled against his bonds. "You must let me go! She could be in danger! Untie me!"

"When will you stop?" John shouted. Rising to his feet, he marched toward the man and wrenched at his collar. "Would it were my decision! I would see your corpse hang from this very tree, and so help me if you so much as speak that lass's name again, I swear by the spirits, I'll do it! And sure as daylight, I'll leave you no foothold to slay my master!"

"You think I wish to be set free to kill the Rebel?" Gisborne's brows raised wildly, as he wrestled under the ropes, gritting his teeth. "If I wanted him dead, would I not have done away with him already?"

"Dare you seek to pierce my understanding? Not one of us has forgotten your accursed history!"

"And history's curse is that is never be amended. Still, cannot a man make alteration of his future?"

"Oh, so you would have all forget it? All the people, good people, you sent away to prison and to the gallows, now you are discharged of accountability? And you cry for what wife you've claimed, but of my wife, the very one you took to settle debts that you devised and forced on me, you would have such blood washed from your hands?" John shouted, throwing his fist hard across the man's face, the blood of the captive on his hand. "Mark my words, you blackguard, your end is near!"

***

Sifting through Sherwood, the sunrise beat down overhead.

How swift they ventured along the hidden path, yet not so far in the distance stood a league of soldiers. The smoke from their camp swirled high up into the air, and the noise of metal clanking about, and men's voices grumbling low, echoed through the eaves. Quickly, Robin pulled back the reins, as the horse slowed down to a trot, cautious to remain undetected. And as the men were making

371

enough of a racket themselves, they would not so easily hear the outlaws slip by.

When the threat was long behind them, the men continued on, and the horse was set to galloping once more, wild and free. Finally, three grand trees caught the young lad's eye.

"There, master! Westward!" Jack pointed, his eager eyes brightening as he beheld the sight of those trees once more. Just as the words had left his lips, and the thought of his comrade waiting for them cheered his venturous spirit, the scent of smoke filled his lungs. "Do you smell that?" Jack sniffed the air.

"Yes," Robin answered. "That is no bonfire."

As they moved through those trees and onto the land that stretched before the cottage, the waning cloud of dark smoke hung above them. Beyond, they perceived where the cottage had been, smoke still rising from the rubble, and beneath, nothing left but the burnt and brittle frame.

"I thought my father said it was abandoned," Jack whispered. "Will would have no cause to do this, no one would have cause to burn down this home. This must be the sheriff's doing."

"Aye, you may be right," Robin nodded, his eyes staring sharply forward.

Suddenly, a thought took hold in Jack's mind. "Will... he stayed behind. What if..." his eyes shone woeful, looking back at his master, as each took in the realisation.

"Search everywhere!" Robin cried frantically, as he dismounted, and bolted toward the rubble. Cautiously he stepped over a pile of ash where there once had been an entrance.

Jack bounded away over fragmented bits of wood and stone, the smoke still rising in places here and there, breaking free in puffs as he stepped through. But sprinting across the centre of the home, the lad made too hard a step, so that his foot was caught fast amongst the remains and a whirl of ash rose up against his face. As the outlaw aided the lad, he cautioned him to step slowly and lightly, for they must continue searching and any further delay would surely hinder their cause.

On his feet once more, the lad stepped watchfully, listening keenly to the creaking from the frame high above, the wind letting it sway here and there, as bits of soot flecked his hood. Stooping low, Jack brushed away some rubble, finding very little to satisfy anyone's doubting thoughts. Then, a peculiar shape caught his eye.

Presently, he knelt down and dug below the debris, as he groped toward the object. Picking it up, he studied the item and knew it well. Silent, he stared, fixed by the weight of the object in his hands.

"Have you found anything?" Robin called back, as he walked through the frame and out into the garden.

For a moment, the delay in answer did not deter him, for as he walked out over the soot-laden grounds, he thought he saw a figure in the distance; a grand, white figure. But as he followed unto the edge of the wood, the creature was nowhere to be seen. His green eyes surveyed what forest lay before him, and all such pondering proved idle. For it was in this moment he recalled his word to his comrade, and how behind him, the land laid quiet. Thus once more did he call out to the lad, as he drew unto the rubble. "Jack!" He cried. "Have you found anything?"

No answer met his ears.

Approaching the wounded frame, the outlaw saw the lad kneeling, and his head bowed. Swiftly, the man inlet beside him, awaiting his comrade's answer.

"Master," Jack sighed, rising up and holding out the dagger. "It belonged to him... didn't it?" He whispered.

Taking the blade in his hands, Robin brushed the charcoal off the handle, and there was no doubt, it belonged to their kinsman.

"No... no, he can't have," Robin shook his head in disbelief. Clenching the dagger in his hand, he brought it to his heart.

How the men lingered amongst the ruins to shed what brief and silent tears they must, for so unsure and yet unmoved were they in this conclusion, that they had lost so beloved a brother. With haste and much toil, the outlaws departed and journeyed toward their camp once more.

***

The sun grew steadily higher in the skies, the morning now fled, and the heat of midday shone down upon them. Gisborne sighed, his neck ached bitterly, and from all his struggling, he had scratched the skin on his wrists, now raw and burning and bleeding. And John, who sat for a time in dormant rage, took no further notice of the man but kept to his whittling. Each silent, each eager for the outlaws to return.

Then, fast approaching, Robin and Jack approached the camp.

"You're back!" John leapt to his feet, yet as he saw no other, his expression grew puzzled. "What of Will? Did you not find him?" But as the man and the lad dismounted, John observed their red eyes and grim faces. Gripping his master by the shoulders, he stared with all unease. "Where is he?"

Robin only shook his head, his eyes heavy. With a deep sigh, he retrieved from his pocket, their brother's dagger, smeared with charcoal. "He's gone," he whispered.

Hesitantly, John took the blade, "But... how? How did this happen?"

"There was a fire, father," Jack stepped forward. "The whole cottage was burnt down to nothing."

"No!" Gisborne cried, his heart racing beneath his chest. "Tell me this is not true!"

Robin nodded, "Everything was destroyed."

"But did you find anyone? Or any sign that Múriel had been there when the fire happened?" The captive begged.

"We've lost William! Our William!" John roared, setting his hand over his heart, his blue eyes brimming. "How do we know this wasn't a trap set for him by you and that devilish sheriff? How do we know you weren't intending for Robin to get caught in that fire?"

"Have you no sense?" Gisborne growled back, "I am as much a victim, too, if my wife was left there," his voice cracked.

"Enough with all this rubbish!" John determined, drawing his sword, ready to slay the man.

"Stop!" Jack interjected, standing before his father. "Aye this man is a villain, who has caused grief enough for all of us, but you cannot kill him. We still do not yet know whether any of this was of his doing," he said, as his father let angered tears fall down his face.

"Aye, lad," John sighed. "We will wait for Alan and Tuck to return. Then, we will decide his fate."

As their master nodded, together, Robin and Little John looked on with one final callous glare at the captive, their very cores loathing him without measure.

The hours passed, and the sunset painted the forest in hues of crimson. Despondent, Gisborne stared into the flames of the campfire, as John and Jack made ready the noose, and Robin strutted past them with an armful of kindling.

"Robin," Gisborne called, his voice solemn and earnest. "Can you not spare me, for Múriel's sake?"

"Many whom I have loved are dead at your hand, and you dare entreat reprieve?" Robin's eyes shone worn and empty, staring back at the man.

"I swear I did not do this... but I am sorry for the loss of your comrade."

"Do not offer me counterfeit condolences," he sneered, moving toward the hostage. "You have been as a plague and a pestilence, devouring all that is good and pure and precious. Do not venture to seek your stars, Gisborne, for surely if they be sound in their own right, they will not mark you."

Suddenly, the rustling of leaves and heavy breaths drew nearer, as Alan and Tuck raced through the forest and finally came upon the camp.

"A'Dale!" Gisborne shouted. "Have you any news of Múriel? Is she alive?"

Alan, though panting, grinned broadly under his dark beard, merry and mirthful as ever, as he glanced at Guy. "Let Will tell you of it himself."

"Will?" Robin looked in astonishment, as the others stared dumbfounded, for bounding into the midst, their brother came forward and fell to his knees before the men; breathless.

"You're alive!" Robin's eyes lit up, as he embraced the man of copper hair. "We thought you had died in the fire! We found your dagger in the cottage!" He said as he pulled back to show him the blade.

"Oh! My dagger! I wondered what that noise was," Scarlet smiled. "But no, dead I am not. Starved as a dog, but not dead."

"But you're covered in blood," Jack mumbled nervously. "What happened?"

"I am well, truly, 'tis not my own," Will shook his head. Then, drawing to his feet, he sprinted toward the captive and began cutting away at the bonds. "Guy, I've much to tell you," he said.

"What are you doing?" John raised his grey brows wildly. "His fate is already sealed!"

"And yet I shall cut him lose no matter what any of you say. He's told the truth, and I've proof enough to vindicate him." Will proclaimed, still working away at severing the rope. "It was unbelievable, Guy. She was simply unbelievable!"

"What do you mean? Have you found her? Have you found my wife?" The man stared in such bewilderment, as his heart knew not to rejoice from despairing.

"You actually found the lass?" John questioned.

"Aye, I found her, and this," the man said, revealing from his pocket, the silver brooch.

Gisborne's eyes widened at the sight, and such did all the men about gaze on at the trinket. "But how? How did you come to find her?"

"Oh, let him tell you what you need hear," Tuck waved his hand, as he sat down.

"Tell me what?" The captive wondered, finally breathing a sigh of relief as he was freed from his bonds and given the treasure.

"Here is how it went; John and I had gone to the cottage. We found it, but the whole place was a wreck. There was furniture knocked about everywhere, and John fled as he had thought it just some old abandoned pit, but I stayed behind to-"

"We know as much already," Alan rolled his eyes. "Get on with it."

"For pity's sake, I've not said more than two words together," the man scolded. "Now, I stayed behind because I had found a cradle and the silver brooch in the bedchamber. I knew she had to be the very one Claudia was looking for; there was not a single doubt in my mind. Thus, I searched about the kitchens and saw a bit of linen stuck fast in the frame of the back door. When I opened the door, there were before it, tracks that led out into the woods, and thus I followed them. The tracks went on and on until I found her."

"Was she alright? Is she alright?" Gisborne implored, grasping the outlaw's shoulders.

"Aye, she was safe, when I found her by the river. But as she knew me not, she was terribly frightened, so I quickly told her who I was and that you had sent me. Howbeit, she outright confirmed that you were her husband, and told me of the black riders that had come to the cottage, and 'twas for this reason she fled. Then, just as the dawn came, she had the child," the outlaw grinned.

"What?" Guy whispered, his expression brighter. "She did?"

"Well, when I found her she was in labour, and really in the thick of it-"

"And you stayed with her all the while?"

"I couldn't leave her by herself," he said. "This is why I was lost for hours, and sure as I live, she was unbelievable! I've never seen a woman stronger or braver than she."

Much to everyone's surprise, Gisborne smiled heartily and suddenly embraced the outlaw.

"You are a friend indeed, Will," he said, beaming with excitement, as he stepped back. "How is she? Where is she? How is the child?"

"She and the child are well enough," Scarlet nodded. "She told me to tell you that they are at Aldred's cottage. And I went out and called upon Winifred, so no doubt she is there now tending to your wife. I could not leave her without a physician. I had intended to bring her back to your cottage, but by the time we reached it, it had been destroyed. Thank the stars she remembered that old cottage.

But that is why I was gone so long, and why I look as I do. I had to carry her and the child all that way, but they are safe, Guy."

"Good... good," Gisborne sighed. "Thank you."

"Well, congratulations," Alan embraced the man. "And born on the twenty-eighth of August. A day of good fortune, indeed," he winked.

"And what does that mean?" Will scoffed. "How on earth is the twenty-eighth of August of any luck?"

"It's the same day that I was born," Alan chuckled, though his comrade merely huffed in response.

"But I must go to her! I must go now!" Gisborne thought, as he raced toward his horse, then paused in his steps; thinking. "Robin," he said. Turning back, he faced the Rebel, with the unspoken words lingering in his eyes. "Robin, all I ask is for your forgiveness," the man entreated, holding out his hand; waiting.

How the outlaw stood; his arms folded across his chest and his eyes stern as he looked back at the man. "Get out of my sight," he said. And turning his back toward the man, he paced away.

"Come now, master," Alan chided. "Can you not make peace with him?"

"He might've been telling the truth, but it changes nothing," Robin hissed.

Suddenly, through the forest, an arrow shot into the midst of the camp, and a symphony of hoofs pounded away at the dirt beneath them, drawing all the nearer.

Glancing up, Gisborne met a pair of eyes he did not expect. Petrified, he stared.

CHAPTER TWENTY-SEVEN

THE LAST BATTLE

Grimacing, she remained, mounted upon a black stallion with five soldiers lingering close behind. Her hair wild, her skin sallow, and her eyes of a primal hue in the crimson light.

"You pathetic dog," Claudia sneered. "I had not thought to find you here begging crumbs from outlaws. By and by, 'tis befitting, for when I've found you vagrant and despised, you dare my judgement and sink lower."

"How did you find this place?" Gisborne questioned.

"A simple feat," she lowered her gaze, as the corners of her lips curled. "All accomplished by a single scout. And how fortunate, for here lies double the reward. Slaying you and the Rebel will be a pleasure."

"I've no time for your games," he said. Retrieving the bow, he readied his arrow.

Quickly, she trotted aside as the troupe stormed after the outlaws. With one shot, Guy felled the first horse, its rider flung to the ground. Without a breath, Little John and Jack were after the soldier and drawn high above, their weapons shining.

Swift, a second arrow was loosed by Robin, as Claudia's stallion was pierced in the leg, the horse wailing madly; its head jolting every which way. Thus it sent its master back, flat to the forest floor.

Tuck, Alan, and Will each gripped fast their swords as they advanced toward two soldiers, who drew forth their weapons; steel against steel, amidst the fray. Though Tuck was old, he was keen enough and his feet ever agile as he wielded his sword against one of the soldiers, dodging every attack. And at last, when the moment struck, he gashed the blade into the man's leg, just as Alan came up from behind and drove his sword through the rider's back. And so it went, as one by one, the soldiers were defeated.

Yet Robin chased on ahead through the battle unto Claudia.

Dauntless, one of the riders galloped toward Gisborne at full speed, his spear outstretched and a cry of war upon his vicious tongue. Stalwart and strong, Guy stood his ground, bringing the bow and arrow up, loosing the arrow, he shot the rider in the shoulder, the man sent tumbling off his horse. For a moment, the soldier faltered as he made to stand, for what bruises were suffered in the fall, yet, he was quick to find his feet once more and sprinted forward. Bereft of his spear, the soldier caught the archer off guard, and swung his fist sharp across the man's face and hard against his stomach. Flung to his knees, Guy lost hold of his bow, and his enemy was cunning, for he drew forth his dagger, ready. Yet, rising up once more, the archer wrestled against the soldier with all his might, keeping the knife at bay, and forcing the soldier down against the rocky ground. The blade slipping from the blackguard's grasp, Guy wasted no time in seizing it and slit the man's throat; his foe vanquished.

Amid the battle, the dreaded woman had taken up her sword, as Robin cast aside his bow, to wield his blade. Dirt smeared upon her face, and caught up in her tangled hair, she glowered.

"Why must it come to this?" Robin said, panting as the sweat dripped from his brow.

"Oh, you have been a pebble in my shoe for far too long!" Claudia fumed, wielding her weapon against the outlaw, though he blocked her blade skillfully. "You and that blasted Marian!"

"Marian?" He shouted, wincing, as his side was still sore from his recent injury.

"Yes, that Saxon whore, the very one you corrupted."

"How dare you speak such things!" Robin howled, his sword halting another blow.

"Oh, but I know all about your seductions and the child," she cackled.

His face flushing white, the man stared astonished as both he and the woman stepped back for the sake of respite, breathing fast and hard, and both weary from the fight.

"What," he shook his head. "How could you know?"

"Don't mark her, Robin!" Guy called, darting forward. "She only makes to dissuade you of your senses!"

"Ah, but you are one to talk, indeed," she smirked, wiping the blood from her lip. "You, the man with neither heart nor conscience. I'm surprised the Rebel hasn't put an end to you, given your attachment to the lady."

"What does she mean, Gisborne?" Robin pressed, his eyes heavy with affliction and anger.

"He's not spoken of it? Oft times she went to him in secret, confessing of her plight," she grinned. "Did you not know, that Marian was confiding in Sir Guy all the while? How she did beg him to keep her and the child safe?"

"She went to you, to seek your protection?" Robin cried. "And you deceived her?"

"I loved her, and gave her my word I would not tell a soul," Guy said.

"*Loved her*? What fouler words could fall from your mouth…and still, you willingly handed her over to Rothgar?" The outlaw roared, readying his sword against the man. "You devil!"

"Surely as I live, I did all in my power to protect her," Guy petitioned.

"Ha! But did you not consider that someone might notice all those moments you two stole away deep in the night? That those conversations were not shielded from all ears?" Claudia smiled, a wicked glare in her pale eye.

Lunging forward, Robin pinned the woman to the ground, his hair hanging over his face as the sweat trickled from his jaw, and the sinews of his neck tensed.

"What did you do to my wife?" He shouted; his face red, and his hands clutching at her wrists such that the whites of his knuckles were bursting. "What did you do to her?"

"You," Gisborne's eyes widened. "You were the one-"

"Yes, I told Rothgar of her debauchery, of her treason," she laughed. And then, as a sudden storm, her expression hardened. "Guy was pledged to *me!* He was mine; the wealth was mine. All was *mine!*" Claudia cried, the vein in her forehead pulsing. "And before the world, he said he would not have me, all for a Saxon cow. That revolting little country whore. She deserved to die, she and that wretched little half-breed."

As the man backed away, horrified, the woman groped about the ground. Finding the sword, she swung it all the wilder, as the outlaw took the defensive and merely attempted to block her blows. Yet, as her rage increased, untethered, Robin's resistance dwindled, for he lost his footing and tripped backwards over a rock which jutted out from the ground, wounding his side. Viciously, the woman raised up her sword, ready to deliver the final blow.

"No!" Gisborne cried out, rushing forth.

Thoughtlessly, he grasped the woman's blade in his bare hands, halting her attack; the weapon fixed above them. Staring hard at the woman, he saw in her only hate and malice, as she gnashed her teeth, shrieking and warring against him; the blade digging into his palms, though he held firm and would not relinquish it.

"Let go, you hellion!" She cried, wrenching at the hilt.

"Claudia, don't do this," Guy held fast the blade, his hands raw.

"It must be done, and I will have glory!"

"Don't be a fool," he panted as his arms began to shake, the blood dripping down his wrists. "There is no glory in bloodshed. There is no glory in lawlessness!"

"He must die!" She howled. "I will have his blood!"

"Never. Not while I stand! If you slay him, you slay the prince of men!" He cried. Yet as the blade cup deeper, he could restrain it no longer.

Thus, did the woman regain her weapon, the blood upon it glinting in the evening sun. Then, just as she made to strike the man, an arrow flew. Stuck fast, it pierced through the base of the woman's throat. Gisborne stared astounded, and as he turned, he saw the Rebel standing proud with his bow in hand, for he found the strength to rise again. Desolate, Claudia choked, the blood dripping down her lips and past the feathers at the end of the arrow. Letting go of the sword, it hit the ground at her feet, and she beside it fell.

It seemed a moment and an eternity, staring into the eyes of so much darkness, now so swiftly faded into the void. How the man felt such pity, and yet, all at once was his mind given reprieve. For all of her, and every measure of it was finished.

"It is over, friend," Robin sighed, placing his hand upon Gisborne's shoulder.

"Yes," the man whispered, letting out a deep breath. "It is over."

Wearied, he glanced up to meet the outlaw's eye. For each having borne much of sorrow, having borne much of shame, their eyes outright revealed it. And while no word was spoken between them, each knew what the other had resolved. A contrite recompense, a quiet and sombre accord, and all offences mended.

Then, looking down, Robin saw the archer's hands. "Tuck! Come quickly!" He called.

In much haste, the old man came to their side and examined the man's hands; a deep, clean cut across each palm and several cuts at the flesh of his fingers. Breathless, the rest of the comrades approached.

"You cannot ride like this," Tuck shook his head.

Gisborne clenched his jaw, as his fingers trembled. "Please... I have to see my wife," he sighed.

"And you shall," Alan nodded, as he drew beside the man.

"John, go fetch a needle and thread. Alan, if we've any drink, fetch it now," Robin ordered.

Swift, the men heeded their master, and when they had returned, Alan brought a flask, and John followed not far behind with needle and thread. Kneeling beside Gisborne, the outlaw held up the drink. "Don't leave a drop," Alan said, wrinkling his nose in disgust as he glanced down at the severed flesh of the man's shaking palms.

"Stop! First, the wound must be cleansed," Tuck said.

"But this is the last of it," Alan sighed.

"Quick, give it to me!" Tuck took the flask from the outlaw and poured it over the man's wounds. "I'm sorry, but we must clean the wounds or else my work will be of little use."

"Do what you must," Gisborne winced; the liquid stinging.

"The work will take some time. Can you manage?" Tuck asked, gleaning the final drops from the flask to prepare the needle.

"Just do it," the man said. Holding his breath, Gisborne waited as Tuck held his hand, the needle ready.

"Wait!" Jack called out, "Take this."

Cutting off a length of leather from his jacket, the lad rolled it tight and held it out. Anxious, the man bit down hard on the leather, the veins in his throat bulging, as Tuck looked up at him. Gisborne nodded, and the old man pierced through the flesh of his hand. Miserably, every muscle tensed, his hands shaking uncontrollably. Firmly, Alan held down his forearms to keep them still while the old man worked. For Robin and the others stood back, sickened at the sight. Stitch by stitch, the man panted in agony. Peering down, he could see in places the very bone of his fingers showing through the torn flesh, and then he closed his eyes once more.

"I cannot watch this," Little John said, covering his mouth as he turned away.

"Just a few more stitches," A'Dale encouraged, though Tuck had hardly finished stitching up the first palm.

Gisborne moaned fiercely, clenching his eyes shut. Though at first, his hands were shaking, now his arms began to tremble.

"Alan, you must hold him still," the old man warned.

"I am doing all I can!"

"Would someone please go and fetch this man some ale!" Robin cried as he held his own aching side.

"Master, that truly was the last of it. I swear," Alan replied.

"Are you absolutely certain?"

"No, I took my sweet time searching o'er hill and dale for a blessed pint!"

"For pity's sake, go and fetch whatever you can find!"

"But master, if I go-"

"I'll hold him down. Now, go!" Robin said, and with all haste he knelt beside Gisborne, constraining the man's forearms.

Fleetly, A'Dale leapt to his feet to search the stores. There, John sat, rubbing at his temples, his grey hair hanging.

"I can't stand the sound of it," John said. "The moaning like that of a wild beast."

"Have you no respect?" Alan returned. "That man is the only reason Robin is still alive. If he were our brother, I know right well you would be the first by his side. Now, is there anything left to relieve the man?"

His moustache curling, John rolled back his shoulders. "There may be a flask behind those chests in the corner," he pointed, trying to ignore the distant howling.

"And are you to sit there all day as a daisy, or will you help me?"

"Aye, very well!" The man complained, hurrying over to the hoard of chests alongside his comrade, searching amongst the supplies and spoils and stores.

Finally, John picked up a small, rusted flask, and held it out to his friend.

"A little drink is better than no drink," Alan's brows flung up, as he took the flask and dashed away.

Hastily, when the outlaw returned, Guy spat out the role of leather, and Alan brought the flask up to his lips. The liquid was thick and bitter and stung at the back of his throat; sweat rolled down his face as he swallowed the final swig of it.

"The leather," Guy exhaled sharply. As A'Dale retrieved it, the man bit down again, breathing deep as he readied himself for Tuck to finish his work. Ragged from his plight, he did not realise how he had been gasping for air, his breathing rough and hastening, his mind fading and the voices about him growing distant.

"Guy! You must slow your breath!" Tuck shouted, his voice blurring out of range.

Then, he fell.

***

The morning light was gentle and new, the air filled with all the sweet scents of dew covered grass. Thrushes sang and whistled amongst the branches, and the wind swirled through the boughs of the treetops. It was nearly the seventh hour, just as the sun was beginning to warm the world, though a chill whispered in the air of the autumn soon to come.

"Wake up, my friend," Alan's face hovered above the man with the light of morning greeting the forest behind him. "Wake up."

Languid, he rested with his back against a tree and gazing down, his wounds were bound in strips of white cloth. Though his hands were bitterly sore, laying upon his lap, he gently curled each finger to form a fist, then slowly opened his hands, over and over again.

"What happened?" Gisborne sighed.

"Tuck nearly finished when you lost consciousness, but at least it is done," Alan lowered his chin. "Surely, you're one of the most fearless men I've ever seen."

"Foolish, not fearless," he mumbled.

"But you saved my master, and that was no feat of folly," the outlaw returned.

Reflective, Guy nodded. "And, what of Claudia and the riders?"

"Everything was burned last night," Alan answered.

"Good. But Alan, please, help me ride out to Múriel. I must see her," his eyes begged.

"Aye, we'll leave shortly. Wait a moment," Alan smiled, springing to his feet.

Soon, he stood by Scarlet, and together they made ready Gisborne's horse and the other that had remained unharmed in the battle; two gallant horses. As the two men with horses lingered behind, Robin stepped forward and knelt before the man he had once deemed his enemy, his eyes now calm and steady and kind.

"You're faring better," Robin said. "That was a gruesome fight."

"Indeed," Guy admitted, dropping his shoulders. "And what of you?"

"Well enough. I ought to thank you... I owe you my life," Robin sighed, his green eyes pensive.

"No, you owe me nothing," he said.

"But what you said about me-"

"I meant every word," Gisborne answered, his tone so sincere. "I did not see as I do now. Forgive me?"

"You've no need to entreat me for any forgiveness, you've already proved your honour," the outlaw aided the man to his feet. "Come, my friend, let us bring you to your family."

CHAPTER TWENTY-EIGHT

LIGHT ON THE WATER

Four great men, upon their steeds, did ride.

Galloping wildly, they ventured on through the forest, past the sacred gate of elders; the trees of such wholesome green, and every tender leaf as little sails blown here and there in the caresses of the wind. Hoofs stamped the ground, and the good woodland earth kicked up along the path as the creatures valiant, passed. And what an air, what liberty, to fly across the way, ever looking onward.

At last, lying still in the ease of the early morning, the old cottage stood. The smoke from the hearth rose up and swirled above the chimney top and dawn's pleasant sighs mingling with the fresh scent of everything green about that quaint little home, and the faint sounds of a child's cry from within. But the cottage was not so free of threatening chains, though the morn would have them so sustained, for what echoed beyond was the clamour of the sheriff's men.

Cautiously, the four dismounted from their horses. As Guy beheld the dwelling, how everything within him yearned to cast aside discernment and bound away freely toward it. Nevertheless, the men stepped lightly across the leaf-laden ground, veiled in the shadows. Nearing the only window at the back of the cottage, Robin tip-toed ahead, searching about with keen eyes. With no soldiers yet in sight, he whistled three notes, light and merry as a songbird, the notes his companions knew so well. This was the signal for the others to follow. As Robin led the men, carefully they crept around the cottage unto the entrance. Suddenly, the outlaw caught sight of two guards on horseback, following the road before them, passing by the home.

Firmly, he raised his hand and the others halted, quieting their breath until the trotting hoofs faded away beyond them. When the riders were surely gone, and no other suspicious eye could perceive them, the men hurried to the door. Once more, Robin whistled three notes, yet this time, his tune proud and steady, heralding their presence.

The door creaked open, as a hand drew around the edge of the frame. Pulling the door back, Winifred glanced cautiously, and finding familiar faces, she waved the men inside, and softly closed the door behind her.

"Clever indeed you took your time, many a soldier has come passing by, and all the stuff of trouble," she said, fitting her hands upon her hips as she looked on the man with the copper locks. "And clever you sent for me when you did. I fear what may have happened if she was left here on her own."

"How is she?" Guy drew forward, his blue eyes longing. "Where is she?"

"Go on," she said, pointing to the modest chamber at the back of the cottage. Without a moment's delay, the man dashed across the way.

There, upon a bed of white linen, he saw... her. Her face glowing, her long hair cascading down her shoulder, and her eyes alit with such boundless joy. Embraced so gently, the infant lay in his mother's arms, his little cheek pressed against her chest as he slept.

"Guy," Múriel whispered.

"I'm here, my darling," the man sighed. Drawing to her side, he laid a tender kiss upon her lips, and as he took in the warmth of her smile, he then glanced down, his eyes brimming.

"Our son," she said. "Guiscard."

"Guiscard," he said, a smile upon his lips, "A name of strength." As Múriel held the child forth, the man shook his head, revealing to her his wounded hands. "I can't," he said, as he let a tear roll down his face. "I was not with you when I should have been... I've failed you."

"No, you have not failed me," she encouraged so affectionately. Thus, in his arms, she placed the child, and in that very moment, all shadow dispelled from his heart. Gazing down upon the child, the man smiled so richly.

"Hello, little one," Guy whispered, his voice as deep and sure as the dawn sweeping over the forest.

At the sound of his father's voice, the child opened his eyes, and how the man stared in wonder, for a pair of bright silver eyes greeted him, and knew him. Cradling the infant in his arms, the man brought the child up and placed a kiss upon his little nose, and in turn, the child cooed, reaching up with his little hand to touch his father's bearded cheek.

Soft, the three outlaws drew unto the chamber, and the lady's eyes shone full of gladness. "Thank you, Robin," Múriel said, "Thank you for bringing my husband back."

Now Robin could scarce find the words to speak but bowed his head in return.

"Would... would you like to hold him?" She offered, her voice, so calm and sincere.

Hesitant, Robin looked toward Gisborne, and when the man nodded, he stepped forward and took the infant from the man's arms.

Small and fragile and temperate, Robin feared for holding one so precious. All that he had longed for; all the simplicity and quiet of a normal life, all the future that had fallen from his hand.. against such woes, nought was left that could diminish this cherished instance. For though he would never walk this path, these were the lives he fought so fervently to protect. Lives, so full of promise.

"You are a blessed man, Gisborne... I envy you," he sighed. Though it almost pained him, dutifully, he placed the child back in his father's arms. "You have been given a rare gift, never lose sight of that," Robin cautioned, as a bittersweetness shone behind his eyes.

"Never," Guy promised, and embracing the child in his own arms once more, there was no grander feeling.

Turning back, the outlaw bid his men follow, and as they turned away, Alan gazed back over his shoulder, a little smile on his lips as his eyes met Múriel's. And sensing his thought, she nodded. With a playful grin, Alan turned toward the hearth.

At long last, the man and his wife were alone, and so shared their wild tales of what had happened, each, in turn, shocked and horrified, then relieved and comforted. And there were tears to be shed when Guy spoke of Eleanor's fate, for Múriel could not be spared such a rightful sorrow, but in his arms, she found it bearable. What tears fell o'er it fell much as the rain, and when the storm had passed, the rain with it ceased.

Upon the bed, Guy lay beside Múriel, her head nestled in the crook of his shoulder, as their son lay sleeping in her arms. Having shared so much of all they had endured, the lady had yet to speak of her encounter with the white stag. Still, as he knew her through and through, the man perceived the hidden pondering of her mind, and after some persuasion, she confessed it to him.

"But what do you suppose he meant? Why would he say this to me?" She whispered.

"I cannot tell," he sighed, his brows furrowed in deep thought. "Perhaps we may not know for some time, though there has never been any doubt in my mind that he is trustworthy."

"Oui, vous parlez bien," the lady smiled, breathing lightly as the man laid a kiss upon the crown of her head.

"Nous saurons un jour, ma chérie," he whispered.

And there, they slept for a time.

***

As Winifred worked to prepare breakfast, the three men sat round the table by the hearth of the fire; the flames dancing as the song of morning enchanted its rhythm.

"Master," Will began, "I know we've brought them this far, but you and I both know they can't stay here long. Not past a day. It was a risk enough taking Gisborne here, and now that they've no home to go back to, couldn't they-"

"No," Robin stared down at the floor, stroking at his beard. "We cannot burden ourselves with... no, we must think of something else."

"How can you say that they would be a burden? If anything, it would be grand for Guy to fight alongside us," Alan leaned forward. "He's proven his worth, has he not? A good fighter and an outlaw nonetheless! He is much as a kinsman already."

"Have you know brains at all?" Winifred scolded, as she stirred and loomed over a large iron pot which hung above the fire. "That ramshackle of a camp, 'tis no place for a young family.

Mercenaries scouting the woods, weapons strewn about, and wild creatures lurking in the shadows… I'll hear none of it."

"Oh, come now," Alan rolled his eyes.

"No, she is right," Robin said, "It's no place for a family."

"Then let us find some new means of shelter! Let us move the camp," Will stood up, setting his hands firm on the table.

"We cannot keep moving and hiding forever, Scarlet," Robin's brow raised as he tensed his jaw. "Claudia sent one scout; one, and we were discovered. Let us not reason like fools and forget Victor will not be far behind. There's not a single place in all of Nottingham that is safe for them. No part of it is safe for us. We live like animals only as we must. It would be thoughtless to inflict such a life upon them."

"Master, what can be done, then?" Alan's eyes grew solemn. "We cannot abandon them altogether."

"I never said that," Robin brought his hand to his temple as he let out a sigh. "They must decide what course to take, of their own accord."

Pensive, Alan stared into the fire, as he let out a deep breath. "But what will become of them?"

"I... I do not know," he admitted, leaning his head into his hands.

"We will protect them, won't we?" Will gripped the man's arm.

"As much as we are given leave to do so. Still, as I have said, this cannot go on forever," the outlaw shook his head.

"Then we must speak with Gisborne now," Alan resolved.

"Let them sleep a while," Winifred said. "They've made enough hard decisions as it is. Give them some time."

Glancing over his shoulder, Robin watched as the man and his family lay so still and peaceful, the morning light shining over them. No, he could not wake them now. He would heed the physician's words. Yet as they rested, the outlaw's mind would know no rest by any means. Robin searched every corner of his mind for any way to bring about a solution for while the sheriff was still in power, surely, Guy and Múriel could not remain.

After they had eaten, the three men departed from the cottage. As for the man and his wife, their son, and the physician, they lingered; the entirety of the day consumed with caring for the child, and the man and his wife both in much need of rest and healing.

***

Three days passed.

On the third day, when Guy's hands had healed a little, Winifred would depart from them. There were far too many in the village in need of her help from all the chaos of the sheriff's men, and she must go where she was most needed, though she was glad to have been of some aid.

That very evening, Winifred took what belongings she required, and bid farewell to Guy and Múriel, wishing them luck. Not long after the healer's departure, as the skies grew dark and quiet, the man heard the sound of three familiar notes whistled at the back window. Swiftly, he leapt to his feet, and though it pained his hand, he opened the door to three hooded figures. Without another thought, he outlaws entered the cottage and drew near the fire, as the man shut the door behind them.

"You've returned?" Guy wondered.

"There is something we must tell you," Robin returned, his expression grave.

"What news have you?" The man entreated.

"You, and your family.... you cannot stay here any longer," Robin said. "Victor knows. And his wrath has been set upon Nottingham. Anyone who was ever suspected of withholding information regarding our whereabouts with us has been killed."

"Four men hung at the gallows already," A'Dale whispered, his dark eyes weighty. "And Cedric, the first amongst them."

"No," Guy sighed, leaning back in his chair.

"Though it may be difficult to accept, your home is gone, and rebuilding it would prove worthless," Robin continued. "This land has grown far too perilous. You must flee England."

"Flee England?" The man's brows raised. "But where would we go?"

"It is but a matter of time before someone happens upon you. Think of Múriel, think of your son," Will urged.

The man thought for a moment, silently contemplating and resolving upon what he had thought they should have done from the very beginning. "Then, we must make for France," he sighed. "I'll speak with Múriel about it when she wakes, but I fear that is our only choice."

"France?" Múriel's gentle voice resonated across the room, as she walked toward the table with Guiscard in her arms.

Standing, Guy slowly set his hands upon her shoulders, though his palms were still sore; his eyes gazing tenderly upon her. "We cannot stay here, my love. I know you would wish to remain, but-"

"Then we shall go," she determined. "I've some family in Josselin, and certainly they would welcome us."

Relieved, the man smiled. "For France," he said.

"Good... good. It's settled then," Robin said. "Now, we can take you as far as Dover, but the journey will be long. How soon can you be ready?"

Guy halted, looking down at his family. For a moment, he feared the journey too arduous, yet the longer they stayed, the higher their risk of being discovered. His eyes set upon her, she knew his heart and nodded though no words were spoken. Taking her hand in his, he sighed and faced the outlaw once more.

"At first light," he answered.

Together they ate and drank, and as the lady sat amongst them, she nursed the child. All night, they discussed the journey ahead; what provisions were needed, how to find Múriel's family, how quickly they could call upon them. All was swiftly prepared to bring them safely to France.

And amidst the conversation and the preparations, finally, Múriel let Alan hold the child, who slept soundly in his arms for two full hours, and when he awoke, greeted the man with a smile... or so Alan boasted.

***

A week had passed since that night.

Robin, Alan, and Will already agreed with the rest of the company, that they would bring Guy and Múriel to Dover, while the others remained to defend the people of Nottingham. And the journey proved toilsome, indeed.

Mounted upon the horse, Múriel held tightly to Guiscard, Guy's arms wrapped around her and holding fast the reins as they strode behind the others. The three outlaws each took their own horses, and set about the creatures were modest provisions.

Early in the morning, before the sun was in the skies, they had at long last reached the very edge of England. Halting at the high white cliffs, they looked out on the expanse of an endless sea as the scents of the salty air swirled about them, and great mists of cloud soared overhead.

Galloping down to the shoreline, there, the men made ready a boat with a broad white sail. As they had finished, Guy and Múriel made their final goodbyes.

"Oh, Will, you shall be dearly missed," Múriel embraced the outlaw gently, and pulling back, she placed a kiss upon his cheek.

Will could scarce feign an answer for his eyes welled with tears, though he tried to hold them back.

"A'Dale, I still don't know how to thank you for all you've done," Gisborne embraced his friend. "And I never quite understood, what was it that Múriel told you, that convinced you to help me escape?"

"Ah, now that is something she shall have to tell you herself," Alan winked. "Farewell, Múriel," he called, as she rushed to put her arm about him.

"Guy," Robin embraced the man, "The forest will be a strange place without you," he smiled. "If you are ever in need, you'll always have friends in Sherwood waiting for you."

"It is an honour to be counted your friend," he said. "I hope we may meet again."

"I have a feeling we will," Robin grinned, his green eyes merry.

Múriel gave one final embrace to the master of the outlaws. "Thank you, for everything, Robin. We shall never forget you," she whispered.

"Before you leave, I have something to give you," he smiled. Removing the ring from his finger, he held it out to Guy. A thick band of gold, engraved with ancient words, and an emerald stone set at its crest. "This belonged to my father, and to his father before him. A symbol of my lineage, of the Lords of Locksley. But, I've no son to whom I may give it, and those days are long behind me," he placed it in the man's hand, "Here, my comrade, my fellow lord. May you bear it proudly, and may many sons come to bear it long after you have gone."

Guy bowed his head, and setting the stone upon his own finger, he embraced the outlaw one final time.

As they bid their friends farewell, the man, along with his wife and child, rowed across the sea, the roaring waves rolling beneath them. Broad was the sail that filled with the salted air, giving the vessel wings. Standing upon the deck, Guy held Múriel in his arms, as she held the child in hers; the wild winds whipping their brown and raven locks into ribbons of regal hues.

Gazing back at the shore, Guy perceived them: Robin Hood, Alan A'Dale, and Will the Scarlet, stalwart and dauntless upon their horses. Lifting up his hand, he held it still, as Robin raised his in return, bidding the man goodbye. Yet, something curious caught Gisborne's eye. Sprinting toward the mast, he held fast to it and gained a better view for behind the outlaw, a grand figure appeared, of unfathomable stature; the white stag. From his nostrils, a wave of air burst forth and lifted the ship's sail higher.

Remember, oh, my king! Remember and return!

The voice echoed in his mind, the words spoken to his very spirit. How his heart leapt within him as if new life had been restored. Hastily, he unfastened the golden brooch from his cloak and took from Múriel her silver brooch. Fitting them together, just as he had dreamt, the sun and moon upon them alit with a blazing light as dawn hung above the horizon, calling the magic to waken. Faster and faster the lights spun and finally did it point to the journey's end; ever northward. Bewildered and wholly jubilant, the man beamed with such wonder. And when he looked back, the figure bowed his head, as did Robin, beneath him.

Hirtharon, Guy whispered, *I remember.*

Turning back to gaze upon Múriel, staring deep into her moon grey eyes, she knew they would not go where they had planned, and in fear did she look up at him.

"To France, my love?"

"No," he answered calmly.

"Then, where shall we go?" She clutched his arm, the child held fast against her heart.

Glancing back at the shoreline for the last time, the man watched as the mighty stag drew in one final breath, and blew a great gust of wind from his mouth, a mist of light rushing over the glistening waves.

"Oh, my darling," he held Múriel's beautiful face in his hands, his blue eyes brimming, "That which is must remain, yet that which is becoming must in its season change," he comforted. "There is a season for all things, and this, my precious love, is but the next path to follow on our journey together. A journey to a new life, a good and certain future."

With such passion and unyielding love, he kissed her lips.

Made in the USA
Middletown, DE
25 June 2019